M000046506

Other Titles By

Dyanne Davis

Forever and a Day

Dyanne Davis

Parker Publishing, LLC

Noire Allure

Noire Allure is an imprint of Parker Publishing, LLC.

Copyright © 2007 by Dyanne Davis

Published by Parker Publishing, LLC
P.O. Box 380-844
Brooklyn, NY 11238
www.parker-publishing.com

All rights reserved. This book is protected under the copyright laws of the United States of America. No part of this publication may be reproduced, stored in a retrieval system, or transmitted in any form or by any means—electronic, mechanical, photocopying, recording, or otherwise—without the prior written permission of the publisher.

This book is a work of fiction. Characters, names, locations, events and incidents (in either a contemporary and/or historical setting) are products of the author's imagination and are being used in an imaginative manner as a part of this work of fiction. Any resemblance to actual events, locations, settings, or persons, living or dead, is entirely coincidental.

ISBN: 978-1-60043-004-6

First Edition

Manufactured in the United States of America

Dedication

This book is dedicated with love to Alvena McNeil, one of the many victims of the wrath of Mother Nature in the past year. The aftermath of natural disasters have been fierce and felt worldwide. Hurricane Katrina was one of them.

In the face of life altering changes, Alvena has gone through this tragedy with so much grace and faith that she's put me to shame with my petty complaints about life. She has held to her faith and sense of humor, and as unbelievable as this might seem, she's remained a source of comfort to many, giving her shoulder for others to lean on when her own was sagging under the weight of loss. Alvena, you are truly a magnificent spirit, and I'm honored to know you.

Acknowledgements

To God, I give all honor and glory above all others. I thank you for the lessons. And I thank God for bringing the people into my life who have enriched my spirit and increased my capacity to love.

To my baby sister, Jackqueline Jackson, who looks first at the acknowledgements and gets upset when she doesn't see her name there. And never mind that she's already had a book dedicated to her. I've been ordered to put her name in every book. LOL. So now I want her to see her name is surrounded by my version of lights. You're nuts and I love you. (You didn't think I was going to do it did you?) smile

To the Parker Family, I'm glad to be included in this venture.

To my editor, Deatri King-Bey, author of *Caught Up* (wonderful read by the way). You made me work harder, and dig deeper than I wanted to go, but your comments and suggestions have resulted in a stronger book. Thank You.

To Anne Frances Bank, my Virgo sister. Thanks (and you know why).

To Sarah Stone, your spirit and growth is a joy to my heart.

To all of the families touched by Katrina in Alabama, Mississippi, and Louisiana, and that includes the thousands of victims and the thousands of volunteers. May we never have to ever hear of another disaster anywhere in the world.

To everyone else that I may have known in any of the lives that I've lived or will live. Thank you. (I was ordered to keep this short)

Bill and Billy you remain as always the two most important people in my heart. I love you both.

Prologue

July 2004 — Baton Rouge Louisiana

A war game is underway at the States Emergency Center called PAM. It's an exercise to show what would happen if a major hurricane would strike on the Gulf Coast. The estimated results of the PAM exercise:

Death Toll: 61,000

Injured and sick: 500,000 Homeless: 380,000

People evacuated from the hurricane zone, 1,000,000

Buildings destroyed: 500,000

In the war game, PAM crippled state and local government, and the federal government had to come in and take over.

Thirteen Months Later:

Wednesday August 24th 2005 11 AM (ET)

In the central Bahamas a tropical storm is spotted. Miami issues an advisory of possible hurricane conditions in the next thirty-six hours.

Thursday August 25th 2005 3:30 ET- The tropical storm has now been classified as a hurricane and it's named Hurricane Katrina.

In Bensonville, Arkansas, an emergency resource team is getting things needed in case of emergency. Katrina's winds hit speeds of 75 MPH — it's now classified as a category 1 hurricane.

6:30 PM

Hurricane Katrina pummels the coast of Florida and heads inland. She leaves fourteen people dead and causes 460 million dollars in damages. For a category 1, she packs a serious punch.

Forever and a Day

Katrina draws energy from the warm waters of the Gulf of Mexico and reenergizes.

Friday August 26th 2005 11:30 AM (ET)

Katrina strengthens to a category 2 hurricane and could become a 3 within the next three hours. Her next target—anywhere from the Florida Panhandle to Louisiana. Along the Gulf Coast, the Red Cross and Salvation Army are on the move. They open shelters and mobile feeding units. The news about Katrina is spreading.

Friday August 26th 2005 5PM (ET).

Katrina is northwest of the Florida Keys. With every passing hour, she sucks in energy. She's now a category 3. State and federal officials from Washington, D.C. to Louisiana know Katrina is coming. A state of emergency is declared in Louisiana and Mississippi. The U.S. Coast Guard puts helicopters, planes, and cutters on standby. Oil Companies evacuate rigs out in the Gulf Coast. Katrina is expected to hit the Gulf Coast in seventy-two hours.

Chapter One

Friday August 26th 7:00 PM.

The smell of jambalaya fought with the gumbo. "Mama, don't put in any okra." A useless request, there would be okra in the gumbo, but with so much more food to eat it wouldn't matter. The smile appeared on her face before she could stop it, and Torrie relaxed for just a moment to enjoy the different aromas. Taking a deep breath, she inhaled. The scent of catfish wafted throughout the house. The hush puppies were piled high on a platter, waiting for the hurricane party.

"What if this one's for real?" Torrie turned toward her sister. "The weather reports say it's going to be bad." As expected, Kimmie, her sister, laughed at her.

"There's no need to fear. How many times have we been through this, a million?"

"Not a million." Torrie stopped and swayed, putting her hands on her hips. "Besides, this one feels different. I'm scared."

"There is nothing different about this storm than from any other. We're going to have a party. There's going to be some rain, maybe a little flooding, but nothing major. Come on, Torrie, you know how it is."

Torrie turned and stared at the gathering crowd. She walked toward the kitchen. The smells pulled on her and the laughter filled her heart, but something loomed in the far recesses of her mind. Doom. She dismissed this feeling, but it came back. Something was wrong. This party was the same as any other. The ninth ward had huddled and prayed through this many times. She wasn't sure if it was the governor, the mayor, her constant dreams, or a combination of all of these, but she was truly worried.

Forever and a Day

She shoved a warm hush puppy into her mouth. Torrie bit down, savoring the taste. Her stomach growled, alerting her of the hunger she denied. "Everything looks good," she whispered. "Look everybody," she reached for a glass, then tapped it several times with the back of the butter knife, stopping the swarm of voices and laughter. The sea of brown faces turned toward her.

"What's up?" more than one voice inquired.

"We have time to leave New Orleans before the hurricane is scheduled to hit. Let's have the party tonight and tomorrow go someplace else, maybe Lake Charles, maybe…maybe…I don't know. I'm going to call around and try to find someplace to go for a few days until the hurricane passes. I don't feel safe. What if the levee breaks?"

Laughter rang out, a dozen voices drowning out her words.

"Please, the levees will never break," said Auntie Mattie. "They will hold regardless. We are blessed by God, his favored people. God doesn't have any doing with the poor, only the rich. He will not touch our homes, don't worry."

"Have you spoken to God?" Torrie insisted stubbornly. "Did He tell you he wouldn't destroy our homes?" She faced her Auntie Mattie waiting patiently for the answer.

"The Bible said the world wouldn't be destroyed by water but with fire next time. The hurricane, honey, that's water, and I'm not afraid. Hurricane Katrina is not gonna bother me."

"What if it does, Auntie?"

"Look, if you're scared pray and God will put your mind at ease. But we're trying to have a party here, baby, you're putting a real damper on it."

She tried but the feeling wouldn't leave, then the chills started, and she was taken back as she always was to when she was four and huddled in a corner at nursery school. Torrie could remember Jake's face as plain as day. Only a few months older, he'd come to the corner where she was cowering and had removed her hands

4

from her face. She'd stared into his golden brown eyes, and he'd smiled at her.

"Hi, my name's Jake. I'll sit with you," he'd said. "You don't have to be afraid. I'll protect you."

The two of them had sat hand in hand, looking at each other until the storm passed. When Torrie cringed at loud claps of thunder, Jake smiled and squeezed her hand. "I won't let the thunder hurt you, Torrie," he'd boasted, puffing his chest out. And somehow, she'd believed him.

Torrie had gone though many storms with Jake. She'd even had her first kiss with him during the middle of a thunderstorm. They'd been to a mall and had gotten caught in a thunderstorm, her body had trembled at the sound, and Jake had put his arm around her, laughing at her, telling her as he'd done a hundred times in the past that he'd protect her. Only that time something was different, the way he'd held her was different. His voice had become husky and low, and she'd suddenly felt hot, unable to breathe. She forgot about the storm when she'd stared at Jake. His eyes held a look she was unfamiliar with, but she had some inner knowing of what was coming.

She tilted her head up at the same instant his lips came down. He kissed her tentatively at first, then bolder. Things she had no way of knowing surged through her. Heat shimmied down her spine, and she felt Jake's body harden as he pulled her close.

The result of the kiss had also been Torrie's first brush with classism. Jake's neighbor, Torrie later learned, had snatched Jake away from her and asked what the hell they thought they were doing. He'd threatened to tell Jake's parents he'd been seen kissing on a Thibodeaux girl from the ninth ward out in public. Name and skin color meant so much in New Orleans. Not as much as it had in the fifties, but the remnants still remained. Torrie was still amazed that strangers, like Jake's neighbor, could look at her face and know that her name was Thibodeaux.

Forever and a Day

The abruptness of being pulled apart by a stranger surprised Torrie. Jake's face had turned red. His eyes, which had had that funny look right before he'd kissed her, changed. He was angry. Torrie had cringed. Jake was in trouble for kissing her, and when he moved further away from her, Torrie had seen another look in Jake's eyes. Shame.

She'd stood for a moment watching his eyes dart back and forth from her to the man who had broken them apart. Fury blazed from Jake's eyes. Whether his emotions came about because of her or his neighbor, she wasn't sure. With a sob in her throat, Torrie ran from the mall and hadn't stopped running until she got home.

Her friendship with Jake changed that day. They no longer laughed as easily or shared their secrets with each other, and eventually their communication almost stopped. Two years after their kiss, Jake left town, and Torrie only heard from him occasionally: on her birthday, Christmas, and when it stormed. Of course, he had called to tell her he was in love and a year later to tell her he was getting married. And, he called five years ago telling her he was divorced.

Torrie glanced toward the phone, wondering if Jake was listening to the news, wondering if he'd call. She smiled; of course, he'd call. He always did, and she'd assure him she was no longer a child, no longer afraid of storms. But they'd both knew she was lying, a lie between old friends that could be accepted. After all, they lived in different worlds, and Jake could no longer protect her from the storms.

"Damn," Jake swore as he looked at the weather report. He'd called Benjamin, a meteorologist for the *Mississippi Times*, to ask if he thought the possibility of a major hurricane was imminent. He wanted to affirm if all the reports he'd heard were true. The Big

Easy was always threatened with such news. The news from
Benjamin was grim. Yes, yes, and yes. This time the authorities had
it right. The mayor was not just blowing smoke up anyone's behind,
and the governor had done the right thing in ordering the populace
to evacuate. Jake immediately thought of Torrie's dire predictions
and dreams she'd had since early childhood that New Orleans
would be destroyed. He'd always told her she was too pessimistic,
waiting for the shoe to drop, and nothing would happen. He
glanced again at the television, remembering how many times he'd
promised to protect her, to not allow any old hurricane to destroy
their town.

"Damn," he muttered as he paced his office. Why the hell did
he care anymore? In the twelve years since he'd left home, she'd
never initiated a conversation, had never sent him one letter, one
card, not on his birthday, not at Christmas, nothing. If he didn't
keep in touch with her, she wouldn't care.

He groaned, aching deep in his chest. He still cared about her.
He'd cared about her when he was five, and he cared about her at
thirty. When he'd called to tell her he'd fallen in love, he'd cared.
When he'd told her he was getting married, he'd cared. And five
years ago when he'd called to tell her the marriage hadn't worked
out, he'd cared. But in none of the conversations he'd had with her
through the years, had she ever shown him more than the polite
conversation one has with an old friend. If it hadn't been for the one
incessant vision he'd had of the two of them, perhaps he would have
stopped calling her years ago.

The only time Jake saw glimpses of the friendship he'd valued
so long was when he heard a storm was coming. During these times,
Torrie seemed genuinely glad to talk to him, even expectant. He'd
calm her down, and they'd laugh over her silliness. The only time
since he'd been gone he'd not called her during a storm or threat of
a hurricane, was when he'd been married. He had the first year,
then he'd stopped, calling Torrie only on special occasions. He'd

decided he couldn't worry any longer about talking her through the storms.

Once his divorce was final, he'd slipped back into his old pattern as easily as one slipped into a comfortable pair of loafers. He knew Torrie. He knew she was probably watching the weather reports like a hawk. And he knew she would be scared, but he also knew she wouldn't leave New Orleans, wouldn't seek safety. That sickened him with worry. For once, he was taking Torrie's dreams seriously. *Damn*, he thought for the third time and dialed her number.

Torrie smiled when her phone rang. She knew, without checking, that it was Jake. She was glad he'd called her cell instead of the house. Flipping the phone open to answer, she went out to the porch. She didn't talk to Jake often, but when she did, she liked keeping his calls to herself.

"Hey, Jake," her voice trembled. "You've been listening to the weather reports, haven't you?"

"Of course. I know what a chicken you are." He sucked in a breath, wishing like hell the picture he had of her was something more than the eighteen-year-old girl. He groaned and shooed away the thought. "Torrie, I've checked around with a friend of mine who's a meteorologist. He says this one's for real and going to be big. Have you given any thought to getting out of there?"

Torrie chuckled softly. The fluttery feeling she always got when she talked to Jake filled her chest and warmth flooded her body. She tried to shake the feeling away, but when she couldn't, she gave in to it. Jake was a thousand miles away. She'd not seen him in twelve years. He was a Broussard, and she was a Thibodeaux. He lived in New York, and she lived in New Orleans. And nothing more than that first kiss would ever happen between them.

"Torrie, are you paying attention to me?"

"Yes, Jake, I was just remembering."

"What?" he asked, knowing very well what she was remembering, the same as he, the first and last time he'd comforted her through a storm, and their first kiss.

"I'm not that afraid of storms anymore, Jake."

"Liar."

"Well, let's say for two years I learned to go through them alone." Damn why had she said that? She'd never allowed herself to even think it. The only time Jake had not called to talk her through a storm was the last two years of his three year marriage.

"Torrie?"

"I'm sorry, Jake, I shouldn't have said that. I didn't mean it." A moment of silence filled the space between them. They both knew it was a lie. "I've missed you," she found herself admitting. "I've missed our friendship."

"That's hard to believe. You've never made an attempt to keep it strong. If I hadn't called you during these past twelve years, I don't think you would've given a damn."

"That's not true. I appreciate your calling me. I do. Hearing your voice helps." Torrie smiled, allowing it to seep into her voice, "Even though I'm no longer afraid of the storms."

"Liar," Jake repeated, and they both laughed.

"It's been fourteen years, Torrie. Are we ever going to talk about it?"

"Jake, please, why do we have to dredge up the past?"

"Because for two years I tried to tell you I was sorry. I was sixteen."

"So was I."

"I didn't mean it. I don't know what happened."

"I do. You kissed me remember, and you were embarrassed and ashamed you had."

"I never meant to hurt you."

"I know. Look, we were kids." Torrie's throat loosened, and she wondered why Jake wanted to discuss this now. Afterward, she hadn't seen him for two months. In the two years before he'd left town, they'd never discussed the kiss, nor in the twelve years since then. Why today?

"I've been thinking about your dreams, your premonitions."

"About the town being destroyed?" Torrie sighed and raked her fingers through her hair. "Jake, you always told me I was being silly, that premonitions were not true, and I think you're right. Look how many storms we've had. We're still standing. Don't worry about me. I'm fine."

"I do worry about you." He felt a tightening in his chest. "I've always worried about you. We're friends and friends worry about each other. Are we still friends?"

For a moment, Torrie didn't answer: Friends kept in touch, they called, they occasionally saw each other's face. She'd not seen Jake's face in many years. Sure, she'd seen him in the paper and once on television when he was working on the Bush campaign. But she'd not seen his face in person. She supposed they were still friends. "Yes, Jake, we're friends."

"That took a long time for you to answer."

"I had to reconsider what makes a friendship." She laughed. "No matter what happened, I will always be grateful to the little boy who promised to fight the elements for me, to protect me from the storm. You were so ferocious. I picture you sometimes, and now I know you are fierce."

A thud landed in his belly and warmth spread through his chest. Jake wondered if he'd really heard her. If she was admitting to things, maybe he had more reason to be afraid than he thought. It meant Torrie wasn't just scared, she was terrified.

"You've been thinking about me?" Jake asked.

"Yes."

"Are you still having the dreams?" He waited.

"Yes."

Fear clutched him for her safety. "Why don't you leave for a few days? Maybe go to Texas. You could even fly up here to visit me. I'd love to see you."

"Would being in New York make it different?" *Oh God, why did I go there?* Torrie hurriedly sought words to cover up what she'd never meant to ask. "Jake, New York has storms, and my dreams would still happen there."

"I know…I just thought…I have a bad feeling about this, Torrie. For the first time since we were kids, I have a really bad feeling. I don't want you to be in the way of a hurricane. I don't want your dreams coming true. I want you to be safe. I'm worried about you."

"Have you called your family?"

"Not yet."

Silence. The only sound was the leaves blowing in the wind. For a moment, Torrie watched as the wind continued to whip the leaves about her feet. She moved her left foot, kicking gently at the gathered leaves waiting for Jake to say something.

They both understood what he'd said without using any words. She was the first person he'd called. He worried about her, but Torrie didn't want him to worry about her out of misplaced childhood guilt. Their families tolerated their friendship when they were younger because their hormones weren't involved. When that changed, so had the friendship.

"Jake, let's get this out of the way, okay. It doesn't matter about the kiss. You didn't force me to kiss you. I knew you were going to, and I wanted you to. I never hated you for kissing me or for what happened after the kiss. God, our being friends in the first place was a long shot. We both know how it is. You lived in the Garden District, and I lived in the ninth ward. If you hadn't had relatives in the seventh ward and my aunt had not worked at the nursery school you went to, we would have never met. I appreciate that you've kept in touch through the years and that you worry about me, but if it's because of some silly guilt, you don't have to. I'm not your responsibility. I never was."

"Is that the reason you've never picked up the phone to call me in all the years I've been gone?"

"How do you know I've never picked up the phone?"

Jake's throat hurt. His first kiss had rocked him to his soul and stolen his life. He'd been unable to forget Torrie or her taste. Since he'd left home, somehow, he'd not made many friends and not one female friend, not because he'd avoided it, just because that was the way it was. He was friendly to everyone, but now as he talked to Torrie, he was reminded how colorless his life seemed, in more ways than one. He knew why he maintained contact with Torrie, she connected him to his past, a much more innocent time, and somewhere in his heart she'd been embedded since he was five and she was four and three-quarters. He couldn't let go of that, even if she didn't reciprocate.

"You were the first girl I ever kissed."

"I know that, you dork."

"I wasn't ashamed of kissing you." Again, Jake found himself waiting. "Torrie, can't we talk about this? I'm so tired of having the kiss between us. We can't seem to move on."

"We've both moved on, Jake. You have a full life, and so do I. You've been married and divorced; you don't call that moving on? I have a thriving daycare business and own my own home. I'm doing well; that's moving on."

"You know that's not what I meant."

"Jake, I thought you called about the storm, to offer me comfort. This wasn't what you called about, so why are we talking about this?"

"Because it was never settled, because there's a hole in my heart where our friendship used to be, because I still hurt having you think I was ashamed of you."

"You were," Torrie said softly.

"I was ashamed," Jake admitted. "I was ashamed I kissed you for the first time in public. I was ashamed my neighbor caught us. I was ashamed of the words he used and I was ashamed I didn't speak up, because I hurt your feelings, and you ran away. I didn't talk to you for two months and I didn't know how to make things right for us again. As for being your friend, I was ashamed of having breeched our friendship. I was your friend, your protector. I had no right to kiss you; and, yes I was ashamed but not for the reasons you think."

A long sigh came across the line, and Jake slumped into a chair.

"Okay, Jake, let's say this and put a period behind it. I was embarrassed, too, to have allowed you to kiss me in public. And yes, I got scolded, too, from everybody about being careful what I did out in public. You weren't the only one. I didn't want our friendship to end on a bad note. And I called you a dozen times in those two months, but I didn't hear from you. I sent you letters."

"I never got any letters. I never knew, Torrie."

"You had to. When you came back around you told me you were sorry over what happened, but it couldn't happen again." Torrie knew the words he'd used by heart, his…'we can only be friends' speech. "Jake, you made yourself very clear."

"Exactly what did I make clear to you? I swear I've been trying to figure that out for years." Jake sucked in a breath, wishing like hell there had been a letter. Her emphatic statement puzzled him.

"Are you for real?" Torrie couldn't believe it. "Jake, don't do this, not now. Is this your new way of distracting me from the storm?"

"This has nothing to do with the storm."

"Isn't that why you called?"

"It was but…"

"But."

"Torrie, what did you hear me say?"

"It's been fourteen years," Torrie answered. "Do you really think I remember every word you said that long ago?"

"Of course I do. You have a mind like a steel trap. You remember word for word." He laughed, knowing she remembered.

"You said we could only be friends."

Jake searched his memory. "Yeah, I did, and you cut me off telling me you agreed we could only be friends. That wasn't what I meant. What I wanted to tell you was that we could only be friends until we knew for sure. It was storming, Torrie. I was doing what I'd always done, talking you out of being afraid. Something happened that day, something different. And, somehow, I haven't been able to get over the feeling that I failed you and I took advantage of you and your fears. I wasn't telling you there couldn't be more for us. I had only wanted to tell you I valued our friendship too much to risk it, that we needed to be very sure."

"Why are you bothering with this now? It's been so long, a lifetime ago."

"I don't know," Jake admitted. "Suddenly, I feel so afraid something might happen, that your dreams might come true. I don't want anything bad to happen to you, and I wanted to make sure you know I have always valued you and our friendship."

"Just stop. You're talking as though you think I'm going to die or something." Torrie laughed. "I'm not going to die." When he didn't answer, a shiver ran down her spine. "Please, Jake, you're scaring me. Stop, okay?"

A strong breeze blew across Torrie's face. She felt the dampness it carried and wrapped her arms around her body to ward off the chill. She took a look around. An eerie feeling touched her, as though the wind whispered a secret. Another strong breeze pushed her several steps. She didn't want Jake to know, but not only was his call scaring her, but also the rapid change in the weather.

"What were you doing when I called?"

"What do you think? I was getting ready for the hurricane party." She heard his groan. "We're strong here. God always protects us, and the levees have been reinforced many times. Nothing is going to happen. I've been silly," Torrie said, parroting the words of her family, words she didn't really believe. "Come on, you've always said it. Listen, I'd rather go back to the other conversation. That was easier to handle." Torrie laughed, thinking Jake would do the same. When he didn't, she knew this was serious. "Everything will be okay," she repeated.

"I want you to promise me you'll leave."

"No one else is leaving."

"I don't care. I want you to."

"I'll think about it."

"We okay?"

"We're always okay. We're friends, remember?" Torrie sucked on her teeth, remembering their beginning. He'd been her hero. In some way, he would always remain in that position. "Thanks for calling. I enjoyed talking to you, as always," she whispered softly, then hung up.

The moment Torrie walked back into the house, a plate of piping hot catfish was shoved into her hand. She smiled and inhaled the steam. So, the family had decided to comfort her with food. Why not? She'd had the same dreams most of her life, and so far they'd never come true. She bit into the fish and smiled in satisfaction, which turned into a grin when someone handed her the bottle of hot sauce she hadn't asked for.

Yeah, she would party tonight, and she would enjoy every minute of it. She tried to let go of Jake's words, his feeling of doom, but couldn't. "Hey everyone, tomorrow I'm going to leave. Seriously, this time I'm not joking. I'm going to call around for a room and wait out the storm, hurricane, whatever it turns out to be. I'm leaving until it's over."

"That's crazy," several voices chimed in. They all knew she'd been talking to Jake.

Torrie pressed on despite the objections of her family. She agreed with Jake. Another shiver claimed her, rocking her to her soul. She closed her eyes and clenched her teeth, waiting for it to pass. When it didn't, she opened her eyes and looked out on the varying sea of brown. Her stomach muscles twisted, causing her pain. Would life even be worth living if she saved herself and lost her family? Her sister eyed her strangely. Torrie smiled and reached an arm out to her sister, pulling her close, breathing in the scent of the sister she'd spent so many years with.

"Come with me," she pleaded softly, "just for a few days." A lump quickly filled Torrie's chest at the thought of losing Kimmie. "Please don't make me go alone. I'm your baby sister. Remember, you're supposed to protect me," Torrie whispered, using the same words she'd used as a child that always made her sister give in. Torrie shivered, hoping it would work this time. She kissed her sister's cheek, nuzzling herself into the warm brown skin fragrant with the smell of cooking. "I love you, Kimmie, don't make me go alone."

"Torrie," her sister said about to scold her, but she saw the fear in Torrie's eyes. "Okay, I'll leave with you. I need a little vacation anyway. You call tomorrow and see if you can get us a room somewhere. We'll just consider it a little break, a little vacation."

"Kimmie, what are you doing giving into her like that?" Their mother frowned at both Kimmie and Torrie. "She's just trying to wrap you around her little finger, like always. You know she's just scared of the storms. She's always been afraid. Nothing's going to happen. Now she's got you all worked up. You're the big sister. You're supposed to talk her out of this nonsense, not help her with this foolishness."

"Mama, I don't mind going." Kimmie shrugged her shoulder. "Maybe Torrie's right. Maybe we all should leave for a couple of days until the storm passes."

"Torrie, what did that boy say to you?" Her mother turned and glared in her direction.

Torrie snuggled even closer to her sister as she glanced sideways at her mother. To her mother, Jake would always be "that boy." He'd been Jake until their kiss though. Torrie had never told her mama what had happened. She'd only told her sister, but her mother knew, with the instinct mothers have, that Jake had hurt her deeply. And to her mama, Jake had been reduced to, 'that boy'.

"Jake talked to a friend, Mama, a meteorologist. He says that the hurricane is the biggest he's seen. It's major, and he thinks we should all leave home until it's over."

"Well, tell me something. Did that boy say where we're supposed to go? We're just supposed to pick up and leave our homes open to whoever wants to come and pick them clean? I don't think so. Torrie, you're too old for such nonsense. I've told you a million times, baby, your dreams are only that. Look around you, baby. You've got most of your entire family around you. Do you really think we'd let anything happen to you? We'll always protect you. You don't have to worry, and you don't have to listen to that boy. He may be talking to a meteorologist, but I know the Lord has no problems with us, and he's been doing a good job of looking out for us. If things get bad, we can always go to the church just like we've always done. We'll have a party for a few days, have fun eating, dancing, playing a little bit of whist, and wait out the storm. There'll be so much laughing you won't even hear the noise from the wind. I promise, now come on, stop."

The confident smile on her mother's face was what Torrie saw, but this time it wasn't enough. They didn't understand. Jake thought she would die. He didn't try to talk her out of her fears as he'd always done. There was a reason for all of them to be afraid. Jake was afraid of nothing, and this time even he was afraid. It was time to do something different than they'd all done. It was time to seek higher ground. Or at least ground that wasn't in the path of the storm.

"No one's talking me out of this, Mama. I'm going to find someplace out of the path of the hurricane." Torrie looked around the room at her family. "I want you all to come." She shrugged her shoulders when they laughed at her. "I have a feeling this time the hurricane is going to be really bad."

"Torrie, you've been saying that since you learned to talk. You're just afraid. Now that boy called and got you all worked up over nothing."

"Maybe, maybe not, but either way tomorrow I'm outta here." Torrie sank her teeth into another piece of fish, wishing as she always had she could return to a time when she could look into Jake's eyes and not be afraid. That time had passed, even Jake was afraid. And the knot of fear, now her constant companion, was more than enough to worry her.

The next day's weather reports were worse and so was Jake's mood. He'd had a nightmare the night before, one he didn't want to relive. After talking to Torrie, he'd called his family in New Orleans, pleading with them to leave, but they refused. What the hell was wrong with these people, all of them, his family, his friends? He thought of Torrie, and his stomach tightened as though he was about to retch. This sense of premonition had never happened to him before, but he decided it was just his nerves. His skin crawled. He couldn't eat, sleep, or even sip water. He was so frigging worried about everyone. They had televisions, were they all blind? He remembered the hurricane parties he'd attended many years ago. Now he knew how asinine the idea would appear to the rest of the world.

"Damn it," Jake muttered loudly, kicking his slipper across the room as another announcement of impending doom crossed the airwaves into his home, making the fear he'd had before seem as nothing. Terror filled every cell in his body, most of it for Torrie. He closed his eyes and held the phone for a moment before dialing. The nightmare flashed before him, and he shuddered hard. *If anything happened to Torrie.* He shook his head and dialed her number. "Torrie, where are you?" he asked the moment she answered.

"I'm still in New Orleans. Jake—"

"New Orleans! Do you just want your damn dream to come true? Maybe I can talk some sense into your family." He clicked the end call button and redialed to Torrie's family home. He hung up before anyone could answer; knowing no one would listen to him. He tried to dial Torrie again, until he realized she'd turned off her phone.

Kimmie looked at Torrie and gave her a half smile. "Why didn't you just tell him you were leaving today?"

"He didn't give me a chance. Jake always bombards everything and everyone. He got into the right profession." Torrie laughed. "Tearing down houses with a bulldozer is right up his alley." She absentmindedly pushed her foot back and forth, making the porch swing she was sitting in with Kimmie move a bit faster.

"What about him working with Bush?"

"It's his life. He can do what he wants to do."

"You don't still have a crush on him, do you?"

Torrie smiled. "I never had a crush on Jake. He was my friend, nothing more." She lifted her glass of lemonade from the wicker table beside the swing. Taking a sip, Torrie allowed her thoughts to stray to her feelings for Jake. She swallowed the feelings of want that always surfaced when she thought of how much Jake really meant to her. From the corner of her eye, she saw Kimmie tapping her fingers against her thigh, waiting for an answer. Torrie got up from the swing and walked across the porch. She stared out on the neighborhood, not wanting to see the look her sister would be giving her for the lie she'd just told.

"Is that why your heart has been broken for fourteen years? You forget, little sister, I was the one you ran to when he made you cry. I don't know about you, but I've never forgiven him for hurting you. I don't know how you could have continued being friends with him."

"I loved Jake…as a friend," Torrie amended. "I didn't want to be angry with him."

"And what did you think he wanted? Sometimes I wish I had told Mama what happened. She would have beaten your tail for running after that boy. Two months you called him and sent him letters, and not once did he call you back, then he just waltzed back into your life, and you allowed him. Hell, that was the first time I ever wanted to slap the hell out of you. You didn't even demand an explanation."

"I didn't have to, Kimmie. He told me he wanted to be friends again. I wanted him to be my friend."

"You wanted a lot more than that."

Torrie looked at her sister. "I don't know if that's true or not. I'd never had any different feelings for Jake until a moment before he kissed me. I don't think he felt any different about me either, not until then. We never had a chance to see if there was more."

"Is that why you allow him to keep calling you all the time, because you wonder?"

Torrie thought about Jake, about the years of friendship, about the hurt, and then back to the little boy he'd been. "Jake's a part of me. He made himself a part of me when I was four. Why do you think I stopped teaching and opened the nursery school? Because of Jake. He shouldn't have been the one to comfort a frightened little girl; it should have been the teachers. I always used to think the first grade teachers were the most important people in a student's life. That's why I taught first and second grade until I figured out nursery school teachers are the most important. I want to make these babies feel safe from the moment their parents drop

20

them off. I love what I do. Jake and I have both found our callings. I comfort and Jake bulldozes." Torrie laughed.

"Still you didn't answer the question. Why didn't you just tell the boy you're leaving? Are you hoping he'll worry so much he'll come here to make you leave?"

The thought had never crossed her mind, or had it? Torrie glanced up. "There could never be anything between us. I would like to see him again before we're both old, but he's never come home once since he's been gone."

"How do you know, Torrie? Maybe he just didn't come looking for you. Maybe he stayed in the Garden District…then you wouldn't know would you? You don't run in the same circles. All of his family moved to East New Orleans. He'd have no need to come around."

"He still has a couple of cousins around here."

"If you're going to be talking about Jake the entire time we're gone, I'm not going with you." Kimmie glared. "I mean it. He's hurt you twice. I'm not going to give him a chance to hurt you a third time. You're right. You're my little sister, and I'm going to protect you. If you don't have the sense God gave a billy goat, then I'll have to look out for you. When this is over, we're going to find you a man and get your tail married. You need some fine brother to get your mind off Jake."

Little did Kimmie know that no fine brother could get her mind off Jake. Not in the way Kimmie thought anyway. No one could take the place Jake had in her heart. Torrie laughed. "If you're so good at finding men, then why don't you have one?"

"May I speak to Torrie?" Jake had given up the idea of letting the matter pass. His conversations to himself hadn't helped, his words that she was a grown woman, to leave her alone did no good.

It didn't matter he'd not seen Torrie in twelve years or that she'd hurt him with her indifference. He had to try until he got her to agree to leave. Maybe then this sick feeling in his gut would ease.

"Who is this?" the voice on the phone asked.

Jake knew darn well, they all knew who he was. He'd called the home for over twenty-five years. "It's Jake."

"Jake who, and what do you want with Torrie?"

"Who is this?" Jake asked pretending not to recognize the voice of Torrie's cousin Trey. Two could play that game.

"You called here, what do you want?" Trey asked in his sullen voice.

"I want to speak to Torrie." Jake was almost screaming now. "Why are you people not taking this hurricane warning seriously? Are all you people nuts or what?"

"You people?"

The phone was snatched and the tone sounded different. Damn, he'd been on speakerphone. *Oh hell.*

"Jake, what do you mean calling here and talking like that? Trey had you on the speaker. You should have at least had the sense to call me on my cell."

"Torrie, I didn't mean it like that, not the *you people* comment. Besides, you weren't answering your cell. But I did mean it when I asked if you're all stupid there. There's a damn hurricane coming. If you don't have sense to get out now, you are stupid."

When the phone clicked, Jake threw it across the room. "Damn stupid people," he screamed. He didn't give a damn if Torrie heard him. He was talking about all the people in New Orleans who chose to ride out the storm same as they'd always done. His family was also part of the stupid people.

His relationship with Torrie was already strained. He took in a deep breath and blew it out, then he dialed her home, intending to apologize to whoever answered. "Hello," Jake said and ignored the, "It's that uptown boy again," Torrie's cousin muttered. The phone was slammed down, reminding Jake of a time his calls had been welcomed into the home. But the kiss had changed everything.

For the count of ten, Jake hesitated. This was almost not worth the aggravation, but because of Torrie, he would risk it. Jake called repeatedly, each time getting the phone being lifted and slammed. Okay forget Torrie's family, it was Torrie he wanted out of there. The rest of them could stay and drown as far as he cared.

He dialed her cell. "Torrie, get the hell out of there."

"Jake, my whole family is pissed at you, ready to kick your butt. I can't talk to you now."

"Don't be so damn stupid, Torrie. There's a hurricane coming, and it's no joke."

"The levee—"

"Don't tell me about no damn levee," Jake thundered, slipping back into his southern drawl automatically. Somehow, Torrie brought out all things in him, all the things he'd tried a lifetime to forget. "If you need money, I'll wire it to you."

"Thank you, massuh. I'sho grateful for that."

"Now you *are* being stupid," Jake yelled and slammed the phone down.

Chapter Two

Torrie kept one hand on the steering wheel as she drove away from the bank. This was the first time since she'd rented the safe deposit box she'd ever taken the contents outside the bank. She rubbed her free hand across the smooth metal surface of the locked box. A chill ran through her, but it had nothing to do with the temperature of the metal. She could feel her sister's eyes looking at her. She couldn't do anything about that, but she couldn't leave the box behind, in light of her reasons for leaving.

"What's in the box? I've never seen anyone have an actual locked box stored in a lock box at a bank. Torrie, you're strange. One of either would have been enough. Why both?"

"You're not going to like the answer," Torrie warned as she parked in front of her house and got out of the car. She looked up and down the street. Everyone was ignoring the warnings from the mayor. People laughed at his impassioned pleas as though they were a joke. Torrie had witnessed the agony in the depths of Nagin's eyes. Her soul had carried the burden for longer than she cared to remember. She sympathized with the man. He was in charge of public safety, and no one listened, no one believed. Torrie shivered, she wasn't leaving because of the mayor's warning, not even because of her own dread. She was leaving because Jake was afraid for her.

A ball bounced against the car, startling her. Torrie turned toward the group of children and blinked. "Kimmie, oh my God, the kids. How could I have forgotten the kids? Listen, I'm going to the school. We have to convince more people to leave. I have the two school vans and they each hold twenty."

"Don't take this too far, okay?" Kimmie warned. "We don't even have a place to go yet."

"It's not as though I haven't been trying. I just haven't had any luck. Half the time the calls didn't go through, or no rooms were available.."

"Then why in the world are you trying to convince people to leave when you have no place for them to go?"

"I have to do something." Torrie looked up and down the street, trying to hold back her emotions. She needed to remain calm in order to figure out what to do next.

"Torrie, you need a plan."

"I have one. We're going to leave."

"That's not a plan."

"Stop looking at me like I'm crazy. I'm going to keep trying to find someplace to go. But even if I don't, I'll still feel safer in the car traveling away from here."

"Like I said, don't take this too far."

"Too far? I can't just leave my babies like this. What kind of a person would I be? What kind of teacher?"

"If you go around scaring the hell out of people, when this is over everybody's going to yank their kids out of your daycare. If you want that, then you go ahead and act like a fool, a crazy woman. Who the hell do you think wants a crazy, insane woman taking care of their kids? Torrie, your daycare is the only one open on the weekend. Think about it. People need you."

For a moment, her sister's words slowed her down. But only for a moment. Okay, she was behaving like a raving lunatic. She would have to get it together. She sucked in her breath. If she could convince her sister her feet were firmly planted on the ground, she could convince others. She pasted on a smile. "You're right, Kimmie, I'm sorry." She glanced at the ball she held in her hand. She looked at the child with the impatient slant to his shoulders, the defiant dare for her to keep his ball. She smiled, then tossed it back to him.

"As a Christian, I feel obligated to tell everyone we're leaving, and alert the families of all my babies that I'm closing the nursery school until we get back."

"Why?" Kimmie stared at her as if she'd suddenly grown a second head. "You can leave the school open. You have teachers who can work until you come back."

Tiny shivers flapped around her heart. Mama was right, Kimmie was doing this to appease her, not because she thought there was any real danger approaching. But she didn't care why her sister thought she wanted to leave or that she thought Torrie was crazy, the main thing was Kimmie would be with her out of harm's way.

"I can't very well head to safety and leave my staff in danger, now can I?" Torrie asked, making her voice sound as reasonable as possible.

"These people need their paychecks. You can't just take that from them. And the parents need to go to work. What are they going to do if you close, if they have no place to take their kids?"

"Then they take their kids away from New Orleans. I will not dock the employee's pay. But I'm not leaving without telling everyone why." Torrie carried the heavy metal box up the stairs to her bedroom. "And don't start with me about the box. It goes where I go."

Torrie's heart was breaking. One pair of dark brown eyes after the other looked at her first in amusement, then fear, then utter disbelief.

"You're closing? What are the parents going to do? Torrie, it's just a storm. It will pass," Ann said.

"I'm praying it will, but if it doesn't...Listen," Torrie stopped and looked around the office, which was crowded with all the teachers. Kimmie was the only one out with the kids, Torrie wanted to give this little speech only once. "I'm paying everyone's salary for the days we're closed. It shouldn't be but a few days. Maybe I'm being silly, but the weatherman said this hurricane is a category five storm. The mayor thinks we should all leave, and so do I. I'm paying Roy and Michael to drive the school vans. They're taking their families, but there is still room for some of you. The rest can drive their cars. We can all leave together. Whoever wants to go, sign your name on the list. We'll meet back here and leave around three. If you're coming, pack light. Bring food and clothes for a few days."

Torrie passed the list around, sighing when no one put their name on it. "Look everyone, what if this storm isn't like always? You do remember the levee broke in the ninth ward back in 1965. I love you guys. Please, don't make me be the only person from the daycare who leaves."

"Torrie, you just don't want to look silly, do you?"

Torrie turned toward Ann who made the remark jokingly, but Torrie could sense mounting fear in Ann. The fear made its way to her eyes. Torrie passed the list again to Ann and smiled in relief as Ann scribbled her name across the page.

"What the hell do I care?" Ann said, trying to go for amusement. "If the boss lady wants to pay me for taking a vacation, then hell, I'll go."

"I'd go, too, Torrie, but we don't have money for a vacation." Suzette looked down.

The moment was building, but Torrie had to find a way to make this happen. She didn't have enough money to cover everyone in the town, but she did have enough for her staff for a few days.

"Give me a couple of hours, and I'll take care of everything. I'll pay," Torrie promised, knowing she would even if she had to borrow from her sister. The single sheet fluttered between the tips of her fingers as she held it out.

"Leroy won't leave." Maggie shrugged her shoulders. "He's a deacon. He thinks we should just have faith."

Forever and a Day

Then let Leroy stay here, and you take your kids and run. Torrie closed her eyes and looked away. She couldn't say those words, no matter how much she thought them. *Still.* She sighed as she turned back. "Look, I know none of you expected this, and it was wrong of me to think you could make a decision so quickly. Call Leroy," she glanced in Maggie's direction, "tell him I'm paying for everything." She saw the frowns on the women's faces. "This isn't charity. I can't leave without knowing you guys are planning to leave or come with me. I'm going to worry myself to death unless I know you're safe. We're family. I want my family with me." The frowns changed into expressions that showed their understanding.

"I have a baby shower on Sunday."

Torrie blinked before she could process this statement. She almost laughed. "Latrice, you have four babies. We've had showers for all four of them." She attempted not to frown as she looked at Latrice's eight-month pregnant belly. "Don't you think one baby shower is enough?" Torrie finished.

Immediate silence filled the room. Everyone had showers for each baby, no matter if it were ten or more. Torrie had crossed the line, and she knew it. She was sounding as if she were insulting Latrice and all the other women who had baby showers for more than one baby. That wasn't her intention. Still, the idea that a baby shower was more important than leaving the path of Hurricane Katrina, than protecting the lives of those four little babies already here and the unborn, that was just plain...Torrie thought of Jake; it was stupid. But she was allowed to think it. Jake had crossed more than one line when he'd said it.

"Latrice, don't you think I'm looking out for you and your babies? Come on. Go with us. We'll have you a shower when we get to wherever we're going."

"Where are we going?" Latrice asked.

Now that was a very good question. Where was Torrie taking all of these people like she was some modern day Messiah leading these people out into the wilderness? This shouldn't have even been a concern. The mayor had issued a mandatory evacuation. Many people had already left the city. She'd badgered her own family relentlessly until she'd convinced several cousins and two uncles to leave. They'd already headed for Texas. She'd work on the rest, but for now, she wanted to convince her employees to leave. If she could, she'd try and get the entire city to leave.

Since the party, she'd done nothing but beg her family to leave, only to have them laugh at her as they'd watched her calls become disconnected. The phone service was straining under the sheer volume of calls and wasn't working most of the time. None of that mattered to Torrie. She was leaving with or without a place to stay. And she would do like her mama always told her: she would pray things would work out.

"Don't worry," she made her voice sound self-assured and confident. "Just sign up so I'll know how many rooms we'll need, and I'll get the place for all of us." *Please God*, she prayed. "Listen, I'll be back here in a couple of hours. I want to go convince more of my family to leave."

"If you're trying to make room for us in the vans, what are you going to do if your family decides to come or your aunts and their families?" Latrice looked from Torrie to Kimmie.

"Daddy has that big truck," Torrie answered. "As for my aunts. Auntie Mattie is the only one who needs a ride. The rest have transportation, but I still have to insist first come first served. Sorry. I'll pay for the gas for those who are caravanning. Just know the center is closing until the threat of the hurricane leaves."

Walking toward her sister, Torrie was determined to hide her nervousness. She eased closer to Kimmie, making sure to keep her voice low, digging her nails into her sister's arm to warn her to keep quiet. "I have to pay for rooms for everyone. I promised I would." She ignored the dread on her sister's face. "What choice do I have? I have to do something."

"Did you suddenly become rich and we don't know about it?"

"What was I supposed to do?"

Kimmie sighed, and she put her hands on her hips as she glared toward Torrie's office door. "They're going to take advantage of you. They all know you can't afford this."

"They didn't ask me to pay, I volunteered."

"Yeah right. *'Torrie, I don't have money for this.'* This whole city knows what a softie you are. Who are you kidding?"

"If I'm a softie, I learned it from you." Torrie stood for a moment and smiled at her big sister. "I have the money for a few days."

"Did you empty your accounts? Is there money in that locked box of yours that you keep hidden?"

"What's in that box can't pay the bills, but I can't leave here without it. And no, I didn't take all of my money, just most of it. Now come on, we need to go and find someplace with some beds since we're taking people with us. Maybe we can get Mama and Daddy to give in and come." Kimmie laughed and Torrie frowned. "That wasn't a joke," she said.

"That's why I laughed. Honey, your tears are not going to work on them, not when it comes to leaving. If they didn't up and leave when we were kids, they sure as heck won't leave now. And if you don't hurry up, I might change my mind." Kimmie didn't try to soften her glare. "I can't believe we're leaving home because of Jake."

Torrie walked out the door with Kimmie close behind her. She refused to comment on her sister's remark. As for leaving because of Jake, his fear was an excellent reason to leave.

Torrie tried not to look at her sister as she sighed in desperation. Every place she'd called had no more vacancies. She was having the same results as last night and was getting frustrated. She wasn't the only person who'd thought of leaving. Good. But still, it didn't help in her quest to get a safe place for everyone to stay. She sighed and hung up the phone. Her gaze connected with Kimmie as her sister paused from packing her tarot cards, stones and other trinkets she used in her spiritual reader shop. She wondered if the high shelf Kimmie was placing them on would be high enough.

"I can't find anyplace to stay," Torrie said softly.

"Try Sam Houston Jones State Park in Lake Charles."

"The park? I never thought of the park." She calculated the difference in trying to pay for a large group. People could pile in on top of each other if necessary; she wasn't as worried about physical comfort as she was about safety. Kimmie's smiling at her as she dialed the operator to get the number gave her the will to continue. Within a matter of minutes, she had booked twelve cabins. She charged them to her credit card and was told she could bring tents and RVs. The price was just right.

"Turn that up." Torrie pointed toward the television. Mayor Nagin was speaking.

"You need to leave, this is not a test. This is the real deal. I don't want you to panic. We want you to be ready; we want you to be safe. We want you to be calm. Hurricane Katrina is no joke. There is an evacuation order in place. When it hits there will be nothing we can do. It is a category five. I suggest every one of you get a ride, call a friend, and get out of New Orleans until after the hurricane passes."

Torrie and Kimmie stared like twin statues at the television. Torrie listened for a moment longer, then blinked. "Did you vote for him?"

"No, did you?"

"Yes. I think he's trying to get rid of some of the corruption, and I think he's right in this."

"Would you think it were corruption if your name was Broussard?"

Torrie thought about it. "I have to admit, I've wondered how it would be to receive special privileges because you're a shade lighter than someone else. And I won't lie, I've wondered what life would be like if I had a privileged name." She didn't add "like Jake." She didn't have to.

"Have you ever wondered how living in the Garden District would be?"

Jake's not living in the ninth ward has always been a sore spot. A person would have to be born and raised in New Orleans to understand how class worked; the place was a country into itself with its own rules and definite prejudices. Everything was done according to the ward a person lived in. Though political graft ran rampant throughout the city, privilege all came down to the power in a name. Torrie's family name of Thibodeaux carried no such power, but Torrie had always been determined that wouldn't matter. She'd worked hard and had a good life, which should count for something. And anywhere else in the world it would, except New Orleans.

"Kimmie, I'm not sixteen. I'm not wishing things were different. I love my neighborhood and my people. Don't make this about Jake. You told me not to talk about him, so don't keep bringing him up."

"That's going to be kind of hard to do since we're leaving because of him. When this hurricane passes, you will still be from the ninth ward. It doesn't make a bit of difference that you now live in Mid City. Baby sister, you're from the ninth ward, and Jake will still be from the Garden District. He will always be a Broussard and you won't."

A sharp pain pierced Torrie's heart. *If only.* Now was not the appropriate time to talk about this. She ached all over, but mostly her heart ached. The hole Jake had mentioned existed in her also. In all the years Jake had been gone, Torrie had not once given in to the urge to call him, to ask him to come home. Nothing. Hadn't her actions earned her sister's respect? How much stoicism would she have to show in order to erase the two months she'd played the fool for Jake?

Instead of searching for an answer to Kimmie, she dialed the phone to her nursery school. "Maggie," she spat out the moment the phone was answered, "type a flyer and print, about a thousand. Make them simple, bold type, just say that Sam Houston Jones Park has space for tents and RVs, and the price is reasonable for anyone wanting to escape from the path of Hurricane Katrina."

Torrie gave Maggie the number to call. "And, Maggie," she continued, "could you call a few guys? I want them to go around and stick them on the doors." Torrie glanced at Kimmie. Her sister was shaking her head as a sullen and sad expression appeared on her face. "You can't take everyone with us, Torrie."

"You're right, I can't take everyone, but I can try and make sure as many people as possible know about the park."

"Don't you think people heard Nagin?"

"They heard him, but most of them won't listen to anything he has to say. They probably won't listen to me either, but I have to try."

Two hours later, Torrie had taken her sister to pack a small bag and packed her own. She met with her staff, a couple had changed their minds. She hugged each of them, telling them to not wait too long. She paused when she came to Latrice. "Let me take the kids," she pleaded, "I'll take care of them."

"My kids stay with me."

"No offence, Latrice, I just...I don't—"

"Okay everyone, come on," Kimmie said, cutting her off, knowing her pleading would accomplish nothing. It had all been said, and Torrie's tears wouldn't change things.

The first drops of rain started as the school's vans and the cars loaded with people Torrie had convinced to leave followed behind them. She had one stop to make. She'd never intended to bring a caravan to her parent's home, but somehow everyone was following her.

By the time Kimmie and Torrie climbed from the car, the rain was beating harder. Her mama met them at the door with two baskets. Without asking, Torrie knew they were loaded with food.

Torrie kissed her father and went into her mother's arms, holding on for dear life. She was trembling, afraid, not wanting to let her mother go. "Mommy" she pleaded, not caring she was crying like a two year old. "Please, Mommy, come with me. Please, Mommy, I need you." Her mother tried to push her away, but Torrie refused to be pushed. She held on tighter. "Mommy, listen to me. This is going to be bad. I won't be able to stand it if anything happens to you."

"Nothing is going to happen to me, child. I'll be here when you come home."

"What if you aren't?"

"I'll be here, Torrie. I promise you. I've never made a promise to you that I haven't kept."

"But, Mommy, you don't have control over the weather."

"I have control over my word, and I've given you my word, nothing will happen to me. Now you and your sister go. Why are all those people following you? Did you convince them to leave?"

This time when her mother attempted to pull away, Torrie allowed her to. She looked at the growing caravan. "They believe me, Mommy. Why don't you?"

"It has nothing to do with my believing you, baby? I just don't believe there's a need to leave. Don't take me for an old fool, Torrie. I would never put myself in the path of danger. I just don't think there's any reason for us to go, baby, but I understand that you do, and I want you to. Don't worry about us. The good Lord will take care of us. He always does."

"But, Mommy?"

"No buts. You go on with your sister. You got all those people waiting. Go on now."

Torrie touched her mother's hair, her fingertips outlining her mother's face. The tears fell from her eyes as she ignored Kimmie pulling her from her Mama. She whispered softly before glancing over at her father. "Daddy, won't you come?" She looked again at her mother. "Mommy, please keep the promise, okay?" Kimmie pulled her down the steps of the porch. The rain was pouring now, buckets of it. Kimmie climbed behind the steering wheel and screamed at her. "Let's go, Torrie."

This dreadful feeling, this immense weight crushing her throat hurt. She couldn't leave. Torrie stood in the rain, looking at the porch, at her parents and her aunts and cousins who had gathered. She felt the shudder to her soul. She reached for her cell to call Jake.

The wind picked up speed. She was drenched so much the smells of New Orleans clung to her and to her limp, wet hair. It filled her pores and battled with the elements. The humidity claimed her. She looked upward. The sky was as dark as her fears, too dark for so early in the afternoon. His face floated before her. She had to tell him she couldn't leave. She prayed he would answer.

"Jake," Torrie moaned, "Jake…"

"Torrie, are you still in New Orleans?" He heard the tears in her voice. The howling of the wind over the wires fused his increasing fears. "Tell me you've left. Please, tell me that you're somewhere safe."

"It's raining, Jake, hard, I'm not going to be able to leave my family. I can't…What would I do if something happened to them?"

"What would I do if something happened to you?" Jake's hand clutched the phone. "Please leave now."

"My mama won't leave. How can I go? She's standing on the porch looking at me, smiling. You tell me, Jake, how am I going to leave her like that?"

"I'm coming down there, and I'm taking you someplace safe."

In spite of the pain in her heart, Torrie laughed softly. "You can't. There's a hurricane coming. I don't want you getting hurt. I don't want to worry about you."

"But don't you understand I'm worried about you?"

"I can't leave."

"*Oh God,*" Jake held the phone against the side of his face. An agonized wail filled his spirit, and he groaned aloud. He was watching the news. This was bad. "I love you, Torrie," he whispered. "I've always loved you."

"I love you, too, Jake."

"Not that way, Torrie. I mean I've always loved you. You should have been the one I married. Don't let me lose you, not now. Just tell me you're going."

She really wanted to tell him, but she kept looking at her mother, watching as she went to the screen door and still watching her as her cousin Trey bounced down the stairs and opened the back door of her car. Before Torrie was even aware of his intentions, he'd lifted her in his arms and tossed her into the back seat. He locked the door, then dove into the front seat. "Drive, Kimmie," he ordered, "damn it, just drive."

Shudder after shudder claimed her body. Torrie rocked back and forth, watching her parents until the blinding rain made it impossible. She cast tearful eyes at the phone, having forgotten Jake.

"Jake," Torrie called almost in a whisper, then louder when he didn't answer.

Silence. The phone was dead.

Chapter Three

I love you Torrie. Why had it taken so long for him to say those words? Jake had always known he was in love with Torrie, and that had happened long before the kiss. Long before he'd known about lust, he'd loved Torrie.

He looked at the dead phone and fell to his knees, praying for Torrie's safety, wishing he'd been bold enough to admit his true feelings to her years before or that he'd at least admitted it to himself.

He had admitted his reasons for leaving New Orleans after he'd kissed Torrie. The intensity of his feelings for her changed rapidly, scaring the hell out of him. He constantly thought about touching her in places he knew were forbidden. She was a good girl and his friend. And he'd do everything in his power to keep it that way. Besides, she'd only wanted to be his friend. He'd had no choice but to get the hell out of New Orleans. For the two years he'd remained in New Orleans after he kissed her, his feelings had only grown, and he'd been afraid of what he'd do if she never reciprocated the feelings. He'd wanted her so badly, his body ached constantly. That was the lust. He loved her so much the thought of defiling her forced him to leave home to leave her virginity in tack. He'd had no choice but to get the hell out of New Orleans.

Through the years he'd kept up the painful act of being her friend, always ready to go to her should she ever call. She'd never called and he'd never gone. Tonight she'd called, and as he would have done for the past twelve years, he was going to her. Come hell, flood, hurricane, or high-water he was going after Torrie. He had to make sure she was safe.

Forever and a Day

Torrie lay with her head buried on the cushions of the car. She knew they had waited too long to leave. She wondered if the cabins she'd paid for with her charge card would still be open to them. A lot of other people had left before them. She had no idea if they would even be allowed to leave on the I-10 West. From what she'd heard, the contra flow had worked initially. She had talked to a few friends who'd been turned back and had to find another way to go out of New Orleans. Right now, she could only pray they would make it.

When they crawled onto the I-10 West, Torrie breathed easier. She glanced in the mirror and caught sight of her sister watching her. "I'm okay," Torrie assured her. "Sorry about the meltdown." She chuckled, waiting for her sister to join in, to call her a baby. She moved her head a little to look at the side of Trey's face. He sat with a rock hard expression on his face, not saying a word, but Torrie could see his knee bouncing up and down. He was either nervous or angry; she didn't know which.

"Was that Jake on the phone?" Kimmie asked.

"Yes. He told me that he loved me," Torrie whispered.

Her glance darted back to the rearview mirror, catching Kimmie watching her instead of the crawling traffic in front of her. "Whenever you get tired, Kimmie, I can drive." She cringed at the look that passed between Kimmie and Trey, and then she knew. The silence wasn't about them leaving town in the middle of an upcoming hurricane. No, it was about Jake.

Torrie held the phone to her chest. Despite worrying about her parents' safety, beside her fears, there was a tiny spark building somewhere inside her spirit. Jake loved her. She would use those words to ride out the storm even if he took the words back later. For now, she'd allow them to run freely through her. Somehow, Jake found a way to put her mind on something other than her dreams of the storm. *Jake loves me.* Her heart skipped a beat.

Three hours later, the car was still quiet. It was unlike any of them to not talk, not joke, not even belittle her worries. Now Torrie wished they would. She wished her phone worked. She wanted to let Jake know she'd left. Besides, every time she'd checked to see if her cell phone had a signal, she heard the double sigh from the front seat. No one bothered to ask if she was checking on their parents.

The light flutter that always filled her when she talked to Jake was now trying to take hold, making her feel safe in the midst of the storm. Torrie fell asleep, dreaming of five-year-old Jake promising to take care of her. She smiled at the memory.

Five hours later, Trey was waking her. "Come on out of there, Torrie, or do I have to carry you too?"

Torrie blinked. Wiping the sleep from her eyes, she looked up at the lighted office of the state park. She stretched as she climbed out of the car and looked at the straggling caravan before going into the office to collect the keys. Sixty dollars a night wasn't too much, she thought, not for a cabin. She held the handful of keys. Neither was the seven hundred and twenty dollars a night for the cabins for the few cousins, employees and friends she'd convinced to come. When they got the instructions to the cabin, the mood lightened.

She glanced at the phone on the wall, ignoring Kimmie's glare, and marched toward it. When she dialed her parents, she sighed in disgust. The phone was dead. "Mommy's phone isn't working," she said in Kimmie's direction, then turned her back and dialed.

"Jake, I'm safe," she said when his answering machine kicked in. "I'm at Sam Houston Jones State Park. You didn't need to worry about me. By the way, I love you, too," she said softly. "I'll talk to you later." An emptiness overtook her. She'd wanted to hear Jake's voice again, wanted to know if he'd really said those words, if he'd meant them.

Torrie licked her lips and pushed past her sister. "He was worried about me. I had to let him know I'm safe."

"I heard you, Torrie."

"So what?" Torrie stopped on her way to the counter. "So what if you heard, Kimmie? What harm is there in telling him I love him? He's a friend."

"That wasn't what you meant."

Torrie paid for the pralines and soda, determined not to get into an unnecessary fight with her sister. They were words, nothing more. Sure, she meant them, but she was still in Louisiana, and Jake was in New York. He was doing as he'd always done, helping her through the storm.

Torrie passed out the keys and maps of the state park, and then climbed into the driver's seat of her car. The cabin was a lot more than they'd expected with one bedroom and two extra beds in the outer room. A nice size kitchen with a microwave, refrigerator, and stove, it also contained a table, chairs and large countertops. The sun porch in the back was a bonus. She flipped through the papers she'd been given and dicovered a place to wash their clothes and a store. Though after tomorrow they'd more than likely go to town for groceries. They would be here for no more than a couple of days. Torrie would do as she'd promised; she'd buy the food for all of them. A couple thousand dollars would be well worth the price for her peace of mind.

Trey plopped the baskets loaded with the remainder of the food her mother had packed, onto the countertop and looked at her. "Since we did all the driving to get here, you can warm up the food, you little chicken." He thumped her head and Torrie smiled. Trey was no longer angry. She glanced at Kimmie. Her sister was shaking her head at her, a look of sadness in her eyes.

"I'm not stupid," Torrie said, going up to her sister and kissing her on the cheek. "I won't get hurt. I promise. It's just the storm, trust me. Jake is not going to have any more effect on my life than he's had already. He's just a good friend, Kimmie, that's all. He wanted me to leave, I have. Now it's over, and we'll go back to the way it was; calls on my birthday, Christmas, and during storms.

That's all. Can't I have two days a year to think of him?" She hugged her sister's trembling body close.

"Don't take that from me, Kimmie, I know all about the way things are done. I just want those two days. I just want my memories of him." She pulled back and stared into her sister's identical brown eyes. "Do you want to deny me that?" Kimmie's arms closed around her, and Torrie snuggled close.

"Mama put in a whole thermos of jambalaya and a loaf of sourdough bread. Let's eat, and then we can play cards." Torrie could tell the smile was coming. "I'll share my pralines," she teased, "and Mama probably even put in some pecan pie to make our waiting easier."

Jake ignored the steadily sinking feeling. This was crazy. He had no business being on the Gulf Coast with a hurricane chasing his tail. It was plain stupid, idiotic. And there was nothing else he could be doing at the moment, but going after Torrie. He'd wasted a lifetime not telling her he loved her. He'd promised to take care of her, and he was going to do just that.

He could barely see through the sheets of rain coming down. Hell, if he lived through this, it would be a miracle. He only hoped Torrie's mother had not lied to him. She hadn't cared for him. Still, he hoped that as serious as this hurricane was she hadn't sent him on a wild goose chase.

He glanced at the clock on the dash. He'd been driving almost non-stop since he talked to Torrie. He'd gassed up when necessary and made only three pit stops. His stomach was growling, but he didn't want to take the time to eat. He wanted to get to Lake Charles and hold Torrie in his arms, look into her eyes, and make sure she was safe.

Forever and a Day

The thought occurred—what if Torrie didn't feel the same about him? She'd said she loved him, but he was sure she'd meant as a friend. The only picture he had of her was the eighteen year old he'd left. Jake wondered if her skin was still the same creamy chocolate it had always been. He wondered if her smell would be different. He looked out the window at the cold rain pouring down on his car and wondered would the magic of that first kiss claim his soul as it had fourteen years before.

He got on I-10, wondering why traffic was coming from the other direction. Well, one thing was clear, the journey to Lake Charles was definitely an adventure. Most sane people were home in bed where they belonged. Then again, most sane people didn't have to worry about their one true soul mate being out in this mess alone. And he'd bet it was even less of a possibility that people had allowed years to pass knowing in their heart and soul they'd found the one, yet not claiming them. Jake wanted that chance; he needed it. A shiver slithered down his spine, and he clenched his teeth: Torrie would be fine, he would get to her, he would not allow anything to hurt her, and together they would ride out Hurricane Katrina.

He blinked rapidly several times, glad to hear the pounding rain. Jake remembered the eerie dead silence of a hurricane before it actually hit. And he remembered the sounds when the winds would pick up again. Torrie had once told him the winds sounded like a can opener prying open the house. He'd agreed and knew first hand how the entire house would vibrate, how it could be felt inside every room, how a person tried to drown out the sound with singing hymns or doing second line dancing. This distraction did not work for long, because after some time everyone would end up huddled together in silence.

Jake remembered the hurricane he'd been caught in and waited out at Torrie's house. The two of them had stayed as far from the windows and doors as possible. Torrie wouldn't eat a morsel of the sumptuous hurricane party food until Jake told her nothing was

42

going to happen. She wouldn't join in on the second line dancing. She wasn't interested. And she hadn't felt like dancing, not even when Jake begged. Her eyes had pleaded with Jake to take her seriously. He did take her seriously and he tried so hard to reassure her that she would be fine, that nothing would harm them as long as they were together.

During that hurricane, Jake had been welcome in the home, or at least tolerated. But when the hurricane was over, his father had looked at him in disapproval and reminded him of their background. He'd been fifteen. When he'd turned sixteen, things had changed.

Jake had wanted to ask his father exactly what the hell he'd meant. He'd always known there was something in his town, the underbelly of society. He didn't ask many questions, but now as an adult he knew what he'd witnessed involved corruption, bribery, and the insane idea of the Autocrat club in New Orleans that most inhabitants believed in, the damn paper bag test. If you were darker than a paper bag, you didn't belong. If your name had the right consonants, you could make legal troubles go away. It was a men's club, and membership was by invitation only. The Broussards were long-time members.

Jake remembered how his Uncle James had calmly walked into another man's home and just as calmly shot him to death along with Auntie Sally, his wife, who'd been sleeping with the man. His uncle had spent less than an hour in jail. When Jake tried to ask his father about it, all he'd gotten was a raised brow and, "If you ever need your name, you will be glad you have it. We have more than New Orleans, Jacob."

There was power in his name, and power in the lack of color in a black person's skin. That one was more difficult for Jake to accept. He'd heard of the marches for freedom and of Dr. King, but he wondered if Dr. King had meant that black folks should forget such foolishness as segregating themselves. He wondered if that only applied to the Europeans.

Forever and a Day

Jake saw the lights up ahead. *Finally*, he thought, *another car.* At least he wouldn't have to go there in his mind, wouldn't have to separate the members of his family into boxes; mulattos, creoles, whites, light skinned, high yellow, and those that didn't pass the paper bag test. He wondered for how many years his own family had been relegated to less because they didn't live in the Garden District. He wondered about his family living in East New Orleans, which was actually a part of the ninth ward, but because they didn't want to be associated with the people in the ninth had completely renamed the area. And then there was Mid City.

Everything was all crazy. When anyone else looked at them, they were still all black. Even Jake with his high yellow complexion and golden brown eyes was still considered black. Unfortunately that difference along with his family name and money had made Torrie think he was ashamed of her. *God.* He sucked in his breath. He'd never answered her question.

Yes, New York would make a hell of a lot of difference. Sure black folks were color struck there as well, but at least in New York no one gave a damn if your name was Thibodeaux or Broussard. There they would both be the same. It shouldn't have to be like that, but that was life, as he'd known it on the strange little planet he was born on called New Orleans.

Jake's mind lingered on Torrie. *Thank God she's left New Orleans.*

Please, God, let her be sleeping someplace safe in the park. He pushed the worry away that something might have happened to her on her way out of New Orleans.

Knowing the three-hour trip would take forever and for Torrie it would be a nightmare, he cringed inwardly. She would be filled with terror no matter what happened. And she would hold it all inside. Jake knew, even though she told her family of her dreams, she'd only shared with him the true devastation she'd witnessed. Another shiver tried to claim Jake, but he resisted it. Nothing had happened to Torrie; she would be okay. *God in heaven*, he prayed, *let Torrie be okay.*

Torrie waited for the eerie silence before shaking off the sleep. They were three hours from the hot spot and over an entire day away from the hurricane. Torrie looked around the room, pushing Kimmie's leg off her back, smiling at the memory of the way Kimmie had always slept, taking up every spare inch of space. She wondered if any of the other families who had come with them were awake and hungry. She should have taken care of it last night, but she'd been too exhausted to think.

She went into the bathroom and took a quick shower, running the comb through her hair with one hand while she brushed her teeth with the other. She needed to go to the office and take care of provisions for everyone. She didn't want anyone to have to ask her about breakfast. She wanted them to feel as independent as she could possibly make them.

"Where are you going, Torrie?" Kimmie woke, her question sounding sleepy. "It's still dark outside."

"I just want to go to the office and take care of food for everyone."

"It's dark outside, wake up Trey."

Torrie laughed for the first time since they'd begun their little odyssey. "Wake up Trey? You've got to be kidding. I'm a big girl. I can go outside, get into the car, and drive all by myself."

"If you were such a big girl, why didn't you drive here by yourself?" Kimmie asked, throwing the pillow at her.

Torrie laughed and walked out the cabin. When she came back, she noticed a brand new SUV parked several cabins away. She hadn't noticed it the night before and wondered why she did now. Torrie stared for a moment at the vehicle, her heart racing when she noticed the New York license plate. *Jake*, the name repeated in her mind before she gave up on the foolishness and reentered the cabin. Turning on the radio, she took out the recently washed bowls and laid out pastries, fruit and cereal.

Torrie stood shaking, her eyes on the radio as though she could see the announcer's face. Images from her lifelong dreams swirled inside her mind. Trey stuck his head from under the covers. "Turn it up," he said softly.

Within seconds, Kimmie had opened the door and was looking at Trey and Torrie. "I hope Mama and Daddy are okay."

"They will be, they promised," Torrie answered and moved toward her sister. A knock at the door stopped her. She moved to answer the door, but Trey moved quicker.

Light streamed into the room ahead of the early morning visitor. Torrie could feel the catch in her throat. She glanced upward at the tall muscular man that filled the doorway. *Jake*. Her heart pounded. *"Torrie,"* she heard him call to her.

Jake had knocked on over two-dozen cabin doors, going inside to look around, even when he hadn't been invited. The most the manager at the desk had been able to tell him was that Torrie'd paid for a dozen cabins. When he recognized the people in the rooms, he'd chatted a moment or two with all of them, his feet itching to leave but not wanting to seem rude. It was bad enough he wasn't liked simply because he came from the Garden District and had the fortune or misfortune of having the surname of Broussard.

"Torrie," Jake said softly the moment the door opened. He sensed her essence before he actually saw her. Trey's scowling face once he recognized him was more than enough of a clue his presence wasn't welcomed. Jake stood for a moment, barely breathing, just looking at her. She'd changed into an even more beautiful woman than she'd been as a girl. Her skin was still chocolate brown. He saw the instant she knew it was him; she smiled and his heart seized. She ran to him.

Jake pushed Trey aside and with two strides was swinging Torrie in the air. "Torrie," he breathed deeply, letting her down at last, holding her face between his hands. Torrie was all the words he seemed capable of saying.

"The hurricane, you came," Torrie whispered softly. "Jake," she touched his face, "you came." Then her voice became as lost as his as he crushed her against his chest.

Chapter Four

The smell of rain and sweat along with the unmistakable odor of French fries clung to Jake. This was real; it wasn't a dream. He was standing in the cabin with her and holding her so tightly Torrie thought he might break a rib.

"Torrie, what's wrong with you? Remember you're not alone. Trey and I are standing right here."

Kimmie's voice barely seeped into her mind until she heard the chuckle in Jake's throat. She pulled away to look at him. He'd changed, matured. He pulled her back and held her even closer, whispering in her ear, "I didn't drive all the way from New York to find you and have you leave my arms so soon."

Torrie trembled. She could hear the news announcer, Trey and Kimmie were speaking in worried angry voices, but she couldn't make out what they were saying. She could only concentrate on Jake. She felt his hands lightly massaging her back. When one hand moved, she stared at him knowing what was coming—the same way she'd known at sixteen. *Can't Jake ever kiss me when we're alone?*

His eyes stared into hers, as though he were trying to absorb her soul, as if by osmosis he would become a permanent part of her. Didn't he know he would always be a permanent part of her?

"Torrie," Jake said a moment before his lips touched hers, lightly at first, testing, tasting. He ran his tongue over her lips and she shivered. His mouth became glued to hers, and Torrie gave into the wish she'd kept buried for fourteen years. She kissed Jake, battling his tongue for dominance, drowning in his sweet nectar. They kissed until they had no more breath, then Jake drew away slowly and pressed his forehead against hers.

"Damn," he said, "that was better than I remembered. It was worth the trip."

"What'cha doing, Jake Broussard? Slumming?"

Jake eyes lingered on Torrie for one long moment. He grinned down at her, hoping the "later" in his thoughts was conveyed to her. They had so much to talk about. He slid his hands slowly down Torrie's arms and turned to face Trey.

"Even running from a hurricane, you save your best insults for me. Thanks, Trey." Jake noticed the twitch in Trey's jaw, the squeezing of his hand at his side that immediately closed into a fist. Jake wasn't worried. He didn't drive from New York to fight with Torrie's cousin. But he had no intention of allowing the man, who'd once been his friend, to annoy him.

Torrie touched his arm, and he knew she wanted them to stop the masculine posturing. He eased his own stance. "Hello, Kimmie," he said to Torrie's sister. "I'm glad you all made it out safely."

Now that he was here, Jake wondered why he'd never thought about Kimmie being with Torrie. She'd always fancied herself as Torrie's other mother, always protecting her. He supposed the ten year age difference was a factor in her role. But in the case of storms and hurricanes, it was him who Torrie came to, not Kimmie.

The way Kimmie glared at his arm around Torrie, he almost thought to move it, but he smiled instead. "Were you able to convince the rest of your family to come here?" he asked, pulling Torrie over to the sofa in the sitting room.

"A few, you know how it is." Torrie sat on the sofa, her attention split between the radio and wanting to ask Jake a thousand questions. "I wish I could see what's going on," Torrie said softly, studying Jake's face.

He could grant her wish, but he hesitated, knowing what would happen the moment he said anything. He leaned in close and whispered, "If you want, I have a TV in my truck."

"The black SUV?"

He looked at her. "How did you know?"

"I don't know…I saw it and…I thought it looked like something you might drive."

Jake felt the tiny tremble in Torrie's hand. She'd felt him there. The connection between them had always been uncanny. The tension in the room was growing. Jake actually wished they could go into his SUV and talk, but this was bigger than Trey and Kimmie's dislike. This was about the city, something they all had in common.

He skimmed the pads of his fingers across the back of her hand and smiled. Her kiss was still the kiss that touched his soul. Not a single woman even came close to capturing that special place in his heart. That place had been reserved for Torrie.

He caught her glance toward her sister and was aware of the question in her mind. "Kimmie, Trey, if you want to, I have a very small television in my truck," he said, downplaying the top-of-the-line screen he'd had installed. "The picture might not be that great, but we could perhaps catch something on the news about what's happening at home."

"Home?" Trey, smirked. "It's our home, Jake. You haven't been there in over twelve years."

"It doesn't make it any less my home." Jake tore his eyes away from Trey. He felt Torrie tense beside him. "Whatever's between us, Trey, we can talk about later. Right now I suggest we put our differences aside." He stood, pulling Torrie up with him as he rose. "Do you two want to come with us?" He left it open to them. "Come on, Torrie," he said, pressing the back of her hand gently with his thumb when he felt she might not go. Twelve years. How the hell had he allowed so many years to pass between them?

He opened the passenger door for Torrie and helped her get in, allowing his hand to slide down her arm again. His heart shuddered. *God, thank you,* he thought, as he walked around to the driver's side. Turning on the engine, he immediately clicked on the television, ignoring Kimmie and Trey who had finally come out of the cabin and were climbing into his vehicle as though it was a one-way ride to hell.

Picture after picture of people trying to escape New Orleans flashed on the screen. They silently watched. The tension of misunderstanding and hatred melted away leaving the common line of worry about family left behind.

"Did all of your family get out, Jake?"

He slid his eyes toward Torrie, wanting to touch her, to kiss her again, to tell her how sorry he was that he'd wasted a lifetime of not having her. "Yes," he finally answered, worrying the spot in the center of his top lip with his tongue. "I finally convinced them to go to Texas, but a few distant cousins from my mom's side of the family wouldn't leave."

"What are you saying, people in the ninth ward don't have the sense to get out?"

"Did you hear me say that?" Jake turned toward Trey. "I said I have some distant family who wouldn't leave. Look, this fighting is ridiculous. And over what, Trey? A job that I took when I was sixteen? Let it go, man."

"Jake, do you have a cabin?" Torrie interrupted their argument.

"No, they're all taken, but I can sleep in my truck."

"There's an extra bed," Torrie offered.

"Hell no!" Trey's hand thumped the back of her seat. "Hell no!"

Torrie sucked in her breath. She had no intention of mentioning who was paying for the accommodations. She didn't want to go there with Trey, but she would if she had to. Jake was not sleeping in any damn truck. Not when there was an extra bed in the cabin. He wasn't sleeping in the truck even if there wasn't an extra bed.

"Jake, you're welcome to share the cabin with us. Thanks for coming." She reached out her hand and turned up the volume as she watched the waters pour over New Orleans. She shivered, not being there, but feeling the affect in her spirit. Jake's hand reached out for her, and his eyes found hers. An image of devastation from her dreams flashed before her, and she closed her eyes to forget. When she opened them again, Jake was staring intensely at her.

"Torrie," was all he had to say. He knew what was happening to her, knew the visions she'd had for so many years.

She shook her head yes and lost herself in his eyes. His calm manner bespoke of the little boy who'd promised to protect her. She attempted to smile; but couldn't as she looked at the pictures coming across Jake's screen.

"Wow," she heard her sister say softly and glanced at her. Kimmie's eyes were closed, and Torrie knew she was praying. She closed her own eyes and prayed as well.

After a couple of hours of watching the news, Torrie glanced at Jake. "I think I've had enough for awhile." She glanced toward the cabin door. Feeling the immediate tension, she smiled in Jake's direction. "I haven't been to the park lately. Do you want to take a walk around?"

Before the words were out, he was opening her door and helping her out, ignoring Kimmie and Trey entirely. Torrie didn't blame him; neither of them had said more than a dozen words to him.

"Torrie," Kimmie called to her, sternly, "remember our talk and your promise."

"I'll remember." Torrie closed the door and walked away with Jake.

"What promise are you going to remember?" he asked.

"That I'll be careful of things in the park that could hurt me."

"Liar, we both know she's warning you against me."

Jake bumped her with his shoulder, and they both laughed. The air between them was much lighter without the tension from Trey and Kimmie.

"Jake, it was too dangerous, your driving here alone like that. You didn't have to."

"But you're glad I did?"

Now how the heck did he expect her to answer a question like that? Her heart skipped a beat, then fluttered when he smiled. When his hand reached out and touched her face, Torrie almost forgot the reason Jake was there.

"Why didn't you ever come home?" she asked.

"You've never asked me."

"I didn't ask you this time."

"Yes you did, Torrie. You knew when you picked up that phone and called me, I would come. You've always known. Why haven't you ever called?" He stared at her. "Tell me."

"Tell me why you've kissed me twice?" Torrie walked ahead of Jake, then stooped to pick a flower and turned back. For a second Jake's eyes traveled over her, stopping to rest on her lips. He wanted to kiss her. "Are you going to answer me? Why the kisses?"

He gave a gentle smile. "The first time was my burgeoning awareness of you as something more than a friend, my awareness of my own lust." He clutched her hand tightly. "The second kiss was an acknowledgement of my love for you."

How could she lie after what he'd just said? Yes, she was glad he'd come after her. "You're amazing, Jake. I can't believe you came here knowing how bad this could get."

"And I can't believe I haven't done it sooner. It's never been the same talking you through bad weather over the telephone."

"But it helped." Torrie turned to smile at him and saw the intense look in his eyes, the one that said he wanted to kiss her again. But this time she was ready. She just couldn't keep going around kissing Jake, and then not seeing him for another twelve years. She needed more than that.

"How was your drive, the weather...I mean? How long did it take you?"

Laughter met her question, and she couldn't help but smile. Of course, he was aware of what she was doing. "You can't just keep kissing me. The first kiss when I saw you in the cabin was okay. That was just…well…a hello kiss. We need a better reason to keep doing it."

"A better reason?" Jake's brow arched upward. "Like what?"

"I don't know," Torrie answered. "But think about it; you've kissed me twice."

"And you've kissed me." Jake stared at Torrie as the gentle breeze lifted the curls on the side of her ear. The temperature was already in the upper seventies and would soar even higher. A faint glistening of perspiration hovered just above her lips. He moved closer and wiped it away with his finger "I plan on kissing you again."

"Like I said, you've kissed me twice now, and I don't know if you had a real reason for either. Was there?"

"Don't you know? When we were kids you always knew what I was thinking."

"But we're not kids anymore."

"I still feel the connection."

"So do I, especially now that you're here. But I've been wrong about so many things. Besides, there's so much happening to me. My emotions are on overload.. I don't think I can just trust an on-again off-again link. I need to hear you tell me why you keep kissing me. And I need to hear you tell me while knowing I'm safe."

Jake spotted a park bench and extended his hand to Torrie. When she smiled up at him and sat down, he sat beside her. Gently rubbing her hand, he sighed in satisfaction, his gaze lingering on her, her ears, her nose, her forehead, her cheeks, and then her lips. Was there a reason for kissing her? He felt a primal groan fighting to come from his gut. "Torrie, I meant what I said. I do love you. I've always loved you." He stared into her eyes. She'd closed herself off to him. I meant it when I said it, and I mean it now."

"This is romanticizing things, Jake. We don't even know each other, not really, not as adults. You got carried away worrying about me, and I was scared to death to leave my family behind. I panicked and my mind clicked on you. I had just wanted to talk to you, to tell you I couldn't leave. I never expected you to come after me."

Torrie rubbed his hand that lay over hers. "Jake, if anything had happened to you, I would never have forgiven myself."

"What do you think about me? Why do you think I came?"

"To be my hero, to show me that no little old category five hurricane was going to stop you from protecting a friend, calming my fears, quieting me and listening to my dreams."

He stared at the slight tremble of her lips. He wanted to pull her close. "I came because I'm tired of pretending, tired of living my life as though it's okay you're not in it. I've known since I was five, Torrie. You've known, too. I love you. Look into my eyes and tell me you don't love me."

He watched as she licked her lips, wondering if she would lie or if she'd deny their connection.

"Of course I love you. You're my friend."

She'd taken the easy way out. He smiled, not blaming her. The kiss she'd given him had not been one of friendship; like it hadn't been one of friendship back when they were sixteen. So okay, he had to do some groveling, probably a lot of it, to get back in her heart. He'd hurt her, and he'd never made up for it, not the way he should have.

"You sure you don't mind me staying in the cabin for a couple of days? I want to catch up with you, and then drive back into New Orleans when things calm down and check on the family who are still there. Do you mind?"

Heat showed in her eyes, and it shimmed up and down his spine. He was a goner and so was she, but she was cautious. *Wise move,* Jake thought. He was in the mood to make love to her right then and there. That feeling hadn't changed; the years had done nothing to lessen his desire for her.

"I suppose we can get to know each other again as adults. Until then, I don't think we should do any kissing."

Jake laughed at her words, then swallowed as he trailed his fingers up the left side of Torrie's cheek. His lips followed the path of his fingers. He planted airy kisses on her cheek, kissing only the corner of her mouth. He felt her tremble and grinned.

"Jake, you're not playing fair."

"That wasn't kissing."

"I know. It was a lot more potent. Come on, we need to talk."

"Can I hold you, and share our dreams and our nightmares?" He opened his arms and folded her in them as her head came to rest on his shoulder.

Kimmie's pacing body was the first thing Torrie saw when they returned to the cabins. Her sister ran toward her instantly, sending Torrie's panic back up.

"Kimmie, what's wrong?" she asked, rushing to her sister.

"I was worried to death about you. Our home is in the path of what you've convinced me is a major hurricane. According to the reports, there's less than twenty hours before it hits. You were the one who was so worried, who wanted to leave, and then you disappear. What did you think? You knew I would be worried."

For a moment, Torrie felt two instead of thirty, and being scolded in front of Jake annoyed her. She could feel Jake tense beside her, ready to battle Kimmie along with the elements. This wasn't his fight. Her family was her business.

"I was with Jake," she began.

"And that means what? We know nothing about him. Nothing new that is, and the old leaves a lot to be desired."

For a second Torrie could only stare at her sister, wondering what the heck was the point of her tirade. She caught the way

Kimmie and Trey kept casting glances at each other. For some reason, they feared her being alone with Jake. And Torrie was aware their worry had nothing to do with her physical well being.

The high pitched sounds of Kimmie's voice was beginning to attract attention, people came from their cabins, something else drawing their attention, something other than the hurricane bearing down on their city. This was not New Orleans. This was not a ward war, and Torrie had no intentions of letting things escalate to that point. She glanced quickly at Trey, saw his smirk, then her eyes sought Jake's. There was anger there, the same anger he'd had when they'd been chastised for kissing when they were sixteen.

Torrie was responsible for many of the people in the cabins, she'd begged them to come, had paid for them, and if she could have brought more, she would have. She wouldn't allow the people she felt responsible for do anything to Jake.

Torrie glared at Kimmie, her hands splayed on her hips. "When you're done, let me know," she said in a deadly calm voice filled with authority. Torrie gave her sister one more glance before turning to the others gathered there.

"The hurricane is fast approaching New Orleans, if you haven't heard already. If you have another place to go and want to do that, then I suggest you go. We should all be grateful we're here, and we should all be praying for everyone who wasn't able to leave. I know none of you could care less now about family names, skin color, or wards. We are all one, all running from the danger. We're all a family." She turned slowly around. "And if you for one moment think the park will not toss out trouble makers, then go ahead and cause trouble. I will not lift one finger to assist anyone who gets tossed out. You're on your own."

Torrie turned slowly from person to person, leveling them with a firm look. "I think we should all pray together," she said and began praying, knowing others would join in. When the prayer was over, she reached for Jake's hand. "For those of you who don't know, this is Jake Broussard. New Orleans is his home as well as ours. He stands to lose as much if not more than us. We all have our lives, let's be grateful."

Torrie sighed and sucked in a breath. "I'm sure in a day or two after the hurricane hits, we can all go home. Let's make the best of it until then." She walked toward the cabin, her limbs trembling in anger over Kimmie's public confrontation. She was not a child and resented being treated like one.

The moment the door closed behind Kimmie and Trey, Torrie walked to the two of them. "I meant what I said. This is not a war zone. Keep your problems with Jake to yourself. If you don't want to sleep in the other twin bed, Trey, drive up to the office and see if something opened up. I doubt it, but Jake's staying." She looked at Jake. "Do you drink coffee?" she asked, going for the chicory her mother had put in the bags. Right now, she needed something a bit stronger.

Jake stared at Trey and Kimmie. Trey's lips curled in a sneer while Kimmie's eyes were wide, the anger barely contained. He wondered when the hell had this change occurred? When had the baby sister changed roles with her older sister? Was it because Torrie was a big contributor to the family coffer? She hadn't said the words, but he'd gotten the impression she was paying the way of lots of people and the unveiled threat had been that she would pull it. He stopped the smile about to come to his lips. Torrie was right; they didn't know each other as well as he thought.

For two hours, Kimmie spoke not one word to Torrie, not one blasted word. She'd even avoided looking at her, and when Jake took off for a drive into town, Kimmie still refused to speak. The only reason Torrie had not gone with Jake was because she and her sister needed to talk without Jake there.

"Kimmie, I have done nothing wrong."

"You call kissing him like a hooker in front of us the moment you saw him nothing wrong?"

Kissing him like a hooker. Torrie couldn't stop the smile that crossed her face. This was nonsense. How the heck exactly did a hooker kiss? If a male hooker kissed like Jake, then Torrie might be inclined to investigate. She could only shake her head at the accusation, without answering her.

"You haven't seen him in twelve years. Do you remember what happened the last time he kissed you?"

"We were sixteen. We didn't even know what we were doing."

"And that's why I'm worried. Now you do. You've been yearning for that boy for fourteen years. If he didn't make a move toward you in the two years he was home before he went off to college, why is he doing it now? If he cared so much about you, why didn't he ever come home? Why didn't he ever tell you he loved you before all of this?"

"He's slumming," Trey broke in. "His big family name means nothing here in the park, Torrie. Do you think he's going to stay here with you? Hell no, he's going to ride his butt back to New York in that big fancy SUV of his."

If screaming would solve anything, Torrie would have screamed at the top of her lungs until she lost her voice. "Jake is my friend," she repeated. "If we decide to take it farther, it's our business. You're my big sister, and I love you, but whom I choose to give my body to is my business. It's my choice. I've never questioned your's."

Immediate hurt filled Kimmie's eyes, and Torrie swallowed. She'd not wanted to hurt her sister or remind her of her bad choices. She was forty years old, unmarried and childless. She'd had affairs Torrie had not approved of, but she did want her sister to know this was her life.

"Jake didn't come here to raid my pantry," she said. "He was worried; he didn't want me to go through this storm alone."

"Alone, Torrie? Didn't I come with you so you wouldn't be alone? Didn't Trey? Now that Jake's here, we don't count? Is a Broussard the only one worth anything?"

Torrie blinked several times, trying to summon just the right words. She had no intention of hurting Kimmie but her comment had struck a nerve. She glanced around. Her gaze fell on the pastel cushions of the rattan chairs on the back porch. She walked the few steps to the porch and motioned for Kimmie to follow. Then she sank her body down into the soft cushion, thinking how nice this cabin would be if it were just for a vacation. She patted the spot beside her and waited for her sister to sit. Torrie reached out and touched her sister. She leaned her head on Kimmie's shoulder focusing her gaze on the view outside the window

"I'm sorry. I shouldn't have put it like that. I know even without Jake, I'm not alone. I'm glad you two are with me, but you both know how I've always been about storms. You know how Jake was always able to get me through them. I meant he didn't want me to go through the hurricane without him. It's the worst it's been since Hurricane Betsy in 1965. This is Jake we're talking about; of course he'd be worried."

"He wants you, Torrie. I saw it in his eyes and in the way he touched you. He came for more than to protect you. He was looking at you like he was a hungry lion, and you were the meat he was going to feast on."

"You seem to forget I have a part in this. For your information, Jake and I only talked. I know we don't really know each other. I know it's dangerous to allow what's happening to influence us, but he's still my friend, and I'm going to make sure he stays here until it's safe for him to leave. That much I know, Kimmie." Torrie looked toward Trey who'd joined them uninvited. "As for you, Trey." Torrie began turning to face her cousin. "You jumped in the car with us and came here of your own free will. Jake used to be your friend. What did he do to make you hate him so much? You've said worse things to me, and we're blood. Jake was never like most of the people who looked down on the lower ninth."

"You think that's true?" Trey bristled. "You think your precious Jake didn't have privilege because of the Broussard name, because of his high yellow complexion? You think he didn't accept those privileges as though they were nothing? You think he ever gave a damn about our supposed friendship when he wasn't in the ninth ward? For heaven's sake, Torrie, don't be so blind or stupid. If Jake's cousin hadn't worked over at Little Angel in the seventh, and if his mother hadn't been so busy being a social butterfly to take care of her son, he would have never been driven over there."

"But we did meet," Torrie said, moving from the porch and going back to the living room with Trey and Kimmie close on her heels.

"He wouldn't have ever met you, and he damn sure wouldn't have been at our house for no hurricane parties. Sure, Jake claimed to be a friend to both of us. The difference between us, Torrie, is that I got over it. I grew up and saw Jake for who he really was, a Broussard. You, on the other hand, have tried hard to forget where you come from to make yourself more acceptable to Jake. You might live in Mid City now, Torrie, and you might have a business over there, but, baby, when anyone looks at your face, even in all your paint and fancy clothes, they know you're from the ninth ward."

"Would you stop following me?" Torrie turned to face her cousin, putting out a hand to stop him from walking into her. "Back up, Trey. I have never acted like that, like I was trying to forget where I came from. I have a right to better myself. It's my life and what I've done with it was for me, not Jake. Just because I moved doesn't mean I've forgotten who I am. And who I am has nothing to do with where I live."

Trey grabbed Torrie's shoulders, holding her tightly, forcing her to listen to him. "If you think Jake wants more from you than an easy piece, think again."

A light knock sounded on the door, and Jake opened the door, coming in hefting a box on his shoulder. The conversation ceased as their eyes focused on the box. He'd bought a television. A good thing, but Torrie could see from the smirk on Trey and Kimmie's faces they thought Jake was rubbing his family's money in their faces. She knew he was doing it so they could all watch what was happening. Trey had relaxed his hold on her. Torrie thought of shoving him as she moved past him to stand by Jake, but didn't. Jake and Trey didn't need anymore of a reason to start a fight. A nagging thought attempted to creep into her mind, but she shoved it away. There was no truth in what Trey had said. She wasn't trying to make herself over for Jake. Her lips still tingled where Jake had kissed her. She wasn't just an easy piece for him. She wasn't.

It wasn't that Jake had been eavesdropping, but as loudly as Trey had been shouting, anyone within a mile of the park could have heard. Jake had decided to knock before Torrie could answer. He didn't want to hear her answer yet. He didn't know if he was ready for it. She'd said she didn't trust their connection completely. He hoped she trusted it enough to know she would never be an easy piece for him, that Trey was way off on that one. He came in with the television, refusing to meet Torrie's eyes, not wanting to know if the look had changed. The only thing he wanted to see in her eyes was the look she'd given him when he'd first arrived. Jake didn't think he could tolerate anything else.

As for Trey's question, Torrie was not an easy piece. But did Jake want to make love to her? Hell yes! He wanted her so badly his teeth ached. He'd had to clench them tightly to keep the lust inside. Damn, it was going to be hard. The only time he'd felt safe in allowing his erection free rein was in his truck going toward town. He almost wished he had some way to tie it down, but it couldn't be helped. He'd been in perpetual heat for the two years he'd remained in New Orleans.

Not until Jake had messed things up did he realize he'd made all the wrong moves concerning Torrie. He was determined he wouldn't mess up this time. He wouldn't scare Torrie. He wouldn't give her a reason to think all he wanted was her body. He set the television on the kitchen counter and plugged it in, ordering the erection to go away. His body was determined to make it hard as hell for him to win Torrie's love.

Jake took a quick glance in Torrie's direction, knowing he already had her love, but she had always been stubborn. She wouldn't just fall into his arms because she loved him. She would make him work to regain her trust. She had said as much, and Jake was determined to do just that. He would come home on regular visits as soon as this business with the hurricane was over. He'd make the Big Easy his home again if he had to.

Torrie's gaze met his, and the groan he'd held in fell from his lips. Damn. She was making it hard for him to be cool. Jake thought of his family. He'd left home for another reason, wanting to make his own way, not because of his last name. No way in hell would moving back to the Big Easy keep it like that. He'd never know if his business was because of his reputation as a fair and good contractor or because his family demanded he be given the contracts.

Jake licked his lips. Hell, being away from Torrie again wasn't an option. He would have to find a way to move his business to New Orleans and court her properly until she understood he wanted the whole enchilada.

Torrie could see the muscles in Jake's back strain and knew it wasn't from the weight of the television. He'd heard the conversation before he'd entered the cabin. She was sure of that, and he was restraining himself. She smiled to herself, ignoring the sullen looks from her family. Of course, Jake wanted her, but she wasn't just a piece to him, and she damn well knew it. No man came a thousand miles in the storm for a piece of tail, not that Torrie would mind giving into her urges. She'd always wondered what they would be like together. She knew she wasn't married or in a committed relationship because of Jake. And if she had to hazard a guess, she'd think his marriage had failed because of her. The time had come for them to admit the truth to each other as well as themselves. That Torrie agreed with, but she wasn't rushing into things.

God, he was fine. She turned toward Kimmie, wondering if her sister could read minds. She'd said they would find Torrie a fine brother. Well, God had not made them any finer than Jake. He was a brother, and he was hot. Even more beautiful than the little boy who'd stolen her heart.

Torrie stared at Jake, knowing he knew, knowing it was making him nervous. She chuckled, allowing the sound to resonate through her body before letting it out her mouth. She saw the tremor that it produced in Jake and laughed again. From the back she could see him lick his lips, trying to get that naughty erection of his under control. Did he really think she didn't know? She cast her eyes on his firm behind. The budge from the front caused the material around the rear to tighten up.

Torrie was emboldened by what she could produce in Jake. Too bad she hadn't known of her feminine powers fourteen years ago or even twelve when Jake left town. She would have turned up the power to the ninth degree like the ward she came from. And she would have given him her body as she'd given him her heart.

When Jake claimed her, no one would doubt that he wanted her for life, that he loved her, that she was his true soul mate. No one would doubt their love, not the Broussards, her parents, Trey, or Kimmie. Until then she'd remain cool.

Torrie's plan worked just fine until Jake turned around and stared at her, his eyes once again holding that strange look, the one she now understood, the one that said he was on fire and wanted her. If clothes could melt, she'd be standing there butt naked. Jake was scorching her with his golden brown eyes. *Damn.* He grinned, showing white, even teeth and Torrie grinned in return.

That link between them, he'd known she was staring at his behind and every inch of his body from his strong legs to the top of his short-cropped hair. Black jeans were almost an overstatement of masculinity on Jake. He looked too damn good in them. Torrie shook her head, trying to come out of the trance Jake induced. After all, her plan was to keep her panties on, well, at least until she was sure.

Torrie didn't know how long they would have stayed staring at each other if Kimmie hadn't marched past her and shoved Jake out of the way to turn on the television.

"People, there's a hurricane report. I think it might be something we all want to look at. Maybe the two of you will cool off."

And it should have, but it didn't happen until a minute or two later. Torrie sank into the cushions on the couch. Jake sat beside her, but now both of their hormones were under control. How could they think of anything else in the face of what they were seeing?

"*We're facing a storm that most of us have long feared.*" It was Mayor Ray Nagin. They all sat bunched up, watching the screen. "*This is a once in a lifetime event,*" Nagin added.

Trey looked around the room before muting the sound. "He sounds like the hurricane is a show or something. An event, what does that mean exactly?"

"Trey, don't," Torrie said softly. "He's just trying to impress on people how serious this is, that they need to leave."

"The governor already said that, but hell, Torrie, did anyone think about how the people were supposed to leave? Most of them don't have anyplace to go. Who are you going to run to when your entire family lives in the same damn neighborhood?" He glared in Jake's direction.

"Not everyone has the money to leave," Trey continued. "Especially people living in the wards, and definitely not the lower ninth. What the hell are they going to do, where are they going to go?"

"Not everyone will leave even if they have money." Jake answered Trey's glare with one of his own. "You keep alluding to it. Let's put it on the table, Trey. Yes, I have money. Yes, my name is Broussard. Yes, my family has privilege in New Orleans, but New Orleans is not the entire world. Do you think in New York anyone gives a damn that my name is Broussard, or that I come from New Orleans? Hell no, you want to know what people think when they learn where I come from? Do you want to know what they're interested in? They ask me if my family practices voodoo. Hell, I have never known one person in my entire life that did. They ask me about the graveyards, are there ghosts? Do I believe in vampires? Why? Because some damn writers get it in their heads to write about that crap, and they write about it happening in New Orleans. And do you want to know what else, Trey? They want to know if all the women down here show their breasts all the time, or if they only do it at Mardi Gras?"

Kimmie glared at Jake. "I hate that outsiders know nothing about us. Cajun food, gumbo, naked breasts, and voodoo. I have to agree with you on that. And to be honest, Jake, it galls me to agree with you on anything. I can't believe the dumb-ass questions people ask or the things they think, as though we're not God-fearing people like the rest of the world. I'm not saying voodoo isn't practiced here, but it's practiced all over the world. There might be a different name for it, but if a rose, yada yada ya'll know the rest.

"Hell, if I knew voodoo I'd change things," Kimmie said angrily waving her hands and pointing a make-believe wand toward the ceiling. She turned toward Jake. "If I could really put a hex on someone, I know a couple of people I would have done it to."

"I'm on your side in this," Jake answered her not too well-veiled threat.

For a moment, Kimmie forgot her opinion of Jake. "In this I know we're of the same mind, Jake. But the whole business of voodoo gets me riled up. If anyone in New Orleans had any magical powers, we wouldn't have had to run from a hurricane. We wouldn't be one of the most economically disadvantaged areas in the entire country. If I really knew voodoo I would do something else for a living instead of giving out spooky readings on Bourbon Street to tourists who come looking for it. Why do you think I scare the hell out of them with their readings? They expect it, and I enjoy doing it." She glared at each of them as if they were the tourists she despised.

"Kimmie, no one thought you practiced voodoo. Jake didn't even know you had a shop up town. I've never told him that. Besides, like you said, you're only play acting, pulling a con, making a living on the stupid assumptions of people. I for one am glad you do it. It serves them right for looking down on us and thinking we all go around with a chicken foot in our purses." Torrie breathed hard. "Jake, I thought that part would be different for you."

"It's not." He held her gaze. "And it's not the New Yorkers I blame. How can I when in our very own city if people really knew the dirty truths, they'd wonder how can we complain of social injustice, how can we slam Simi Valley when we do the same thing to each other." He cut his glance to Trey. "Not everyone left who could afford to, Trey, and they all have their reasons."

"Mama and Daddy had the means to leave. Daddy has that truck with the huge tires he drives through mud and floods. Besides that, I begged them to leave. That's not why they didn't leave, Trey. They just don't believe a hurricane will be as bad as everyone says."

"Turn the sound up," Kimmie ordered. "Look what's happening."

The four of them watched in silence as the Saints Superdome was being opened and people lined up to get inside. Torrie tried the phone again and winced when the call wouldn't go through.

"That's not a safe place to be," she said. "Mama and Daddy wouldn't go there, would they?"

"Bring enough food, water and medicine to last up to five days."

"What did they say? Did anyone hear?" Torrie asked knowing none of them had heard the entire report. They were so busy fighting over the right thing to do they were catching only about every fifth word the mayor was saying. Torrie felt her stomach convulse. This was a bad idea, she knew it. Her body began to tremble.

"Torrie," Jake whispered. She turned toward him, but couldn't answer. Images were flashing before her, her nightmare, and they wouldn't stop. She could feel Jake rubbing her hands, crooning softly to her.

"Torrie, they'll be safe there. It's a strong structure."

She fell against his chest. "Jake, I never wanted to have these dreams. I never wanted them to come true." She shook her head back and forth. "Hold me tight, Jake, and make it all go away."

Such a silly childish wish. Jake could not make this go away. This was also a part of her dreams.

"Why can't the people get out now?" Torrie whispered. "They still have almost fifteen hours!"

"How the hell are they going to get out?" Trey snapped. "You want to go back and get them?"

Jake stood up and reached for Trey. "You leave her the hell alone. She's worried and she's scared. I'd say she did a damn good job of getting people out, she got your trifling ass out, and you want to badger her, make her feel guilty."

Trey's jaws were tight, but somehow the anger in Jake stopped him from getting physical. "Trifling, you have no idea what I do, Jake. I'm a teacher, that's not trifling."

"It's not the job that makes a man trifling, Trey. It's his actions. The way you're treating your cousin makes your ass trifling in my book."

Torrie lifted her chin and stared at her cousin. Jake had a point. Trey didn't need to bite her head off because he didn't like Jake. She tilted her head to the side, giving him a chance to apologize. Instead, he snarled at them and walked out the door, slamming it behind him. Kimmie glared at her and Jake.

"Look, Torrie, you wanted us to stay all cooped up in here. I suggest you put a leash on him." She jerked her head in Jake's direction before marching out the door.

Jake took several deep breaths before calming down. Trey's jacking around with him was one thing, but Trey's messing with Torrie in front of his face was not going to happen. Sure, he'd been offered jobs, and he hadn't even been looking while Trey had begged for jobs and never been given one.

Jake paced around the room, wanting to knock something over. He wished like hell he'd never accepted the damn job Trey had wanted, that he'd had the good sense or even the loyalty to say no. He knew Trey had really wanted it, and he'd admit he'd been selfish. Jake had only wanted the job to buy a present for Torrie with his own money. It wasn't until he'd accepted the job that he'd learned Trey needed money to buy clothes, money to stay in school. When Jake had tried to explain and to get Trey to take the job instead of him, Trey had slugged him for his efforts. He'd thought to hell with Trey and had told him he'd never get the job anyway because he was too black.

Jake glanced in Torrie's direction. Why shouldn't her entire family distrust him? A couple of days later he'd carried his precious gift to Torrie and had kissed her. He'd never given it to her, she'd run away, and he'd not talked to her for two months, the lesson drilled into his head about his place in the town and Torrie's.

Those lessons had brought those hateful words to Jake's lips. Those words had been drilled into him by his father for years after the neighbor who'd caught them kissing had told his father as he'd threatened to do. Those same lessons had been pounded into Jake's head for the two months he hadn't seen Torrie. He'd called repeatedly and he'd tried to visit her, but Kimmie had always told him Torrie didn't want to see or hear from him. He'd been forced to wait until she did.

It was the words learned from a lifetime that he'd uttered to his friend, and had hated himself for ever since. Words he had not believed, but said anyway with the knowledge that words had the power to destroy. They had destroyed his friendship with Trey.

How was he ever going to make things right with Torrie when he couldn't make them right with Trey? Torrie was at least two shades darker than Trey. He loved her dark chocolate complexion. He always had. He glared at the door Trey and Kimmie had stormed through, knowing what was really behind their hatred of him—the words he'd uttered fourteen years ago and the fact they came from a Broussard.

"Torrie, I should probably leave. Maybe see if I can find something in town. I don't think it's going to work. Not all of us together like this." He saw the pulse jump at the base of her throat.

"Don't leave me, Jake."

God, she was killing him. "But, Torrie, you know something is gonna jump off for real if Trey and I are under the same roof. Hell, Kimmie looks like she wants to take a swing at me. I didn't come to cause you more stress."

"I'll be stressed if you leave."

Her voice was whispery soft and her eyes liquid pools of desire a man could drown in, that he was drowning in. She swiped her lips with her tongue, and he groaned. "Torrie, this is going to be so damn hard."

"I know Trey and Kimmie they can be—"

"No, Torrie, it's me and you. Let's put our cards on the table. I love you. I want you, and by God I would be your servant if you'd give me another kiss."

"My servant?"

"Your servant," he answered, moving in.

Everything sensible in Torrie was screaming no, but her heart was screaming yes. The desire in Jake's eyes fueled the desire in her. The two of them alone...God, they were a lethal combination, more deadly than the elements. Her panties were wet and they shouldn't have been. She should be concentrating on her worries, on her sister and her cousin or on the group of people she'd convinced to follow her. She should be thinking about that, but she was lost in the gold of Jake's eyes, in the way his muscles rippled beneath the black sweater, his legs in the black jeans.

Torrie could smell his breath. Peppermint. She felt his heat. God she was lost. If she didn't know better, she'd believe she was born wanting this man. So much about him had changed, but so much about him remained the same: the way he made her heart race, the way he made her feel safe and loved and wanted. She stared into his eyes, thinking of another emotion Jake produced in her. She now felt desired—and saw desire mirrored in Jake's eyes.

"One kiss," Torrie said, coming to her senses, "one kiss and you're my servant. One kiss, and you'll stay with me until the hurricane passes?"

His lips moved slowly down toward her own. His breath smelled so sweet, and she wanted him so badly. "One kiss, Jake."

"Torrie, you do know you don't have to give me a kiss to get me to stay, don't you? All you ever have to do is ask something of me, and it will be given if it's in my power to give it. I would still like the kiss, but only if you want to kiss me."

Jake smiled as her eyes shuttered and closed. Torrie was playing it safe, being able to say she'd never given him the permission should things not work out, wanting to make it all his decision. Hell, he'd take it. He nibbled her bottom lip, tasting it with the tip of his tongue. He slid down on the floor to rest between her thighs. He could smell her heat rise up to meet him. She was wet for him. He grinned and took her. Her mouth, warm, wet and inviting did magical things to him., his semi-erection swelled until it was rock hard.

Torrie shuddered, arching her back, and he moved over her, gathering her in his arms, pulling on the sweet nectar hidden in her lush mouth. How could any sane man have denied himself of this treat for all the time he had? Her body, pliable and warm, melded against him, heat fused them together. The kiss, totally erotic, totally sweet and so filled with a promise that Jake broke. He wouldn't push it further. Not here. Not when any moment Trey or Kimmie could walk back in. Torrie would be embarrassed and ashamed. He'd done that to her once, and he didn't intend to do it a second time. He ended the kiss and pulled her closer to his body, allowing his own tremor to absorb her shudders.

"I am your servant," he whispered in her ear and laughed softly, forcing his long body from the floor to sit beside her. She reached to touch him and a groan came out instead. "I'm trying to be honorable, Torrie. How about moving away? Go make some coffee, please, because I've only got about five more seconds of pride left in me, then I'm going to be begging you to let me make love to you. And I will kill Trey if he tries to stop me. So for all our sakes, please, go make the coffee. This cabin is not nearly large enough for the two of us as it is. I need to breathe and you need to move away."

"But, Jake, this cabin is plenty big. Look around, a living room, well-stocked kitchen, and an enclosed back porch." She paused before adding, "It also has a very large bedroom. It's big enough…"

She smiled and Jake grinned. Yeah, Torrie was working it. She was aware she had him aroused. Jake wondered when Torrie had turned into this wanton creature. The thought crossed his mind that he'd thought he would be her first, that she'd somehow know and wait for him. He shook his head as he watched her. He no longer thought that. Her look and the sway of her body told him she was much more experienced than the sixteen-year-old girl he had kissed.

Jealousy quickly consumed him. He didn't give a damn about having been married. He wanted the thought of any other man putting his hands on Torrie banished from his head for good. His masculine pride was almost his downfall. He wanted nothing more than to forget the words he'd uttered and take her so that she'd know despite who ever she'd allowed to enter her body that Jake, and he alone, was meant for her. He heard her laugh, that damn connection—it would be now it chose to work. He shook his head as she turned to grin.

"Have you always imagined me here longing for you, Jake?" Torrie asked. She turned back toward the kitchen thinking of their earlier conversation. If she knew voodoo, Jake would have been unable to perform on his wedding night or any day after. She laughed and got the water. Better not to go there. She couldn't even look at him right now. The picture she held in her mind was potent enough: his broad shoulders and tapered hips, his hard belly, his oh so firm behind.

Torrie sighed, knowing Jake's physical attributes were not important to her. She'd fallen in love with his smile and his eyes. They both still contained innocence and warmth. She would hold on to those things. This time things would be different. He'd said all she had to do was ask, and he'd do her bidding. He'd come through a storm because she'd called. She wondered if she asked if he would move back home when this was over.

Torrie could feel his eyes burning through her blouse. She could feel his wanting of her across the room, and it gave her a tremendous feeling of power. Jake was hers as she would be his, and this time she wouldn't allow him to blow it.

Chapter Five

T
he hurricane has hit folks. I repeat, the hurricane has hit New
Orleans with gale force winds. At this moment, I'm unsure if it's
the five that was predicted, but it's the worse I've witnessed.
Power lines are down all over. It's bad, people, really bad."

Torrie rubbed sleep from her eyes and woke Kimmie. "The
hurricane hit," she whispered in her sister's ear. Just then another
announcement came over the wires.

"New Orleans was damaged less than expected."

Her hands tented together automatically, Torrie prayed. "They
say it wasn't so bad." She turned the radio down. She'd heard all she
needed to hear. "Come on, let's get up and watch what's happening
on the television."

Without waiting for Kimmie to answer, Torrie went into the
bathroom and took a quick shower, then brushed her teeth and her
hair, glad she had a fresh perm. The last thing she needed was to
wrestle with her wild mane of untamed hair, not with Jake only a few
feet away.

Torrie could smell coffee brewing before she opened the
bedroom door. She glanced at Kimmie's figure still huddled beneath
the covers and wondered who'd made it. *Jake.* Trey would never do
anything like that. He thought cooking was woman's work and
would go hours wanting a cup until someone broke down and made
it for him.

"No damage figures, but it certainly wasn't the kind of end of the
century storm everyone predicted."

Torrie glanced at the name, Peter Whoriskey of *The Washington*
Post. She smiled at Jake, then crossed her legs and sat on the couch.

He handed her the cup of coffee. She sighed in pleasure as she took the first sip. It was perfect.

"As I walked through downtown New Orleans today, things are a mess. Water in some places is a foot or more. I do know some people are out and about, but only a handful."

"What about the levees?" Jeffery Brown, the man interviewing him, asked.

"They appear to be a substantial success."

Torrie began to cry, she raised her eyes. "Thank you, God," she repeated over and over. She felt Jake's arm around her. "Thank you for being here, Jake." She took another sip of her coffee, feeling much better than she had in a week. The worst was over. Her dream wasn't coming true. The levees had held up against the hurricane.

"Any cars out?" Brown asked.

Whoriskey answered, *"A couple of cars. We got a flat in the car I was riding in because of all the debris. I saw some others stalled in a few feet of water. Even some of the high riding vehicles are having problems.*

"Not Daddy's truck," Torrie said softly. She looked at Jake. "Don't ask me why an old man would want a truck like that, but his tires have to be ten feet tall."

"Ten feet, Torrie?"

"Well, I know Daddy's truck can handle a little bit of water."

"But it's over and if he didn't leave during the hurricane, Torrie, do you really think he will leave now it's passed? I know your father and how stubborn he is. I also know you have that same streak in you. Naw, he'll likely stay there and ride it out until things are dry and clear."

"So we took a four and we're still there." Torrie smiled. "Would you have come if it had been less, Jake?"

"If it had been a measly little old thunderstorm, I would have come…if you had bothered to call me." He stared at her lips full and lush. He wished she had called him sooner. "Why didn't you ever call me on my birthday or send me a card?"

Forever and a Day

The metal box under her bed was Torrie's proof Jake remained in her heart and her thoughts. She kept every card Jake sent her. She had bought him a card for every birthday and Christmas. She'd even written him letters, and locked them in the box, too. She knew she was being silly, but she'd allowed herself this one thing. She couldn't let go of her connection to him.

"Did I ever tell you I finally went to the Autocrat Club?" Torrie smiled. "And I got in the club. I guess they threw out the brown bag test for the night." She saw him cringe. "Okay, we know it's a men's club, but I still went. A friend, who was invited by a member to one of the Friday night fish fries, invited me. They had the best fish I've ever tasted: fish so good it would make you slap your mama, potato salad, string beans, bread, pound cake. The music was good and I had a good time."

"What's this all about, Torrie? I didn't ask about the club. I asked why you haven't sent me one damn birthday card in twelve years."

"Remember, I just said the fish was the best?" She waited while he stared at her. "You know my mama, and you know how good she cooks right? I've always wondered if the fish was really as good as I thought, or because I had been denied going in there to try it. I don't even know why I went, except I went with a friend, a friend who's about as light as you, Jake. She has that long straight hair. You know, good hair, and she got me into the club."

Torrie could feel bitterness creeping in and didn't want it to. "She's not even from New Orleans. She's from Honduras, and she was my pass to get into a club in my hometown. Do you have any idea how I felt? I'm not saying that if some man invited me to the club I wouldn't have been allowed in. I'm just saying, I was never there until my friend was invited. At first when I got there, I kept waiting for someone to throw me out...I kept thinking Kimmie would have a fit if she knew we'd gone there. So would Mama and Daddy. I've never gone anyplace I wasn't wanted except to that club, and I only went one time. It was good, but I would never go back because I had to use someone else to gain entrance."

She saw the irritation in his eyes. Her meaning had not been lost, but then again, she hadn't intended it should. "Jake, there are so many things I've wanted in my life, so many things happened to me. Like you said, I inherited my daddy's stubbornness. I don't have to go after everything I think I might want. Some things have to want me first. That's important to me. I'm not an exotic treat or a walk on the dark side. It irritates me when people think otherwise. And there have been others who've thought that, Jake."

"You have the nerve to sit here in my face and tell me that's what you think. I didn't drive all the way here because I thought you were some damn exotic treat? You know better than that. Why the hell are you still trying to push me away?" Jake snatched the half-empty coffee cup from Torrie's hand. "If you want coffee, go get it yourself." He walked to the sink and dumped the still hot coffee out, then rinsed the cup and stormed out the door.

Torrie stared after him, wondering why she'd told all of that to Jake. She glanced over toward the beds and saw Trey watching her, knowing he wasn't asleep. She saw the door to the bedroom was ajar and knew Kimmie was behind the door listening.

"You went to the Autocrat Club?" Trey asked, sitting up.

"Yeah," she answered.

"Why?"

"I'm not sure. Maybe it had a little to do with being told I couldn't get in. It doesn't matter now. Once I went, I found it was no big deal. I didn't want to go anymore. I got the wanting out of my system."

"What about Jake? Are you saying you don't want him?"

Torrie turned as Kimmie finally came into the room. "I want him," she admitted. "You guys don't have to worry about me with Jake. I'm not easy. I've never been, and I'm not about to change now. Am I glad he came, that I got to see him, that I kissed him? Hell yes, but I'm in control of my mind." *If not my body*, she thought.

"Jake loves me," Torrie continued. "And I love him. Still, I'm aware it takes more than love to make a relationship work. If we're going to have a future we have to start building a strong foundation. I told that stuff to Jake to get it out of the way, not because I'm uncertain of his feelings for me, because I'm not. It's the intensity of my feelings for him that frighten me. I also want to clear something up with you, Trey." Torrie glared at her cousin. "As for Jake, let's get real. You both know he didn't come all this way just for a piece of tail. Jake loves me. But he still needs to remember that my name is Thibodeaux and his family cares about that even if he doesn't.

Jake fumed. He walked several miles, trying to get rid of his increasing anger. He should have known when Torrie began her crazy story about the Autocrat Club it wouldn't be good. He'd seen it in her eyes, in the tremor of her body, the way she'd moved away from him. And when he'd searched her eyes, he'd known what she was thinking.

That damn remark he'd made to Trey when they were kids. Damn. It was as though he'd said it to her. If he could erase those words, he would. If he could erase what had happened after their first kiss, he'd erase that also. Hell, if he'd known a sixteen-year-old girl's heart was the most fragile thing on the face of the earth, he would have never hurt her. He'd tried to make it up to her through the years, but she'd never allowed him to really talk about it. Even with the calls he'd made over the years, they weren't the same. He hadn't felt that indestructible connection as strongly until she'd finally called him.

Damn straight, more than the storm brought him to her side. He knew they could finally put the things in the past behind them. Jake would give anything to be able to finally find forgiveness for his wrong against her.

A hard shudder overtook him and stopped him in his tracks. He wasn't confused. He wasn't just saying he loved Torrie because he wanted to atone. Jake continued walking, annoyed with Torrie and himself for allowing her to put doubts into his head. Hell, he didn't care about being a Broussard. He didn't care about any of that. *Me thinks thou doth protest too much*, the words spiraled through his brain. Trey and Kimmie were poisoning Torrie's mind against him. Hell, he could be just as stubborn as she was. He also didn't go anywhere he wasn't wanted. The next time he kissed Torrie, she would be the one asking him to do it.

When Jake returned to the cabin, he could feel the tension emanating from Trey, Kimmie and Torrie. He attempted to ignore the three of them as he went to the kitchen and took a chair, bringing it next to the couch where Torrie sat. He glanced toward her before sighing and looking at the screen.

"The news has changed," Torrie said quietly. "There are reports of a couple of leaks in the dome. There's water there also. They have no idea how long the people can stay there." She turned the sound up.

"There are bodies floating in floodwater," the reporter said with a look of awe on his face.

"Is this true?" Jake asked, knowing they didn't know anymore than he did.

"According to Reuters, this is what Nagin said, but I don't know if it's true," Torrie said, shrugging her shoulders. "I hope not." She glanced at her watch it was a quarter to eleven. "The reports before said the water was only a few feet. Bodies can't float in just that little bit of water. If it's true that would mean…"

"Have they said anything about the levees?" Jake asked, stopping Torrie before she could complete the thought that was on all of their minds. If the water were rising things would only get worse.

Forever and a Day

Everyone's main concern was always the levee that protected the cities. Many people didn't know New Orleans had been built in a sort of bowl. The Mississippi River, Lake Pontchartrain, and the Gulf of Mexico surrounded the city on three sides. As they listened to the reports, talk of Lake Pontchartrain gave them the most worry. The Army Corps of Engineers seemed confident, however, that things would be fine. The levees would be shored up and they would hold.

"The water in Lake Pontchartrain continues to rise, racing and eating away at the dirt levee beneath the concrete floodwall built to protect New Orleans from disaster. The water has receded on occasion, and when a breath that has been held is let out, it rises again. We just don't know."

Torrie was worried. Passing her hand over her face, she shook her head. The visions again, she didn't want to give into the terror, but it was strong and just as vibrant as the pictures she was seeing on the television. She listened closely to Col. Wayne of the Army Corps of Engineers.

"They realize the gravity of the situation. They're not sparing any resources on getting this fixed. We're confident the corps will come up with a solution to this problem quickly. Sure, there are some damaged highways and flooded streets, but we're working on things."

Jake glanced toward Torrie. She trembled, and her eyes were glazed over. His earlier anger dissipated, replaced with concern for her. "Torrie," he called out to her, but she didn't answer. He knew very well where she was—lost in her nightmares.

"Torrie," Kimmie called to her also and went toward her.

"No," Jake said firmly. "She needs me for this." He kneeled in front of Torrie and whispered to her, "I'm here, Torrie. It's me, Jake. You're safe. I won't let anything harm you, I promise." He rubbed her temples and kissed her forehead, ignoring the darts of hatred Trey shot him, or the confused hatred exuding from Kimmie's eyes.

Neither had ever believed Torrie, so they didn't know the toll the nightmares had taken on her body. Only Jake knew, and he was the only one who could bring her through. He would save his anger at her for another time when she didn't need him.

"Torrie," he softly repeated, allowing his fingers to massage her temples. "Let it go, baby. Come back now. Let go of the images. I need you to come back now," he crooned and watched as her glazed eyes clouded over and returned almost to normal. Her eyes sparkled with tears, but anything was better than the stark fear. "You okay, baby?" he asked.

"I feel so sick, Jake. It's never been like this." Her eyes sought his, then she looked at the screen. "This is it, Jake. This is my nightmare. They're going to break."

"No, Torrie, the army's working on it. You heard them. The levees are secure. There's no problem. It's rough, but they've got a handle on things."

"No," Torrie insisted, "not this time, Jake. This time they're wrong." She hugged her chest and rocked her body. "Mommy," Torrie muttered.

Kimmie ran for the cell phone and dialed their parents' home. "It's dead," she said, tears in her own voice. "Torrie, what are you and Jake talking about? You're scaring me. Mama always told you your dreams aren't real. Stop encouraging her, Jake!" she nearly screamed.

Torrie's eyes closed as she rocked back and forth. "Mommy," she said repeatedly. Jake pulled her into his arms. She laid her head on his broad shoulder and not one lustful thought crossed her mind. Something bigger than the pull she felt for Jake was happening, and her name was Katrina.

Within a matter of hours, things in New Orleans went from bad to worse. Over half of the families who had followed Torrie to the park left. She didn't know where they were all going, but since the report said Katrina was bearing down on Mississippi and Alabama, it was a good bet they weren't going there. Some said they were going home, despite Torrie's warning.

Jake had rubbed her arm in that calm manner he had, and his eyes had locked on hers. *Let them go,* he was saying in their code. *You've done all you can. You kept them out of the path of the hurricane.*

Torrie sighed, she wanted to go home and see what was happening. Kimmie and Trey had asked her a million times it seemed. Each time she'd shaken her head slowly and whispered to them the time wasn't right yet. The two people who'd teased her the most about her dreams seemed somehow to be taking her seriously. She wondered if they were staying because they wanted to keep an eye on Jake. Torrie didn't care why they stayed, she was just glad they did. Thoughts of her parents sent tears sliding from beneath her long lashes. Not even Jake could stop that.

People filled the cabin throughout the day wanting to get an update on the hurricane. Things weren't looking good; they all knew that. For a time they'd put aside their differences and declared a truce. There were people from all over New Orleans living in the park, black and white, rich and poor. They were all in the same predicament—in danger of losing family members left behind as well as everything they owned. They worried and prayed and sang, anything to keep their minds off the trouble.

When her eyes were so heavy she could not hold them open any longer, Torrie went into the bedroom to try to get some sleep. If Jake and Trey killed each other, she would just have to worry about burying them when she woke. She had barely closed her eyes when she heard loud pounding on the door.

"What's wrong?" Kimmie shot up.

"I don't know," Torrie answered back. "Someone's knocking."

Torrie slid her arms around Kimmie and heard Trey bark toward the front door, "Who the hell is out there banging on this door?"

"It's your uncle, fool. Now let me in."

"Daddy." Torrie bound from the bed, unfazed by the fact she had on little more than panties and bra. "Daddy," she screamed, rushing to hug her father. "Mommy!" She cried holding them close when her father roughly shoved her off her mother.

"Torrie, go put some clothes on your naked body." Her father bellowed.

The burn of embarrassment stung, she'd forgotten but there was still no need for the anger she heard in her father's voice. She turned slowly. Jake stared at her and the look in his eyes told her he was the reason for her father's anger.

Damn, Jake, she wanted to snap at him, *can't you keep that shit under control?* But she didn't. She merely glared. But did he bother to turn away? No. He had the nerve to smile at her and hunch a shoulder. She could feel his eyes burning her back all the way to the bedroom. She passed Kimmie on her way back into the bedroom. Within seconds, Torrie was back out flopping on the living room floor beside her mother. "Mama, you remember Jake. He came to help me through the hurricane." When all she got was a grunt, she pointed toward the television. "He bought it so we could see what's happening." *This isn't working, not the right diversion,* she thought. "Daddy, how did you all get out? Is the house okay?"

"The house is fine. We rode it out just like we told you we would. Got a little water, but as soon as it was clear, fools started shooting. Your mama told me to get some stuff and let's go."

Torrie ignored her father's pacing. She knew his attention was torn between telling them how they'd gotten out of town and trying to figure out what Jake was doing there. Luckily Jake hadn't moved. He stood in the kitchen leaning on the counter top waiting, as they all did, for her father to continue his story.

"Daddy," Torrie called out to her father raising her voice as she did so, wanting to bring his focus from Jake. "I thought the roads were all blocked. We haven't heard about anyone getting out."

Forever and a Day

"Lots of people are staying, but I could smell something wasn't right. Your mama was worried about you, said she had made you a promise, and she wanted to show you she'd kept the promise."

Torrie hugged her mother's knees. "But the highway, Daddy. We heard the highways are broken up and debris is everywhere, and the streets are flooded."

"My truck, baby. That's why I got those tires on that thing. I didn't want to ever be stranded without a way to escape. I had to almost get a ladder to get your mama up in there but we made it. I went the back way. I took Carrolton over to Clairborne and took that over to Jefferson then took the I-10."

"I thought the National Guard was there."

"They were, but they didn't bother us, barely looked up from whatever they were doing. I suspect two old people riding around trying to get out of town was none of their concern."

"Was it a rough trip?"

"It was hell. Sometime I thought maybe we should have just stayed. I didn't feel good about leaving until we pulled into the park. I kept thinking we'd done all this and when we got here you kids would be gone."

"Did my folks leave?" Trey asked as he moved to stand directly in front of his uncle...

"Yeah, they chickened out and left about ten, fifteen minutes after you kids. I don't think they came here though."

Torrie could see the relief in Trey's face. He'd tried to play it off all hard, but he'd been as worried as she was.

"Daddy, you and Mama take the bedroom. Kimmie and I can sleep out here on the couch."

Her father's eyes shifted toward Jake, and then ran quickly over Torrie's body. "I don't think so, you girls sleep in the bed with your mama. I think Jake can move to the sofa, and I'll take his bed."

Torrie had never defied her father—ever—but she wasn't going to allow even her father to make Jake feel he was in the way.

"Daddy, Jake keeps his bed. He's my guest." Torrie stood firm, proud of herself that only a tiny quiver was in her voice. She could see the smirk on Trey's face as the tension in the room built up. She glanced toward Jake and saw the smile. The one that said, *if you want me to I'll leave* but it also said, *I'm so proud of you I could burst.* Torrie sent Jake a smile of her own that said, *you're not leaving. I need you here and I want you.*

She stood and splayed her hands on her hips, facing her parents. "I invited him here, and I want him here. What happened to southern hospitality?"

"You don't expect me to sleep on the couch, do you?" her father asked.

"No, Daddy, I offered you my bed."

"And I told you I'm not leaving you out here. Not with that boy looking at you like that."

Damn did everybody think what she did or didn't do with her body was their business? "Daddy, I'm not sassing you, but I'm grown. I can handle myself. Jake's not a rapist, so if anything happens, Daddy, he would have had my permission."

For a moment the entire room fell silent, then Jake said, "I don't mind taking the sofa."

"I mind your taking it," she snapped. "It's the principle of the thing. You're my guest, and you're staying put."

The line had been drawn. Torrie glared at Trey instead of her father. He'd probably backhand her, grown or not, and she couldn't take it, not in front of Jake. She wanted to tell her parents that if they had not been so darn stubborn in the first place, she could have rented a cabin for them, and had she known they were coming now, she could have re-rented one of the Cabins her employees had left. But, of course, she wasn't going to say any of that. So she waited, not moving an inch, not blinking. She meant what she said. This had nothing to do with lust, but was about right and wrong. And them treating Jake like that was just plain wrong. Besides, she loved Jake, and no way, no how, would she stand by and allow her family to disrespect him like that.

Kimmie was walking behind her. She could feel the breeze from the angry way her body moved. Still, Torrie refused to budge. She remained standing defiantly, her hands still on her hips.

"Did any of you stop to think that the damn couch opens into a bed?" With a snap of her hand, she opened the couch. "Here, Daddy, now you have your own bed. Torrie's right," she threw over her shoulder. "You don't treat a guest like that, even Jake Broussard. I'm going back to bed."

Torrie continued staring at her parents, glad the conflict was over. "Jake, you okay?" she asked, ignoring everyone else in the room.

"I'm okay, Torrie. Go back to bed. I can handle myself."

"That's just it, Jake. You shouldn't have to worry about handling yourself." She glared at Trey before shifting her gaze to her father. "That's not why you're here, but know this, Jake. While you're here, I've got your back." She marched up to him, wound her arms around his neck and kissed his cheek. "Goodnight," she said and walked into the bedroom.

"Torrie, baby, did Jake tell you how he knew where you were?"

Torrie leaned against the door for a moment, listening for the sounds of war to erupt any moment from the front room. "What did you say, Mama?" She looked at her mother, automatically replaying her mother's words. "I don't know. I didn't even ask him."

"He called me."

Torrie looked toward her mother in disbelief. "You told Jake where I was?"

"I didn't see I had much choice. He was so worried, and all I could think about was the way you were crying. I remember the way he used to comfort you when he was little. I told him you were coming here, and I prayed he would get here and find you."

"Mama," Kimmie walked over to where Torrie and her mother stood. "I can't believe you told Jake to come here."

"He was already coming. I just told him where she was so he wouldn't be going on a wild goose chase."

"Does Daddy know?" Kimmie asked.

"Your daddy doesn't need to know everything I know. No man needs to."

"Thank you, Mommy." Torrie threw her arms around her mother, then reached out an arm and pulled Kimmie toward her. "And, Kimmie, for what you did in there for Jake, thank you."

"I didn't do it for Jake. Like you said, Jake is a guest, and that's not how you treat guests." She turned away and climbed in the bed. "I'm not sleeping in the middle," she announced. "I don't care how bossy you're getting. You sleep in the middle."

Torrie walked toward the bed and sat beside her mother, picking her hand up and rubbing it between hers. "Why don't you like Jake, Mama? And since you don't like him, how come you told him where I was?"

"This had nothing to do with my liking Jake or not. I was worried about you, and I knew if anyone could calm you down, Jake could. Besides, Jake did something to hurt you. You tried to hide it from me, but I heard you crying. And Kimmie would not have treated Jake the way she did if it had not been something serious." Her mother narrowed her eyes. "I've had my suspicions. Did he get you pregnant?"

Torrie gasped. "Pregnant! No, Mommy, nothing like that. He kissed me, nothing more."

Her mother stared at her a long while, not making any comment. Torrie was thankful for that. She'd drop the subject.

"Torrie, Torrie, Torrie."

"Not again," Torrie moaned. Climbing from the bed was a feat in itself. She slipped her pants and top on and went out. The worry in Jake's eyes sent a chill through her. "The levee, Jake?"

He led her into the kitchen area before answering. "Yes, baby," Jake answered her at last. He glanced at the back of the television perched on the kitchen counter. "I couldn't sleep," he explained, taking her hand and leading her into the sitting area in front of the television.

"Oh my God," Torrie moaned.

One after one, everyone woke. People began to pound on their cabin door, wanting to see the television. Once again, the room was filled.

"Cascades of water are rushing in through two large breeches in the wall of levees. The Crescent City wedged at the mouth of the Mississippi river below sea level has finally lost its century long battle against the waters surrounding it."

Everything else seemed to happen in a matter of minutes. It was like some disaster movie. This couldn't be real, but was. Torrie watched along with everyone as water filled their beautiful city. She thought of her parents, barely out of there, and her heart lurched as she prayed, grateful they'd made it out. Her eyes went around the room. Jake was watching her.

Hundreds and hundreds of people were stranded. The camera panned on them making their way to rooftops almost engulfed in water. Many had homemade signs, begging for help. She wanted to throw up at the sight of this disaster. They were her neighbors and friends. This was her town. Her nightmare was coming true.

Torrie walked toward the kitchen moving so slowly she felt she was gliding on air. She deliberately tuned out everything around her. She needed something to do, something to keep her grounded without sapping her spirit. She looked out over the ever-increasing group. *Coffee*, she thought. She'd make coffee. She made pot after pot and served them, not knowing what else to do.

After the tenth pot, Jake took the tray from her hand, served it, then took her to the small space the two of them had commandeered in the kitchen. He stared at her for a long time, then pulled her into his arms. "Torrie, I know what you're thinking, and you're wrong. This is not your fault. You were only given a vision, no one believed. You could do nothing."

Jake held Torrie tighter, wanting to absolve her of any guilt she was feeling. Her shoulders shook as she sobbed on his shoulder. His eyes filled, and the tears rolled down his cheeks. He searched hard for words of comfort, but found none.

He thought of his earlier remarks shouted out in anger and frustration, that he didn't care if everyone drowned if they were too stubborn to leave. Thank God he'd shouted those words in his apartment where nobody would hear him. Still, Jake wished he could take back his words. He'd not meant them. Sure, some of the people were stubborn, but most of the ones who didn't leave had neither the means nor anywhere to go if they had. Jake knew that, had known it when he'd gotten angry.

He felt the hard shudder run through Torrie's body. Damn this was bad. She felt responsible, and he had to do something to prove to her she wasn't.

He rained small kisses on her head, brushing back her hair, rubbing her back. When he lifted his eyes, he saw her entire family watching them with tears and fear in their eyes. A tremor of awareness raced through him. Obviously, they now believed Torrie's dream.

Anxiety skittered down his spine. He shook his head at them, thinking *no* hoping they understood. Torrie could not tell the future. She did not have those powers. As far as he knew, she'd had one dream her entire life, and it had played on perpetual rewind.

"Torrie, how will it turn out?" a shaky voice filled with agony called out.

Damn, damn, Jake thought, and turned pleading eyes on Kimmie. Torrie didn't need this right now.

"Torrie doesn't know anymore than anyone else," Kimmie answered, taking the cue from Jake. She looked long at Jake, and he knew she didn't believe her words.

His plans to relocate floated away. He'd have to find a way to get Torrie to come to New York. The two of them could start over in a new place.

"Will everyone get out? Will they rescue them in time, Torrie?"

Torrie lifted her head from Jake's chest to focus on Roy. He hadn't asked any questions when she'd asked him to drive the school van. In fact, he'd thought she was being silly. She glanced around the room, not surprised when she saw the looks on the faces of her friends, family, and strangers. She heard the whispers. The other part of her nightmare had begun. She looked quickly at Jake. He smiled and shook his head a bit to let her know he believed no such nonsense.

"I don't have any answers, Roy," Torrie began and cleared her throat. "I don't know anymore than anyone else."

"You knew we needed to leave. You said it was going to be bad," Trey spoke up his eyes large.

A groan rumbled and came out of Jake. Torrie's hand shot out to still him. She'd had twelve years of taking care of herself. Had he forgotten?

"Trey, do you think that was magic?" Torrie smiled and looked around the room. "Maybe you should ask Governor Blanco or Mayor Nagin. They said it would be bad, remember? The weather reports said it for a week, call them."

"But you had a dream, Torrie."

"So what?"

"You insisted we leave."

"So did the officials. That doesn't make me gifted or anything."

"But, Torrie, you paid for all of us to come," Ann chimed in. "You insisted. You knew, Torrie."

"I listened to the news reports."

"It was more than that," Maggie joined in.

"More than that, you all have got to be kidding."

"Everyone knows you had dreams about this, Torrie, nightmares. So tell us how does it end? Tell us are they going to fix the problem. Will we get to go home in a few days?" Trey pleaded.

She glanced from face to face, disappointment hitting like a stone when she came to her mother. Even she was looking at Torrie in an odd fashion. What answers could she give them? Only one other person in the room knew just how bad it had been in Torrie's dreams, and she was praying as hard as she knew how that those dreams wouldn't come true now.

"Why did Jake drive here if he didn't know this was bad? You must have told him. Jake, tell us, please man," Trey begged. "Jake, man, we need to know."

Unbelievable, they were going around her talking to Jake, a man they'd barely been civil to. And all because they wanted more than what she could give. Torrie didn't have to turn around to know Jake would have her back as he always did.

"Torrie never saw the end of the dreams. She always woke the moment the levees broke. That's all she ever saw."

"Then why was she always so scared?"

"Because any sane person would be afraid. Think about it. Since we were kids, people used stories of the levee breaking in 1965 to scare us into behaving. That's probably what started Torrie's dreams in the first place."

"Are you for real, Jake?"

"Yeah, Trey, I'm for real. Don't you think if Torrie knew more she would have told?"

"That's what you've been so worried about all these years, Torrie, truthfully?" Trey turned his attention to her, his face mottled with worry; his eyes pleading for truth, his voice spoke of hope.

"Were you just afraid the levees would break? You didn't see our city being destroyed or dying?"

Torrie took in a deep breath, then released it as she held her cousin's gaze."That's all I've ever seen, Trey. I always woke up."

"What about earlier when Jake was holding you out here on the couch? You weren't sleeping then. Were you having a vision?"

"You could call it that, Trey, but I didn't see how it ended. I did see the levee breaking and water rushing in, some people on rooftops but that's all."

Hour after hour passed, and the news became worse. Mississippi was hit hard, so was Alabama.

"Many of the refugees are being lifted from rooftops."

The room froze as they all looked at each other, then back at the screen. "Who are they talking about?" Torrie asked, feeling a stab of indignation. "They're talking about us, they're calling us refugees. What makes us refugees?"

"People are taking refuge from the hurricane," Jake offered, trying to sooth her, holding her hand and stroking the tips of her fingers.

"And that make us refugees? I'm a teacher Jake, remember? That sounds more to me like they're talking about political prisoners or someone running from religious oppression, war, or something. I want to know what makes us refugees. I don't like it."

"I know, baby."

"Aren't you upset about this, Jake? Am I the only one bothered by that comment?" Tears filled her eyes. In a way, she was grateful for the diversion. At least it was something to keep her mind off the things she knew were going to happen.

"Of course, I'm bothered by it. We all are, Torrie. It's such a stupid asinine thing those reporters are saying. But you're right.

There is nothing funny about it." He pointed at the hundreds of people on the screen who were waving and begging for help. "They are American citizens, not refugees."

"Yeah black citizens. Ain't that 'bout a blip? People losing everything, then they want to go and strip the last thing from us that we have, like we don't belong to this country or something." A voice in the crowd shouted out.

"Well, we wouldn't be here if it wasn't for that ill-fated cruise we were forced to take." Someone else shouted out, then laughed.

For a short time, the tension in the room lightened, but then reporter after reporter called the residents of New Orleans refugees and their blood began to boil. In one way it was a good thing, people had something else to occupy their minds besides asking Torrie if she had answers. She didn't even have the answer to how she was going to continue paying the bills for the ones who were still left. She'd hoped they would be gone for a few days. Now it looked like it would be a lot longer. She mentally calculated the money in her head as she walked into the kitchen. When she opened the fridge, she knew she needed to get into town to buy supplies. Torrie couldn't suppress the sigh as her eyes connected with Jake's.

"I'm going to take a walk. Do you want to come with me? Get away from all of this for a little while?" Jake asked.

Torrie wanted nothing more than to walk away with Jake and forget everything. She gave him a look filled with longing and hunger.

"Baby, I need to be alone with you. I need to hold you so close to my heart that only one beat can be heard. I need you so badly right now I'm going crazy trying to keep it in," Jake whispered hoarsely in Torrie's ear.

For the first time in hours, Torrie found herself smiling. "Believe me, Jake, you're not doing that good a job of holding it in. Everyone knows what you want to do with me." She laughed, then hugged him and whispered in his ear. "I want those things, too. But right now I can't have them." She felt Jake's erection pressing on her. "But you, my friend, had better go and take that walk. I don't want you getting shot down here, and believe me, Jake, my daddy has his gun." She laughed when she heard his groan. She moaned in return. "Now go on and take that walk and cool off."

Torrie smiled, shaking her head as Jake made his way out the door. When he turned and gave her one last longing look, she couldn't help but laugh and turned away quickly. She'd seen the angry looks. No one wanted her laughing, not in the face of what was happening to their city. But Torrie was thanking God at the moment for Jake because he made her laugh in the midst of such a devastating time. If she kept getting visions, she'd need the laughter Jake induced.

Within a few minutes, Torrie had settled down and again wondered how she would feed everyone. She opened the fridge again. Nothing had changed in there. It wasn't as though by magic more food had appeared. She would have to tell everyone the charge card she was allowing them to use would soon be maxed out. She groaned low. She looked toward her sister, her parents and then Trey, wondering if any of them had brought money with them.

Torrie glanced briefly at the group she'd brought with her, and she made her decision. She'd offered to pay for a few days. This was not going to be a few days by any stretch of the imagination. Everyone would have to kick in whatever they had. That would be best anyway. No one wanted charity.

The door opened and Jake walked into the cabin. His resolution to not look at Torrie failed the moment he entered. She was like a drug to him. He'd not been able to touch her for twelve years, to hold her or to breathe in her unique scent. He felt the jerk and thought, *damn man, you've got to stop that.*

As if a magnet pulled him, he sought Torrie's eyes. She was so damn beautiful and for the first time since he was sixteen years old, Jake was admitting to himself he wanted Torrie in his life. For the first time, there might finally be a chance for the two of them. He loved her, he knew that. He smiled at her; he wanted her. She smiled back; he wanted her forever. *I love her.* When this was all over, he wanted to marry Torrie.

He watched as Torrie returned to peering in the refrigerator, obviously worried about the fast dwindling food supply. Jake also thought they needed more food.

He listened to the steady stream of news reports for a few minutes, becoming annoyed when someone in the room would burst out with an explanation of what was said, as though no one else could hear, and interrupting the commentator. Or maybe that wasn't the true source of his irritation. He grinned at Torrie and walked toward her.

"The park does have the look of a serious refugee camp." He sighed and blew out his breath. "This place is huge. There's one section that has nothing but tents as far as the eye can see and another section with RVs."

Jake stared at the back of Torrie's head before allowing his eyes to move farther down over her back, her round behind, and her beautiful legs hidden in jeans. He needed to concentrate on something else, the horrible conditions in New Orleans, anything. One thing Torrie hadn't lied about, her father definitely had a gun, and Jake would bet money he'd brought it with him. Hell, most of New Orleans owned guns and carried them everywhere. It was common.

When he finally thought he could look at her without salivating, he whispered to her, "Torrie, you've done a wonderful job." He heard her sigh before she turned toward him. "You're lucky you were able to secure so many cabins."

He wanted to offer her help. Torrie tried to smile back at him, but it didn't reach her eyes. She was worried and probably about broke. He wondered how he could manage to buy food for them all without someone taking it the wrong way. People would accept it from Torrie Thibodeaux , but because his name was Broussard; they would see it as charity.

"Torrie," he said loudly over the din of voices. "Do you want to go into town and pick up a couple of things?" He watched as Torrie's eyes swept the room."Does anyone need medicine, anything like that," Torrie asked. "Jake and I are going into town. There's a Wal-Mart where we can pick up some things. We're going for necessities, not junk food, so I don't want to hear any complaints."

Torrie took a deep breath and continued. "Listen everybody, we have to conserve the money we have and pool it together." She took a bowl from the cabinet and went from person to person, collecting whatever they threw into the pot. When Trey threw in two twenties, she gave him a look and stood for a moment with her hand on her hip. He threw in another. Then she went to every single person in the room, saving Maggie for last. Torrie licked her lips, knowing she had no choice but to include her also. She took a breath and sighed, letting it out as she walked toward Maggie. She stood before her. "This is no longer a vacation," Torrie said softly. "Whatever you can put in will help."

Jake stood silently by. This was Torrie's show. He saw a five go in and saw Torrie kiss the woman's cheek.

"Okay, now Jake and I will go get food and supplies for all of us."

His heart ached. He wanted to be her hero. But Jake was so damn proud of Torrie. She knew exactly how to keep everyone's pride intact and not completely drain her steadily depleting funds. He also knew she had found a way without him having to pay. He had to respect her for that. However, if they had to stay in the park much longer, he would have no choice but to foot the bill, and Torrie would have no choice but to let him.

Jake glanced at Torrie. She looked good on the passenger side of his SUV. She belonged there. "Torrie, why didn't you pass the bowl to me for money?" She turned and looked at him for a long moment, making his heart catch in his throat.

"You know the answer to that. You wouldn't have been able to do it right. Too much, everyone would have called you a show off, too little and they would have called you cheap. No one needs to know how much you put in the kitty. But I know you'll at least match Trey." She grinned, "And I know you will not go over that, because you know your money can't buy me, right?"

Torrie grinned and Jake's heart leapt in his chest. The position had been changed or at least shifted. Torrie was now taking care of him. He grinned back at her; he liked it.

A day later, three things happened: the U.S. government declared the coastal region a disaster area and the Sam Houston Jones States Park was declared a refugee site, so Torrie was no longer responsible for everyone. Jake breathed in a sigh of relief. But only a quick one. The other thing that happed was the chaos. Utter and maddeningly ridiculous chaos reigned in New Orleans.

Two steps forward and three steps back. Torrie slid her slender fingers into Jake's hand, glad the two of them were alone in his truck, watching the television there, wanting and needing a little time away from the crowd gathered around the television in the cabin. "Why is everything so distorted, Jake? This is what's shown on the television, and this is what the world sees."

"Torrie, baby, you know it's not just black people who are looting, don't you?"

"Of course I do, but not everyone does. Do you see what happens when a non-black face appears on the screen? The camera moves away quickly as if by design. And that fool with a damn boom box—where the hell is he going to plug it up? There's no electricity. What is he going to do with that?"

Torrie was so angry she was shaking. "Damn, this really gets to me, Jake. Isn't it bad enough people see us as voodoo working, half-naked, gun-touting criminals? Do we have to act like that and prove them right? Do you think anybody is going to go looking for stories of the good, hardworking decent people who live in New Orleans?"

"Of course not. Decent people don't sell stories."

"Forget the news, these people's actions make me ashamed of being black, and it makes me ashamed of being born in New Orleans."

Jake gently pushed Torrie from him and glared at her. "Don't you let me hear you say that again, Torrie Thibodeaux. You're not defined by the actions of a group of people no more than any other racial group. How can you say you're ashamed of being black?"

"You were ashamed of my being black, Jake. You were ashamed of having kissed me because I am black. You weren't so proud of my being a Thibodeaux when you pushed me away." The pain of remembering hurt as much as the first time she'd kissed him and he'd pushed her away.

Before Torrie could protest, Jake grabbed her in a rough embrace and crushed her lips beneath his. It was not a soft kiss, not one filled with love or longing, but a forceful kiss. One meant to right a wrong. She breathed in his breath and moaned. This wasn't going to solve anything. She pushed him away.

"Jake, it happened; don't deny it."

"Damn it, Torrie. What do I have to do? I love you. I'm black. Just like you, and I'm proud of being black."

"That's the reason you called Trey black, because you were proud of the color?"

Jake shuddered in disgust as he felt the tremble in Torrie's limbs. He'd known sooner or later they would have to visit those words. He'd never doubted Trey had told her what he'd said. He licked his lips and exhaled noisily before tucking two fingers underneath Torrie's chin and tilting her face so she would look directly into his eyes. "I shouldn't have done it. I shouldn't have ever said that."

"I'm much darker than Trey. How can you like what you see when you look at me and didn't like it when you looked at Trey?

What makes me different? Is it because I'm a woman, because I have something you want…is it just that…"

"What? Go ahead and say it, Torrie. Everyone in your family has already said it to me. The men in my family go to the women in the lower ninth for sex only. It doesn't surprise me what other people have said about my family, but not you. I never thought you would think I had anything to do with the things my family did. Do I want you because I'm a Broussard and I can have what I want? Is that what you wanted to ask me, Torrie? Damn. For all the talk the two of us have done about our connection, I know good and damn well you don't believe any shit like that."

Jake dropped his fingers from her chin. He looked out the window at the scene in the park. His chest was filled with the pain of knowing just how hard it would be to earn Torrie's trust. "I think it's about time I go home," he finally said.

"So do I." She climbed down from the truck and began walking away from the cabin and away from him.

Jake got out to stop her, but anger rose up in him. "To hell with you," he shouted at her retreating back. "If that's your low opinion of me, Torrie, then you just go to hell."

Slamming the door of his SUV, Jake tore out of the park. It took him twenty miles before he calmed down enough to get off the next exit and turn around. When he returned, he walked around until he spotted Torrie sitting outside on a park bench.

"You're wrong, Torrie. You owe me an apology," Jake said, walking up to her. "You're doing to me what you think the rest of the world will do to all of us. That isn't fair."

She turned watery eyes in his direction, weakening his knees and his resolve. God he loved her. He'd forgive her anything if only she could forgive his one horrible mistake of breaking her heart. He couldn't go back to his life in New York with things like this between him and Torrie. He'd meant what he said about wanting her in his life for good. He watched as her shoulder sagged, and she stood up.

"You're right. I was wrong to lash out at you or to put the things your family has done on your shoulders. I have enough relatives of my own who've done things I'm not proud of either. But that doesn't make it my fault anymore than what's happening at home. Thank you for reminding me of that. I'm sorry, Jake. I just got so worked up seeing what's happening. It's so crazy. I've never understood looting. Now people are shooting guns at rescue helicopters. Why? They can't fly the damn things. Are they trying to take the city hostage? Are they going to take over the rescue efforts?"

"Torrie, I don't want this thing to separate us anymore than we have let it for the past dozen years. This affects us both, Torrie, not just you. I know how it was. But the water flooding the city is no respecter of skin color or of money. Black and white are suffering in this together, Broussards and Thibodeaux, we're in this together."

He sat down, finally pulling Torrie on the bench to sit beside him. He sighed in exasperation. "I didn't come here to get beat up by you. I don't think I need to keep saying this, but because I know you're upset, I'll tell you once more. I was never ashamed of you, period," he said, stopping her words. "I don't give a damn what I said to Trey. I shouldn't have, but it never had a thing to do with you. And no," he said putting a finger that was on her open lips ready to protest.

"No, I should not have said what I did to Trey. I was wrong. But I'm not going to take all the blame for what went wrong with us. At least the two years I remained in town I tried, and ever since I've been gone, I've been keeping us going.

"If I didn't feel our connection so deeply, Torrie, I would have given up long ago. But every time I even thought it, I would picture your face in my mind and I couldn't let you go. Do you have any idea how I've felt for the past twelve years? Do you know how much I hurt that you didn't care enough to even remember me at my birthday? I always waited, always hoped, but not once…"

Jake stared at Torrie for a long moment, loving her more in that moment than he ever had. "Would that have really been so hard for you to do? Yes, I messed up after I kissed you. You refused to let me talk about it, then you judged me and found me guilty. If you had allowed me to talk about it back then, things would have probably been different. Did you only pretend on that first kiss, Torrie? Did your feelings for me change afterward as mine did for you? Did I become more than a friend?"

"Jake, I sent you letters for two months."

"I never got them. I've told you that often enough. You just never believed me."

"Trey told me he handed them to you personally. When did you and Trey have the fight?"

Jake sucked in his anger at Trey, wishing he'd known then why Torrie had always been so adamant she'd sent the letters. This was his fault because he'd never asked. He shook his head, thinking of all the lost years between them. Jake understood exactly why Trey had wanted revenge on him, but Torrie had been the innocent victim. He gave her a look and didn't answer.

"When?"

"A couple of days before I kissed you."

She frowned, then said, "I didn't find out about what you'd said to Trey until two months later when you and I were friends again. I didn't know you were no longer friends when I gave him the letters to give you. If I had known, of course I would have never trusted him to give them to you." Torrie frowned as she put together small pieces of the puzzle that she'd never had before. "Even if Trey didn't give you the letters, what about my calls you never returned?"

Jake was taken aback, his mouth opened slightly, and at first words refused to come. "I did return your calls. Kimmie told me to leave you alone, that you didn't want to talk to me. At first, I didn't blame you when you didn't want to talk about it. Then I was pissed you wouldn't talk to me, that you'd call and was playing games with me when I tried to call you back. You wouldn't even tell me why you were so angry with me or allow me to tell you what I'd been feeling. After I got over being pissed, I was glad in a way I didn't have to tell you what I was feeling, Torrie because it was lust, not shame. I didn't have the words to explain then. I couldn't talk to you."

"How do you know what you're feeling for me now isn't lust? How can you be so sure it's love?" She turned so she was facing him. "We've been though a lifetime together for the bad and the good. I'm so glad you came, but I don't want us to start something because we have nowhere else to turn. There is going to be a lot of rebuilding here, and you have your life. We can do more to keep in touch. I'll do the calling, Jake. When all of this is over in a few months, maybe we'll revisit this and see where we're stand."

"Will you come to New York and visit me?"

"Maybe, but not just to sleep with you."

Jake laughed. "Not for that…but if it should happen?"

"We both know it will happen eventually. There's no getting around that fact. I love you. But I'm warning you right now, I'm not sixteen. I don't just give into things without making sure they're good for me. I have enough willpower to not do anything that will harm me."

Jake pulled Torrie close, hating that she could think for one moment he would hurt her. He played with her fingers, entwining his fingers in hers. "I meant it when I said it's time for me to go home. Can you handle the rest of this alone?"

"I'm not alone, Jake."

"You know what I meant. We know how this is going to end. Can you handle it?" Jake waited. When she didn't answer, he covered his eyes. He wanted her to need him and to tell him so. He wanted her to beg him not to leave. He was hurting. He opened his eyes and looked at her.

Torrie was also hurting. She loved him but was afraid of giving him her heart to break again. He'd have to continue being the one to make the first moves until she was ready.

"Are you ever going to forgive me?" he asked.

"I forgave you a long time ago."

"It doesn't feel like it." Jake snorted. "Torrie, I feel beat up on. You're making me feel guilty for things I never did. If you've forgiven me, I shouldn't be feeling this way when I'm with you."

"I've forgiven you. I'm sorry I keep taking my frustrations out on you. I guess I need to work on forgetting." She licked her lips. "I guess I need to work on believing you. I'll try harder, I promise. Could you stay another day, Jake? I don't want you leaving like this. I don't want you leaving so soon," Torrie finally admitted. "I like having you near."

"If you think you can keep from taking your frustrations out on me, I'll stay a couple more days. If you find you need to scream and yell, we can go off by ourselves and you can let it out. Deal?" He stuck his hand out.

"Deal." Torrie took his hand and lay on his shoulder. "I really am sorry, Jake. You have no idea how all this is for me. Over the years it's gotten worse, the images are sharper, the devastation, everything is unraveling, the worst is yet to come. I don't want to lean on you…you know…I'm not…I'm not going to ask you to stay longer than a day or two."

"But you'll be glad if I do?"

"I'll be glad if you do." Torrie turned away, picking at a blade of grass on her right side. "You know, don't you?" she asked.

" You know how this is going to end? Yes, I know."

She closed her eyes and swallowed. "I never wanted to be right."

"I know that."

Torrie leaned into the bench, reaching her hand out toward Jake. "You've made this easier for me to bear. I'll do my best to remember you're my friend, and not my enemy."

"You don't have to go through this alone. I'm here for you, even after I go back to New York. All you have to do is call me."

"You have no idea what it does to me. When I look at people, I can see the ones who've crossed over in their families. And I don't want to tell them. This is much worse than it ever was, Jake. I can hear the whispers; see the spirits floating around the ones who are left. It's driving me crazy."

"Don't worry; I'm not going to ask you for any information. You're stressed enough as it is, baby. I'll do whatever you need, okay. Lean on me. I'll be whatever you want right now. If it's only a friend you can deal with, cool. I'll be your friend. I won't put any moves on you. I'll keep everything inside."

"Thank you."

"You didn't let me finish," Jake continued, "I'll keep everything inside until you can handle it. One day you will be able to, and I'll be ready." He pushed her head gently down onto his shoulder. "Rest, baby. It's going to be a long time…that much even I know."

The Superdome was no longer a place of safe haven, but Torrie had known it never was going to be. She listened to the reports coming from the various newsrooms: the reported acts of crime, the rapes, the fights. She didn't know how much was true. She had no way to find out. She only knew that a place built to have seventy thousand fans for a few hours had never been meant to house those people for an extended amount of time. The most distressing news for Torrie was hearing the people had no food or water and no place to go to the bathroom.

"*Where's FEMA?*" Everywhere Torrie went in the park, she heard groups of people huddled together asking where the Federal Emergency Management Agency was.

With Red Cross organizing things in the park, the worries on Torrie's shoulders lightened considerably. She no longer worried about how to take care of everyone. Once the word came that it was mandatory that the children in the park be enrolled in school, Torrie no longer worried about the children missing out on their education. She was grateful and considered it a blessing. The children needed the distraction almost as much as they needed their education. Besides, they shouldn't be forced to see so many tears or so much hopelessness in the eyes of all the adults. She could see the excitement as the kids were outfitted with new clothes to begin what for them was an adventure, going to a new school in a new town.

Torrie took in a deep breath and exhaled. The one thing that continued to stress her was the onslaught of news coming from New Orleans. Nothing was getting better. She wished with all her heart the media would do a story about how they had all bonded through the worst devastation the United States had known in years. If the media came to the park, they would be amazed at the amount of unity.

The park looked like tent city, just as Jake had said, but by the grace of God, they were coping. Even the makeshift clinic was well staffed with people and medicine. Too bad the officials in charge of righting New Orleans weren't as efficient at doing what they'd needed to do. Torrie sighed again, looking around her. It was time for action.

"I'm looking for a job," she announced. "Trey, you want to come with me? I'm sure we can get temporary teaching jobs in town." She hesitated before glancing in Jake's direction.

"When I come back," she said looking up at him, "I'd like to take you to dinner tonight. I want some alone time with you before you leave." She licked her lips, and then sawed the top lip with her teeth, hating her nervous habit. Her breath hitched in her chest and she tried to smile but couldn't. The time had come for Jake to go home. He had a business to run. He couldn't be her crutch and the six of them living under one roof was barely tolerable.

"We've got jobs," Torrie announced to the group gathered around the cabins. "There are some jobs in town if anyone's looking. The Wal-Mart might be open to hiring some people part-time. They probably need some help in the park also. I was at the office earlier, and one of the clerks mentioned the possibility to me. Does anyone know anything about medicine or first aid? They've set up additional tents and people are volunteering to take care of the sick. This is going to be hard, but we're all doing what we can to help each other get through this."

When she went into the cabin, she repeated the news, knowing her father was itching to do some work. He couldn't stand the thought of doing nothing, taking government handouts, even for only the two meals a day and free room. It went against everything in him. Torrie was the only one who brought a substantial amount of money. No one else bothered to go to the bank or the ATM.

She thought of her metal box containing her letters and cards to Jake and felt the relief seep through her bones. She was glad she'd brought it with her.

She glanced at Trey who was the only one who hadn't had a chance to pack some clothes. "There are clothes they've put out in the general store. People from all over the country are sending donations, books, toys, more than what we need. So we can get clothes to wear to work. Jake and I are going into town for dinner. He's leaving in the morning," she said and went to shower, hating that Jake was leaving.

Jake stood staring at Torrie. This wasn't the end of them. He did need to leave. He had things to take care of. He wouldn't be coming back as quickly as he thought. He'd done as he'd promised he'd only been her friend, but later when their lives returned to normal, he intended to be more than Torrie's friend.

When he turned back, Trey was smirking. "You're leaving so soon, Jake?"

Jake ignored Trey and walked out of the cabin heading to his truck to wait for Torrie. When she came out, his heart flipped. She was so beautiful, so strong and so sad. Jake hoped some of her sadness was because he was leaving.

He got out of the truck to open the door for her.

She waved him away. "Don't bother," she muttered opening the door herself, and climbing in the truck.

His feathers were a bit ruffled. He'd wanted to bother. He'd wanted any reason to be close to her, to *accidentally* touch her. He'd kept his promise, and it was killing him. Now he was leaving her again, and he had no idea how long it would be before he saw her. Definitely not twelve years, but there would not be a courtship in New Orleans.

The tightening in Jake's groin increased as he watched the liquid slide down Torrie's throat. She'd already told him she wasn't much of a drinker, but this was her third glass of wine. She was nervous about something…that much he could tell. Sure she'd said they didn't know each other well enough as adults for anything more than friendship to happen. But Jake wasn't sure if he agreed with her.

A groan he couldn't control slipped from his throat when Torrie absentmindedly licked an errant drop of wine from her lips. She heard the groan and lifted her eyes. If he wasn't mistaken, he saw desire in them. The bulge in his pants quickly increased. Her body language told him she wanted him. All he had to do was put out his hand and touch her and she would be his. There was one problem; Torrie was getting a bit tipsy.

"When Trey and I came to town earlier to put in job applications, I checked around. There aren't any empty hotels rooms at all."

Almost about to burst, Jake swallowed hard. "Why did you need a hotel room, Torrie?"

"I made a decision."

He waited. She smiled at him with a half-sexy, half-goofy look on her face. Damn, she was more smashed than he thought. He took the glass she was twirling between her fingers and placed it on the table. "Why were you looking for a hotel room, Torrie?"

"Because I can't make love to you in the cabin, too many people." She laughed deep and throaty, giving him a sideways glance and took the last bite of his cake from his plate. She was deliberately toying with him, teasing him.

"I thought you said we didn't know each other well enough," Jake said softly holding her gaze.

"Everyone I thought I knew well enough, I have no idea if I will ever see them again."

Her remark took some of the starch out of his erection. He felt the vein in his neck quicken, wondering at her remark. "Have there been many…whom you thought you knew well enough?"

"There's only been one I've ever wanted…only one."

Jake swallowed hard, and then swallowed again. She couldn't mean. "I thought…why now? Why are you telling me this, and in the same breath telling me there's no place we can go?"

"You have that nice truck out there. The back seat is so huge, we could go park someplace quiet."

Now all of the starch was gone. Torrie had gotten smashed in order to propose her crazy scheme. Did she really think he'd take her in the back of his truck where anyone could walk by and see them? Anger made his nostrils flare. He wasn't a dog, and she wasn't a bitch in heat.

"Torrie, look at me." She turned her eyes on him. "Not like that," he growled snapping his fingers under her nose. "Turn back into Torrie." She blinked, and tears filled her eyes. Jake covered her hand before they could spill. "Listen to me," he said, "you're just scared. Trust me. I'm going home, but you will definitely see me again."

Torrie lost the battle. The tear she'd tried not to let escape slid down her cheek. "Everything's gone, Jake. You're right; I'm so scared. I don't know what to do. Everyone's looking to me for the answers as though I'm their leader, and I don't know what to tell them. If they knew the things I know, they wouldn't survive this. I don't know if I can…not without…once, Jake, that's all I wanted. I've been so good about not giving into my wants or my needs. Now, my world doesn't exist anymore. I don't have the power to make things right. I only wanted something to hold onto. This is not going to get better. I know."

"A different dream."

"Yeah it's happening almost every night. I see more things happening to an already destroyed city, tornadoes, more flooding, more hurricanes. I don't think I'll ever be able to go home again, and it's killing me. I've tried to make the best of it by waiting here." Torrie sniffed and shook her head. "Trey and I checked the computers in town for L4TV. You put in your address. I checked my home and my business address. Everyone's aware of the flooding in the ninth ward, but my business and home is in Mid City…Everything we have, all of our homes are gone."

"Did you tell Kimmie and your parents you and Trey saw pictures of your homes and your business?"

"I don't know how. Seeing the reports on the news is bad enough. Seeing the pictures of where our homes used to be will be unbearable."

"Torrie, they already know."

"I know, but looking at our actual homes, not just pictures of unknown houses, Jake. They're covered to the rooftops with water, my mama's car is floating in the water and so is Kimmie's car. Trey said we had to let them see the pictures themselves."

"This is one time I agree with him."

"I don't know how to fix things. I had some flood insurance on my house and my business. I don't know if they did. You know how it is; so many people don't have insurance. If I tell them and they didn't have insurance, they're going to be crushed. They're too old to start over." She looked into his eyes. "My duty is to them. I have to make sure they're settled."

"I can take care of them for you. I have the money. Let me help you."

"You know I can't take money from you. Right now all I have left is my pride; taking money from you would take that away as well. All I want is to make love to you, Jake."

"Please tell me, Torrie, why do you want me to make love to you?"

"I'm getting a different vision that doesn't involve New Orleans. I don't think we'll be able to stay in Lake Charles for long. I don't know where we'll end up. I don't know if I'll see you again. You're not in my visions, Jake."

She was shivering. He reached over and rubbed away the tears with his finger. His baby was scared. She wanted him to stay and was afraid to ask. He kept his hand on her cheek and stared into her eyes, knowing there was more that Torrie had not shared with him. "You've seen other things, haven't you?" She nodded yes.

"The tsunami?"

She nodded again, fear in her eyes.

"I don't want to see things I can't change."

"I want you to listen to me. Nothing will keep us apart. Do you hear me? Wherever you end up, I will find you. I promise." He squeezed her hand in his. "Come back with me. Come to New York and live with me."

"I can't, I told you everyone is depending on me. I can't just walk away and leave them. Even my parents are looking to me to tell them what to do. There's too much to do here. When this is all over, I have to be close to help them."

"You could go back with me and stay for a couple of weeks, and then we could get to know each other like you want."

Torrie laughed. In spite of the wine, she was aware of what was happening. Yes, the wine had it made it easier to say, but she wasn't as drunk as Jake thought. "You want me to come to New York so we can make love. Don't play the chivalry part now."

"If that were true, I could have easily taken you up on your offer to just do you in the truck." Jake laughed.

"Do me?" Torrie frowned. "I never mentioned anything about your doing me. I wanted to do you, Jake. Ouch," she said when he unconsciously squeezed her hand. "It's too late now, Jake. You turned down the offer, and I'm now officially taking it off the table."

"No," Jake moaned loudly, "please don't," he teased.

"Just for now, you're right about my timing and my reason. I just started missing you before you even left."

"Torrie, were you kidding me? Do you mean you have never ever, even a little bit?"

"Tell me how the heck you could do it a little bit."

"You know…" Jake tilted his head down and wiggled his fingers.

"What I've done or haven't done, Jacob Broussard, is none of your business. Unless, of course, you want to tell me what you've done in the last twelve years." When he didn't answer, Torrie chuckled. "I didn't think so."

"You've never called me Jacob."

"I've never felt the need to, but I sure as heck wasn't making confessions to Jake, Jacob maybe." When Jake turned lustful eyes on Torrie, she laughed so hard he was forced to laugh with her.

When the laughter stopped, they became serious. "Thanks for coming. You can't possibly know how much it meant to me."

"I'm coming back," Jake answered.

"There isn't much to come back to." Torrie pulled in several deep breaths. "I can't imagine how it's going to be when you leave. The cabin will smell different without all that testosterone filling the room each second. Trey won't know what to do without his sparring partner." Torrie lifted her wine glass and held it out toward Jake. "To us," she said.

"To us," Jake answered, taking the wine from her and handing her the glass of water instead. "And just so you know, there is a lot to come back to. There's you. That's all the reason I need."

Torrie had never hurt this much. She was sending Jake back to his home and his business. She was barely holding on, wanting to believe him—that they would be together in the future. She'd grown tired of trying to convince him that in her vision she'd not seen him in her future. He'd looked at her in the same manner he had when he was a little boy and had first offered to protect her from the storm. She'd believed him then, and vision or no vision, she wanted to believe him now. Still, just knowing he would not be there for her to smile at or to touch was tearing her apart.

"Here are some sandwiches and a thermos of coffee." Torrie handed them to Jake and watched as he placed them in the truck. She was imprinting everything about him in her memory, just in case. She ran her hand down the side of his arm, trailing it over his side, stopping it at his behind and dragging it away.

"Jake," she whispered a moment before he crushed her in his arms.

Torrie didn't care that every eye in the vicinity was focused on them. A shimmer of pain shot up her arm. She was trying to force a vision of the two of them together into her head, but it didn't work. The visions never came when she called; they were always unwelcome.

Torrie could feel Jake nuzzling her neck, pushing her hair aside. She felt a shudder claim him. He held her tightly to him. She took in a couple of deep breaths, her vision clouded and her mouth was working, but no words were escaping.

"Oh God, Torrie, come with me please. Don't make me leave alone."

"If I could, I would." She took a steadying breath and willed herself from his arms. But he was pulling as she was pushing, not allowing her to leave.

"You said no more kissing. Are you going to kiss me goodbye?" he asked.

Torrie touched her lips to his and trembled at the connection. Things were going to get much worse before they got better. In fact, she didn't see better in her vision. The thought of losing Jake pulled at her from a primal place. She'd loved him for most of her life, and they'd lost so much time. Now he was leaving again, and there was no guarantee she would ever see him again. For a crazy moment, Torrie wanted to run and get the metal box and give it to Jake. At least if anything happened to either of them, he would know all the years he'd been gone from her he'd remained firmly in her heart.

The thrust of Jake's tongue in her mouth was like a branding iron. The pulling that shot to her nether regions ground out any rational thought. They were the only ones in the park, out in the open for all to see. She thought briefly of Kimmie's remark, that she'd kissed Jake like a whore; she wondered what her sister would think of the way she was kissing him now. Torrie knew what she was doing. She was kissing Jake like a drowning woman.

"Torrie," Jake whispered into her mouth a moment before pulling away, then holding her face in his hands. "I love you, baby. I don't care what your visions reveal. The two of us will come through all of this, Torrie. Now go back into the cabin. I can't drive away and leave you like this." He pulled her to him, and she landed with a hard thud against his body.

"I can't go back in if you keep pulling me to you."

"This is so damn hard, Torrie. I haven't begun to tell you how much I've thought about you and yearned for you through the years. A lot of it just didn't seem appropriate, not in light of everything that's happening at home." He smiled at her. "I get the feeling everyone's thinking we're selfish to be thinking of something other than New Orleans. Everything that's happening makes me sick and it makes me feel so helpless."

Jake stopped and stared at her. "But it doesn't make me stop wanting you, Torrie, nothing could." He gave her his heart with his words. He kissed her, hoping it would satisfy both of them until they met again.

"Go, Torrie, before you make me lose my mind." He turned her around so she faced the cabin and gave her a gentle nudge in that direction.

Jake drove out of the park as though he were being chased by the hounds of hell. He wiped tears from his eyes. He'd thought Torrie had told him everything, but she hadn't. The rest he'd caught when he'd kissed her. He'd never told her he had his own dreams, but unlike hers, she was always in his.

Blinded by tears, Torrie walked back into the cabin, hoping no one would tease her. Her emotions were too raw. All her life she'd never gone after things that might hurt her. And, she believed Jake had the capacity to hurt her, simply because she did love him. And when you loved someone fully, you gave them the power to hurt you.

Torrie knew she should be grateful because he didn't take advantage of her, but she wasn't. She already missed him. Another hurricane named Rita was coming, and Katrina wasn't even finished bearing down on the already devastated Gulf Coast. Torrie sighed, wondering if she and Jake would ever get their chance, wishing she could have gone with him instead of staying with her family.

She walked through the cabin, wanting to sit on the porch and think. She needed to do things but decided to put them off for a while. Of course the moment Kimmie stepped on the porch, staring at her as though waiting for her to say something, Torrie knew she didn't have a choice. She had to confront her sister.

"Why didn't you ever tell me Jake called or that he came by to see me?"

"We're going back fourteen years?"

"We have to. That's where it all started. You didn't have a right to try and keep us apart, Kimmie."

"I had every right. He'd hurt you, and I wasn't going to allow him to do it again."

"But you stayed on me for chasing after Jake, for calling his house, for giving Trey letters to give to him. You already knew what he'd said to Trey didn't you? You were there when I gave Trey the letters. You could have told me they were no longer friends."

"Why? What difference would it have made? You only stayed apart for those two months. When Trey first told me what Jake had said to him, he wanted to tell you. I told him not to. Then when you came home crying and started writing those damn letters to Jake, I told Trey to offer to give them to Jake. I told him to get rid of the letters. Trey was doing what I asked him to do."

"You had no right to interfere."

"I had every right."

"No, you didn't, Kimmie, and neither did Trey."

"It's been fourteen years. It still didn't work, did it?"

"But nothing was the same for us after that. We've never really talked it all through until now. I saw the way you and Trey were looking at each other when you threw that hissy fit after Jake and I had been out talking in the park. Now it all makes sense. You were afraid Jake would tell me he'd called and came by the house. You were afraid I'd finally piece it together. I wasted so much time trying to protect myself against Jake hurting me and maybe I didn't have to. I love him, Kimmie."

An agonized shudder ripped through Torrie's soul. She wanted to discuss this with her sister without the tears, but it was too late. It hurt too much knowing what Kimmie had done, knowing she'd plotted to keep her and Jake apart.

"How could you do it?" Torrie wrapped her arms around her body and rocked, moaning with the knowledge of her sister's betrayal.

"I was just trying to protect you, baby, like always."

Tears were streaming down Kimmie's face. Torrie continued rocking. She was angrier than she'd ever been with Kimmie. But it wasn't anger that hurt the most, but the disappointment that her sister had kept it hidden from her all these years, knowing how she felt.

"I wasn't trying to hurt you." Kimmie sobbed.

"I know that."

And Torrie did know that. Her sister loved her and had always tried to protect her. She held back her tears, too much time had passed and too much was happening to all of them for Torrie to hang on to her anger. Jake was back in her life, and she intended to keep him there. She wiped her eyes with the palm of her hand and stared at her sister. "I love Jake," she repeated firmly.

"Are you sure, Torrie?"

"I'm sure."

"Does he really love you?"

"Yeah, he does." Torrie turned tearful eyes on her sister. "He always did, Kimmie. I know he did."

"He might hurt you again."

"I know."

"Did you...last night...did you?"

"No, I offered and he said no. Jake didn't come here for a piece of tail, Kimmie, he came because he loves me. I'm going to do my best to put all of those doubts in the past where they belong. It might not be easy but I'm going to give Jake a chance. I'm going to give us a chance."

Torrie and Kimmie embraced. She was the only one who knew Torrie had never made love. Torrie had not been able to establish that connection with another soul. She knew that much because Torrie had told her. And she'd told her another man would only be a reflection of what her soul required, that only Jake could provide that. No one knew without her speaking what she was thinking. No one knew her inside out like Jake, and no one but Jake had hurt her and had the power to hurt her still.

Kimmie sighed as she hugged her baby sister. Even their mother had given in and allowed Jake to give Torrie the happiness that none of them could. Torrie had asked Kimmie if she begrudged her that. She couldn't begrudge Torrie her happiness with Jake, not when her own heart had been broken, and she was still pining over her lost love.

Chapter Six

What a mess. Tens of thousand of people stranded in the Saints Superdome, spilling into the surrounding area, unable to leave, nowhere to go. And thousands more stranded in the Convention Center. There was no food, no water and no toilet facilities, yet helicopters were plucking people from rooftops and dropping them into the middle of that madness.

Torrie was amazed life was still going on in the midst of the chaos. She missed Jake like crazy and was only able to talk to him when a signal got through. Yet he found ways to bridge the space between them. He'd been gone almost two weeks and for the past week box after box of supplies had arrived at the park from him. She walked into the cabin after work looking expectantly for another package from Jake.

"Anything new," she said to her parents as she spotted the huge cardboard box sitting on the floor near the couch.

"Another box arrived from Jake." Kimmie answered.

Torrie noticed everyone gathered around when she opened it, knowing Jake would have included things they all could use.

"You're doing a good job, Brownie."

Trey smirked at the president and clicked the television set to another channel as he rifled through the box from Jake. "Can you believe the things he says?"

"No," Torrie answered him. "I can't."

"Baby, I'll talk to you soon. I wish you'd just get on a plane and come to me. I miss you."

"I miss you, too," Torrie said, ending her call to Jake just as Kimmie came onto the porch. She glanced out the window of the back porch before allowing her gaze to shift to her sister.

"I want to go home," Kimmie said. "When can we go home? The city is still filled with water. I can't believe this. This is a real nightmare. Torrie, come on. Second sight is a gift. I wish I had it."

"I don't have second sight."

"Yes you do, and you're scared we can't handle what you see happening. But this is getting too hard on all of us. This uncertainty. I just need to know if there's an end in sight."

Torrie sighed. "I don't have second sight, Kimmie, but I have a strong instinct we shouldn't become too comfortable at Lake Charles. I think we should be ready at anytime to leave here and stop acting as though this park is our home. It's not. Sure we've settled into a routine, and we're trying to get on with our lives, but this isn't permanent."

With the passing weeks, Torrie was beginning to feel as if this new vision would be like the ones she'd had her entire life. Even when the government provided meals dropped to one a day...that was still fine. Most of the people in the park were working in town. As far as Torrie could tell, everyone was trying to make some sense out of the chaos in New Orleans. Some had left, disgusted by the slow progress in New Orleans. They were determined to try their luck in other surrounding states. Torrie and her family hadn't given up on Louisiana. They still hoped they could make their home in the city they'd always known. Even Torrie wouldn't mind finding an apartment in town and waiting to see what happened.

Torrie was even more disturbed when she heard planeloads of people were flown to places like Utah. That was as foreign to someone born in Louisiana as being dropped on a different planet.

She'd talked to Jake several times, and he'd told her he had cousins who had not even known where the plane was taking them until they were in the air. Now Torrie knew why they'd been called refugees, because they were being treated like—non-citizens—people without rights.

Torrie appreciated all the help people of every nationality were giving to the victims. And she didn't want to turn it into a racial thing, but it was hard not to believe no one had known beforehand of the possibility of a levee breech. In her visions, she had seen sheaves of papers being passed to officials. She couldn't make out faces, but she believed her vision now more than ever, and she believed The White House was aware of what happened. Could she prove any of it? No, she couldn't, but did she believe it? Yes.

When she'd first heard the news of Halliburton going into New Orleans, her stomach dropped. The timing didn't bode well. There were many reports about what was and wasn't happening, and Torrie had no way to substantiate any of them. No one could ever be convicted on visions. Jake had told her that and she'd agreed.

Torrie lived for her occasional calls from Jake. She was determined to visit him as soon as things were settled.

Baby, come now. Jake's words warmed her from the inside out. She needed to be desired now more than ever.

A chill had been trailing Torrie's spine all day. She didn't know why, it wasn't as though it had been preceded by any vision. But she'd chosen to heed it just the same. She slept in her jeans and top. Her mother and sister gave her a look but didn't ask any questions and slept in their clothes as well.

When a knock sounded on the cabin door, no one was surprised. When the park ranger told them everyone had four hours to vacate the park because they were in the path of hurricane Rita, they were out in less than thirty minutes.

"At least I don't have to worry about gassing up the vans since Roy and Michael took them to Texas." Torrie said trying to make the situation lighter, to turn their predicament into a joke.

120

"You think you're ever going to see those vans again?" Trey laughed shaking his head at his question. "I don't think either of them are ever coming back."

"It's okay, Trey, I'm just glad they had relatives in Texas. It would have been nice if we'd been able to stay here until we could return home…but…well." Torrie sighed letting go of the thought.

"I liked the school," Trey said softly, looking at her.

"So did I," Torrie replied. Trey was looking so depressed standing by her car staring at the cabin that she went to him and hugged him close.

"It's been a long time since you hugged me like that," Trey said, hugging her back.

"Yeah, I know, way too long." When she pulled away, she held his hands. "I talked to Kimmie. I haven't said anything to you because I didn't want to start things with Mama and Daddy right there in the cabin. And I don't want to fight with you right now, but what you did to me was wrong. We're blood and we're friends. I'm as much your cousin as Kimmie. I just have one question for you. Did you read my letters to Jake?"

"No."

"What did you do with them?"

"I burned them."

Torrie shook her head slowly, bringing her hand to caress her cousin's cheek. "I understand why you did it, but the fact you did it at all pisses me off. But I think even Jake understands."

"He may think he understands, Torrie, but until he's the one on the other end of the prejudice, he can't possibly understand. He thinks because he went to New York after college and started his own company, that his name had nothing to do with it. I'd be willing to bet his daddy had a hand in his success. It was wrong for me to allow you to think I'd given him the letters, when I actually burned them." Trey smiled slowly. "It didn't do any good anyway. The two of you picked up right where you'd left off as though nothing had ever happened."

"You're wrong about that, Trey. When we ran into each other at the mall, it took a few minutes for us to even speak. We just stood there and stared at each other unsure of what to do or say. We'd never been unsure of each other before then. For the two years Jake stayed in town, our friendship was strained. We were distrustful of each other. Even now we're struggling. I'm trying so hard to just trust Jake the way that I did when we were kids. What you and Kimmie did changed our connection. I'm determined to let go of all the old feelings. I'm going to change it back to what it once was."

"What does that mean exactly?"

"It means that I wasn't wrong about the connection between us. I can't see what the future holds for us, but I'm willing to take a chance, to find out if Jake and I can be more than friends."

Torrie turned from Trey and allowed her gaze to linger on her parents, then on Kimmie. She waited while her parents buckled themselves into their hurricane truck—as her daddy had named it. For a second, her sister's gaze locked with hers, and there was such a sadness there. Torrie wished things had gone differently in Kimmie's life. She deserved to be happy, to have a husband and kids, the things she'd almost had. Maybe when all of this was over, that could be changed also. Once Kimmie climbed in beside their parents, Torrie allowed the sigh she'd held in to escape.

"Let's get in, Trey. It's time to go," she said.

"You didn't answer my question about you and Jake. Do you two have a commitment?" Trey slammed the door of the car.

"Until we stop running from storms I have no idea what will happen to me and Jake. I'm too busy trying to stay alive."

As soon as they were on the highway, Torrie took out her cell. Trey had been glaring at her since they left the park, but she didn't care.

"I have to let him know where I am," she said by way of explanation.

"Jake," she whispered, breathing in his calm the moment he answered his phone. "I'm sorry I called so early…I hope I didn't disturb you…"

"The only thing that disturbs me is when I can't get a call through to you. Go ahead and spill it, baby. I can tell there's something wrong. It's in your voice."

"We had to evacuate the park. We're heading for Villa Platt State Park. I'll try to call you when we get there."

"Torrie, baby, come to me."

"Soon, I promise."

"I'm going to hold you to that promise." Jake paused for a moment before continuing. "I love you, Torrie. You be careful, okay? I'm worried about you and I hate being so far from you."

"Don't worry I'm not. I'll talk to you later." She clicked off after hearing Jake tell her again to be careful. She glanced at Trey, noticing the sneer was gone; he swung his head around for a quick look, and then turned his attention back on the road.

"You're not worried?" Trey asked.

"No, not right now." She dialed again. "Daddy, how's everything looking? It's so darn dark out here; we can't really see you guys that well."

"We're okay, baby. Every once in a while I'll blow the horn, and you can follow the sound. Is Trey still driving?"

"Yes, Daddy," she answered, wondering when her father thought they would have pulled over so she could take the wheel.

Trey made a face and started laughing. For the next hour or so, the two of them goofed around and kidded the way they had when they were kids. It was pitch dark, no lights, just miles and miles of country roads. The idea they were being chased by a hurricane only made the night seem darker. The laughter was medicine for them. Behind the laughter Torrie knew they were both worried, but they were leaving that behind them for the moment. They were on the way to their next resting place.

A day and a half at Villa Platt and they were off to their next destination. The State Park was expecting floodwater. This time there was less laughing as they made their way to Meridian, Mississippi. When they stopped for gas, Torrie stole away to the bathroom to call Jake. They were all on edge. She needed to hear from one person who was living a normal life.

"Jake," Torrie whispered wanting to cry, feeling the tears well up in her throat.

"Torrie, baby, what's wrong? Where are you?"

"We're in Meridian."

"Mississippi? But Torrie—"

"I know, as soon as we got here, we heard about the tornado warnings."

"Baby, come to me."

"I want to, Jake, I really want to, but what about my family?"

"Bring them, baby."

"What about Trey?" For a beat of ten Torrie heard nothing, then a rich laughter bubbled over the wires, making her feel better.

"Oh hell, bring him, too."

"Thanks, that makes me feel better. But no one's going to leave. Everyone's waiting to go home. It seems nothing is being done, Jake."

"Baby, that's not true. The entire nation has stepped up. Everyone's pitching in, church groups, everybody's helping."

"I don't mean that. I mean no one's doing anything to make it so we can go home. They just keep saying don't come back, and in the meantime, we don't have any where to go." She took in a deep breath and exhaled it quickly. Being confined in the tiny bathroom was working her nerves. She wanted to move about, to rant and rave but she didn't. What Torrie really wanted was to be near Jake and have him hold her close.

"Where would you go if they allowed you back? Baby, your home, your business, your parents' home, they're gone."

"But I still want to go home." Torrie tried with all her might not to cry or to look into the bathroom mirror. She was afraid of what she'd see. She pulled paper towels down from the container instead and tore them into shreds dropping the shreds into the wastebasket.

"What are you going to do when you get there?"

"I don't know. I just know I want to go home. I'm getting tired."

"You don't have to do this."

Torrie could hear the defeat in Jake's voice. He thought she didn't trust him completely. It wasn't that. She just didn't want to leave and go so far away, then she'd be the one sounding defeated. "Jake, we're going to Natchez. I'll call you when I get another chance. Trey's banging on the door. Everyone's getting short tempered, so I'm going to cut this short. Thanks for being there." She hung up the phone.

Thanks for being there. What the hell kind of comment was that? Where did she think he was supposed to be? What did she think he was going to do? If it would do any damn good, he'd track her again. But he knew for their relationship to work Torrie would have to come to him. Jake groaned loudly. *Damn.* Feeling helpless, he slammed his hand on the desk. "Torrie, I love you. Be careful and stay safe." He closed his eyes and whispered, hoping she would hear him.

Jake's chest tightened with understanding. He'd never missed home more than he did now. All the missed opportunities to return home tore at Jake. New Orleans would never be the same, too much had happened, too much devastation. He was grateful his family was alive. Material possessions could be rebuilt with a bit of luck. Jake couldn't talk to his mother without her crying. She'd talked to many people just days before, and she knew she would not see many of those faces ever again. Many people had left Louisiana for good.

Jake wanted to tell Torrie that no matter what she did, it wouldn't be the same. The people would be different. A lot of them would no longer be there. Sorrow and fear would mar their homes. Jake wanted to protect Torrie from that. He looked down at the phone wishing he'd not waited so long, that he'd made things right between them years ago, then she'd be with him and they'd be married. And she'd be safe.

"Torrie," he murmured as the pain of lost years seeped into his bones, and then his spirit. He swallowed. Torrie was right about one thing; they had to continue living. He had a company to run. His employees depended on their paychecks to take care of their families. If he didn't do his job, they couldn't do theirs, and everyone would lose.

An overnight stay in Natchez brought flood warnings, pushing Torrie and her family on to Hammond where they stayed the night with friends. Everyone was getting tired. Torrie could see the weariness in her daddy's eye. Her parents weren't that old, but they were too damn old to keep running. And so was she, she thought, making a call that might not be appreciated or understood.

"John Tom," she said quickly the moment the deep baritone voice answered the phone, "this is Torrie Thibodeaux."

"Torrie, my God. I've been wondering if you all made it out. I've been so worried. How's Kimmie?"

She smiled briefly, knowing exactly who Tom had been most worried about. "Kimmie's tired. We all are. We got out before the hurricane hit, and we stayed in Sam Jones State Park until hurricane Rita came along. We've been on the run ever since."

Torrie took in a deep breath. "We're all getting tired of running. We need to find someplace to stay on a more permanent basis. I don't think we're going to even be allowed back into New Orleans for a long time." She sighed, feeling the hurt in her throat raw and burning. "Our homes are gone: Mama and Daddy's, Kimmie's, Trey's, mine, my business."

The thought of all they'd lost crowded in on Torrie, and she breathed deeply. She didn't want to press John Tom into doing something he didn't want, something her sister and her parents would want to kill her for doing. But John was the only person Torrie knew who could help them. Well, the only one they'd accept help from. His money wasn't tainted by the Broussard name.

Torrie had made up her mind that life was far too short to waste a moment of it. After she got her family settled she was going to New York and see if there could really be a future for her and Jake.

John Tom's laughing deep voice pulled her out of her thoughts. That wasn't what she expected. "Why are you laughing?"

"Because your sister is going to kill you."

"She's going to have to get in line behind the storms."

"Do you want to come to Harahan, Torrie?"

"I want to be invited." This time when John Tom laughed, Torrie expected it.

"Torrie, I live alone in a six bedroom house I built for your sister. Would you and your entire family please come here and stop running? You're my family, and I love all of you. You're welcome to stay with me as long as you want, forever even."

"There's not going to be any drama? I mean, we'll pay you. I'm not making a barter trade with you Tom."

"A barter trade?" He laughed again.

"You know what I mean. Kimmie gets her own bedroom away from you, and you don't come sniffing after her and don't throw any women in her face."

"You've got a lot of rules for an invited guest." John Tom laughed again. "I don't have a woman, not anymore," he said with longing in his voice. "You know something, Torrie? Sometimes it takes losing something really important to make you know how important it really was. Sometimes it takes that to knock some of the dog out of you."

Some of what Tom said made sense to Torrie. He was a charmer. He was supposed to marry Kimmie, but he'd been busy charming so many other women Kimmie grew tired of it and dumped him. Still, Torrie had remained in contact. He was a good man despite his "charming" ways. She felt a tiny twinge of guilt she'd kept in touch with John Tom throughout the years. Kimmie would not have done it if the situation were reversed. Kimmie had hated Jake on her behalf for fourteen years. Torrie regretted having allowed the situation to go on for so long. She wasn't going to linger over her mistakes now because she was thankful she'd been given another chance to rectify them.

"We'll be out as soon as we can, okay...we just need...thanks, J.T.," she finished quietly.

"Are you going to tell her?"

Torrie's stomach churned angrily. "Not until we're pulling up in front of your door. I'm just going to tell everyone I have a friend in Harahan who offered to let us stay at his home. And that's true." The sound of footsteps behind her startled her. "I've got to go now, but we'll see you soon," Torrie said. She closed the phone, grateful she'd kept in touch, grateful this was one of those rare occasions she could get a call through without being disconnected. She thought of calling Jake, but changed her mind. She would call him after her family was settled, and she was on her way to him.

Chapter Seven

Puzzled, Jake walked away from the bank. He wasn't really friends with the bank president, but knew him and associated with him. Still, the call had surprised him.

The bank wanted to finance Jake to take equipment to New Orleans and help to clean up the city. The plan was laid out and sounded great, but something didn't feel quite right. This was too easy, and he wondered why they chose him. If Jake were home, he would automatically suspect his father's hand in this, but he wasn't home. He was in New York, an entire world away.

Jake called Texas the moment he entered his apartment, Hearing the phone ring relief flooded his body. He was glad his family had a home there and was safe. He swallowed as he waited for someone to answer his call. Money did make a difference, no matter what one thought.

"Hey there, little mama," Jake teased his four foot ten inch mother when she answered the phone. "Is the big man home?"

"Yeah, your father's home. What's up?"

"I was just asked to go home and help with cleaning up and rebuilding the city. I was offered the backing to take some heavy equipment."

"What's wrong with that? It sounds like a good thing."

"Too good," Jake answered. "Why would a bank care about helping? It has to be something more to it."

"You mean them making money. Come on, of course the bank's going to make money, everybody is. That doesn't mean you can't make a piece of it for yourself. Didn't you hear about Halliburton and Trump? I heard there are developers rushing in buying up the land, wanting to build a resort."

"That's not their city there're trying to exploit. It's my city."

"Whatever, son, here's your father."

"What's up, Jacob? I heard your mother's end of the conversation. Seems like you have a way to make some money, and you're being too stubborn to take it, like always."

Jake sucked his teeth. He hated the way his father said his name. It was one of the reasons he'd gone by Jake since he was a kid. After some time, even his mother had starting calling him Jake. Most people didn't even know his given name was Jacob. He'd only told Torrie, and she'd only used the name once. Now hearing his father use his given name, he'd have to make sure Torrie went back to Jake.

"Jacob, are you on the line? Don't tell me you're upset about making money, not again."

Jake and his father would never see eye to eye on things. That was a given. But his father was a savvy businessman and knew a hell of a lot more than Jake was usually willing to give him credit for. Today, Jake felt as though he needed to talk things over with his father.

"I'm not being stubborn," Jake said, "but out of the blue a bank calls me and wants me to help out in Louisiana. What's that about? Why?"

"You always ask too many questions."

"If I didn't, I would be in trouble."

"Hell, you didn't start your company because you wanted to be poor. Every time I try to help you, you throw it in my face. None of the others do it. My nephews and nieces even come to me, even the 'no account ones,' and my only son throws everything I try to do back in my face."

Here we go again, Jake thought, *round number one billion.* "Dad, none of the things I've done were intended to hurt you. I just wanted to make it on my own, that's all."

"And that trip to Louisiana. You were a fool to go chasing after that girl, knowing the kind of weather that was headed toward that area. Your mother was scared to death when she found out what you'd done."

"Would you do everything you could to protect Mama?" Jake asked quietly.

"You know the answer to that."

"And you know I've always been in love with Torrie."

"What about Shelia?"

"I loved her or I wouldn't have married her, but I wasn't *in love* with her," Jake answered. "I didn't realize I was trying to fill a void in my heart." Jake hesitated. "A void only Torrie can fill. In the end Shelia called me on it."

"Good for her."

"Yeah, good for her."

"She was perfect for you, Jacob."

Not perfect, Dad. I was wrong for not examining my feelings for Torrie, and I told that to Shelia. There's only one woman who's perfect for me. There was always just one woman, Torrie."

"You're two different people from two different worlds. That's not going to change. She'll never fit in the family, Jacob."

Jake rubbed his hand across his forehead as he slumped into his favorite leather armchair "I'm not trying to make her fit the family, she fits me."

"You're still looking to be that girl's hero. You like that feeling of taking care of people. You want to be needed, and she likes having you take care of her."

Jake cringed. His father knew nothing of Torrie. She was independent, had always been, but did she enjoy the comfort his presence provided? Yes, he thought, but the feeling didn't fill him with dread but warmth. "I'm not going to lose her again."

"She's going to be like a fish out of water living anywhere besides New Orleans."

Jake wished he could have come back with, "*If she can't live anywhere besides New Orleans, then I guess I'll be moving back home with her,*" but there was no New Orleans to live in. Not right now, and maybe never. "I'm trying to convince her to come here. Maybe she will," Jake said softly.

"If she came to you, it would be to get away from the mess in New Orleans, not because she wants you, Jacob. You're a Broussard. You don't think your name and money mean anything to her?"

Now his father was pissing him off, but that was nothing different. "You know, Dad, since I've made my own way, I don't give a damn if my money means anything to her or not. I'd gladly give her everything I own and make more and give that to her, too. But just in case you weren't aware of this, Torrie had her own business, she has her own finances. She's never asked me for anything beyond friendship." *And she's never accepted anything beyond that,* Jake thought and groaned. "Listen, what I really wanted was to make sure you had nothing to do with the bank asking me to go to New Orleans."

His father laughed, and Jake hated the sound of it. It was there in his voice, him thinking Jake was stupid or weak for not grabbing things without questioning the morality of it.

"Just like your little girlfriend, Jacob, your mother and I have been busy. You may not have cared as much about our surviving the hurricane as you did about that girl, but we've had to start over as well. In case you didn't know it, a lot of our rental properties were damaged. We've lost a lot of money, Jacob. And whether you want it or not, the money we lost was also yours. It belongs to you. Who the hell else do you think I'd leave my money to? So you might as well suck it up and get used to it. Now if you don't mind, your mother has lunch ready for me."

Without saying goodbye or answering Jake's question, his father clicked the phone. Jake wished just once he'd be the first one to hang up the phone. He laughed at his foolishness, wondering if one ever got over wanting the approval of one's parents. Here he'd left home in order to be his own man, and somehow that invisible string between father and son always pulled at him. He'd tried to tell himself it was of no consequence. But he couldn't. He was waiting to hear his father say, "Well done, son. Good job and you did it all without the Broussard name or money."

Jake smiled and walked to the office in his home. He trailed his hand slowly over the furnishings wondering if Torrie would like it when she came to him, wondering what changes she would make. He laughed to himself as his thoughts went back to his father. As usual, his father had made him forget other things. Maybe Daniel Stern, the bank president, had just thought of Jake since they ran in the same circle and he knew Jake was from New Orleans.

Jake had time to think about it. From the looks of things, the last thing New Orleans needed was more bodies in the way. The city was sill underwater and Jake would consider the offer, but his decision would be primarily based on where Torrie would be.

Two calls in one week. A tingle played across his broad shoulders before running down his back. Jake looked around his office, wishing he had the connection with other people he had with Torrie.

"Robert, why me? I haven't done assessments in awhile."

"But you're good at it, Jake, and you have the advantage of being a contractor. You'll know what's a fair price."

A sigh spilled out of him before he could stop it, and he covered his eyes with the palm of his hand. "Shouldn't the fair price be what the homes were insured for?"

"Come on, Jake. We're talking a hell of a lot of those, and you know a lot of those houses were little more than shacks."

"But you took the monthly premiums." Jake knew he wasn't going to get an answer on that one. Everyone was in business to make money. Hell, so was he. But Jake tried his best to give an honest day's work for a day's pay. He didn't believe he'd intentionally overcharged or cheated anyone.

"Jake, with what happened in three states; all of the insurance companies are strained trying to get adjusters out there. Allstate, State Farm, Metropolitan, every single one of them. We're not the only company looking for freelancers. I talked to Daniel Stern, and he said you were going there anyway. I figured since you're going to be there you could take a few cases. You're not the only one I'm sending. I just need some more bodies. What's the big deal?"

"I know a lot of those people, and a lot of them won't appreciate me assessing their property."

"Why?"

Jake sat back in his chair wondering how to explain the unexplainable to an outsider. "In some parts of New Orleans, the name Broussard isn't looked on as one wanting to help. Come on, Robert, we both know people lost everything, just pay the claims."

"Look, if this had been something else, the company could pay out on the policies, but this is a damn disaster. We'd go under…we're trying to help…but…look if you don't want to do it…I just thought since these are your people, you would feel better doing a few claims yourself. I was hoping you'd do it as a favor to me."

Jake clenched his jaw. He owed Robert. When he'd first come to New York, he met Robert by chance while scouring the streets for a job. As if by magic, Robert Ashton had just appeared. They'd hit it off, and Robert had pointed him in the direction of working for one of the country's largest insurance companies, giving him a job as a claims adjuster. Robert also introduced him to Daniel Stern and helped him secure the loan for his equipment on his construction business. Robert had never called in the favor, so this must be important for him to bring it up now. Jake sighed. When you owed a man, you paid your debts.

"You don't find this a conflict of interest?" Jake asked.

"Not unless you plan on trying to bid on the houses, I don't see anything wrong. So you'll go?"

The smile was in his voice. Jake could hear it. He thought he had Jake over a barrel. The thought of going to New Orleans as a claims adjuster for C & J Mutual gave Jake the willies. The people had been royally screwed twice now: first by the hurricane, then by the government. Now their own damn insurance company was trying to screw them as well. "Damn," Jake muttered angrily.

"You'd be doing me a favor, Jake, but you'd be doing an even bigger favor for the hurricane victims. Think of it like that."

"I'm trying to," Jake answered. "That's the only reason I'm considering it. It's just kind of funny you're asking me to do this right now. I'm not sure I'm comfortable with you and Daniel Stern discussing the possibility of me doing this. First him, now you asking, the timing makes me suspicious."

Robert laughed. "Of course people are going to ask favors of you. You come from there, man, and as for the timing, I should have asked you weeks ago. I was trying to be sensitive."

"When do you want me to go?"

"I'm not sure. Things are crazy down there right now. The place is lousy with adjusters; every Joe Schmo who tacked up a sign has people there. Why do you think all the major companies are using freelancers?"

"When?" Jake asked again getting a bit annoyed.

"You should be ready to leave in about a month or so. When the people start going back to look at what's left of their homes, we'll need as many adjusters on site as we can get."

Jake sighed and bit his lip. This wasn't how he'd envisioned returning home—not to devastation and people in mourning. And he'd definitely not thought he'd return as the one with the axe. He would be seen as another Broussard trying to do a hatchet job on them. No one would believe he was coming there to help.

"You're going right?"

"Yeah. I said I'm going. Just let me know when. I have a business of my own to run, you know. Later," Jake said and clicked off the phone.

He carried several letters to his secretary, glad he wasn't working from home today. He checked the work board and reached for a hard hat. Jake needed to go out to one of his construction sites and do something physical to chase away the feeling of impending doom. He hadn't heard from Torrie for several days and had no idea what she was doing or where she was, if she was safe or even dead or alive. Admittedly, he was getting a little pissed at her, too. Here his father thought Torrie wanted to use him. Hell, Jake would be grateful if that was what she wanted. At least he'd know where she was.

For two days Kimmie had not spoken one word to anyone. She'd glared constantly at Torrie, and that was the extent of it. John Tom, on the other hand, was like a little kid running around making them all feel at home, trying to pretend his eyes weren't sliding all over Kimmie's body whenever she came in his line of vision. Her parents had actually seemed grateful to have a place they could stay so they could stop running. Trey had found a job and questioned Torrie when she hadn't applied with the school district. She'd merely hunched her shoulder. Now was the time to tell them, but first she had to make sure she was still welcome. She went into the room John Tom was allowing her to use and quietly closed and locked the door.

Torrie took in a deep breath and dialed Jake's cell.

"Torrie," he said before she could even speak.

"Caller ID?" she asked.

"No, heart ID. I was thinking of you just now and knew it was you calling," Jake answered. Torrie crossed her fingers hoping this was really meant to be.

"Where are you?"

"Harahan. But I'm ready to move on." She heard his sigh.

"This isn't necessary, stop running, Torrie, come to me."

"Okay."

"Okay? Did you just say, okay?"

"Yes, I said okay. Did you mean it, can I come? I'm tired of running. I want to come and see you. I want to live before it's late."

"Of course you can come, baby. I can't wait to see you." Torrie's words rocketed to his soul. She was coming. Then the words of his father came to his mind. A ping of doubt was born, and his heart plummeted. *Damn.*

"Thanks, Jake. I'll try to leave in a day or two. I'll take a taxi so you don't have to bother picking me up."

She was making his head hurt. A bother, were these the words a woman used with a man she loved or a man she thought of as just a friend? He didn't doubt Torrie may be thinking of sleeping with him, something she'd wanted for fourteen years, but now he wasn't so sure if he wanted to sleep with her, not if it was just as a friend, just as her hero or someone she ran to. He felt a twitch in his groin, and his penis jerked in his pants. Jake swallowed. He would have to wait. He'd waited fourteen years. He'd just wait a bit longer.

"Give me your schedule, Torrie, and I'll worry about my time. I want to pick you up," he answered testily, wondering what had happened between the time he'd left her in the state park. Then she'd been in tears, crying, kissing him with pent up passion and desire.

"Thanks, Jake."

He heard the weariness in her voice. She'd been trying to survive. A groan filled him, making him shudder with shame. Hell, he didn't blame Torrie for being tired after almost a month of living in a park. No matter the cabin had all the comforts of home. It wasn't home. She'd lost her home and business and run from another hurricane, a tornado, and flood. She'd traveled over state lines. Yes, she was tired. Jake softened his tone. "Torrie, I want to pick you up, okay? So just let me do that. Just let me know when you're arriving."

"One more thing, Jake. You have two bedrooms, right?"

Yes, he had two bedrooms, and if she'd given him a chance he would have offered her one. "Torrie, this isn't a strings attached visit. You don't have to sleep with me to come."

"I know that. See you soon, Jake."

"Not soon enough, see you, baby," he answered her, and hung up the phone.

Now it was time. Torrie took a deep breath and went into the kitchen where everyone gathered. She looked at her mama stirring the huge pot of gumbo. "Don't put in any okra," Torrie said absently, knowing her mother was going to try and slip it in anyway. For some reason, her sister's glare made her cry.

She was going to miss them. Torrie had always lived within a shout from most of her family. The outside world thought how bad it was everyone had lost their homes; they had no idea how much family actually meant in New Orleans. They couldn't know that generations of families lived in entire communities. There wasn't a house you could pass that didn't have a cousin in it. Now it had been way over a month, and the only cousin Torrie had with her was Trey. She wanted all her people back, the entire neighborhood. Her heart was breaking, and her head was hurting from the frequent dreams. She needed to let go of the dreams, if only for a few hours. And Jake was the only one she felt safe enough with to let go.

She glanced around John Tom's home. He'd built a really nice home for Kimmie; too bad they'd been unable to work on things.

"Torrie, baby, what's wrong? You don't usually break down like this unless there's a storm." Her mother's eyes clouded over.

Torrie shook her head hurriedly. "No, Mama, no storms. I just miss you all so much."

"That's crazy. What are you talking about? We're right here, baby."

"You're leaving, aren't you?" Kimmie asked. "You're going to Jake."

Torrie glanced at Kimmie, then toward John Tom. "Yes," she answered. "You don't know what you've lost until you've lost it. Yes, I'm going to him. Life is too short to not take your happiness when you can."

Her mother's face became a bit harder than it was. "That's not a good enough reason for you to go out there. Are you running, baby?"

"I'm running, Mama, but I'm not running away from anything. I'm running toward something. You all know how I feel about Jake. Let's stop pretending, okay?"

"You're going out there to lay up with that boy, then when he dumps you, what you gone do?"

Torrie couldn't meet her father's eyes. "It's no different from Kimmie living here with John Tom. They love each other, but they have different bedrooms." Kimmie's glare turned to surprise, her mouth dropped opened a bit and her eyes became two huge pools of want as she turned toward John Tom, then toward Torrie not saying a word.

"That's different," her father continued. "We're all here with the two of them."

"I don't need a chaperon, Daddy. I'm grown."

"And I guess that's your answer to everything, you're grown. So now we've lost everything we have, and my baby girl sasses me in front of everyone and takes off to shack up with Jake Broussard."

"I'm not sassing you, Daddy." And she wasn't. But it was time for Torrie to go to Jake. He'd been the one doing all the giving, keeping in touch. It was her turn now.

Chapter Eight

For the entire plane ride, Torrie worried that things would be awkward between her and Jake. Sure, there was passion between them, but they'd had limits, not enough time to be alone. Torrie wondered just how it would be between them now.

She waited at the carousel, almost embarrassed that she had only one suitcase. She lifted her bag and sighed. Everything she owned was in the bag and her precious metal box.

"Can I carry that bag for you, pretty lady?"

At the sound of his voice, her heart raced. *It will be okay*, Torrie thought, turning around with a smile. "Jake." She reached out a hand to touch him but was crushed in his arms. He kissed her as though he was starved for her. After a minute, she pushed him away and looked pointedly around.

"I didn't believe you would come until I saw your beautiful body." He went to hug her again, and Torrie moved away. Jake laughed. "If you think I care that people know how happy I am to see you, you're crazy." She backed up another step, and Jake grinned. "Okay, I get it, come on." He grabbed her bag, wrapped his am around her waist and walked her out the door and into a waiting taxi.

Jake glanced at the one bag he handed over to the driver. "You're not planning on staying long?" he asked. The immediate embarrassment that flared in Torrie's eyes had him wishing he could cut out his tongue. "Listen, I can't wait to show you New York," he said, trying to cover up what her having one bag meant. She'd lost all of her clothes. Damn he should have thought of that. "I can't wait to show you the shops. I want to buy you an entire wardrobe." He felt her fingers squeezing his arms.

"It's okay." Torrie's big brown eyes locked on his face. "It's okay, Jake." He pulled her against him and just held her close. He played with her fingers. A sudden silence he'd never experienced before rose between them. He looked out the window, unable to point out any sights of interests. He was unsure what to do or what to say. How did you point out to a person architecture of interest, places to visit, when their very life had been devastated, when all they'd known their entire life no longer existed?

A knot of pain twisted in Jake, and he groaned low. He'd wanted so much to have Torrie with him, now he didn't know what to do. He felt her squeeze his fingers, and she glanced sideways at him. She was making a silly face, and then she smiled and he knew she was scared, too. They would wait, they'd take it slow.

Torrie glanced at Jake and saw the forlorn look. He was feeling bad about his comment. She smiled at him, deciding to let him off the hook. This was Jake, her friend, she'd didn't come to New York for him to buy her things. She'd come because she needed some normalcy in her life. She needed to ignore the newspapers for a few days. She needed to talk to people who weren't dealing with Katrina's aftermath.

Sure, Jake's home was in New Orleans, but Torrie knew he wasn't going through the same things. She'd heard the Garden District hadn't suffered even wind damage, while her family had lost all they had.

Torrie tried not to sigh. She didn't want Jake to think she was unhappy. Besides, she knew her city wasn't the only one to suffer the recent tragedies. She thought of the thousands of lost lives in the Tsunami, and she thought of the lives lost in 9/11. The entire nation had risen to help, and they were rising to help the citizens of New Orleans.

It wasn't the people Torrie questioned, it was the response time. She knew many thought it was because most of the people were poor and black. She didn't know if that were true or not. But Torrie did know there had been warnings. She also knew all the dirty little secrets would eventually be told after the money was made, after the deals, after many had long forgotten.

Torrie looked out the window on New York, knowing New Orleans would somehow play a big role in the next presidential election. She'd seen it in her dreams. Maybe she'd tell Jake about that.

A shiver raced down Torrie's spine. She'd forgotten the purpose for her trip was to forget, not remember. When the taxi pulled up to the brownstone, Torrie smiled as Jake got out and ran to open the door for her. She looked up and down the block while Jake paid the taxi, and then followed him up the stairs and into the elevator.

Torrie wanted to say wow, but was determined she wouldn't act country. She didn't want him thinking she desired more than him. The thought made her tremble, and she wondered if he'd told his parents she was coming. If they had, she could imagine what they'd had to say.

"Come on, Torrie, let me show you around."

"Thanks," she said. "You have a very nice apartment." She saw him dip his head and not answer. "Jake, you don't have to be ashamed you have nice things. I didn't mean it like that. Come on. You can't help what happened anymore than I can. Do you really think I'd be happier if you were without a home and on the run from the elements?"

Torrie shook her head slowly. "You mean far too much to me. I never want anyone to go through what my family and I and so many others have gone through in this past month and a half. Even so, we were lucky. I know that. It got scary, but I bet it wasn't as scary as some of the New Orleans residents being loaded into a plane and dropped off in what must be for them the middle of nowhere. Think about that, Jake, and don't pity me, okay? I'm here to spend some time with my friend, that's all."

"How long are you going to stay?"

"As long as you want me to."

"Then you're going to be here for several lifetimes." Jake reached for her hand and pulled her into his bedroom, where he'd removed every trace that he'd ever spent a single night in there. "This is your room." He showed her around and watched as she smiled at the lilacs.

"Show me the other bedroom, Jake."

He did, and then he showed her the third bedroom in the apartment. Torrie turned her eyes to his, and he waited.

"You gave me your room, didn't you? You're so sweet…but you didn't have to."

Jake stared for a long moment at Torrie. "Okay, let's get this out the way." He took in a breath and breathed it out hard. He pinned her in place with his gaze. "Yes, I gave you my room; and yes, I know I didn't have to. Yes, I'm going to take you shopping; and yes, I know you're going to object. Yes, I want you here with me so badly that I'm afraid of making mistakes; and yes, I'm afraid even now I'm doing everything wrong. Want something to drink?" When she smiled, he walked toward her and kissed her lightly on the lips.

"What's wrong?" he asked. "Why are we having problems talking?"

"Expectations," Torrie answered. "We don't know what to expect, and neither of us are quite sure why I came. You're wondering if I came because I love you or because I'm tired of running. I'm wondering if you still want me here or if you were so afraid of my being…well, you know of not seeing me again you just shouted out the first words that came to your lips."

"You mean that I love you?"

"Yes."

"Torrie, be honest with me. You know I love you. You've always known. Why are you behaving as though this is something new?"

"Until recently, thoughts of us together were merely a dream. I was afraid to believe they'd ever come true. But you're right. I do know you love me."

"And you love me, right?"

"Yes, I love you."

"Then why is it so hard for you to trust me? Why do you doubt me? Hell, Torrie, do you really think I'd risk my life coming after you if this wasn't real, if I had any doubts we belong together, if I thought I could live the rest of my life without you?"

She smiled. "I doubt because I've had dreams of my future, and you've never been in any of my visions. How could I not worry about that?" Torrie said. She accepted the Coke and sat on the edge of the brocade chair, trying her best not to think how much the chair cost. "All of these years, and you'd never said those words, that you loved me. Things are difficult, Jake. Our home is gone. Of course we will do things that we might not otherwise do."

"If you think that, why did you get on that plane?"

"Because even if I'm not sure of our future, I'm certain of my feelings for you. I've always loved you." She hesitated a nanosecond. "And I want to know what it's like to be with you."

Jake took a deep breath. Hell yes, he knew what Torrie meant, but hell she'd said she wasn't coming to have sex with him. She sure was sending him mixed signals. She was sure as hell confusing him. She'd admitted she loved him, but he saw the fear in her and that fear was overpowering the joy he should be feeling.

"You have no doubts about your love for me?" Jake asked, sucking in a deep breath.

"None."

"Yet you doubt mine."

"Maybe what I'm doubting is my ability to see you in my future."

"I think I feel a bit insulted that you're basing our lives on some vision you haven't had of us. I've proven myself to you over and over, Torrie. Don't forget I'm the one who kept the connection between us. Not you. I'm the one who made the first move to come to you. I'm not jumping though any more hoops, so you'd better decide quickly what you want. We're grown and we've wasted too much time already." He shrugged his shoulders carelessly. "Why the hell are you here?"

He saw her nipples stabbing through the material of her light blouse. He'd definitely have to make sure she had warmer clothes than she was used to if she planned to remain in New York. Jake swallowed. He should turn his head or look down, look up, look away, but he couldn't. His eyes seemed to not want to move. They were glued to Torrie's nipples.

"So I take it you like what you see, Jake?"

He blinked before shaking his head, then laughed as Torrie punched him lightly in the arm and laughed along with him. Just like that, they'd returned to being Torrie and Jake.

"What do you want to do first?" he asked, wrapping his arms around her inhaling the scent of her, the smell of home, and the smell of Torrie.

"I think I'd like a bubble bath and maybe we could order one of those famous New York pizzas I've heard so much about."

"I don't have bubble bath."

"I didn't think you would." Torrie's head slid to the right, and she cocked her head holding Jake's gaze. Now was the time to ask before this went any farther. "If you always loved me, how could you have married another woman?" She watched as his lips turned upward.

"I was lonely."

"So was I."

"You never admitted that to me."

"Neither did you."

Jake sobered when he realized Torrie was serious and not just teasing. "I guess for a while there I didn't see any future for us either, so I got on with my life."

"So how did it happen that at this time in your life you have no one? Did you end a relationship to come to me?"

"I would never have asked you to come to me if I had someone else, and I wouldn't have come—"

"Yes you would, Jake. You would have braved the storm to rescue me, even if you had a woman. I know that and you know it. Let's not pretend. When you were married, it didn't stop your calls...well not entirely."

"You've always known me so well. Why didn't you know me well enough to know I loved you and wanted you to beg me to not get married?"

"Do you really think that's how a woman wants to be courted, to have to beg a man to come to her? Get real, Jake. You didn't do what you should have done years ago, so I've come here to claim you."

"Girl, if your daddy could hear you now, he'd kick your butt all the way back to Louisiana."

"Well my daddy ain't here now, is he?"

"Torrie, baby, you are turning me on. You know that tub is definitely big enough for two, and I feel kind of dirty."

"You are kinda dirty. Now I suggest you stop talking and start dialing your phone for pizza. I'm going to go soak."

Torrie kept waiting for Jake to open the bathroom door. She was glad they'd gotten over their initial shyness with each other. She ran her hand through the water, glad she'd come.

She took in a breath, then allowed her body to submerge beneath the fragrant bubbles. Somehow, she'd known Jake would have a tub large enough for her to disappear. Torrie hadn't enjoyed the luxury of a bath like this in weeks. John Tom had a tub, but not one large enough for Torrie to disappear from view. She brought her head up slowly and took another breath before submerging once again.

Torrie smiled underneath the water as she thought of Kimmie and John Tom. She hoped he'd really learned his lesson and that his doggish ways were behind them. She wanted to believe him. And if he meant it, she hoped Kimmie would give him another chance. Torrie didn't blame her sister for making John Tom earn her love. He'd hurt her.

With that thought, Torrie surfaced and glanced toward the door, wondering if she should just yell out and tell Jake to come on in right this second and join her in the tub. But she'd waited so long for this to happen she wanted everything to be right. An image of her dying popped into her mind. She definitely didn't want to die without knowing what it was like to have made love with Jake.

Torrie had tried hard to push the thoughts of death from her, but with so much happening it wasn't an easy job. She trailed her hand through the water, wondering if Jake was standing there wanting to join her. She gazed at the door, trying to send him a message. If he came in at that moment, she'd end the nonsense. She'd move and give him room in the tub, and she'd make love to him. *If he came in*. Torrie glanced again at the door. "Come in, Jake," she whispered so softly that even if he had been in the tub with her he would have been unable to hear.

Jake stood outside the door whispering, "Baby, invite me in." He was aware he wasn't speaking loud enough for Torrie to hear him, but he had hoped that with their connection she would know he was outside the door just waiting for an invitation. His erection seemed to be growing by the seconds as his thoughts went deeper into what he would like to do with Torrie. It was then he could swear he heard Torrie's voice inviting him to join her in the tub, to come in the bathroom and make love to her.

He put out a hand to touch the doorknob and stopped. He'd told her there were no strings attached, that she didn't have to sleep with him, that she wasn't a piece of tail. Damn, he was trying hard to prove to her that he'd meant it when he told her he loved her. How could he behave like a pig, standing there with an erection? If he went in, she might never believe it was love and not lust. He wouldn't deny that lust played a healthy part in his feelings for Torrie. Hell, he'd wanted her since he was sixteen years old. Feeling that she was calling him was messing with his mind big time.

When the bell rang, Jake could barely tear his eyes from the door. It was the pizza he'd ordered. He should make his feet move and answer the bell. He should stop sniffing the scented air catching the vanilla fragrance Torrie had evidently put into the tub. "Damn, Torrie," Jake said low, "you'd better have on something so ugly that there will be no way it will turn me on." He smiled and went to answer the bell.

"Torrie, the pizza's here, baby. Come on out before it gets cold." He took out plates and napkins and called again, turning to see if she was coming. The silverware he'd just taken from the drawer clattered to the floor as Jake stared at Torrie.

His heart thudded in his chest. No way in hell would this new erection be tamed, so he wasn't even going to try. His eyes were fastened on Torrie's body. He was trying to figure out what she was wearing. The tiny orange top could be anything from a bra to a top, he had no idea. His eyes skimmed downward, the sliver of material covering her hips and about an inch of her thighs were also orange. *Shorts*, he wondered. He tilted his head as she grinned. Damn, all that beautiful dark chocolate encased in orange. He shivered with lust. And his eyes met hers.

Hell yes, Torrie knew exactly what she was doing and what she was doing to him. When she gave a throaty laugh and turned away. He stood watching her as she extended a leg and placed it on a chair in one of those Mrs. Robinson-type moves. Then she began rubbing lotion on her leg so slowly Jake thought he would climax right then and there. This was way too much; she was pushing the envelope here.

He walked over to her, took the bottle from her hand and gazed into her eyes. As he warmed the lotion between his palms, his eyes locked on her lips. Jake refused to drop his gaze until he began rubbing the lotion on her. He heard her *hmm* and couldn't help grinning. "Your other leg, Torrie," he said as he'd finished with the first. He rubbed lotion on that one as well, looking at her as his fingers made their way upward toward her thigh.

"If you go any higher…well…the pizza will get cold."

Jake laughed, thinking for a moment to risk it. He didn't, he kept his fingers where they were for only a second longer, feeling her heat. His eyes were glued to her thighs, to the "V" between them and he shook his head. "Mercy," he said and rubbed downward in the opposite direction. "Is that enough damn lotion, Torrie?"

"Yes," she said, taking the bottle. "Don't be so testy. I didn't ask you to do it, you volunteered. Now you're growling like an old bear as though I put you out, or had you doing something you didn't want to do." She lowered her lashes and batted them at him. "Did I make you do something you didn't want to do, Jake?"

As he swallowed, he moved back, trying to figure out Torrie's game. She'd called him and she'd come to him. She wanted him and now she was teasing him mercilessly. "*Be cool Jake*," he mentally shook himself. *She's testing you.*

"Stop playing games, Torrie, like you said the pizza is getting cold," he said and picked up the dropped silverware and tossed it in the sink with one hand while reaching into the drawer for clean utensils with the other.

"Are you getting cold, Jake?"

"I'm not kidding with you. One second you're hot, the next you're cold. What are you trying to prove anyway? Do I look like a yo-yo?"

"I haven't decided."

"Torrie, stop it," Jake snapped. "This wanton vixen act isn't you. What's up?"

"I'm sorry, Jake." She glanced at the floor then stared at him. "I'm a little nervous. Aren't you?"

He decided not to answer that question. "Come on, let's eat the pizza. I also ordered salad and spaghetti. I didn't know how hungry you were."

"I'm very hungry," Torrie answered, and Jake's head snapped around at the whispery soft innuendo. He wondered what she'd do if he just attacked her and made love to her. She was driving him crazy. He had to get his mind off making love to her.

"Will you marry me, Torrie?"

This time it was Torrie's turn to stand there with an open mouth.

"Will you marry me, Torrie?" Jake repeated, coming around and kneeling down in front of her.

"Let me eat first okay?"

"Why?"

"Because I need to take a breath."

"Why? I haven't been able to breathe since I saw you."

"You know, Jake. I never told you that you had to marry me in order to make love to me. I said you…oh never mind."

"And just who told you that I asked you to marry me because I wanted to make love to you?"

"Well you do, don't you…want to make love…to me…I mean?"

"Of course I do, and you want to make love to me. But that has nothing to do with the question I just asked. And to be honest, I'm offended you've taken my proposal so lightly." Jake slid a piece of pizza onto his plate and sat across from Torrie, watching her eat as though she didn't have a care in the world.

"Torrie, I told you how long I've wanted us to be together. What's so strange about my asking you to marry me?"

"Well, you didn't ask me to marry you before Hurricane Katrina. You didn't tell me you loved me before then, so forgive me if I question you now. Love and marriage are two different things, Jake. Yes, I believe you love me as I love you. Do I believe the next logical step is marriage? No. You've played the hero for me for many years, I think somewhere in that proposal is your desire to take care of me. I don't need you to take care of me, Jake. I don't need the comfort of your bank account and somehow I think you believe that I do."

"You almost sound like my father."

Torrie stopped in the middle of a bite. "You spoke to your father about me?" She frowned. "What did he say? That I wanted to come out here with you because I had nowhere else to go, that I had no money, that I needed you to take care of me?"

"Yes."

"And what did you say?"

"I didn't give a damn what the reason was, I would give you everything I had and then more."

Torrie puckered her brow as she observed Jake. "And you don't think somewhere in that statement there isn't the need to protect me?"

Jake threw down his fork and shoved his chair out of the way. "For Heaven's sake could you please tell me what's wrong with that? I love you. Why shouldn't I want to protect you? Why? Give me one damn good reason, Torrie."

"If you had come home three months ago before all of this happened, I would have said yes without hesitation." Torrie rested her eyes on Jake and shrugged her shoulder. "I can't say yes yet."

"I thought you said you wanted to get on with your life, to not waste another moment."

"That's the reason I came to see you, Jake, not to have you propose. I came to give us time together. I'm not asking you for a promise of forever, just a promise of right now."

"But I'm giving you a promise of forever. I'm giving you a promise of forever and a day. My feelings for you aren't going to change. My wanting to protect you isn't going to change. And my wanting to use my money to help make your life easier is the one thing I can do to make this better. I can't turn back time, but I can help you now." Jake glared at her in disbelief. *This was plain damn stupid.*

"Don't be angry, Jake."

"Give me a good reason not to be."

"Because I came to see you. You asked me to come to you, and I did because I love you, because I want a future with you. As much as you want to help me, I need to make my own money. I just need to secure a future for myself before I can accept what you're offering."

"Damn, baby, I didn't ask you to marry me this minute. I just asked if you would say yes. Will you marry me?"

"Katrina made a lot of difference in both of our lives. We need to wait until we know what's going to happen."

"So what are we going to do? We have no guarantee of when life will return to normal at home. Are you telling me you can't make a commitment to me until then? That's crazy, Torrie."

"I need to go home as soon as the mayor gives the word we can. I have to go and see what's happening. "

"I'm going back also." Jake saw her surprised look and felt some satisfaction. "I've been asked to take a crew down to help clear the debris. While I'm there, another friend has asked me to do a few of the claims for C&J Mutual."

"It's been a long time since you've done assessments hasn't it?"

"Yeah, but he's calling in a favor. He's probably asking every freelance adjuster he knows. He figured since it's my home and I was going to help clean up, we could kill two birds at the same time. No big deal."

"From what I've been hearing, there are more adjusters heading down than the number of people left there. The word is already out they're trying to not pay the claims. Why are you going?"

"Like I said, just a favor."

Torrie remained silent.

"Torrie, let's take it back to the very beginning," Jake whispered, wondering if she would understand. He waited; saw her eyes light and the smile claim her face. God, she was beautiful, and she understood. She reached out her hand for his and headed for the corner, sat down on the polished hardwood floor, and then she placed her hands over her eyes and waited.

Jake took in a breath and held it as he watched Torrie sitting there waiting for him. Simultaneously she broke his heart and lit it on fire. Jake took his place on the floor beside her. He breathed in her scent. *God, please let this work,* he prayed silently.

"Hello, don't be afraid, my name's Jake, and I'll protect you from the storm. I won't let lightning hurt you. I won't ever let anything hurt you ever again, not even me," he added changing the speech he'd given her when he was five. He gently removed her hand from her face and stared into her eyes. "I love you, Torrie, and I promise I'll never hurt you."

Her eyes changed to liquid chocolate. Her lips opened slightly, and she moved closer to him. All Jake wanted in the world was to take a sip from her. Their lips touched, and she trembled. Her lips opened a little wider to allow Jake's tongue to advance.

"Jake," Torrie moaned, knowing she was lost. She drowned from the look in his eyes, finally closing her eyes and giving into the feelings overtaking her. She loved him; there was no denying it. The most romantic thing Jake could have done was to take her back to the beginning.

She was burning up. When Jake's hand slipped beneath her top, she shivered and another moan slid from her throat. His hand touched her breast, and she felt the want fill her. She was going to a place she'd never dared to go. Her head was reeling as Jake pushed her top away and moved her bra to the side. His mouth closed on her breast, and her eyes rolled to the back of her head.

Jake's mouth was trailing hot kisses all over her body. He moved down, pulling on her shorts, trying to remove them. *Finally*, Torrie thought.

"Marry me, Torrie."

"Jake, don't, not now." She felt his hand still, then the kisses stopped and he looked at her. His breath was coming out in hard pants. His golden eyes flicked back and forth between lust and anger. Torrie hoped the lust would win out. She rubbed her hand down his body and pulled him closer, but he pushed away, leaving only the glare that filled his eyes.

"Torrie, I love you. I want to marry you. Will you marry me?"

"Can't we talk about this later, Jake? We have time. I just got here."

"Damn it, Torrie, I'm begging you, and you're giving me shit." His hand shook as he prepared to remove it from between her warm thighs. His fingers didn't want to release her flesh, neither did he. Jake sighed and stood up.

"Torrie, I thought it would be a little different having you here. I have waited so long for this. I wanted to be with you, to hold you, to talk into the wee hours of the morning. I wanted to make you feel safe, but you'll probably bite my head off for that thought. My intentions have never been to jump your bones the moment you came in here or to fight with you. Right now I feel old, tired, and worn out. You're tripping, and I don't have the patience to deal with it right now. So before I do more to ruin our relationship than I already have by telling you I love you and asking you to marry me, I think I'll take a nap. Maybe later when I get up we can talk." He walked away toward the bedroom. Jake closed the door on Torrie, wondering what was so wrong about asking her to marry him, wondering if she'd at least come in and apologize. When it appeared as though she wouldn't, he kicked off his shoes and lay on the bed.

I didn't realize what I'd lost until I lost it. John Tom's words came again and Torrie sucked in the pain of Jake's turning his back on her. She didn't want to lose Jake. She had to let go of the fear, let go of the not knowing what would happen with them. Even if she wasn't able to get a clear picture of the two of them together in the future, there was still now. She had to stop being afraid. She stood at the door, willing him to come back out, to take her in his arms to just make love to her, to just have now. "Jake," she called. "Jake." She knew he could hear her. Tears spilled from her eyes. She screamed his name. "Jake." Still no answer.

Jake lay on his bed listening to Torrie call his name. He wanted so badly to go to her. Jake heard the tears in her voice, he swallowed. This was one time Torrie would have to make the first move. He'd done it for all the years he'd been gone. He'd come to her. Now if she wanted him, she would have to come to him. His stomach knotted as the minutes ticked by, she wasn't coming.

Then miraculously, the door opened and he heard her whimpering sobs, but refused to turn around.

"Jake, please," Torrie begged. "Don't do this please. Look at me. I love you, Jake."

Damn. She'd said the words that would make him melt. He turned slowly and stared at her. "What are you so afraid of, Torrie? Is it me?" She didn't answer. "Torrie?"

"I'm afraid of having nothing."

"That's just it, don't you see? You have what I have."

"I want my own, Jake. I don't want you saving me this time."

"We're stronger together, baby. I know my purpose isn't to save you or for you to save me. But I know we were meant to be together. I believe we were put on this earth to save each other."

"What do you need to be saved from?"

"From being alone, from being talked into joining the family empire, from becoming a New Orleans son."

"That would never happen to you. It's not who you are."

"You never can tell, Torrie. Without you in my life, who knows? Listen," he continued, "we want the same thing, each other. We love each other, and we want to proceed to the next logical step, to make love. I'm not going to sugar coat this. Yes, when I look at you I feel the same lust of that sixteen-year-old boy. But I also feel the love of a thirty-year-old man. I think we're too old to continue playing games. I want to marry you, Torrie."

Jake stared at her while she blinked her eyes in an attempt to stop the tears.

"I'm asking you again. Will you marry me?" When she didn't answer, he lay back on the bed and sighed. "It's obvious we both want the same thing, Torrie, to make love, and it's obvious you want to make love only if I don't ask for a commitment. And it's also obvious that I'm not going to make love to you until you give me a commitment. I guess we're at a stalemate. If you want me to make love to you, you will have to make up your mind about us right here and right now. You have to trust me and trust me not to hurt you. Do you trust me, Torrie?"

"I do trust you in most things, Jake. I really do, and it's not that I think you would do anything to hurt me intentionally. It's…just…Why can't we wait?"

"Because I know what I want."

"I know what I want, too. I really do."

"And you think I should believe you?" Jake sat back up to stare at her. "You trust your heart, but you don't trust mine. That's wrong, Torrie, think about it." She looked so delicious in her orange outfit and chocolate brown skin. Jake couldn't help but love her. He swung his legs over the side of the bed and opened his arms to her. When she rushed in, he held her close.

"This is definitely not how I envisioned our first night together." He pulled her with him. As she lay on top of him, he looked into her eyes, knowing the game was lost. He wasn't fighting anymore. Jake wanted to make love to Torrie as much as she wanted to make love to him. "I love you, baby," he said and kissed her eyelids.

"I love you, too, Jake."

He flipped her over onto her back and gave her a smile. It hurt that she was holding back. He'd wanted her to make a move and she had. She'd come to New York, and she'd come to him now. He wanted badly for her to trust him, for her to know she wasn't just a conquest to him. While he was aware Torrie loved him as much as he loved her, he was also aware she had walls she'd built around her heart. Walls they were both trying to break down by making love. He wished he had the strength to resist her, to not touch her soft skin or to not smell her sweetness. He was a fool for not letting go. Jake didn't possess that much self control. With one hand, he continued to caress Torrie. And with the other, he opened the bedside table feeling for the small square package and grabbed it.

Torrie pulled Jake down to her and kissed him hard—the way he'd done to her. She poured everything that was in her into that kiss, and she didn't let up until she felt Jake's fingers begin their journey to the space between them. He kissed her breasts, and then suckled them once again. The power of what he was doing rocketed through her and flamed her nether regions. She'd waited an eternity to be with Jake. She'd always known he'd be the first, if not the last. If they could do it without talking, they'd be okay.

Heat spiraled down her spine, and Torrie moaned. No man had ever made her moan, perhaps because she'd never allowed any man the liberties she was allowing Jake. When his hand traveled south, feeling for her most intimate areas, Torrie thought she would die from the pleasure. "Oh, Jake, she breathed into his mouth, and desire took over inflaming her senses. Somewhere in the midst of the wanting, their clothes disappeared. She could feel his hardness, his heat scorching her thigh.

"Let me see you," she whispered. "I've always wanted to see you." Torrie took the condom from his hand and slid it over his hardness. Her hands trembled a little and she noticed Jake was trembling as well.

From the look in his eyes, she knew he would not stop no matter what commitment he wanted. Finally, the moment had arrived. Jake pushed in, and for just a moment, Torrie's muscles tightened. She gritted her teeth against the expected pain. She was surprised that it burned. It didn't matter. Torrie wasn't stopping.

"Jake," she said, wrapping her arms about him.

He pumped slowly. "I'm not hurting you, baby, am I?"

"Just a little bit," Torrie answered, readjusting her body to accommodate Jake. She flinched and shook her head at him. "Don't stop," she pleaded.

"Are you sure?"

Heat flooded Torrie's body. The pain was gone. The only thing she felt now was unbelievable pleasure, wave after wave of pleasure. "I'm sure," she answered when she could catch her breath.

Jake stroked going in hard and pulling out. He grinned, finding once again that sweet spot inside Torrie's body, her tightness pulled on him, making him want to let go. But it was her first time. He'd have to hold on for a little longer. Jake could feel himself hovering toward the edge but Torrie was even closer to the precipice than he. Now if he could just hold on.

Jake thrust, moving faster, harder as Torrie rocked against him. When he felt Torrie's body begin to spasm, he held her closer, capturing her mouth in a kiss that told of his love and his passion. He swallowed her screams of pleasure and took her moans of delight deep within his body. While she climaxed, he plunged even deeper into her body, making up for every wet dream he'd had about her, and fulfilling every desire, every want and need.

A shudder began in his limbs and traveled to his groin, then rushed out in an overwhelming roar of passion. The sensations ripped through every cell. His connection of love with Torrie was so strong, he could barely breathe. Jake had never known such fulfillment could exist.

"Torrie," he breathed. "My God, Torrie, I love you. You okay, baby?"

She was crying, holding him. Jake couldn't make out the words. He lifted off her just a little.

"I love you, Jacob Broussard. Will you marry me? I want that commitment."

Jake grinned, holding Torrie close. "Yes, baby, I'll marry you."

Chapter Nine

Jake lay with Torrie sprawled across his chest, unable to wipe the grin from his face. His fingers trembled as he caressed her. The aftershock of their lovemaking bound them together. God, he'd known making love to Torrie would be like that. It was her first time, but it felt like his also. He'd never experienced such a soul connection with anyone. Together they'd soared through the clouds, and they'd come through it stronger than they'd ever been. Satisfied? It hardly begins to describe what Jake was feeling. Sated? Only for the moment. He didn't think he'd ever get enough of touching Torrie or having her touch him.

"Did you mean it, baby?"

"What, that I love you?"

Jake's grin became even larger. "I already know you love me." He kissed the top of her head. "Are you really going to marry me?" He waited while she moved around as if to see him better. She had a funny smirk on her face that worried Jake

"Jacob Broussard, you've waited far too many years to have done what you should have done years ago. You were right. You should have married me in the first darn place, and if you hadn't been so stubborn…" Torrie laughed.

"Me, stubborn, me? Not one phone call, not one card, and you call me stubborn?"

"What if I could prove to you that I never forgot you, that I always cared about you? Would that make you happy?"

"Where's your proof?"

"In my bag."

"And you have to get up to get this proof?"

"Of course I do." Torrie laughed, knowing what was on Jake's mind.

"In that case, I think your proof can wait. How are you feeling? Did I hurt you?"

"Jake, I never knew such exquisite feelings could be made by two people. I think I could very easily become addicted to your touch." Torrie's fingers begin moving, exploring, touching, holding, squeezing. "Of course it takes more than once to make an addiction doesn't it?" She gazed into his eyes that had gone all soft. This was the way her life was meant to be. A brief flash of her family tried to force itself into her brain, but Torrie refused to allow it. All the problems would still be there when they were done.

It was morning before they were done. Sleep had been the last thing on their minds. When they finally drifted off, it was in each other arms. When they woke, they were still in each other arms. Jake tugged on a strand of Torrie's hair.

"Hey wake up. I've got something for you." He watched as a smile curved her lips. "Not that," he teased. "At least not right this second. Come on open your eyes and look at me." One eye opened and Jake smiled. "Both, Torrie."

"Why are you waking me, Jake? It better be important."

"I think you'll like it, but if you don't…well…we'll take care of that." He got out of the bed knowing Torrie's eyes were on him. The only thing he hadn't removed from the room he'd given Torrie was the first thing he'd gone out and bought when he'd returned to New York. It was with her tearful face in his mind that he'd picked it out. Jake retrieved the box and held it behind his back as he walked back to Torrie.

Had she really agreed to marry Jake? God knows she wanted to. But even now after they'd made a commitment, after they'd made love Torrie couldn't get even a clue let alone a vision of her and Jake together in the future. That worried her some. No, her visions weren't always reliable, but they were more so than her dreams, which she now thought were precognitive visions. Either way, she'd seen other things. She'd even had a tiny glimpse of Kimmie and John Tom together. Why couldn't she get something like that on her and Jake?

Looking at Jake, Torrie thought she'd figured out the answer to that. She'd been too afraid of her visions because she'd been wrong as often as she'd been right. If she'd always been right she wouldn't have left one state with bad weather to go to another one with weather just as bad. In spite of her dreams being unreliable she would like to be able to close her eyes and get even an inkling of her future with Jake. Jake was too important to her to not have an inkling. That was the part she couldn't handle. Things she didn't want to know she did. She knew that even after Christmas, New Orleans wouldn't be livable.

Torrie stopped thinking and put her attention back on Jake, where it belonged. She watched his naked form as he came toward her. Her eyes skimmed his body. *Very nice,* she thought...hard chest, flat hips, long legs, and a firm muscled stomach. She grinned as she looked between his thighs. "Very, very nice," she whispered, bringing her eyes up to his, trying to force a vision. Something she knew wouldn't work.

"Torrie, you kind of stole my thunder." Jake knelt by the side of the bed and pulled his hand from behind his back. "No brow beating, baby." He opened the box and waited. Then at last her hand moved toward him and her voice came out all wispy and light, a bit scared, but that was okay. He'd take that, marriage was a scary thing, but the two of them would make it work.

"Jake, it's beautiful." Torrie bit her lip, waiting for Jake to slide the ring on her finger. *Maybe the ring will do it,* she thought. She put it on her finger. Still, no vision. Torrie felt a squeeze of her heart and a stab of pain and wondered what it meant.

"What's wrong baby?" Jake asked.

"Nothing, I was just trying to picture us together, that's all."

"You know we make our own future. We can't leave everything to visions and dreams. I've always believed in your dreams, Torrie, but not about us. You don't see us together, but I do. I've had my own visions, one of you being my wife, one of us growing old together, loving each other, always being faithful, and always trusting, always. I pledge that to you, Torrie, I will never hurt you again I swear."

"And I'll do my best to stop doubting." Jake drew her to him. His lips pressed against hers. The tip of his tongue outlined hers. As his arms encircled her, a dreadful feeling overcame Torrie. She wished Jake had not made that promise. Somehow she didn't feel he'd be able to keep it. She trembled in his embrace. A sense of betrayal washed over her.

"Hold me, Jake," she whispered in his ear. "Just hold me."

It was time Torrie gave her own gift to Jake; time to put his doubts aside. While Jake was declaring his expertise at the stove, Torrie went to her bag and got the metal box. Even though the contents had been for her alone, helping her to feel in some small way more connected to him; she thought he should know he had always been on her mind. The cold metal rested against her thigh as she wondered how Jake would react, she almost felt as if she was giving him some forbidden part of herself. Licking her lips, she decided to put her doubts aside.

"Jake," she called softly, placing the box on the table and waiting for him to acknowledge her. "I have your proof."

Something in Torrie's voice stabbed at Jake. He saw the metal box sitting on the table, the same metal box he'd seen in the cabin, the same one she'd insisted on carrying with her when they went into town. Now she was inviting him to look inside of it. A hard unexpected shudder ripped through him, and for a moment he dreaded what he'd find in the box. It was supposed to be something that would make him happy, but somehow he doubted it would.

He eyed the box, and then stared at Torrie. She was scared also. This couldn't be good. Jake sat down and Torrie took the seat across from him.

"Go ahead, open it," Torrie coached in a voice so unlike hers that his head snapped up and his eyes held hers as he lifted the lid. He blinked as he looked inside. *Letters, cards, envelopes.* He picked up one after the other. They were from him to Torrie. His fingers trembled as he lightly touched the other piles. He knew without picking it up what the other pile would be.

Jake closed his eyes for a moment. *Don't tell me she wasted twelve years of life saving cards and letters.* He could feel the anger shoot straight though to his scalp. He fought to keep the words in, not wanting to spoil their beautiful morning. He picked up one of Torrie's un-mailed letters to him and began reading. *Unbelievable*, the first one lifted from the box was written after he'd called to tell her he was getting married.

For a moment his eyes crossed and the words blurred because of the tears he was holding back. He couldn't believe Torrie was pouring her heart out to him in a letter, telling him how she loved him, that they belonged together, that she should be the one he married.

Jake closed his eyes again and dropped the letter back into the box. He picked up several more envelopes that looked to contain cards. He opened one after the other: birthday cards, Christmas cards, just cards saying she missed him. He licked his lips sucking in the anger as it turned to pain. So many lost years, so many, just one of the cards, one of the letters and he would have come to Torrie.

"Why did you show me this?" Jake asked at last, no longer able to contain his emotions.

"I wanted you to know that I never forgot about you. I wanted you to know I was thinking about you all these years, that I did buy you a card for your birthday."

"But you didn't send them!" Jake narrowed his gaze. "How did you think your giving them to me now was going to make me feel?"

"Happy," Torrie retorted. "I thought you'd be happy or I wouldn't have given it to you."

"Well, you were wrong. I'm not happy. I'm furious knowing that neither of us had to be alone. That we could have been together all this time. So much wasted time, Torrie." Jake pulled in his breath at the look in her eyes and swallowed his rage along with his hurt. "All this time because you didn't trust me, and the hesitation, the reason you wouldn't say yes the first time I asked you to marry me. You really don't trust me, Torrie."

She'd not given him the letters and cards to make him angry. She really had thought he'd be pleased. "I'm working on that, on the trust, Jake. I am."

"Why didn't you just tell me you were in love with me and wanted us to be together?"

"Why didn't you ever tell me?" Torrie was getting angry herself. "You know you could have told me how you felt, too. You wasted just as much time as I did. At least I didn't get married," she snapped. Torrie reached her hand for the box. "If you don't want them, give them back."

Jake's hand reached out and stopped her. "It's mine now. You gave the box to me, remember? It's a gift. You can't take a gift back." Jake got up and paced. "Damn, Torrie, so much time. You're right," he said taking the box from the dining room table in case Torrie got any idea to reclaim it. He took the box to his office and placed it in his safe, locking it there before coming back out to Torrie

"You're right. We were both wrong." He took in a deep breath and pulled Torrie to sit on his lap in his favorite leather chair. "No more, okay. No more not talking. No more not trusting me?" He kissed the hollow of her neck, sliding his tongue out just a bit in order to capture the taste of her on the tip. "No more worrying because you don't have a vision of the two of us together. No more, Torrie, do you understand? Yes, Katrina brought us together. I admit that, but damn, baby, we should have been together all this time."

Jake's thoughts returned for a moment to the contents of the box and the fistful of envelopes he'd first pulled out. "You know that and I know that. You wanted it and I wanted it. Just like you were burning with desire for me, and I've been going mad for the past fourteen years wanting you."

This was crazy, he and Torrie fighting over the past, her glaring at him, her angry and hurt and him feeling the same. He shook his head and took in several breaths, releasing them as he buried his lips in soft fragrant skin.

"Our past is just that, Torrie. Do you understand me? No more of what we didn't do. It's over, we begin our life right now." He lifted her hand and kissed the ring he'd placed on her finger. "This is our beginning." Jake wrapped his arms more firmly around her as he places little kisses along her jaw line before heading for her lips. "I wanted to show you New York, but I've been worried if it would be insensitive. I don't want to mess up with you. I've—"

"Been so worried about me and pitying me for losing everything, that you've forgotten I have a degree and business skills. I'll survive, Jake. I'll start over. It's not as though I have a choice, now is it?"

"No, but at least you won't be starting over alone. We can do it together."

She gave him a smile, then a kiss. Torrie didn't want to start another fight, not so soon anyway. Yes, she would marry Jake, but not until she'd reestablished her business and rebuilt her home. Jake had a business and employees he worried about, so did Torrie. Sure, she didn't have a job for them to go to anymore, but she still worried about them. Her bank account was a little plumper from the twenty-three hundred dollar check she'd finally received from FEMA. And she'd filled out and returned the papers to get back all of the money she'd paid out for everyone at Sam Houston Jones State Park. Once it had been declared a Disaster Recovery Center, she'd been told her money would be refunded.

Torrie took a deep breath, deciding to go with the flow. She relaxed in Jake's arms, accepting his embrace. She didn't need to talk to him about any of that now. She wasn't allowed back into New Orleans, but when she was, she was positive her insurance company would be there. Every other insurance company was there or heading there. Even Jake was going to be there doing assessing. And with the entire world watching, as small as they were, even Rediflex Mutual would have to have people there, and they wouldn't dare try and renege on the claims. No, Torrie wasn't worried. It wasn't a vision she relied on concerning that matter, just plain good old intuition.

Chapter Ten

Torrie hadn't called her family in two weeks. At that time, only Kimmie would speak to her. Her parents were so angry that she'd gone to shack up with Jake they weren't speaking to her. Trey didn't voice his opinions, but Torrie knew them.

Now it was time to call home, or as close to home as Torrie could get. Jake was leaving in a week or so to return to help with the clean up and the assessments. Torrie was almost afraid to return to New Orleans with him, but she'd made up her mind. She dialed John Tom's home and waited, hoping it would be Kimmie; it wasn't.

"Hi, Mama." For a few seconds the line was quiet, then her mother sighed as though she'd just given up. "Does Jake love you, baby?"

"He asked me to marry him."

"What did you say?"

"What do you think I said? I love Jake."

"I thought you said you weren't going to rush into anything."

"I don't know if I would call twelve years rushing. Considering all we've been through, Jake and I have taken it very slow."

"What about that second bedroom Jake has? Did he put you up in there?"

Torrie could laugh. "Jake has three bedrooms. He cleaned out his own bedroom and gave it to me. He took another room. We've been all over New York. He's taken me to see his company and the sites he's working on. He's going home soon. He's helping with the clean-up effort in New Orleans. He's bringing in a crew, and I'm going back with him." Torrie was rushing her words, not wanting to go any farther with her mother about her personal life. "Mama, can I talk to Kimmie?"

Torrie played with the strands of her hair as she tapped a foot impatiently, waiting for her sister.

"Hello."

"Dang, Kimmie, what did you do, stop to wash your hair?"

"Hey, you waited long enough to call back. I guess that means you're having a good time. And I took exactly three seconds to come to the phone."

Torrie grinned from ear to ear. "Kimmie, go outside." Torrie waited a few seconds. "Did you do it," she asked. "Are you some-place where we can talk?"

"Yes, I'm outside," Kimmie said with slight irritation. "Girl, you don't have to tell me. I already know. You did it, didn't you?"

Laughter erupted and spilled from Torrie's throat. "Kimmie, oh my God, I can't believe it. I love him so much." Torrie gushed; glad Jake was taking a shower alone for the first time since she'd been there. She'd told him she wanted to call her sister, and he'd under-stood.

"Kimmie, Jake asked me to marry him. He gave me the most beautiful ring. He'd already had it picked out and here waiting for me. Kimmie, he does love me."

"You got off the subject real fast. Come on back to it. Torrie, was it worth all those years of pining over that boy?"

"It was worth every second. We are so good together. It's like magic, like we're in heaven. I love it. I love making love to Jake and I love him…have you and John Tom?" The silence made Torrie laugh so hard that tears ran down her cheeks. "Mama and Daddy thought they had to watch out for me, and here you are right under their noses." Torrie laughed again.

"We haven't done it here. We've gone out," Kimmie said indig-nantly.

"Kimmie, it's okay. I'm glad you and John Tom are back together."

"We're not back together. We just slept together. Just because you're having sex with a man, doesn't mean he's going to be true to you. I should know. I've been through that mess once. Hell, a lot more than once with that fool. I'm not going to do it again."

The wistfulness and the sadness came through the phone lines as though her sister was standing right beside her. Torrie could see Kimmie throwing her chance for happiness right out the window. She wasn't too old to start over, to marry, or even to have babies. Kimmie needed someone else to mother besides Torrie, someone else's virginity to watch out for.

"Kimmie, I think John Tom has changed."

"You're too willing to believe that. When a man hurts you, you have to remember or you'll repeat your mistakes."

"I know you're talking about me; I get it. Jake was sixteen, Kimmie. I love him. Besides, if I don't forgive Jake how am I am going to find true happiness? And you forget, people can change." Torrie wanted desperately to change the conversation. "I gave him something."

"Yeah, I know."

"No, the metal box I had. I gave it to him."

"What was in it?"

"It had all the letters I've written to him over the years and never mailed, all the cards I bought for him."

"I don't believe it. You mean to tell me you've been pining over him all these years and all you did was write letters to him and never mail them? Torrie, you need help. Please tell me Jake didn't open the box."

"I thought he would be happy to know I'd not stopped thinking about him, that I'd always loved him just as he loved me. But he wasn't happy about it. He was angry and hurt I'd wasted so much time. He's right. All those wasted years of remembering how he'd once hurt me, all those years of protecting myself so he couldn't hurt me again. And you know what, Kimmie, all I have to show for it are a lot of lonely years and empty arms. All I got for my protection was this incredible ache in my soul. My heart was so raw I swore I didn't need a man. I don't want to remember when Jake hurt me anymore. I just want to think about him loving me. It took me awhile to realize why I kept pushing Jake away, why I never reached out to him or asked him to come home. I don't want to live in the past holding on to old pain. I want to live for the future."

"Then you're a fool, baby sister. If you don't remember he can hurt you again."

"Kimmie, listen to me. What you're saying now isn't about Jake, and we both know it. It's been five years. I know John Tom was a dog and slept with anything that breathed. But I also know even then he loved you. I think he's changed. I think losing you changed him. You see he never married anyone else, and he could have."

"About that, you had no right to just bring me here, and while we're on it, I think it was pretty disloyal of you to have maintained a relationship with him all these years. You shouldn't have."

"Then that makes us even. You had no right fourteen years ago to try and manipulate my life, but I figured you did it because you loved me and thought you knew best and that's what I did. I took you to the home of a man who loves you and our family."

"But all of these years and you've never said a word to me. I can't believe you didn't tell me you remained friends with him."

"I liked him, I always have. He was the big brother I never had. He's been there for me when I needed him through the years just for a man's point of view. Besides, if I hadn't kept in contact with him, we wouldn't have had anywhere to go. Mama and Daddy are too old for all that running nonsense. I know John Tom didn't change overnight, Kimmie, but he changed long before I took you to his home, a home he built for you. I'm just saying, if you just settle for sex with him, you'll be cheating yourself and cheating him. Give him a chance to make it right. I'm not saying you've got to make it easy for him."

"Like you made it easy for Jake?"

Torrie stopped and shook off the hit. "Kimmie, just let me be happy for another week."

"Okay, Torrie, you've got your week. Even though you're being a selfish little brat. Mama and Daddy are having all kinds of trouble trying to get a damn trailer to live in, and you haven't bothered to call in two weeks. Nagin's still telling people to keep their asses out of New Orleans, and then the next damn day he's on the news telling folks to come home. Come home to what? Is he crazy? Where the hell does he expect people to sleep, in the damn feces-covered streets? But I know I shouldn't bother you with any of that. You're in New York making love to Jake, sightseeing, shopping, you can't be bothered."

"That's not fair. I've been there for everybody my entire life. I didn't come to Jake until I made sure you all had someplace to stay." Torrie remained perched on the edge of Jake's bed in disbelief. She'd known Kimmie more than likely wasn't going to be happy, but she didn't think her sister would accuse her of not caring. "I said I'm coming back to be with you guys."

Kimmie took a deep breath and continued. "Why should you, you have a ring on your finger, and you don't have to worry about where your next meal is coming from or even if you're going to find a job. Did you even think to ask about Trey? That boy is worrying himself sick. He's working, but still worried that any day the hurricane victims will be seen as just a novelty and the school board will decide they don't need the extra teachers they hired. Have you given that any thought, Torrie? Have you ever thought Jake's father might have different plans for his son and his marrying a Thibodeaux might not be in those plans?"

"I didn't call to fight with you. I just wanted to check in with you. But I was hoping you'd finally let go of some of your own anger toward men and took a good look at John Tom. Even though you can't be happy for me I am happy to hear things are progressing for you and John Tom."

172

"Turn on Jake's damn television and return to planet earth. A lot has happened since you left. A hell of a lot, and if you thought things were going to get miraculously better, think again, baby sister. They're a hell of a lot worse."

Kimmie clicked off the phone, and Torrie held it for a moment looking at it. Her mother was not even as hostile as Kimmie had been.

Torrie felt the tears sliding down her cheeks and looked up. Jake was staring at her. She wondered how long he'd been standing there.

"Are they angry we're getting married?"

"I'm not exactly sure why Kimmie is angry. She seems angry that I left and that I haven't called again." Torrie pulled her gaze away. "I just wanted to take a little vacation away from all of it, Jake. I was never planning on staying here forever. Kimmie told me things are worse in New Orleans." Torrie bit her lips. "I've purposely not listened to any news since I've been here. I wanted to be happy."

"I wanted you to be happy, too, baby," Jake said, walking toward her. "I've played a part in keeping you so busy you didn't have a chance to watch the news. I didn't think either of us needed a constant reminder. My parents have called me everyday, that's reminder enough."

Torrie looked surprised. "I didn't know your parents had called. Do they know I'm here?"

"They know."

"And?"

"And this is my home. I pay my own bills. I make my own money. I may be a Broussard, but I'm my own man."

Torrie tried to smile. "So I guess that means they disapprove." She slid over on the bed, staring intently into Jake's eyes. "Can we watch some news?"

"Livingston Disaster recovery center closes."

Torrie glanced at the screen, and then back at Jake. "You can turn it off now. I don't need the news. The pictures are in my head.

173

Does that make me wrong? My family keeps their concentration centered on New Orleans because that's our home, but a lot of the people in Alabama and Mississippi are still hurting also. I still see it, Jake. They're still living in trailers there, too."

"Kimmie made you feel guilty for being with me instead of in the trenches with them, didn't she?"

Torrie didn't want to admit it, but she did feel guilty. She'd had so much joy in the last three weeks with Jake, and she'd purposefully stolen the time because she couldn't get a fix on a future. Maybe if she could see them together she would have watched the news and would have gone home sooner, but she hadn't. She wanted now for herself and for Jake. "Does my bailing out make me a bad person, Jake?"

"You didn't bail out, and you know the answer to the other part, baby. You're not a bad person. Sometimes the only rest you get is the rest you create."

Jake pointed at the screen. "Look, we have one more week. Nothing we do here is going to change anything in one week. One more week, baby, that's all I ask for." He held her gaze. "I know you're worried about what's going to happen to us. I know even with the ring you don't have a vision of the two of us together. I want to tell you something, and I want you to hold on to it. Hold on to the vision I've been holding on to for years. It's of the two of us together, married and happy. It wasn't a dream, Torrie, it was a vision and it happened a long time before the hurricane. That's why in the face of your seeming not to care about me, I continued to call. A vision of us kept me going."

"Even when you were married?"

"I'm ashamed to admit this, but yes, even when I was married. I just knew you wouldn't allow me to marry another woman. It was a stupid game I played and lost because you didn't ask me not to get married. Sheila, my ex, told me she didn't feel the soul connection with me. I knew she was right. I only had the soul connection with you, baby. But I did love her. That was when I decided not to call you." He shrugged his shoulder. "I vowed to be a better husband, to try and make that soul connection with Shelia. After all, my wife wanted me, you didn't."

"Since you ended up getting divorced, what happened?"

"You can't create that kind of connection. In the end, Shelia thanked me for trying, but told me my heart was with you." He stared at Torrie. "That's why I'm telling you it doesn't matter you can't get a vision of us. I have it."

"Are you just telling me what I want to hear?"

"I'd never do that. I love you, Torrie. I have never lied to you, and I'm not about to start now."

"So your wife knew about me?"

"Of course she did. It would have been unfair marrying her without telling her. She accepted it in the beginning; after all, I only called you a few times a year. You never called me. She didn't see it as a problem."

"And then she did?"

"Not my calling you or sending you cards, just my wanting you, my loving you. Sometimes I'd give her a compliment, and she'd say I was thinking of you."

"Do we look alike?"

"Not at all."

"Then how, why?"

"She said she could see it in my eyes, hear it my voice when I said she was beautiful. She said it was you I was thinking of and talking to."

"Was she right?"

"I didn't think so. But were you always in my thoughts? Yes. Could I erase you?" He smiled. "Hell no. And believe me, I tried to, but your face wouldn't go away and the visions of us kept getting stronger." He kissed her. "That's enough about the past. Shelia and I are friendly, not friends, but we do speak when we see each other. She's happily married now and has two kids. Things happened the way they should have for both of us."

Forever and a Day

Torrie accepted Jake's kissing, thinking how the two of them had lead parallel lives. She'd been asked by more than one boyfriend, *"Who are you thinking of?"* when they kissed her. It had always amazed her that the memory of her first kiss was evoked whenever she kissed another man. And more amazing to Torrie was that the men knew.

Chapter Eleven

Like Torrie, Jake knew going back to New Orleans was going to put pressure on all of them. Just the idea of going to Torrie's home and taking a look around at all she'd lost would be hard for Torrie and hard for Jake to watch. Jake had watched CNN each night when she'd fallen asleep. What he saw convinced him they were doing the right thing in not watching the news. They had one week left. Jake planned to make his presence so much a part of her life she'd never be able to live without him.

Jake hadn't even bothered to ask Torrie if she wanted to fly home. He'd given instructions to his team and had made arrangements for the heavy equipment to be shipped. Now he and Torrie were loaded into his SUV and heading home. There was an uncertain silence hovering between them. Jake could feel the difference as surely as he could feel the November chill. He thought about the sweater he'd bought for Torrie and had tucked in his bag. Before they reached home, she'd more than likely need it. She might fuss a bit but she'd be warm. He smiled at her.

"It's a long way to New Orleans, baby. Are we not going to talk the entire trip?"

"I didn't know we weren't talking, Jake. I'm sorry. I'm just thinking, wondering, wishing." Torrie smiled slightly. "Thanks for allowing me to come and visit. I had a nice time."

Oh hell no! Now she was back to thanking him as though he were just some guy off the street. "I think we need a pact. From now on, no holding things in anymore. No going back to how we were, okay? Things are different now. Whatever happens, we're in this together. You and I, Torrie. We're getting married. We're in this together."

She nodded her head a little and looked out the window. She couldn't look at him and lie right to his face. Torrie knew where Jake was heading. He wanted to throw his money at her situation and make it go away. She would fill out whatever papers the government had ordered, and she would do whatever the insurance company said. Jake must be forgetting she was a teacher. She had a means of making money.

"You do know things will be different when we return to Louisiana. I hope you're not crazy enough to think I'm going to shack up with you when we get home. New York is one thing, grown or not, I'm not about to throw that stuff in my daddy's face."

Jake pulled to the curb and used his hand to turn Torrie's face around. "I'm not kidding with you, Torrie. Don't get any ideas of leaving me out of anything. I'm going to be with you every step of the way. Of course, I don't expect you to just move in with me, but I also do expect to make love to you when we return to New Orleans. We're both grown, and we're getting married."

"I know that…but there are so many things I have to do. I have check everything out. I have to go into my house and see if I can salvage anything. Trying to think beyond that is hard."

"FEMA said the first time people go into their homes, they should have someone with them. I think you should have me. I want to be with you." He narrowed his eyes and tried not to glare. "I am going to be with you, Torrie."

"How do you know what FEMA said, Jake?"

"I heard it on the news."

"You didn't tell me you were listening to the news."

"I wasn't trying to keep it a secret. I just happened to hear a few things, that's all. But you're trying to sidetrack me. Are we in agreement?"

"Yes, Jake, we're in agreement." Torrie started to turn away, but Jake's fingers on her chin prevented it. He wasn't buying it. Torrie's heart thudded, God, she loved him.

She blinked and drew in her breath. They were getting married. Torrie smiled. She'd have to work on the partner thing, but she was determined to do as much as she could to allow Jake in without losing herself.

"We're a team, Jake Broussard. We're getting married, and nothing and no one can stop it, even us. And vision or no vision, our futures are intertwined. I will not push you away." She saw the worry line smooth out on his face.

"I love you, Torrie," Jake whispered into her mouth. She breathed in his breath as she accepted his kiss along with a prayer.

Ten miles outside of town, Jake could sense the edginess in Torrie. "You want to make a stop anyplace before we go on?"

"No, Jake, I have to do this."

"You sure you're ready?"

"As much as I'll ever be," Torrie answered, accepting Jake's hand. The feel of his fingers squeezing hers was needed warmth. They rode the next few miles in tense silence, bracing themselves for their first foray into New Orleans.

They had driven for several minutes inside the city when a low muttered, "damn" came from Jake. Torrie turned to look at him. The gasp came out of nowhere. Torrie wasn't prepared, though she should have been, had thought she was.

Her dream, her nightmare had come true. The television and newspapers should have prepared her. But seeing it like this, her home. "Oh God," Torrie groaned and felt the knot in her belly growing larger, twisting her intestines. "Oh, God, Jake." She felt his grip tighten, and she heard his murmuring identical to her own. For a moment, she'd forgotten this was Jake's home also. She looked at him staring in shock out the window. His eyes came around to hers as he slowed down.

"Torrie, this is so damn hard to see. Are you sure you want to go and see your house now?"

"I have to, waiting a day or even an hour longer will not make an iota of difference. If you don't want to go, Jake, just drop me off, and you can pick me up later."

"You're not going alone," he growled. "We're a team."

Torrie grit her teeth. She was not going to turn this into a fight. "You're right. We're a team."

"Then don't talk to me with your teeth clenched."

"If you stop growling at me, I won't talk to you through clenched teeth." Torrie stopped in mid-sentence and looked at Jake. "I don't know where we are." A tear slid down her cheek. "How are we going to find my house, Jake? This looks worse than a war zone."

"Don't worry, baby, we'll find it." Jake silently thanked God his truck could easily ride over much of the debris still littering the streets, though he tried to miss as much as he could. Damn, all of this time, and it looked as though not much had been accomplished: a means of making money, homes smashed like so many tinder boxes, broken toys and clothing everywhere, the stench was so overpowering he wanted to throw up. He didn't want to go in Torrie's home or her business or any of the other places in the area. He heard Torrie groaning, and knew what he wanted or didn't want, wouldn't matter. He would go into hell and back with her.

He searched the area, looking for workers in order to obtain the throw-away outer covering for him and Torrie to wear over their clothes. He wasn't taking her anyplace without protective garb. A sigh of relief seeped out of Jake when he finally spotted a FEMA truck and went to get gear. When he got back in, Torrie was staring at the items. She was licking her lips and blinking in an effort to hold back her mounting fears.

Jake tossed the things in the back seat and rubbed her hands. "Torrie, can you handle this?"

"I don't really have a choice, do I?"

"You have a choice." When she looked away, he pulled her back to look at him. "You have a choice. We can get married right now, today, and you never have to bother with this. We can leave here right now and go back to New York. You don't have to put yourself through this." He touched a finger to her lip. "Don't answer me now, just remember that."

With patience, Jake finally found Torrie's home. He took a breath and looked at her, this time deciding not to say a word. He knew no matter what he said, she would have to view things for herself.

He went around to the passenger side and gave Torrie the protective covering. If he could wipe the pained expression from her face, he would. She was staring up at her home. His line of vision followed hers. It was obvious the locks had been broken to the iron gates. The front door was left standing wide open for any criminals to come in and help themselves.

Torrie was trembling. Jake wanted to fold her in his arms and take her back to New York. But she would hate him if he did, and knowing Torrie's stubbornness, she would never submit to it.

"Why are the gates broken?" Torrie asked, not quite recognizing the sound of her own voice. She felt as though she were in a dream and waiting to snap out of it. She'd worked so hard to make her home beautiful. She glanced at Jake. He'd never been in her home, and now the first thing he would see would be…Torrie stopped her images of what they would find. She stared at her yard, blinking furiously to keep back the tears. *Oh, God,* she thought. "Jake, I had so many flowers. My yard was beautiful."

"Baby, I know," Jake said, trying to comfort her. "I know, Torrie," he repeated.

Torrie swallowed. It felt like she was being given something she didn't want. Jake wasn't patronizing her. That much she knew, but still he didn't know how pretty her yard or her home was. So why was he saying, 'I know baby?'

"They broke my gate," Torrie whispered.

"They had to make sure there weren't any bodies inside."

She looked at Jake for a moment, then walked up the stairs of her home. For five minutes, Torrie stared through the open doors, wanting something to hold onto. The room she was looking at couldn't possibly be real. It had to have been manmade, something created for a movie set, something someone wanted to turn the stomachs of moviegoers because it was definitely turning her stomach.

"You don't have to."

Torrie walked into the house, cutting off the rest of Jake's words. She stepped in, looking from the floor to the ceilings. The ten-foot tall walls had watermarks reaching all the way up. She stood in the middle of the living room, wanting to leave, yet unable to make her feet move. She blinked. Something was smeared on the walls. She looked around, slowly taking in the entire downstairs.

"Oh God!" Torrie moaned softly. *Mold.* "How can it be like that, Jake? It looks like someone took a putty knife and layered it on."

She glanced in the corner at her piano: the one she had never gotten the lessons to learn to play, the one she'd bought because she thought it gave her home more class. Torrie closed her eyes as the tears seeped beneath the lids.

Kimmie had teased her unmercifully for buying the piano, saying she was trying to be uptown. She wondered if that were true. But she'd remembered thinking of Jake the day she bought it and hoping one day he'd see it. Now it was destroyed.

Torrie held her arms around herself. She was about to break down. She felt stupid and maybe even materialistic; something she'd never thought she was. But she was looking at the destruction and knowing Jake would never know how nice she'd made her home. The knowledge that she was worried about that made the tears flow even faster.

Torrie walked slowly, looking at the overturned furniture. She walked toward the kitchen and saw the refrigerator face down in the muck.

"Be careful," Jake warned, "the floor, baby, it's slick ...I'm sorry," his voice broke. "I think it's...baby, it's feces."

Torrie backed up a few steps and looked through the kitchen at the cabinets. She couldn't figure out what was wrong with the wood. It wasn't just the water damage. Then she spotted the bottles of empty cleaning products splayed on the floor. She wondered if the spilled liquid had reactions with whatever else that had come into her home and made this caustic mess.

"Torrie," Jake was calling her, but she didn't want to look at him. She had to do this. If she saw the look she knew would be in Jake's eyes, she wouldn't be able to continue. She had to finish this, see it all.

"I'm okay, Jake," she answered. Moving to go up the stairs to her bedroom, Torrie wanted to scream, to tell Jake to leave her alone, to stop calling her name. It was like someone raking a nail over her flesh. He didn't want her to go up, didn't want her in the house, and didn't want her contaminated by the ceiling-high mold.

Is he crazy? Torrie wondered. She didn't want to be contaminated, but she loved her home. She'd bought it and every stick of furniture with her own money. A sob tore at her throat. She'd always wanted Jake to see her home, now he never would. He'd never see it, not the way it had been.

She took in a deep breath, gearing up for what lay ahead. She put one foot in front of the other and made her way up the stairs. The sound was different. She paused wondering if the stairs would hold, wondering if her mere presence in her home would cause it to cave in. She could feel her limbs trembling harder than they had before and prayed for strength.

Torrie bowed her body in half, rocking back and forth to balance herself. And then she took the next step and the next before Jake could stop her. This was killing her, but she had to see it all. The entire wall leading to the bedrooms was also covered in mold. She stopped walking and stared at the walls. She had hoped the mold hadn't come all the way up. She remembered she'd seen her roof under water on L4TV. She'd seen it a thousand times over in her visions. *I should have been ready for this.*

Doors were broken off the hinges, clothes scattered about, closets opened, no hurricane had done this damage, no water. The flood had some help, the human kind. Torrie looked at the pictures on her mold-covered walls.

Jake reached out to touch her. She pushed his rubber gloved hand away. She was determined; she'd come this far. She had to see the rest. She looked in each room until she felt as though she would suffocate. Then she reached the upstairs bathroom and saw the waste that covered everything. The scream Torrie had been holding inside bubbled out of her. She screamed, shaking her head at Jake. She didn't want him comforting her or touching her. She wanted out of the house. She'd seen enough.

"Lord, enough," she whispered softly. She closed her eyes and rocked. When she opened them, she realized if she didn't leave soon she would break.

"Move, Jake. I have to leave." She was trying to keep the hysteria from her voice. "Move, Jake," she said again as he backed up a step, enough so she could exit. Torrie made her way out the door, went to the corner of her once pretty yard and vomited, leaving more human waste to add to the pile covering her property. Her body continued retching. She felt she would never stop. Her throat was raw. It burned all the way to her abdomen. Her arms wrapped around her body, she could only rock and moan.

"Torrie, baby, you have to take those things off," Jake pleaded with her. She could tell he was worried about her. Unable to meet his eyes, she did as he instructed and begin removing the protective coverings. But Jake wanted more from her. He wanted her to leave the area. She couldn't, not yet. She still had to look at her nursery school where her babies had come everyday for the last three years. The place she'd come to think of as her replacement for Jake. The babies she'd claimed as her own because she never thought she'd have the chance to have any with Jake. She had to see the hope she'd accepted when she'd given up on a life with him.

"I have to go and see my business, Jake."

"Torrie."

For the first time since they'd gotten out of his SUV, Torrie met Jake's eyes. "You know I have to," she said.

Since Torrie had told him about the nursery school. Jake knew somehow the two of them were connected to it, their past, their beginning. Jake also knew this would be a lot worse for Torrie than what she'd seen so far.

"Hold your face up, Torrie," he said and poured water from the gallon bottle he carried, and then he poured water over his own face. He went to the back of the vehicle and got them clean towels, and then sanitary wipes.

"Just tell me where the nursery school was," he said and held the door open for her. Jake wanted to hold Torrie close to his heart. She was looking so fragile as though she would crumble. He didn't touch her, afraid if he did, she would shatter into a million little pieces. She needed her strength to get through what she must. When it was done, he would give her his strength.

Jake closed the door after Torrie was seated. He took another look around. The sense of loss overcame him. He'd waited twelve long years to come home, and now his home no longer existed. He wasn't just thinking about his house, but the entire city. He didn't see how it could ever be the same. Television cameras had not been able to capture the real devastation, the broken hearts, and the life-long dreams. His eyes swept the terrain. The television cameras hadn't been able to capture how bad things really were and this was two and a half months after Katrina.

They'd picked their way across now unfamiliar roads with so much garbage strewn about that Jake couldn't believe they were in America. Surely, they had to be somewhere else. He'd always thought of New Orleans as a different planet. Now Jake was sure it was. This wasn't the New Orleans he'd grown up in. This wasn't the New Orleans he'd planned to return to for the last twelve years. Jake shuddered and leaned against his truck, breathing hard. He had to be strong for Torrie; she needed him.

"There it is," Torrie said quietly, pointing at the huge colored balls that somehow had managed to cling to the rooftop. That was one of the markers that had told her it belonged to her when she'd looked it up on the Internet. This was what she'd been so proud of, what she'd always wanted to tell Jake. She turned to him.

"Jasmine was my first baby who came to my nursery. Her mother didn't have the full fee, but she reminded me so much of myself I didn't mind reducing the fee for her. Then as I got other kids, there was a little boy who hovered around Jasmine. They used to always play together, but not because she was afraid, Jake. I tried to ensure my babies were not afraid when they were in my care." She blinked several times. "But those two…they always reminded me of us." Torrie shrugged. "He's not light bright and almost white though." She tried to laugh. "If their friendship had lasted, they wouldn't have had any problems. They have the same surname."

"Torrie, don't do this."

She looked out the window. "I don't know if all of my babies are safe, Jake. I've tried finding them on the Internet. I've been praying so hard." She swallowed a lump in her throat. "I don't want to do this. I don't want to see what it looks like in here." She was shaking her head as she reached for clean gear in the back on the seat. "I can't take this place being destroyed. It means so much to me. You don't understand."

"I understand baby," Jake said, reaching for his own clean gear. "This place was a reminder of us. We're going to get through this. That's a promise."

"No one looks like they're doing anything, Jake."

"I didn't say the government was going to get us through. I said we're going to get us through. I'll rebuild your home and your business."

"You can rebuild if the insurance covers it."

Damn. Jake groaned and turned away. He'd almost forgotten part of the reason he was there was to be an insurance adjuster. How the hell did he tell Torrie that most of her loss in her home and business probably wouldn't be covered? In a place like New Orleans, known for floods, everyone was woefully underinsured for flood damage because of the expense. Jake took in a breath and asked, "Are you ready to go inside?"

This time the door wasn't standing wide open, but it did appear stuck, not budging as Torrie twisted on the key. Jake gave a quick look at Torrie. "Do you want me to force it open?" he asked. When she nodded, he lifted his foot and kicked, pain went through him as Torrie winced. The door flew open, and he glanced at her.

"I'm sorry, baby," he said.

She tried to smile. "I know, Jake."

This time Torrie couldn't stop the stream of tears as she looked at the rooms. The cots jumbled up and smashed, the toys, everything, even some of the kids' clothing lay in the muck. She moved toward her office. The computers were missing, the lamps broken. What the hurricane hadn't destroyed had been looted.

This was the last straw. She wanted to do this without tears. She wanted to be strong. She didn't want to see Jake hurting for her. Suddenly, it no longer mattered. Torrie's resolve melted. She could feel her ability to be strong fluttering. She loved Jake with her whole heart, but she didn't want to need him. Torrie stared at Jake unable to deny the truth. She needed him. Her heart was breaking, her dream was gone, crushed, lost, and destroyed. And what wasn't destroyed was apparently stolen.

Torrie threw her arms out wide to the heavens and screamed as loud as she could. She continued screaming, even when Jake gathered her in his arms. She screamed until no more sounds would come from her throat. She stood there shaking, not able to control the pain or make it go away.

She felt Jake lifting her in his arms. And she couldn't protest. She thought of the contamination factor and cried even harder. Now she had to worry about making Jake ill. Still, Torrie couldn't stop. Her tears mixed with her moans of pain. The grief was just too much to bear. She truly understood why FEMA had warned people not to return to their homes alone. She didn't know what she would have done if Jake were not there with her.

"Put me down, Jake. I don't want to make you sick."

"I don't give a damn."

"I do," Torrie said, stopping her sobs long enough to look at him. "Put me down." When he held her even tighter, Torrie buried her head in his shoulder and sobbed some more.

Put her down. Torrie was crazy if she thought he could let go of her right now. Jake had to hold on to her or lose his own sanity. *Damn, my poor baby.* He leaned against the side of his truck, rocking her, and praying that the worst was behind them. He kept Torrie in his arms until her sobs dissolved into whimpers. He wanted to kiss her so badly that he ached. But she was right, they needed to remove their face masks, gloves and everything else creating a barrier between them.

At last Jake placed Torrie on the ground and began stripping away her contaminated garments, then walked to throw them into a makeshift pile nearby. He came back with a can of germicidal spray, then finished decontaminating them.

"I feel so dirty, Jake. I want a bath. I feel too dirty to even get back in your truck." She looked at the leather seats. "What if being in my house and my business makes you sick?"

"What if it makes you sick?"

"I had a reason for being there, you didn't."

"You were my reason. You were there, so where else was I going to be? You want to try to find a hotel and take a shower?"

"All the hotels are filled with the…" Torrie stopped as though puzzled. "What are we calling our people now, the evacuees? I know they've been put up in the hotels. We don't have anyplace to go. Maybe we could ride into Harahan and take a shower at John Tom's." She looked at him and shook her head. She'd forgotten, once again, that this was also Jake's home.

"I'm sorry, Jake," Torrie rubbed his arm. "I was being selfish. Did you want to go take a look at your family's home before we go?"

"No, baby, enough looking today. Let's ride over to Harahan."

He opened the door for Torrie, and guilt washed over him. He didn't want Torrie with him when he went to look at his home. He knew there wasn't any damage, not from the wind or the water. Every stick of furniture was in place; that much Jake knew from his frequents conversations with his mother. His home had survived Katrina and Rita. Torrie didn't need to know that. She already thought the rich got richer and the poor poorer. He didn't need to prove to her she'd been right. Besides Jake needed to check on his construction crew. Some were staying in trailers on the Broussard property. Some were staying in some of their rental property.

"We can drive over to Bourbon Street and go to Café Du Monde and have some coffee and some beignets. I heard they're open."

"I don't want to sound mean, Jake, but I don't care if Café Du Monde is open. That doesn't mean anything to me. They got what, a little flood water?"

"What about your sister's shop?"

Torrie blinked and shook her head as though gearing up for something unpleasant "I guess we could go and take a look at Kimmie's shop. I just...I don't..."

"It should be okay, Torrie. Like you said, there was mostly flood water, but if we're doing it, maybe it's just better to yank off the bandage all the way." From all Jake knew and had since found out about Kimmie, he didn't think even a flood would dare to cross her path.

"I wonder if Kimmie has seen it yet?"

"Your sister, of course she has."

"You think she saw my home?"

Jake didn't answer.

"She was trying to protect me, wasn't she? That's probably why she got so angry. She knew what a mess I was coming home to, and she probably thought I should be home taking care of things."

Torrie glanced out the window. "I guess I should have been here." She didn't speak again until they were standing in front of Kimmie's shop with the iron gates firmly locked, the strong smell of bleach emanating from the building. Torrie smiled. Yes, her sister had been there.

Torrie rubbed her finger continuously across the beautiful diamond on her left hand. She loved it, but in the face of what she was seeing, it somehow seemed obscene. She covered the ring with her hand and looked out the window before closing her eyes. The thought of the gifts she'd bought for her family now seemed so impractical. When she'd bought them that had been her intent, to give them something frivolous, something that would take them away for a moment from what they were facing daily. Guilt came at her in waves. It had been selfish of her to take off and leave the rest of them alone to fend for themselves. She removed her hand from the ring. The proof of her selfishness sat on her finger.

Jake saw from the corner of his eye that Torrie was touching the ring. She was wondering about her decision to marry him, having doubts. This had nothing to do with them; that much he knew. It had to do with the haves and the have-nots. Jake was a have. Torrie had been on her way to being a have. Now he could tell from the defeated slump of her shoulders that she considered herself, once again, one of the have-nots.

He covered her hand and sighed. *Damn.* Why the hell did the entire eighty percent of the destroyed city have to be the have-nots? And why were eighty percent of the have-nots black? Jake said a quick mental prayer of forgiveness. This shouldn't be about color, race, or class. Every single person living in New Orleans was tied in this together. Black, white, brown, or yellow, in this they were all family, and they had all suffered. Jake wished not a single solitary person in his city had to suffer. Damn, this was hard and going to get harder.

"Jake, if you have something else to do, you don't have to come in with me."

Jake sucked in his breath. He wouldn't allow Torrie to push him away. He wouldn't let her words create a fracture between them.

"Did you hear me, Jake?"

"I heard you."

"And?"

"And you're not cargo. I'm not just dropping you off."

"But…you know…a month…there's going to be questions."

"And I know how I plan to answer them. Anything the two of us did together, Torrie, is none of their business." He glanced sideways at her, "and if anyone pushes the issue, that's exactly what I plan to tell them, your daddy's gun notwithstanding."

"I don't think I feel like dealing with anymore right now, Jake." Torrie pulled her cell from her purse and dialed. "Kimmie," she said when her sister answered, not giving her a chance to talk. "I'm home. I've gone to see my house and the school. I went by your shop. I didn't go and see yours or Trey's or Mama and Daddy's house. Jake and I are on our way to Harahan. I just want to take a bath, okay? Tell Mama that for me. Just let me bathe, and then I'll talk: no hugging, no kissing, nothing, okay, Kimmie? I don't want to be touched until I bathe."

Torrie snapped the phone close and heaved. She rocked slowly back and forth, holding on to her sanity by sheer will. She didn't want to fight with Jake, and she didn't want to fight with her family. Her energy was gone, and she needed to feel clean. She continued rubbing the ring, trying to force a vision that wasn't coming.

If wishes really came true, right now the only vision Torrie would be having would be one of her and Jake. She prayed she could see her and Jake as easily as she could see the mayor making a remark in the coming months that would destroy his career. How she wished that as easily as she saw Michael Brown finally getting angry and admitting he'd told his bosses the New Orleans levees would be breeched, that she could see Jake by her side.

She could see a newspaper headline associated with Brown from FEMA, and that was in February. Maybe it would take longer for her and Jake to have a future, she didn't know. But she'd had this dream of devastation for years. She'd had other dreams she'd never told Jake about, and they were almost exact to the second, so why wasn't she seeing her and Jake?

"Torrie, you're going to be okay. I promise you—"

"Don't make me promises you can't keep," she interrupted.

Her voice made his skin crawl as a chill swept over him. Jake glanced quickly at her. "Torrie," he called her name softly. When she turned to him, fear made him shudder. Jake touched her. She was trembling. Then her body began to shake so hard he thought she was having a seizure. He pulled over to the side and put the truck in park. "Torrie," he said, reaching for her.

"Don't touch me, Jake, not right now. Don't touch me."

He pulled her into his arms, easing her shudders, taking them into his own body. "Baby, baby," he murmured.

"Let me go, Jake."

"I'm not going to let you go. I'm never letting you go, never. Do you understand me, Torrie? I've waited too long to be with you. I'm not giving up so damn quickly. Yes, our city looks like the pit of hell, and it is our city, Torrie. And hell yes, it looks like not a damn thing has been done, but I'm here now, baby. I swear to you my crew will work day and night. You'll see some progress. I won't stop working. Do you hear me, baby?"

"I hear you."

"I'll rebuild your home with my bare hands if I have to."

"What about the rest of New Orleans?"

"Torrie, tomorrow I'll start working. And I'll do everything as quickly as I can. I'll do my best to give the most for the homes Robert wants me to assess."

"What about the ones that didn't have insurance? What are you going to do for them?"

His chest ached as he held her close and kissed the hollow of her neck. "I can't help every person, Torrie. Even I don't have that much money. This problem will be way more than I have. But I can find a way to help cut through the red tape. I can do that, baby. If there is something else you want me to do, you tell me, and I'll do it. I just want to keep you safe and happy."

Jake pulled away. "And I want to keep you sane. If I could have done anything about your visions when we were kids, I would have." He felt the burning in his lungs. "If I could do something about them now, I would. I would take away all the visions and replace them all with my love. I love you, baby, just remember that. No matter how rough things get, I love you."

He held her and allowed her to cry. She needed that. Jake knew Torrie wanted to go into her family with dry eyes and holding her head up. *God, please let her get though this, let us.*

She'd never in her life felt weak until now. Torrie had lived the last twelve years without Jake in her life, knowing he was her soul mate but not prepared to beg him to love her. For so many years, it had looked as if friendship would be the only thing they had. Jake's marriage had put an end to Torrie's most vivid wishes. Still, the life she'd built had always had Jake somewhere in it. When she went to college, when she'd become a teacher, when she'd started her business, and when she'd bought her home.

Through all of it, Torrie always thought of Jake, hoping one day he would see what she'd made of herself. Torrie's throat was tight with tears. She didn't want to bring it out into the light. She was ashamed of having ever thought it, more ashamed of having lived her life because of the thought. She'd gotten angry when Kimmie had accused her of it, but had always known in some way it was true.

Torrie may not be able to pass the brown bag test, but she knew without a doubt she wanted entrance into the circles she was denied simply because of her complexion. Torrie wanted to be good enough for Jake.

It hurt that she'd ever had the thought and it hurt like hell that the thought had come to her as she viewed all she'd lost. *You're back where you started, poor and from the lower ninth ward.*

"Oh, God, please forgive me," Torrie prayed silently. She hugged Jake tightly to her. She didn't want to feel less than him. She knew she was just as good as Jake. Torrie knew that in her heart, but right now looking at all she'd lost, it was hard to keep that thought in the forefront of her mind.

Now Jake was making her promises, promises she wanted to accept. God it would be so easy to just say yes to him. But he'd wonder forever, and if he didn't, his family would.

The Broussards were probably one of the snootiest families in town. They'd even looked down on their own kin who'd lived in the lower ninth ward. She'd tried her best to forget what Trey had said, but now the words burned in her brain.

"Torrie, you're being so damn stupid," Trey had shouted and dragged her by the arm to the hall mirror. "Look in the mirror, girl." He'd shoved his face alongside hers. "He called me black, Torrie. He said I couldn't get the damn job because my skin was too black. Look at your face, Torrie. Look how black you are. You're way darker than I am. If he feels like that about me, what do you think he thinks of you?"

"Torrie, baby, I love you."

Torrie heard Jake's words as he rubbed her back, once again shutting out Trey's words. She wouldn't allow anything else to cloud her knowledge of his love. So okay, she didn't have a vision of the two of them together, but then again, she hadn't had visions of a lot of things. She hadn't had a vision that her parents would find them in the park. And she hadn't had a vision of Jake driving through the night to rescue her, but he had.

"Torrie, you promised you wouldn't shut me out."

"I don't want to. I really don't."

"Then don't?"

"I'm trying, Jake."

"You're going to have to try a little harder. This will take the both of us working together. You can't just tell me to drop you off and leave. What the hell is that about?" he asked softly, against her skin. "You have no idea how much it's going to kill me, knowing I can't keep you safe in my arms tonight. I have reasons to worry, Torrie. You kept your feelings hidden from me, locked away in a metal box. I don't want to them be put there again. I want you to openly love me. I don't want you treating me as the enemy. I didn't have a damn thing to do with this hurricane." He hugged her tight. "Baby, I'm so sorry for your loss. I really am."

"I know, and I know I'm acting irrationally."

"Not irrational."

"I am but…granted, I have a reason. I thought I could handle anything. I was already dealing with the worst possible hurt in my life." She looked at him. "It wasn't easy for me to live without you. You have no idea how I waited for your calls." Torrie stared into Jake's eyes. "Don't worry, Jake, I have no plans of letting you go."

"Then why did you want me to just drop you off and leave you there?"

"I don't know, momentary lapse knowing everyone's going to question me. I didn't want them taking potshots at you."

"But why were you rubbing the ring as though you wished you weren't wearing it?"

This time Torrie did smile. She should have known Jake would call her on that. "Okay, you've got me. I love my ring." Torrie looked down at the ring, then back at Jake. "Just for a moment it seemed inappropriate for me to be wearing it. I…I…I…damn, Jake, you know how it's going to get."

"If wearing your ring is the first hurdle, and we can't get through that, then, baby, you can see why I'm a bit worried." He lifted her hand. "Do you really want me to just drop you off, Torrie, and leave without even coming in the house?"

"It's an arguable point now. You've already said you weren't going to do it."

"That wasn't my question. Is that what you want?" She shifted. He grabbed for her, holding her head in place, pinning her with a stare.

"I want you to come in and take a shower and eat, and then hold me and never let me go," Torrie finally answered.

That was the answer he needed to hear. He gave her a quick kiss and pulled back on the road.

"Jake, I'm sorry for acting as if this only affects me. It's got to be rough on you. I'm sorry for making you worry so much about me that I didn't take the time to know how this had to be for you. I know it's hurting you. You haven't been home in twelve years, and this is your first view of home. I'm sorry, Jake. I really am. You're right, we're in this together."

"That's John Tom's house two doors down," Torrie instructed. She sucked in a breath and licked her lips. The fifteen minutes from New Orleans to Harahan seemed to have passed by in a matter of moments.

"How do you know him, Torrie?"

She'd forgotten she hadn't told Jake about Kimmie and John Tom. "No need to worry, Jake. He's Kimmie's ex, a skirt chaser. They were supposed to have gotten married five years ago. Kimmie caught him one too many times and dumped him. I kept in touch and called and asked him if we could come and stay with him."

"Was it easier to ask him and go to him than it was to ask me?"

Torrie took a breath; relationships of any kind were hard. She supposed a new love, or an old love just beginning to grow was even harder. Jake, in some ways, was as insecure as she. "Jake, when I called John Tom and asked if we could come, I had already made up my mind to come to you."

"Why didn't you call me first?"

"Because I had to get my family settled first, and we both knew they weren't about to come to New York. Even if Kimmie and my parents had agreed, Trey wouldn't have come, and I wasn't going to leave him. We left New Orleans together; we were all going to be safe together. You of all people should know me better than that."

"Would you have eventually come to me, even if things hadn't happened the way they did, if Katrina had never hit, if the levees hadn't broken?"

"What can I say that either of us would believe? I do know after I saw you again, I wasn't going to be a fool and go back to the way it had been for the past twelve years. So yes, I think eventually I would have come to you, Jake."

"That's all I wanted to hear. Give me a kiss before we go in and face your father's shotgun." Jake bent his head slowly, allowing his tongue to reach out and taste her before he pressed his lips against hers. He felt a tightening in his chest, and then in his groin. "You're my salvation, Torrie. You've given me a reason to be. I won't let you down, baby. That's a promise I'm going to keep. You may not see as much of me as either of us will like, but I need to start clearing some of the debris around here."

"How are you getting permission so quickly?"

"It was already in the works," Jake answered, getting out of the truck, opening up the back, and then coming around to open the door for Torrie. "Just know that sometimes it does pay to have a father with connections. I've run from those connections, now I'm using them to help. Okay?" He stopped and looked at her. "This is how I can finish things. You cool with that?"

"I'm cool with whatever you have to do to allow people to come home and begin to rebuild their lives. Just don't turn into a typical New Orleans son, okay?" She glanced at the bags Jake was taking from the vehicle. "I don't think I want all of that stuff right now."

"Torrie."

"No, Jake, no gifts, not now." She walked away from him toward the gate, then suddenly she turned back. "One thing at a time, okay?"

Torrie rang the bell and waited. She took three steps back when her mother answered the door. "Let me shower, Mommy," she said, holding up her hands, "then I'll hug you. I feel so dirty right now. I don't want to touch you like this." She looked into her mother's eyes. "Have you been home? Did you see our house?"

"No, baby, but your daddy has." Her mother leaned into Torrie and kissed her cheek before Torrie could complain. "Kimmie told me I didn't want to go, and the way they behaved when they got back, I decided to take her advice. Come on in," she said, moving back, casting a glance at Jake unloading bags from his SUV.

"He needs a shower, too," Torrie answered, "and maybe you could give him something to eat. Please, Mama, no questions just yet."

"Did Jake go by his folk's house?"

"Not yet. I think he was so worried about me he just wanted to get me out of New Orleans." Torrie closed her eyes and shivered. "Mommy, I need a hug from you so bad." She shook her head, tasting her tears in the back of her throat. "Just give me ten minutes to shower and let Jake use the other bathroom. Is Kimmie home?"

"No one's home but me. Kimmie and John Tom went off some place after you called. I don't think your sister thought she could see you and not hug you, so she left. Trey's at work, so is your daddy. He's got a part-time job."

A wave of relief washed over Torrie. She rushed away before she broke down in front of her mother. At least the one good thing was her mother had not seen all the things they'd lost. Torrie had not been able to go and look at the home where she'd been raised. Even with Jake by her side, she didn't think she could handle that right now.

"When Jake brings my bag in, could you bring me some clean clothes into the bathroom?" Torrie asked over her shoulder. She thought about waiting for Jake to come in, to be there to soften whatever hostility there might be between her mother and Jake, but right now Torrie was doing the best she could. She'd have nothing to fight with if she didn't get under the water and wash the horror away. She needed a return to sanity.

Jake's eyes swept the living room for Torrie. He glanced in the connecting room. "Where's Torrie?" he asked.

"She's taking a shower," her mother answered with a bit of frost in her voice. "She wanted me to show you to one of the other bathrooms and allow you to take a shower." The woman glared at Jake, then planted her hands on her hips and glared at him some more.

"What do you want with Torrie, Jake Broussard?"

"I want to marry her," Jake said without hesitation. "I'm in love with her. I always have been."

"Then why did it take you so long to come and claim her?"

"I was a fool." Jake shrugged his shoulders, wondering what answer he could give to appease a mother who thought he wanted to hurt her baby.

"Things happened when we were kids that neither of us knew how to handle. Things happened with Trey. I said things to him I shouldn't have. Things I never meant, but I've always loved Torrie."

"That much I believe. You used to be such a nice little boy."

Used to be. Jake smiled at the words. "I've always remembered how nice you were to me, how much you treated me like family. I know some of the things that have happened in town since I've been gone. I know how you feel about my family. I'm a Broussard. I can't change that, and I wouldn't want to," Jake added. "I'm proud of my family, just as you're proud of yours. I'm sorry for everything you've lost. I'm going to do my best to work and speed things up here, to clear up some of the debris so rebuilding can begin. I didn't come back to try to hurt anyone. I only want to help, that's it. New Orleans is my home also. Will you give me a chance?"

Ernestine didn't answer Jake. She took Torrie's bag to the bedroom. She took in a breath, refusing to glance back out the door, knowing in her mother's heart how much Jake meant to Torrie. The boy did love her baby. It was in his eyes, in his running out with a hurricane on his behind. She'd seen the way he'd looked at Torrie in the cabin.

Ernestine couldn't help but chuckle. She'd seen the way Jake looked at Torrie when he was a little boy and hadn't had sense enough to know the feelings he had in his heart for her. And she'd seen the way her baby had looked at Jake the same way when she was just a little bitty thang. If ever two people had been meant to be together, it was those two. She sighed. It wouldn't be easy for them. She didn't want Jake to hurt Torrie. Still, in the face of everything that had happened, everything they'd all lost, she didn't know if she had the heart to take something else from her youngest child.

Another sigh escaped her, and Ernestine looked at Torrie's bag and opened it at last taking out clean underwear, then a blouse and jeans. She knocked on the bathroom door, put them in there and closed the door. Jake waited patiently; he deserved the treatment he was getting.

"Torrie said you wanted a shower."

"I do, thank you." Jake pulled in a deep breath. "There is something I need more than a shower." He watched as Torrie's mother narrowed her eyes suspiciously. "Torrie's family is everything to her. You're the most important people in her life. If there isn't some kind of truce, Torrie won't be happy, we both know that." Jake took in another breath and allowed the air to be released slowly. "She loves me, ma'am. I promise you, I won't hurt her. I only want to make Torrie happy."

Jake waited, only silence greeted him. He knew Torrie's mother loved her, and she wasn't as hard as she pretended to be. If she were, she would have never told him where Torrie was heading when he'd followed her to the state park. "If you think it's best I don't love Torrie, that she'll be happier without me in her life, I'll understand. It won't stop me from trying to convince her otherwise, but I'll understand."

"You'll understand?"

"Yes. But if the only thing you're holding against me is something I did when I was a kid or something my family may have done, then I won't understand. All I'm asking is that you give me a chance to show you I mean no harm to Torrie."

"Jake Broussard, you think you know how to get around me, don't you? You don't have to convince me you love my baby or that she loves you. I've always known that. You took something from Torrie when she was just a kid, and she has never quite gotten it back. I hadn't seen that spark in her until you showed up at the cabin. That alone tells me how much she wants you in her life."

"So what's the problem?" Jake asked softly.

"Torrie's been gone a month. I'm not asking any questions I already know the answers to. But I do know you've taken something even more precious from her this time. That child has always been a daddy's baby. He's still hurting over her sassing him. She went against her family for you. In a way, she chose you over us. And I know if you hurt her again what with everything else that's been happening, that spark in her might die out for good. I'm afraid to put so much power over my daughter into your hands. You may love Torrie, but your folks don't. I don't want my baby girl to go through such nonsense. She's been through enough already."

Jake stood with his mouth slightly open and his hands at his side. He didn't have an answer. Torrie's mother was right. His parents didn't want him with Torrie; that was no secret. But Jake wasn't controlled by his family.

"Know this," Jake answered at last. "There is no battle that will take place where I'm not at Torrie's side. I will never allow anyone to disrespect her. I can't promise you how anyone else in my family will accept the news, but I can tell you that if Torrie isn't welcomed and accepted, they will not be welcomed into our lives."

Jake closed his eyes for a moment, then opened them again. "Just so we're straight, I'm not telling you I'll give up my family. I love them same as Torrie loves you all, but I won't allow anyone to ever mistreat Torrie in my presence."

He stood in silence and could almost see his words taking effect. When she sighed and shrugged her shoulders, Jake felt relief thinking she would give him a chance.

"Jake, I believe you. If you had told me you were going to turn your back on your family, I don't know if I'd trust you or if I'd want Torrie with you. Good or bad, family is family, and you don't turn your back on them. I want my baby to be happy, and for whatever reason, you seem to make her happy. I'm willing to wait and see. You hurt her, and it won't have to be my husband who you'll worry about coming after you with a gun." She turned. "Grab your bag, get yourselves some clean clothes and take that shower."

Jake noticed she took him on the opposite end of the house. He wanted to laugh. It didn't matter to Torrie's mother what they'd done or in what state of undress they'd seen each other. She was just as determined nothing was going to happen under her roof, albeit her temporary roof and definitely not under her watch.

Within fifteen minutes, Jake was showered, dressed and sitting at the dining room table eating leftovers and eying the bread pudding. He kept glancing down the hall, wondering what had happened to Torrie.

"She's still showering," Torrie's mother answered. Their eyes met. "It was bad, huh?"

Jake shook his head and held the woman's gaze. "Yeah, it was really bad."

"So, Jake, you said you were back here to help. How?"

He smiled at the abrupt change in conversation. "I'm working for the bank. I brought my crew down to clean up some of the debris. Nothing much can get done until the place has been cleared." He sighed and decided to tell the rest. "I'm also doing a favor for a friend who owns an insurance company in New York. The company has a lot of claims down here. I'm acting as one of the freelance claim adjusters for them."

Jake saw the stiffness in Ernestine Thibodeaux's shoulders and hurried the rest of his words. "He knew I was coming back and thought I could help. There are so many claims every insurance company is begging for help from each other."

"Yeah, I know all about that. It seems everybody, even next-door neighbors, have a different adjuster, but they all seem to be here to do the same thing. They don't want to pay. They're doing their best to cheat us out of what we've got coming. What about your company, Jake? Is that what they want you to do?"

"New Orleans is my home. I don't want to see anybody cheated. That's why I took the job. I'm going to get every penny I can for the claims I work."

"We're not much worried about the pennies, Jake. We want the dollars."

Jake laughed a little at her words and prayed her family was insured by State Farm or Allstate.

Water washed over her face. She'd been in so long, the water was turning cold now. Torrie had stood beneath the water crying for so long she was weak. She'd washed her hair three times. Each time she rinsed it, she still felt dirty and started over. Her skin was now stinging and raw from the scraping she'd done. She knew she should climb out of the tub, but couldn't. She thought of burning her clothes, but that would be wasteful and just plain dumb. Jake would be out there waiting for her, wondering what she was doing. She almost laughed. She should be out there protecting Jake, being his hero. She had no idea if anyone else was home.

When the water became too cold for Torrie to bear, she reluctantly climbed out and toweled off, then walked to the adjoining bedroom. She dressed slowly, looking around the room as she did so. She smiled at the purple flowers on the border surrounding the walls. Each room had been decorated with Kimmie in mind. J.T. had changed, Torrie thought, again feeling hopeful about her sister's future. When she finally dressed she walked out into the dining room. She did feel better. She looked from her mother to Jake and back again, waiting.

"Go ahead, show me the ring."

She brought her hand out and showed the ring to her mother. Torrie's eyes sought Jake's, and she smiled. Her stomach flipped a couple of times while she waited.

"It's beautiful, baby."

"Thanks, Mama."

"Jake and I talked, baby. We're going to put our differences aside. We're both going to wait and see what happens. Now give me some sugar."

Torrie smiled and welcomed being enfolded in her mother's arms. "I can't believe how it looked, Mommy, all the pictures, everything." She trembled as her mother stroked her hair and held her, rocking her back and forth. This time Torrie didn't cry. She'd cried enough.

Chapter Twelve

With a sigh of relief, Jake stood in the middle of the entryway of his childhood home. His soul was so covered in emotions it was hard to separate them. He wouldn't lie. He was glad his home had been spared and his parents had not had to go through what Torrie and her family were going through.

He walked deeper into the house and closed his eyes for a second. This was his home, and as happy as he was that his home was untouched, he felt ashamed of feeling that way. His parents could easily afford to rebuild if they'd needed to and yet they were spared. His heart ached for Torrie.

He thought of the look of compassion in her eyes when he'd left her in Harahan. She thought he was going alone to view his home when he hadn't wanted to tell her his home was untouched by either hurricane. It was impossible to believe there was no damage in the Garden District. Sure, Torrie knew the damage was minimal at best but he knew she didn't believe there wasn't any. Jake took another look around his home. Nope, no damage.

"I'm home," Jake called. He smelled food coming from the massive kitchen and knew the housekeeper had been waiting for him to get home. The moment he'd told his mother he was returning home and staying in the family home he'd known she would make sure everything was ready for him. He couldn't stop the smile from coming to his lips as he thought of his mother giving instructions on what to cook for him. Money did make a difference. Jake sighed, went out to the kitchen and greeted the housekeeper and cook, asking both about their families.

"Most of mine made it through," Bessie said without looking directly at him. "We're not sure about everybody. They're still holding unidentified bodies, and people are having a hard time trying to locate them."

Tears appeared in Bessie's eyes. Jake went to her and held her. "I'll be around for a while. I brought my crew to help in the clean up. I'm also doing a favor for a friend of mine who owns one of the insurance agencies in New York, and had some of the homes down here insured. He thought I could help people with the paperwork, maybe help to speed up the process for some of them." Again suspicious looks followed Jake's words. He pulled back, wondering what the hell he didn't know? What had his father done to keep people from trusting Jake?

"I took Torrie Thibodeaux over to Harahan. I'm beat. Just give me to morning. Make out a list of all your relatives who're missing. Tomorrow I'll start doing an Internet search to try and find them or…" Jake lowered his voice, "if worse come to worse, we still need to know everyone's whereabouts…I'm going to do my best. I have some contacts who can help me cut through the red tape. Just let me sleep tonight, okay."

"Okay, Mr. Broussard," Bessie answered. "Your dinner is ready. I can bring up a tray for you."

"Give me a couple hours, Bessie, then you can bring me up a tray." Jake walked up the stairs, grateful to be free of the reeking odor of rotted meat and things gone bad. A shudder made Jake stop and close his eyes. If he lived to be a hundred, he would never forget the smell or the sights, and he would never in a million years forget his sorrow at the sound of Torrie's heart breaking.

"Mr. Broussard, the men and equipment are here. We've got FEMA out here telling us we don't have permission to be here."

"Damn," Jake cursed. *Couldn't this have waited until I was at least out of the bed?* "Stay put, I'm on my way." He dialed Texas, making the necessary call to his father. Now was time to use his privilege. Hell, he'd always been a little ashamed of being a member of the Republican Party, but he'd had good reasons for his allegiance. Initially Jake believed in the base philosophies of the Republican Party. But now the party seemed to have turned into a network of blood-sucking cronies who filled positions or had them made up for them. Either way Jake now considered himself to be independent. But his father had powerful connections, and he was now calling his father to use those powerful connections.

He thought of his promise to Torrie not to become a typical son of New Orleans. He'd do his best to keep that promise. But right now only a typical son would be able to wield the clout needed to get things done.

By the time Jake arrived on the site where he'd instructed his men to go, it seemed the long arm of Cannan Broussard had twisted the necessary arms, and the FEMA people had allowed the men to start doing the job they'd come down to do. *Damn fools*, Jake thought, *what the hell is wrong with everyone?* There was so much paperwork nothing was getting done, everything having to be done in triplicate when all they needed was several good crews with equipment, and they could take care of the whole damn place.

Jake flipped his hard hat on his head and walked over to his foreman. "Rick, get these men started." Jake surveyed the area. "I have other things I need to take care of. I'll be back in a few hours." The list was growing so long and there were so many balls in the air Jake prayed he wouldn't drop them.

He needed to call Robert and have him fax him the list of insured he wanted him to handle. He'd been put off a couple times when he'd asked for the information. Once Torrie had arrived in New York, getting the list hadn't been Jake's top priority. Now it was. He needed to get to work cleaning up some of the debris as well as trying to do the assessments for Robert. Jake rubbed his hand across his brow, thinking of all the things he needed to do. His promise to Bessie was moved up on his list of priorities. He needed to start making contacts to see where the bodies were being kept and helping Bessie, if need be, to identify her kin.

Three hours later, Jake had one thought on his mind; how the hell to get out of the job he'd taken on and the favor he owed Robert? He'd checked the list a dozen times, hoping that if he looked again her name wouldn't be there. A knot the size of New Orleans twisted his guts. He'd thrown the sheets of paper down after spotting Torrie's name, now he had no choice but to pick it back up knowing what he'd find. Chances were if C&J Mutual was Torrie's insurance company then her parents, Kimmie, and Trey would have the same company. That was the way it was done in families.

"Damn," he shouted, wishing he had something to throw. C&J Mutual wasn't the name Torrie gave him as her insurance company. He groaned knowing what had happened. Lots of times small companies sold out. But usually the clients were notified. He sighed in disgust, knowing because of the legalese many of them failed to read the entire letters. If he were being honest, he was also aware, more often than not, important information was shoved on the back in the very last paragraph and in small print. He sighed again, knowing none of this mattered. Who knew what had happened? He sure as hell didn't. Maybe C&J Mutual just hadn't bothered to change the name.

"Damn," Jake swore again. He was screwed. This was definitely a conflict of interest. If he didn't keep the job, Robert might find someone who would try to stiff Torrie and her family. If he did keep it, they would think Jake had stiffed them. It wouldn't matter what he did, one way or the other, Torrie stood to get hurt. A burning sensation began working its way from his stomach to his esophagus.

He couldn't tell Torrie, not now. He'd have to put her off for a while, get as much work done as he could on the clean up and see what he could do about helping Torrie. First, he needed to go over her policy to check for loopholes.

Jake groaned as he made his way to the kitchen for some milk to cool the burn in his throat. Torrie was too damn stubborn to wait for long, so was the entire family. He'd have to talk with Robert, and have him tell Torrie and her family when they called that they needed to be patient. He had to have time to figure out a plan. Whether he liked it or not, he was a Broussard. His father's contacts were also Jake's. He just needed time to think.

The milk did nothing for the burn. All Jake could see was Torrie heartbroken and in tears when he'd taken her to her home. Regardless of what he had to do, he wouldn't see her hurt like that again if he could do something to prevent it.

He drank the milk, then refilled the glass. Already, his conscience was beginning to bother him. No possible way should Jake assess Torrie's property. He had to think of something, some way to fix this. The situation, as it stood now, was beyond unethical. It would put him firmly on the path of being a true son of corruption, a true son of New Orleans.

After he drank the glass of milk, the burn remained. How the hell was he going to keep his promise to Torrie never to hurt her, and he was already plotting a way to lie, to keep things from her? *Damn*, he thought and poured a third glass of milk.

"I am getting sick of this run around," Torrie said to the agent on the phone. "You didn't have any trouble taking all of our money. Now that it's time to pay out on claims, you have no answers."

"Ma'am, we're trying. FEMA is allowing limited adjusters in the area."

"That's not true," Torrie fumed, trying her best to subdue the irritation in her voice. She was determined to try to persuade the man on the other end of the phone to cooperate.

"Listen, I came back to the area, and I have a friend, Jake Broussard, who works for an insurance company as an adjuster, and he's in the area." A moment of uncomfortable silence made Torrie pause. She caught a quick flash, an almost vision, an image of Jake. She let it go. She'd been thinking about him, talking about him, that was the likely explanation.

"Excuse me," Torrie tried again. "Like I said, there are at least a thousand other claims adjusters in the area. Why aren't you here?"

"We are there. We have more than twenty adjusters in the area."

"Then why haven't they gotten around to me and my family?"

"I have to get back to you on that. We're sorry, and we do understand you're frustrated, but you must understand we have thousands upon thousands of insured. We're even having some of our adjusters helping out some of the other companies."

"Maybe if you're short staffed you should have your adjusters working strictly with your own clients. We're the ones who've been paying you."

"We're doing the best we can. Call us back in a couple of weeks, and maybe we'll have better news."

With that, the man clicked off and Torrie screamed to the top of her lungs. "A couple of weeks." Her patience was wearing thin. She glanced at Trey and blew out a breath. "I'm tempted to ask Jake to handle this for us. I'll bet his father could make those jerks get their butts down here. That man has pull everywhere."

"We don't need Cannan Broussard or Jake." Trey stared at Torrie as though she'd lost her mind. "The Broussards are not our friends, Torrie. I'm curious about something. Jake's been back in town for weeks. Has he taken you to his family's home?"

Torrie blinked at Trey's question. They'd all been so busy she hadn't really thought about it. No, Jake hadn't taken her to his home. She hadn't asked and he hadn't offered.

Trey was smiling. "I didn't think so," he said. "Do you want to know why? His home is untouched, Torrie, nada, zip, or didn't you know that? He still thinks he's too good to have you in there. Don't forget the lower ninth has no business in the Garden District."

"Trey, that might not be the case," John Tom spoke up. "It could very well be the boy is feeling bad that his home is still standing. Don't you think I feel bad?" John Tom looked at each of them in turn, and then at Trey, holding his glance, his eyes never wavering.

"You don't think I feel guilty as hell?" His voice dropped an octave. "Well I do, and most of you like me." He glanced at Kimmie. "If I could, I would give anything to not have this happen. You guys think you're putting me out, but I'm so damn grateful to have you all alive and living here. I feel God has blessed me, given me another chance."

His eyes slid over to Torrie. "No, maybe Jake hasn't invited you over to that big house in the Garden District. But that boy loves you, Torrie, think about that. And if I'm feeling guilty that my house survived and I have the woman I love here with me, how must he feel?"

John Tom turned slightly as he moved his gaze to Kimmie, not turning away when she glared at him. "How do you think Jake feels, Torrie?" he asked. "Most folks in New Orleans hate his family. And almost everyone in this house has something bad to say about him. Now his home is still standing, and yours is destroyed, and here he has more than enough money to make things right for you. But if he mentions doing anything for you, the entire family just glares at him."

John Tom got up and paced from the dining room to the living room then back again, shaking his head as though he didn't know what else to do. He came and stood in front of Trey. "You don't think Jake's feeling lucky, now do you, Trey?" he asked, and then looked at every person in the room, finishing with Trey. "That boy is hurting, so think again. Broussard or not, New Orleans is his home, and you've got to give him credit. I've been going by there, and I see the difference his crew has made. I also saw that he got someone to gut your house, Torrie."

Torrie was shocked. "I didn't ask him to."

"No, but it needed doing. He also gutted the nursery school. And I heard through the grapevine he pulled some strings and they allowed him to fill out the paperwork for the thirty thousand dollar grants to have your home and your business elevated. The boy is trying to do his damn job, and everyone's giving him shit for it. Some folks want a hell of a lot more than their places were worth, and they're blaming Jake for not giving it to them. Everybody keeps forgetting there's a difference in homeowners insurance and flood insurance. No one down here has enough flood insurance. The insurance companies would go bankrupt if they gave full coverage on that. And it was the flooding that destroyed everything. Remember that. Jake's having a harder time than he should, Torrie, just so you know that. Cut the man some slack. And you too, Trey. Jake is on our side."

"Not our side, Tom," Trey came back. "You have a home remember? You didn't have your place destroyed."

"I remember." John Tom looked at Kimmie and sighed loudly before walking toward her. "Listen, we're both too damn old to act as stupid as Trey. You had good reason to dump me. I don't blame you. I wouldn't have respected you if you hadn't, but, Kimmie, I always loved you."

Torrie glanced from her sister to John Tom .She couldn't believe what was coming. She stared at her mother and prayed with all her heart her sister wouldn't be a fool. She held her breath in anticipation, waiting for it to continue.

"You know, Kimmie," John Tom continued. "You aren't too old yet to have some babies. We always planned on it. I'm ready to settle down and get married."

Torrie waited with bated breath, wanting to shout yes for her sister. Right there in front of everyone, John Tom went to Kimmie and dropped down on one knee.

"Kimmie, will you marry me? I promise I'll love you always."

"Get up, fool," Kimmie sputtered, looking pleased and embarrassed at the same time. "It wasn't your love I was questioning, but your fidelity. When you can pledge that, maybe I'll think about it."

"I promise I won't screw around on you ever again."

Torrie laughed when the light shone in her sister's eyes, and she accepted John Tom's kiss. She gazed at the two of them while a clear picture of them married and happy flashed before her. Torrie didn't want to feel the onslaught of sadness. She was happy to have a vision showing her sister would be happy. But now she wondered more than ever why she could see nothing about her and Jake. She hadn't heard from Jake in two days. She knew he was busy, but was he too busy to call her? And this time she hadn't waited. She'd called him and he hadn't returned her calls.

"I know she keeps calling," Jake snapped, "just keep stalling her."

"She's threatening us," Robert snapped back.

"Tell her you're really trying, that you're sending more agents, that there are so many cases the agents already here haven't had time to get to her. Tell her we'll take care of her by the first of the year."

"Jake, I sent you out there because I really needed the help, man. This thing you have going with one of the claimants is not my problem. Just go to her house and assess the damage. If you don't think you can be objective, tell me now. This is the company's money you're playing around with. Now, are you up to the job? Are you going to complete it?" Robert asked, not disguising the anger in his voice.

Jake groaned. "I will. I just want to finish what I'm doing. You knew my primary function was going to be clearing debris. I'm doing the claims on the side like you asked of me, when I have a chance. That was the deal. Remember?"

"Jake, I hope you know not to let whatever you've got going with this woman interfere with a fair assessment. We don't want you just giving money away. If you can't handle it, give me the word, and I'll give the cases over to one of the other adjusters I already have there."

"Look, Robert, you asked me to do you a favor. Damn it, I'm doing it. You hold Torrie and her family off until the first of the year."

"That's a long time, Jake. People are already filing complaints against us. They're talking about not being home for Thanksgiving, now you want me to tell her she won't get any help until after the New Year."

"I didn't tell you to tell her like that. You're much too smooth to tell her anything so stupid. Use your charm. Make her believe you're doing the best you can. You can do a better job than that, okay?"

"What's the problem, Jake? You've taken a look at her home right? Why the hell couldn't you just assess a value right then and there?"

That was a fair question, besides, Jake knew it was coming. It was also one he had an answer for. "Look, the area Torrie's house is in, the homes were worth more, but it depends on how quickly the area is cleansed of the debris and if her home can be raised. That plays a huge part in her assessment. I've pulled in all the favors I can, trying to get someone out here to tell me if they can raise the house or not. They can't get here sooner than the first of the year. Just tell her that, man. Tell her we're trying to get her top dollar for her property. Tell her you've heard maybe her house can be raised.

Forever and a Day

Just tell her something she will believe until I get someone out here to tell me if there's any hope."

"What about the other homes you asked me to hold out on? Are you trying to get those raised, too?"

"Naw, her parent's' home was little more than a lean-to. You know, a shotgun house. Your typical add-on. I took a look at the place. You should never have issued him flood insurance as an underwriter, even if FEMA was partially covering it. They should have had nothing but bare minimal."

"Then just do his claim and tell him that and get on with it. These people are calling the office three, four times a day. I'm getting tired of having the calls rerouted here. I'm tempted to just have them answer the phones at C&J Mutual."

Jake exhaled out of frustration, then took in a hard breath. "Don't do that. If people didn't know their insurance company was sold before all of this happened, they sure don't need to find out now."

"Fine," Robert answered. "You've got a point. What about this Trey guy, how's his house?"

Trey's home had been almost as easy to assess as Torrie's. Too little and Trey would think he'd fudged, too much and he'd think the same damn thing. "I haven't had a chance to get there," Jake lied. He wasn't ready to deal with Trey to tell him that his property wasn't worth more than twenty, thirty thousand dollars at the most and that it in fact excluded damage done by flood. The twenty thousand was the most Jake could see Trey getting for his contents. There were so many clauses in the policies Jake would be stretching things to give even that much.

Double damn, Jake thought. Why hadn't people thought better of what they were getting? Torrie had the most coverage, and even she would be out of luck. She owed the bank a hell of a lot more than he should probably give her on the claim. Either way, Torrie was screwed.

"I just talked to Ms. Thibodeaux a few hours ago. I don't think I'm going to have any luck putting her off for much longer. I only took her call because she was driving the office crazy, and I knew you were stalling for time. But, your time's running out, Jake. That woman is so damn insistent. I wouldn't put it past her to come here in person."

"Look, Robert, just give me a few more weeks. New Years will be here before you know it. As soon as I can find out if her property can be raised, I'll assess it. Just stall her as long as you can."

"I'll do what I can. I'm not making any promises."

Jake said his goodbyes without a guarantee and hung up. If he had any luck at all, he would convince Torrie to marry him by the New Year, and his problems would be solved. She'd have to accept his help once they were married. They would move to New York, they could start over there. *Sure you can*, his conscience screamed at him. And do you really think she'll leave and marry you when her parents have no damn place to go, or Trey for that matter. Torrie felt responsible for all of them.

And Jake felt responsible for Torrie. He couldn't even look at her or hear her voice without the guilt threatening to choke the life out of him. He'd tried to think of solutions, but was getting nowhere. Really and truly, Torrie's parents' home should be condemned. The structure had been so weak, he'd been afraid to go into it.

That's what happened to a lot of places people just added on to without having a professional do the job. The add-on had no real sturdy foundation to speak of. *Damn, if only.*

If only what? He wondered. Even if he'd been home and had started his construction company in New Orleans, who would have listened to him when he would have made suggestions? Who would have had the money to implement them?

Jake sighed, it had been two days since he'd talked to Torrie, and all because he was trying to help her, working day and night to fix things.

Forever and a Day

He dialed Torrie's number, feeling numb from fatigue. Too much was happening. He wondered if he should bother her. He looked at the time. Torrie was still in class. He sighed and left Torrie a message on her voice mail as he drove out to the area his crew was working. *Still so much work to be done*, he thought, as he looked around. If he had a thousand more machines, right now Jake doubted he could finish the job. They were racing against the unknown and the known. They all knew in a few months hurricane season would begin again and the government would have done nothing with the levees.

What if it were all for nothing? In June the rain water and another hurricane could come rushing through the already destroyed city and finish it off. Jake wished he knew what to do. If God was willing to tell him, he sure as hell was willing to listen. He wondered if Torrie was having any visions about the future. If she was she hadn't said. Then again, he hadn't asked. He'd been too busy avoiding the truth to discuss anything real with her. What a mess. What a rip-roaring, jacked the hell up mess.

Chapter Thirteen

A chill gave Jake his first warning when he pulled into the driveway. The big Lincoln parked in the driveway was the second. *Damn, why are they home?* He'd told them he would come to Texas right after Thanksgiving. He let out his breath in a rush and prepared to meet the lion.

"Jacob, we've been calling you for two hours. Didn't you get our messages?"

"I was busy," Jake said, meeting his father's eyes before allowing them to flit away. "You didn't say you were coming home. I told you I was coming to Texas right after Thanksgiving."

"We do own this house, boy, and we are allowed to come back to it. Besides, your mother wanted you with her for the holiday, not right after, so we came home. We needed to check on things. So, what have you been doing?"

The words were innocent, but to Jake they sounded like a reprimand. Something in his father's eyes told Jake this was not just a visit home. He talked to his parents almost daily. Not one of them had mentioned coming. Jake gave his father a wary once over. "Where's Mom?"

"She's around. Why are you staring at me like that, Jacob?"

"No reason. I'm puzzled, that's all."

"Too puzzled to show affection? Or are you not glad to see me? I know you didn't hightail it to Texas to make sure we were safe, not like you did with that girl, anyway. But I had thought at least my only child would be happy enough to see me that I would get a hug."

For a nanosecond, father and son stared at each other before Jake made the first move and embraced his father.

"So how is Tora doing?"

"Torrie, Dad, you know her name."

"Fine. How's she's doing? Has the adjuster settled her claim yet? Is she and her family planning on moving on?"

The hairs on the back of Jake's neck bristled. Something was wrong, too many questions from his father about Torrie was one indication, the feeling in his gut, another. "Why would I know about Torrie's affairs or those of her family?"

"Didn't you tell me you were also down here to act as an insurance adjuster?"

Jake honestly couldn't remember if he'd talked that over with his father or not. Perhaps he had, but something was still wrong about his father's question. "I didn't tell you I was on Torrie's case nor did I say I was with her insurance company. There are a lot of insurance companies around here, so what would make you think of all the insurance companies I would end up working for the one insuring Torrie?" A strange sensation settled around Jake's shoulder. Something was definitely wrong.

"Why are you dodging my questions, Jacob?"

"Would you mind calling me Jake?" Jake lifted his head higher. "Like everyone else?"

"Yes, I do mind calling you Jake. I'm not everyone else. I'm your father, and I didn't name you Jake, I named you Jacob. What's wrong with you? Why are you acting so suspicious?"

"Because I am. What's going on?"

The noise from the kitchen cut off Jake's next question. A second later, his mother came through the door calling his name. He didn't need any encouragement to pick his mother up from the floor and swing her around.

"Boy, put your mother down."

"No," Jake responded, laughing as he swung his mother again and hugged her tightly. Her, he was glad to see. "What are you guys doing here? Why didn't you tell me you were coming?"

"Your father wanted to surprise you."

Jake glanced around at his father. The man was cool; he'd have to give him that. He didn't flinch, not one little bit, but coming to New Orleans to surprise him, Jake didn't think so. Besides, his father had said it was his mother's idea. That she'd wanted to spend Thanksgiving Day with Jake. Now even that was suspect.

Something about the timing, something wasn't right, and he had a sneaky suspicion it had to do with Torrie. Well they might as well get into it, no use in putting it off.

Jake held onto his mother's hands. "I have good news." He smiled and caught the flicker as she glanced quickly at his father. They knew. How? Jake dropped his mother's hand and moved to sit; part of his mind was reeling. What the hell was going on? How did they know? He hadn't told them, not that he was trying to keep it a secret. But he'd intended to tell them in person when he went to Texas. He crossed one leg over the other and stared at both his parents.

"I'm getting married."

"When did this happen?" his father asked, coming to take the seat opposite him.

His mother attempted a smile. She gave a tiny shrug, then took the seat on the left of his father.

"I asked Torrie to marry me about two months ago."

His father reached into the pocket of his jacket for a cigar, one Jake knew he wouldn't light. It was a ritual before he lectured Jake. Strange something so meaningless could so easily strike fear into Jake's heart as a boy. It always meant his father was disappointed about something.

Jake blinked at the crooked smile on his father's face, aware he knew exactly how that gesture affected his son. Jake sat back in disbelief, surprised the two of them had engaged in this little dance for so many years. Even as a boy, his father had never hit him, just the cigar and the disappointed look on his face would be enough to get Jake in line.

Laughter pulled at him. He laughed softly, as though he'd finally gotten the meaning to some intimate joke. Jake blinked again. Even as an adult, his father had done the same thing, and Jake had given in. The dance of father and son would never end. Jake knew that now.

He caught the look that passed between his parents. His father loved him, that Jake was sure of, but he hadn't been quite so sure when he was younger. He'd always been so busy trying to earn his father's love he'd overlooked the fact he already had it. His father just didn't know how to behave in any other manner. He liked control over everything, from his business to his family. And he liked order. Jake doing something his father disapproved of was out of order. But it had never been about the love.

Jake shook his head slowly in understanding, the firm hand-shakes, the hugs through the years, even the one that they'd shared a few moments before. There was genuine emotion in that embrace.

The answer was crystal clear. Somehow his parents had found out he was marrying Torrie and had come to change things. Jake glanced at the candles on the mantle and at the box of matches that had been placed next to them for as many years as they lived in the house. He went for them, stood in front of his father and struck one, holding it directly under the cigar, calling his father's bluff.

"You may as well smoke that one, because this routine of ours isn't working any more. I'm marrying Torrie."

His father's eyes met his. Jake saw the surprise, the amusement, the respect, and then the determination of the older man to win.

"Congratulations, Jacob."

Oh, he was good alright. "Thank you," Jake answered, blowing out the unused match. He took his seat and waited while his father ran his fingers up and down the cigar as though it were an instrument. *New technique*, Jake thought. Did his father really think at thirty he'd be so easily unnerved?

"Are you planning on moving back here, Jacob?"

222

"We haven't discussed it; there hasn't really been much time."

"Two months and you haven't found time to know where you want to live? What are you afraid of: that maybe your father might be right about something, that maybe New Orleans is the only place that girl can live?"

"Torrie," Jake corrected his father and stared. "In case you haven't noticed, a lot is happening here. There's a lot more to think about than where we live. Torrie's waiting to settle her affairs."

"I wonder why that hasn't happened." His father narrowed his eyes and gave Jake a direct look. "There is one thing women don't forgive and never forget, Jacob. They hate to be lied to. When that happens, they won't believe anything you have to say, not even a lie detector test will make them believe you."

He knew. *Damn it*. Jake had no idea how but he knew his father knew and his father wanted him to know. The same chill Jake had experienced earlier returned.

"Why don't you bring Tora here for dinner after church on Sunday? If you're marrying her, we may as well start to act as if we can get along with her. Besides, if you're going to make her the second lady of the manor, she needs to see what's in store for her."

"Let me be clear about something. I'm not going to allow you to disrespect Torrie. You know her name, so stop calling her Tora. And I didn't say Torrie and I would be living here."

"Well you sure as hell can't live in her house, now can you, Jacob? It's unlivable."

What was there to say? Anger rose like a swift cloud between them, each glaring. Jake refusing to back down, only he didn't know what he wasn't backing down from. But he did know something was going on with his father and he believed it involved Torrie. And Jake didn't like it.

"Jake," his mother called to him, "that's a good idea. Why don't you invite Torrie over to dinner and give us a better chance to get acquainted. I do remember her from when you two were kids. She was a pretty little thing."

Forever and a Day

Jake watched as his father's head swiveled around, and he glared at his mother. "Well she was, Cannan, and her name is Torrie," his mother continued. "If Jake's getting married, we're going to support him. He's our only child. I'm not losing him because you don't like who he's marrying."

"You don't care about this, Mom...that I'm marrying Torrie?"

"Not enough to lose you, Jake."

"I didn't say I had objections," Cannan Broussard retorted. "It was my idea to invite the girl here. I just don't think the two of you are as compatible as you think. The things you've done, Jacob, tell me you're concerned as well. I want you to be happy, son. I always have."

"Since when?" Jake asked, his voice escalated in surprise. "You've had me jumping through hoops my entire life."

"Is wanting you to be the best a crime?" His father pulled his chair directly in front of Jake and sat back down, looking eye-to-eye with him, sitting toe-to-toe. "I've always been proud of you. I've wanted the best for you. If you want to convict me for that, then go ahead. I'll never stop being proud of you, Jacob, never stop wanting the best of everything for you. I'm your father."

Speechless. His father had left him totally and utterly speechless. Proud of him. Words that Jake had resigned himself to never hearing from his father were now leaving him breathless. He licked his lips, battling the urge to bawl like a baby. God! Jake didn't want his father's words to have that much power over him, but they did. "You've never told me you were proud of me."

"I didn't know I had to. I thought you always knew."

Thought I knew. Jake sat in stunned disbelief as his father eyed him with curiosity. Somewhere in Jake's brain the word "setup" echoed, but the overwhelming joy battled with it and won.

"Jacob, everything I have, that I've worked to attain was for you. It's been so difficult at times trying to help my only son who didn't want my help. Still, it's all for you. I want you to be as respected and feared in your business dealings as I am. Not being afraid of doing

224

your job, Jacob, is the way to do that. Sometimes we all have to do things we may not want to do, things that are hard, but we have to. You're a man. You are a Broussard, Jacob, and you have to make your own name respected in your own right. So far you've done a splendid job, son."

Son, damn his father was laying it on too thick, finally the cloud was lifting. He should have heeded all the signs. Jake's mind flew back over the string of coincidences that had happened in the past few months. He thought of Torrie coming to visit him. If she hadn't come when she had, maybe he would have been able to pull things together sooner. He'd been so blinded by being with her after all the years of wanting her that there was no way in hell Jake had even thought to figure out the puzzle. Now it was clear.

"You own the insurance company."

"We own it. C&J Mutual. Cannan and Jacob. I'm surprised you never guessed."

A thud filled his chest as his eyes shuttered close. Jake covered his face with his hand. Thinking of his chance meeting with Robert. "You set that all up, the meeting with Robert, the job?"

"You wouldn't allow me to help you outright. Your mother was worried about you."

Jake turned his attention to his mother for verification. The look in her eyes was enough. "Why?" he asked, stunned.

"I didn't want you struggling with no one looking out for you. You were so determined to make it on your own, to stay away from us."

"Mama, I have a degree in engineering. I wasn't going to starve."

"You are my baby. I wanted to help you, so did your father. That's the only reason we did it, Jake. It wasn't like we knew any of this would happen years later. It's not like we planned it, Jake, you know that."

Of course he knew it. Jake paced back and forth. "I don't believe it. Why didn't you ever tell me?"

"Jake, you didn't even work there for that long, just a few years and doing work for them on the side only occasionally. Then you started your own construction company, and there was no need to tell you," his mother said softly.

His heart fell even lower at the mention of his construction company. Another coincidence, something that had happened way too easily. "Who secured my business loans?"

The look on his father's face and the silence in the room was his answer. Jake Broussard, a self made man, hell what a laugh. His father had helped him the entire time.

"I never should have come back here. Do you have any idea how this looks? How it will look when Torrie finds out? Damn," Jake swore and blinked. "Sorry, Mom." He swallowed down his anger. He needed answers now.

"What did Robert do, call and tell you I wasn't doing my job?"

"No, he thinks you're doing an excellent job...in most instances. He just said you had a problem with four of the claims and the staff was being harassed by the customers. He didn't think you could handle those four customers. He wanted to know if you knew them, if you had a personal connection. He just wanted to know since you're excellent at your job, why all of a sudden you couldn't do your job when it came to those four customers. He gave me the names."

Jake stared at his father, feeling what he'd felt his entire life, his father's disappointment. But none had ever been as acute as this and he remembered just a few moments before the joy he'd felt at his father's pride in him. Damn him for wanting it, but Jake wanted it back.

"Do your job, Jacob. Good or bad, this is your company, your decision. If you want to give charity to the claimants, it's your money. Just remember there will be repercussions. People talk, they will know. Besides, you think you're helping your girlfriend and her family. She's going to ask you why you didn't just turn the file over to someone else. There were other people from the company here.

You should have given it to one of them in the beginning. Robert made you that offer several times. Now it's about too late, Jacob. Now you need to finish what you've started."

Jake walked from one end of the room to the other. He stopped when his father came behind him and placed his hand on his back.

"I know you can do it, Jacob, or I would not have sent you here to do the job." He took Jake's shoulders and turned him to face him. "If you fold now, you will have to fire everyone at the agency who knows about this, because no one will follow a weak leader. It's your company. Fire them if you want, Jacob. I will not stop you. But you've always made me proud, make me proud in this. Do your job, son."

The words his father said were true. As an owner of the company, he definitely couldn't be seen as weak. He glared at his father, not even having to ask how he'd managed to accomplish all of this or when. Cannan Broussard was a true son of New Orleans. He was proud of that fact and always had been. And here Jake had been so determined not to go the same route. He groaned, thinking how easy it had all been. From the moment he'd hit town he'd used his father's muscle to get things done. He'd told Torrie he wouldn't become a part of the corruption, but he already was. And now it looked like he would slide even deeper into it.

"Torrie's going to hate me if she finds out about this."

"She can't hate you for doing your job, for being a man. If she wants you to give her money her business isn't worth, then you have your answer, Jacob. It's not you she wants, but your money and your name. The decision is yours." His father walked out the room and his mother followed.

Why the hell hadn't he listened to the warning signs? Jake was pissed. He didn't know who to be more ticked at, himself for not having known all this time, for thinking fate had just stepped in and handed him a job on a silver platter, he'd gotten his bank loans without any trouble, or that he'd been asked to return home.

He wondered if his father had known all along Torrie's property was covered by them. *Hell yes.* Of course, the old man knew. He was smarter than Jake gave him credit for, and Jake had always given his father credit for being a savvy businessman. Damn, his father was testing him in more ways than one.

He wanted to see if Jake would fold, if he'd be afraid to put Torrie's love to the test. A groan filled him and he took the stairs three at time, stripping his clothes the minute he was in his bedroom and going into his private bath. Anger toward his father created a steady pounding in his temples. If only he'd given Torrie's file and those of her family to someone else. He'd only been trying to get more money for them. Now finding out he owned the company, Jake groaned. No one would believe he hadn't known all along. His head was throbbing now. No way was Trey or the rest of them going to believe Jake hadn't deliberately put them off in order to help them. They were going to believe he was there to slash them to pieces.

Jake stood beneath the hot spray of water, thinking of Torrie. He still needed a little more time to help her. He had to figure out a way to give Torrie and her family money that didn't come from him. Torrie had already warned him concerning this issue. If he could give them the money, it would be the easiest way to handle things and the surest way to lose Torrie.

Would she be happy to have her claim finally settled or would she be angry he'd known and not told her? She was going to be pissed and Jake didn't need a connection with her to tell him that.

Wrapping himself in the huge towel, he sat on the bed and called Torrie. "Hey baby, I'm sorry I've been neglecting you. I've been so damn busy. I've been keeping my promise to you to clean away the debris so the rebuilding can start." A lump formed in his throat, and he closed his eyes against the pain. "I miss you, baby," he said around the lump.

"I miss you too, Jake."

"What's wrong? You sound kind of funny." Jake didn't know if he were beginning to feel paranoid or if Torrie really did sound funny, probably more than likely it was his guilt.

"It's getting so hard to keep doing this, living someplace I don't own or my parents don't own. It would even be different if I was living with Kimmie or Trey, but I'm not. John Tom is nice to us. He's like family." Torrie sighed sucking in all the pain. "By the way, he asked Kimmie to marry him."

"What did she say?"

"She called him a fool and told him to get off his knees."

"Seems like all Thibodeaux women have trouble saying yes to the men that love them."

"Jake."

"What is it, baby?"

"I'm scared."

"Why, Torrie?"

"I don't know. I'm still having these half visions of the future. I don't see us."

"I thought you weren't going to go on visions." Jake clutched the phone tightly. "I love you, Torrie. If you're worried because I haven't called—"

"No, Jake, it's not that. I keep getting these flashes of us fighting. I don't know what they mean. I'm being silly probably," she said.

"If you doubt us, I would definitely have to agree with you and say you're being silly."

"Why haven't you asked me to come to your house? We've been back here for weeks." Torrie sucked in her breath; she hadn't wanted to be the first one to mention it. But something wasn't quite right.

"I was going to ask you to come over for dinner this Sunday after church."

"I wasn't fishing for an invitation," Torrie answered, wishing now she hadn't said anything.

"No baby, my parents came. They asked me bring you over to visit them."

"That wasn't my question, Jake. Why haven't you taken me there before now? Was there a reason?"

"There was a reason, perhaps not a very good reason, but a reason just the same."

"What was it?" Torrie couldn't stop herself from pressing. She bit her lips. "Why didn't you want me to come to your house Jake?"

"Torrie, you do know the Garden District wasn't touched, don't you?"

"I'd heard it wasn't, so what?"

"How do you think it made me feel to know you and your family had lost everything and my home was dry, not even wind damaged. Did you think I wanted to throw that in your face?"

"Did you think I would be jealous your house was okay?"

"Not jealous, Torrie…just…look…this was my own thing. It had nothing to do with you. I didn't like knowing it. I was ashamed of it. I know we can't do a damn thing about the elements, but somehow I feel like I failed you, baby. That's all it was."

"We're going to have to work on the dynamics of our relationship, aren't we? I know I've always allowed you to take care of me. I'm not going to lie. I liked it. But come on, we're getting married. I'm a lot stronger than you think. You don't need to keep protecting me."

"I like doing it."

"I know you do. Stop it, okay."

"I don't think I can…not right now."

"You're hiding something from me aren't you?"

"I guess you could say that. Don't ask me right now what it is. There's a problem, and I'm trying like hell to figure out a way to fix it." Jake removed the towel from his body and climbed under the cover, clicking off the light.

"Baby, I didn't call to talk to you about problems. I wanted to tell you how much I miss you. I want to ask what you're wearing

230

right now." Jake's voice turned low and husky. "Do you have on that little orange number that turns me on?"

Torrie laughed at Jake's wanting to use phone sex to change the topic. She'd wait for him to tell her whatever he was hiding. "So your parents want me to come for dinner on Sunday?"

"What does that have to do with what you're wearing?"

"Jake?"

"Yeah, after church." He chuckled. "I'll come to church with you and bring you over to my house."

"Thanks, I don't think I want to walk into your house alone."

"Baby, you've got me. You'll never be alone. What church are you going to, Torrie?"

"St. Peter Claver, over in the Treme area."

"Is that Father Mike's church?"

"Yeah, you've been?"

"He was there before I left. Don't you remember I used to go there with you? What does this make for him, about nineteen years?"

"Twenty," Torrie corrected. "I forgot you went there with me."

"I wonder why?" Jake laughed remembering how he'd teased Torrie mercilessly while they were in the church. It was no wonder she didn't remember. They'd never done anything even halfway resembling spirituality when they went to church together.

"Is he still wearing his dashiki, pretending to be black?"

"He's still wearing it, but it's not because he's pretending to be black, Jake."

"How many of us are wearing them?"

"He's a good man and a great preacher, he sounds Baptist. I go to the gospel Mass, okay? Am I not going to see you until Sunday?"

"I really shouldn't, Torrie. You distract me too much. I tell you it seems the piles are multiplying. The more we haul away it seems more is there the next day to take its place."

"I wish I could have an adjuster as conscientious as you. I'm getting the run around with my company. Listen, Jake, I hate to ask this, but do you think you could put in a call to my insurance company? Maybe you can get me an answer as to when they'll be assessing my property. So many people have already heard. It's like my entire family has been singled out and shoved to the back of the list. It's beginning to feel deliberate. I don't like that feeling."

"Give me the info." Jake made noise as though he were going for a pen and paper. "I'll take care of it." After he repeated the information back, Jake sighed. "I'll take care of it, baby, now get some rest and stop worrying about it. I'll see you Sunday. I'll pick you up, and we can go and have breakfast first, okay?"

"That's fine. Thanks, Jake. For the call I mean. I'm getting frustrated, and I know they're blocking my calls. All I'm asking you to do is make a call, Jake. You understand what I'm saying to you?"

"Of course, I do…but sometimes it takes a little more to get things done."

"I know. But I don't want to lose my friend to corruption. That's important to me, more important than you making the call. Can you handle it without going there?"

"I'm trying."

"Trying?"

"I meant I'll try."

"Don't do anything stupid. You know I'll find out. I'll talk to you later. I love you, Jake."

"I love you too, baby." Jake hung up the phone and groaned. Damn, this was getting worse.

Torrie trembled with dread. Jake hadn't written the number down. She didn't know how she knew, but she did. He'd simply repeated it back to her. *What was that all about? Why was he sounding so strange? Okay, he was tired. That was it; he was tired.* At least he remembered the number. He'd probably written it down after they hung up. But why, Torrie wondered. *Why did he make such a show of opening drawers, pretending to get pen and paper? Why had he done that?* She'd not thought of it until they'd disconnected. Then the clear sounds of what he'd done came to her. She couldn't ignore the momentary silence on the line to her insurance company when she'd mentioned Jake's name. Torrie began rocking back and forth, knowing she didn't need to have Jake make the call. She knew the name of her claims adjusters.

"Jake," she murmured softly, "oh my sweet, sweet Jake. I don't blame you for not wanting me to know." She thought of her parents, Kimmie and Trey. "Oh God!"

C&J Mutual. Torrie felt sick. "Jake, you need to tell me the truth. I know it already, Jake. I know."

Chapter Fourteen

"There's Ms. Mary and her grandson Darcell." Torrie turned to Jake. "I'm teaching her grandson at the MAX school." She smiled at the blank look on Jake's face. "Come on, Jake, you remember Ms. Mary. She worked at the daycare when we were kids."

Torrie pulled Jake with her toward the woman. "Ms. Mary. Hello this is—"

"Hello, Torrie, you don't have to tell me who this is. This is Jake Broussard. Tell me, Jake, how's your family doing?"

"They're doing fine."

"You don't remember me, do you?"

"No ma'am." Jake smiled.

"I'm not surprised. Even back then you had eyes only for Torrie. I'm not surprised you two are together." She glanced at Torrie's engagement ring. "Are you two just now getting together?"

"It did take a long time," Jake said. "We both made a few wrong turns." He glanced at the lanky teenager beside her. "So, Darcell, Torrie tells me she's one of your teachers at the MAX school. I don't think I've heard of that." Jake frowned as Torrie laughed while Darcell begin to explain it to Jake.

"St. Mary, St Augustine, and Xavier. M for Mary, A for... You get it?" Darcell asked, looking at Jake.

"I get it. Why are they calling them the MAX?"

"Well, after Katrina and everybody left, they brought the schools together sort of to bring the kids back into the area. They got a motto and everything. 'Taking it to the MAX.' I'm glad I'm graduating this year, because who knows what will happen if we have another hurricane. St. Augustine had the most water damage, because it's near the London Street Bridge. Who knows? Even St. Mary, the all girls' school, had damage. I don't know if they could take much more either. The only school that wasn't damaged is Xavier, and it will go back to being Xavier Prep."

Darcell shrugged his shoulder. "It's in the Garden District and didn't have any damage at all. You know how that is," Darcell said. "It's in the rich white area, so they wouldn't have any damage."

"Some black people live there, too, Darcell." Ms. Mary said, giving her grandson a look he chose to ignore.

"Yeah, but if they do they have money, so they're like white. I don't know why my family is separated and my mama is living in Shreveport. My entire family is scattered everywhere. Before we all lived just a couple of blocks apart. Now my aunts, uncles and all my cousins are living in different places, and I don't get a chance to see them. Even my brothers and sisters are not here with me. I'm only here to finish school. Now I have an aunt living in Baton Rouge, one in Boca Raton, and another in Dallas. And my grandma lives now in Harahan. I had to live with her to finish out my school year."

Torrie could tell Darcell was angry and unmindful of his grandmother's warning. His life had been destroyed, and he needed answers just as they all did.

"I want my family back," Darcell said, looking at Jake as though Jake had the power to make it happen. "Father Mike preached a good sermon, but all his praying isn't making things change. Why did my whole family have to be broken apart? I miss my aunts, my cousins, and my brothers and sisters." He looked from Jake to Torrie, then to his grandmother. "I love you, Grandma, but I miss my mother. I want to go home. I want things back the way they were." Darcell strode angrily away, and the three adults stood looking after him, feeling the exact same sentiment.

"I'm sorry," his grandmother apologized to Jake, knowing that somehow Darcell sensed Jake lived in the Garden District. "I'm really sorry," she said again and walked away. "He's usually not like that. He's so well behaved; he's angry and hurt and doesn't know what's happening. And I don't have answers for him," she said and continued out the door.

Jake stared for a long moment at the door the teenager exited. What went wrong? Why was everyone blaming his family and him for every bad thing that had happened? Fine, people were angry, maybe even jealous, because the homes in the Garden District had not been destroyed. Did they think God had spared them for some reason? If that were true, had no one thought that the punishment of those who'd survived Katrina would be that the rest of the city would hate them because they hadn't lost anything of material value?

He gazed around the church, unable to look at Torrie, not wanting to see if her eyes held some of the same thoughts as Darcell. Ms. Mary had been nice. He wondered if there was a hidden meaning behind Torrie's dragging him over to meet them, surely she hadn't thought the reception would be different.

"Jake."

He waited until Torrie called his name a second time before he turned to look at her. He stared at her for a moment, trying to decipher the look in her eyes. "Was there something behind that little meeting, Torrie?"

"I thought you'd get a kick out of seeing our old preschool teacher."

"And what about her grandson?"

"What about him?"

"Surely, if you're his teacher you knew how he felt about everything. It's like he had a personal vendetta against the Garden District."

"He's seventeen, Jake, his world has been destroyed, and he feels everyone's lying to him. How do you expect him to react?"

"I haven't lied to him. I don't even know the kid."

"That doesn't matter. To Darcell you are one of the haves. To him you're a liar." Torrie held Jake's gaze, her vision not wavering.

It was a question she'd asked, not a statement. Jake ran their last conversation through his mind. He couldn't remember anything, and then he thought of Torrie asking him to talk to the insurance company on her behalf. "Baby, I talked to the adjuster. He told me he's overloaded with cases and he's going to get to you as soon as possible. It might take him a few more weeks."

Jake stopped at the look that filled Torrie's chocolate brown eyes. He pulled her to him and rubbed her back. "Don't worry, baby. It's going to be fine. You don't have to deal with them anymore, I'll take care of it." He felt her tremble beneath his touch. "It's okay, Torrie, I promise you."

The words almost stuck to the roof of his mouth. Here he was, lying to her. Even more disturbing because he was doing it in church.

"Torrie, baby, you listening?"

"I'm listening." Torrie tilted her head. "Well, Jake, if that's the answer you received from the insurance company, then it doesn't look like you had any more luck than I did." She rubbed her thumb over her ring and a sensation of pain passed through her, forcing her to bend with the ache.

"Baby, are you okay?"

No, she wasn't okay. She moved away from Jake, unable to bear his touch, she watched him.

"Are you upset with me about something?"

"Should I be?" she asked.. "I love you, Jake, I really do. I want nothing more than to spend the rest of my life with you, but I don't want to start things off with a lie. Isn't there something you need to tell me?" Finally, she had the strength to look up at him. She saw pain flicker in Jake's golden eyes. She saw him swallow. Awareness of his lie to her filled his eyes. He'd been caught. Torrie was hurt because Jake lied. She stared at Jake and waited.

"Do you think I would hurt you, Torrie?"

"Lying to me hurts me, Jake." He moved toward her and pulled her into his arms.

A shiver of uneasiness whipped through Torrie. She closed her eyes and swallowed. Jake had returned for her. She remembered him coming through the cabin door and her sister saying she'd kissed Jake like a whore.

She stared at him, feeling for him what she'd felt that night in the cabin when she'd finally held him after twelve long years. He risked his life for her. And now he was doing what he'd always promised to do. He was trying to protect her...that much she knew.

Torrie pulled air in between her teeth as she made her decision. She should say the words now and stop playing games using innuendos, or demand that Jake say them. She couldn't pull her gaze from his. "Out with it, Jake."

"I own C&J Mutual and C&J Mutual owns Rediflex Mutual."

Torrie's mouth opened in surprise. This wasn't exactly what she'd expected. This was worse. "I just thought you were the claim adjuster assigned to me."

"How did you know?"

"I'm not stupid. I can't believe you own the company? Didn't you know that?" Torrie turned from Jake trying to think. "How can that be?"

"It happens all the time. My company bought yours." He tried to ignore the glare. "I didn't know when I took the job. Don't you remember I asked you the name of your insurance company? I was afraid of this very thing happening. One in a million chances. I thought 'no way'." He sighed. "Yes way."

"Why didn't you just go ahead and do the claims?"

"None of your flood coverage is enough. I've been trying to have someone tell me if I could raise your home so you could get more. I was only trying to help. I promise that's all I've been trying to do since we came home."

"You don't think you can be fair. I know, Jake. You're torn between wanting to help me and my family and doing your job. I understand, but you know how I've been about them not sending anyone. Why would you allow me to keep making the calls, going crazy, getting so angry when you knew you were the adjuster? Jake, my family and I have been living in limbo. We all need to get on with things. We need to know what to do. I need to put my life back together, to know what my next step is."

"Just give me a little more time, Torrie. I'll take care of things. I'll take care of you." He reached for her, but she moved farther away, and Jake had no choice but to swallow the hurt. "I know you don't want to be taken care of, but I need to, that's my job. It's always been my job since we were little."

"We're not little anymore. Besides, it was never your job."

"It was."

"Then that was what you decided, maybe what I encouraged. And even if it were, it shouldn't have been. Whatever, Jake. It's not what I want anymore, and you damn well know that. I will take care of me, and I will find a way to take care of my family without your help."

For a moment, Torrie allowed the simmering anger to surface. "Do you have any idea how my family will react to this knowing that things could have been handled weeks ago?" She took in a breath and held it before exhaling. "It would have been so much easier if you had just told me the truth in the beginning, or even if you had turned the job over to someone else? There has to be more than one claims adjuster. You shouldn't have taken the job."

"I wanted to, Torrie. I've been trying to find a way to do this without you finding out, without your entire family finding out. I know they're going to think I'm sticking it to them no matter what I do. And we both know Trey's not going to believe anything I say."

"Something else is going wrong. What is it?

"My father set up this whole thing. I didn't know C&J Mutual was for Cannan and Jacob. My father came to find out why I was holding up on your claims."

"In this case I have to agree with your father. What did he say?"

"He told me to just do my damn job!" Jake couldn't help but wince at his father's words. Hell, he wanted to do his damn job.

What made either Torrie or his father think he didn't? He just wasn't ready to do his job if it meant hurting Torrie. Why the hell couldn't either of them understand?

"He's right. You should have done that from the beginning. I would never blame you for doing your job."

"And your family?"

"There're going to find something to blame you for no matter what you do. But I know better. You're a good man, Jake. You were a good little boy, and you've turned into a man I'm proud of, one I'm glad I know, and one I'm thankful has the good sense to know he loves me. I don't want your trying to play superhero for me to spoil what we have. I'd rather have nothing and have you tell me the truth than to have you fix things for me, Jake. I don't want charity. I never did. I worked for everything I have. So did the rest of my family. We only want what's due us, that's why we paid our premiums. Just do that, Jake, okay?"

"Are you going to tell your family?"

Torrie's eyes snapped closed and she wanted to scream. How was she going to tell her family now? They already didn't trust Jake. She didn't want to give them any more ammunition, but she wouldn't keep them in the dark, she couldn't.

"It's not so easy knowing is it? I tried to get you not to press me."

A tear rolled down Torrie's cheek, and she wished for a moment she had not pressed. Torrie moaned as her body swayed. Jake held her and she didn't move away. She looked around at the now almost empty church not feeling the peace she usually found there. *God what a mess*, she thought again.

"I love you, Torrie. Just give me a little time to try and help your family."

"How much time, Jake?"

"No later than the first of the year." He heard the groan that came from deep inside her body and held her tighter. "I'll take care of everything, baby. Just give me a chance."

"A chance to do what, make some shady deals to give us more money? Do you really think that's what I want?"

"You could make this a lot easier by letting me help. Yes, I have money and connections, Torrie. So what? If I want to use it to help you, I will."

"Don't you get it? You've got to stop taking care of me!"

"Don't you get it, Torrie? This is who I am."

"I told Kimmie you like bulldozing things, but you can't do it to me. I don't need you to run interference for me. I'm not a child, Jake, don't treat me like one."

They both sighed, and then Jake shook his head slowly. "I know you're not a child. I'm not trying to run your life. I'm only trying to protect you. And you're not going to stop me from doing that, so don't even try." Right there before God and all, Jake pulled Torrie into his arms and held her close.

"You two okay?"

Torrie opened her eyes to look at Father Mike. "We're fine," she said, moving from Jake's arms, allowing the engagement ring to be seen by the priest. It was bad enough to think what thoughts might be running through his head. She wanted him to at least know they were engaged. When a smile appeared on the man's face, Torrie felt the tension ease from her body.

"We're okay, Father. We were just about to leave." Torrie answered.

"I wasn't trying to rush you out but I noticed you talking for a while and you seemed upset. I just wanted to know if you needed anything."

"Nothing's wrong," Torrie said unable to look at the priest. When she spoke she allowed her gaze to travel the length of the church before returning to rest on the priest.

"You're getting married, Torrie?"

"Yes, Father."

"Praise God! In the midst of it all, life goes on and love wins. I hope you're planning on my doing it. I'd love to marry you and Jacob."

Jake turned surprised eyes on the priest. He'd forgotten Father Mike had also called him Jacob. But that had been many years ago. "I didn't think you remembered me, Father. It's been a long time, and I didn't come all that often."

"No, you didn't, but when you did you were always with Torrie, and I always kept my eye on you because you couldn't keep your eyes off her. I wanted to make sure you two didn't get into any trouble." He shook hand with both of them. "Anyway, when you're ready, you know where I'll be."

Jake stared after the man. "We could do it right now, Torrie, let's go into his study and get married."

""That's not going to solve anything. It will only make matters worse. We don't have to run away like little kids who've done something wrong. I don't want to start my life with you that way."

For a beat of ten, Torrie stared at Jake. There were more questions she knew she should ask him, like how long had he known? Had he been the one to give the orders to give her the run around? She took in a deep breath and exhaled it, no need in getting into this before she met his parents as his fiancée. She was nervous enough about that already. It wouldn't do for them to have tension between them. Cannan Broussard was a man known for seizing his opponent's weaknesses and using them against him. Torrie didn't plan on walking into Jake's home at a disadvantage.

"Tora, welcome to our home."

"Torrie," three voices corrected Cannan Broussard at once.

"Don't start," Jake warned his father. "Torrie came here for dinner and for the two of you to get to know her as the woman I'm going to marry."

Torrie stuck out her hand. "It's nice to see you again, sir," she said, wanting to stop Jake. She didn't need him to protect her from his father. She saw a flicker of something in the man's eyes. *A challenge*, she thought.

"I'm sorry, Torrie." Cannan smiled. "I forgot your name. I didn't mean any disrespect."

"Good," Jake answered for Torrie, "because if you had I'd be forced to take Torrie home."

Jake's arm slid around her waist, and he pulled her close. Torrie breathed easier. She gave Jake a grateful smile for knowing what she needed at the moment. She turned and caught the look that passed between Jake's parents and wondered what it was about.

She glanced at the man while they made small talk, moving with Jake into the parlor, his hand holding hers firmly. She couldn't help but smile. Jake was prepared to do battle for her the same as always. This time Torrie didn't think she'd need him. She could handle Cannan Broussard herself.

An hour later, she wasn't so sure. The man had practically come out and accused her of wanting to marry Jake for his money, and he'd done it all with a smile pasted on his face. She'd gone toe-to-toe with the man, answering him with the same pleasant voice he'd used with her, until she'd finally asked if she could go to the bathroom. She needed a moment to regroup.

Torrie marched past Cannan and back into the living room, taking her seat beside Jake determined not to glare, to paste a smile on her face, and go through with this. She glanced at Jake who was still sitting by her side, but she could sense the tension emanating from him and the pleasure that tension brought to his father.

She smiled at Cannan. Did he think he could so easily put a wedge between her and Jake? Torrie moved her hand slowly across the couch toward Jake. When he took her hand and gave her fingers a squeeze, she smiled at him, putting all her love into the smile. The look he gave her in return melted her heart and her resolve. They stared for a long moment into each other eyes. They were in this together,

Torrie smiled politely, turning her attention to Jake's mother. "You have a lovely home. I'm happy you and your husband were able to leave New Orleans before the hurricane or the levees broke. Although even if you had stayed, you would have been fine." Torrie smiled. "Most of New Orleans wasn't so lucky, but I'm glad our entire city wasn't destroyed."

For a moment, her comments seemed to have some effect on both of Jake's parents. They looked around the room and appeared a bit uncomfortable.

"Did all of your family get out, Torrie?" Jake's mother asked.

"Yes, they did. Thank you."

"I hear Jake followed you, risking his life for you. Did you ask him to come?" Cannan asked.

"I would never ask Jake to risk his life for me," Torrie stated simply. She turned toward Jake and smiled at him before turning back to his mother. "I love, Jake. I would never want him in harms way to protect me."

"Torrie, would you want Jake to put himself in harms way on his job to protect you?"

For the first time the man was correctly pronouncing her name.

"Jake and I have talked about his being the adjuster for my family's policies. And I know you and Jake are C&J Mutual. To answer your question, do I want Jake to overvalue our property? No, I don't. Do I think Jake is an honest enough man that he'll be able to give us a fair appraisal? Yes, I do."

"Are you saying you're not upset that Jake hasn't done this already, that he didn't put your family at the top of the list of homes he had to appraise? You know if he had, you would know where you stand by now." Cannan grinned. "I guess that doesn't much matter, you're marrying Jake. You don't have to worry about how much he gives you for your property."

"Dad, stop it—"

"No, thanks just the same, Jake," Torrie cut him off. "Mr. Broussard, if Jake had moved us ahead of other claimants, that would have been favoritism, and I don't want that. Of course I want my claim settled, but no one is giving me anything. I paid for the coverage. As for marrying Jake, we've agreed we won't get married until all of my financial affairs are settled. I made my own way Mr. Broussard, I don't need your son to take care of me."

The man scratched his chin, then he took out a cigar and ran his fingers over it. Torrie frowned slightly.

"I seem to remember Jacob always protected you. Right?"

"I'll take that one." Jake put his hand on Torrie's arm. "When I was five years old, Torrie stole my heart. I've always loved her, and I will always want to protect her from everything and anyone who wants to harm her. Torrie and I are a team. To be more specific, Torrie neither needs nor wants my protection or my money, only my love, but she has all three." He shrugged his shoulders. "That's just the way it is."

"And, Jacob, you think you'll be able to do your job where she's concerned? You sure the company shouldn't send in another man?"

"I can do my job. I've always done my job. I've never cheated either a client or a company, and I'm not about to start now."

"Good." Cannan smiled. "I'm pleased to know you're not going to squander my money and give it away to charity."

Jake squeezed Torrie fingers so tightly she lost the feeling in them. *One, two, three,* she said mentally. *Calm down, Torrie. The man's trying to provoke you, calm down.*

"Excuse me," Torrie said, rising to make yet another trip to the bathroom. She held onto the gold gilded pedestal sink her eyes fastened on the pink flowered wallpaper, and groaned with the knowledge of why the bathroom looked so familiar. She'd seen pictures of it in a local magazine and had copied the design in her own home. She bit her lips trying to keep the tears back. Maybe Kimmie was right. Maybe she had been trying to be uptown.

"I'm not going to tell you again," Jake said doing his best to keep his voice low enough so Torrie wouldn't hear. "Stop being rude to Torrie."

"I have done nothing to the girl except try and be polite?"

"Is that what we're calling it nowadays, grilling her, almost saying she's marrying me for my money?"

"If you're not going to ask her these questions, someone has to."

"Not you, Dad. She's not marrying you."

"But she will be marrying into the money I made."

"We don't need your money."

"Too bad, you have it. And you have my name and everything that it means."

Jake got the meaning. *Corruption thy name is New Orleans.* Everything was done undercover. Jake thought of the many opportunities the city had lost because of all of the corruption. He'd even been told Disney World would have been in New Orleans, but the longtime tradition of corruption ran them away as it had many more economic opportunities. He'd always known his father was a true son of New Orleans. He'd just never wanted to admit it.

"You're a son of New Orleans, Dad, not me,"

"No, don't you think the mere fact you're here working on two different projects is a conflict of interest? Don't you think your being the one to assess that girl's property isn't a bit suspect?"

"But you set all of that up, Dad."

"You are a son of New Orleans, Jacob. You're my son. You're smart, stop pretending you don't know what I'm talking about."

"I don't know." Jake tried to figure out what his father's statement meant. What else could Cannan Broussard be involved in? Then it hit him.

Cannan grinned at his son before turning toward the door on hearing the click of Torrie's heels. "Are you going to tell Torrie, Jacob, or should I?"

"Tell me what?" Torrie reentered the room. "Is there something else you should tell me, Jake?"

Jake glared at his father. "Let it go," he said, then turned to Torrie. "Tomorrow I'll start on the assessment."

"I thought you wanted to wait until the first of the year."

"If your home can't be elevated and it has to be destroyed, the bank holding your mortgage will more than likely take over the land. There isn't enough …Torrie, basically, the bank owns your land."

Torrie and Jake both turned toward Cannan Broussard, the man who held the actual deed to Torrie's property. He owned Torrie's home. Torrie had gotten her loan from Abel Bank. It had long been rumored that Cannan Broussard actually owned the bank. When she'd gotten her loans, Torrie hadn't cared who owned the bank, only that the loan was approved.

Torrie felt suddenly ill. She bit her lip as a sense of betrayal washed over her. She refused to allow Cannan Broussard to see her cry. She'd fight him. "Jake, you have to the first of the year. I plan to rebuild my home, not allow the bank to take it." She stared at Jake. "You're a builder. Do you think it can be raised?"

"I'm not sure. The back portion is on cinder blocks. I want an expert in this field to tell me."

Torrie's heart sank. If her home could be elevated, Jake would have told her, he wouldn't say he wasn't sure. That was the real reason he'd not done the appraisal, he knew she'd lose everything. Legs suddenly weak, Torrie walked past Jake and sat back on the sofa.

"Whatever you have to do I trust you, Jake," she said, not looking at him, thinking instead of her family as the betrayal grew thicker. She could hear her father now saying she was the one who'd allowed the snake into the hen house. *Damn it all to hell.*

Damn. Jake glanced at his father. He should have known. No wonder Cannan Broussard was hated. There had to be something illegal about what the man was doing. He owned a bank that held the mortgages, and he owned the damn insurance company doing the appraisals. Hell. His blood boiled. His father didn't have to wait to see the damage it would do to Torrie. But of course it had been exactly what Cannan had wanted.

"I didn't know about the bank, Torrie."

"Of course you did, Jacob, so did Torrie. You both knew."

Blinding rage filled Jake for what his father was doing. It wasn't so much that he owned the bank but that he was using it to hurt Torrie, that he was trying to make her believe Jake was a part of the corruption.

He would deal with his father later. Right now his primary concern was Torrie. Jake touched her arm and felt the shiver slide through her. She wouldn't look at him until he tilted her chin so her eyes would meet his. "I didn't know," he said. "I didn't know," Jake repeated. "But it won't matter. I promised I would rebuild your home with my bare hands, and I will, Torrie. I will. Don't you dare worry, baby."

Jake could see his father moving around from the corner of his eye. And to think this man's pride in him was all he'd wanted his entire life. He'd had a brief glimpse of that pride. He looked at the pained expression on Torrie's face, and knew the price was too high. He pulled her against him and held her, glaring over his shoulders at his parents.

"Let me go, Jake," Torrie whispered .

"No, baby, not until you believe I didn't know."

"I know." Torrie swallowed, refusing to turn and see his parents staring at them. God how she wished she'd never asked Jake about coming to his home. How she wished Cannan Broussard wasn't his father, and that Jake didn't live in the Garden District. She hated admitting it, but she wished she and Jake came from the same background. Torrie bit her lips. Her eyes were tearing from knowing Cannan Broussard stood to gain her property. She wasn't sure if that were the only reason. The only thing she was sure of was that she wanted to leave.

"Dinner's ready, Mrs. Broussard." Bessie stuck her head in the door as she made the announcement.

"I'm sorry," Torrie said, glancing toward the cook. "I don't mean to be rude, but I think we should do this another time. I'm feeling a bit queasy." She stood and walked toward the door.

Jake opened the door of his SUV and waited while Torrie slid inside. He glanced back at the house. Once again his father had one-upped him, and once again Jake should have been ready for it. He would be next time. If he had to think like his father in order to beat him, he would. The last thing he would see happen would be for his father to take Torrie's property. What had gone down was plum crazy. He was definitely aware his father had staged this moment to tell him he owned the bank. Jake groaned inwardly, what a frigging mess. He walked to the driver's side of the car, got in, closed the door and started the engine.

"Are you telling them tonight?" he asked.

"Yes. I'm not playing around with my family's lives, especially knowing what I now know."

"Would you have given me the extra time if my father didn't own the bank?"

"Yes, I would have given it to you." She stared straight ahead. "But I hope you're not planning on asking me to give it to you now. As it is, Jake, they're going to feel betrayed. I've been telling them they have nothing to worry about, that you're on our side and here to help." She paused hesitating at adding, *that you love me Jake.* Torrie swallowed. "I'm not going to lie to them, not about this, it's too important."

"They're not going to understand I was helping."

"No, they're not going to understand."

"Torrie, I want to tell them."

She stared hard at him. Jake in the house with Trey, Kimmie, and her parents telling them he'd deliberately made them wait before giving them appraisals. Oh yeah that was going to go over real big.

"Torrie?"

"Jake, I don't think it's a good idea. This might be better coming from me."

"But you didn't create this mess."

"Why are you so worried about my family?"

"It's not your family I'm worried about. I don't want us to let this thing come between us. Besides, Torrie, if I don't tell them I'll feel like a coward, like I needed you to fight my battles. I'm a man. I don't need my woman to do my fighting for me. I'll tell them myself, that it was my father who made this mess "

"As I remember, you were always cleaning up the messes I made. I can take care of this. It wouldn't make you any less of a man. I would much rather tell them and let them get out some of their anger before they see you."

"If you think I'm going to put you in the middle of this…" He sighed and breathed in.

Chapter Fifteen

Glares and silence greeted Jake's announcement. He swallowed. "I didn't want to tell any of you about this until I had found a way to help you."

"You mean until you found a way for your father to keep our land. What is he doing, planning on selling all of the land to Halliburton or one of the land developers?"

Jake turned toward Trey. "Do you really think I'd come here and tell you this if that were true?"

"Would you have told us if Torrie hadn't found out?"

"Not until I'd figured out a way to help you."

"I don't want your help." Trey knocked over the kitchen chair he was sitting in and walked with balled fist toward Jake.

"Not in my home," John Tom cautioned. "I'm not having it, Trey. Jake didn't have to come and tell us a damn thing. He has been trying to help; I know that first hand."

"Who the hell asked you, John Tom? You didn't lose anything, I did."

"Leave John Tom alone," Kimmie spoke up. "Trey, you're out of line."

"Calm down all of you. Jake didn't have to tell you any of this. He could have let someone else do the claims. I trust Jake." Torrie went to stand beside Jake and stared into his eyes. "I trust him with my life. He wouldn't do anything to hurt us. He's told me everything he knows, he's not lying to us."

It felt as though a band had encased Jake. He couldn't look at Torrie. Here she was vouching for him, telling her family he wasn't lying when in actuality he'd lied to her for weeks.

"I'll do everything I can for all of you, I'll—"

"We don't want your charity, Jake."

"You won't get my charity, Trey."

"Jake, why didn't you tell me this when we talked a few weeks ago?" Torrie's mother said coming to stand directly in front of him. "You told me you wouldn't do anything to hurt Torrie. But now I'm wondering if I should have taken your words so easily. Maybe I should have made you sign something, but then I guess a contract may not have done anything, huh? You would find a way to talk yourself out of anything."

Jake pulled in a breath as he looked at Torrie's mother. Her voice was shaky. Jake had been fighting so long with Trey that he'd gotten used to it, but Torrie's mother had warmed toward him in the last weeks. He hated to have the woman think he'd deceived her.

He took in a couple of breaths, walking closer to her. "When I came here that first day, I didn't know. When I made you that promise in the beginning, I didn't know about it. I swear I didn't know." Jake dared to look at Torrie. "I came here tonight because I wasn't going to let the blame fall on Torrie. She didn't know and neither did I."

"But it's not unexpected, Jake. Your father has always done business this way."

"But I haven't, Trey."

"But you're his son, man, blood, Jake." Trey shrugged. "It can't be helped."

"I'm going to go now, baby," Jake said and walked toward the door. He walked out the door, not surprised Torrie hadn't stopped him, but hurt nonetheless.

"Jake, man wait up."

Jake met John Tom's eyes over the top of his truck.

"That was some foul shit, brother. I've been speaking up for you, and then you go and do something like this."

Jake waited as John Tom made his way toward him. He licked his lips, wondering if the man was coming to take a swing at him. Jake wished he would, he deserved it.

252

"What's the real deal, man? I don't doubt you love Torrie, but I've had dealings with your father myself. I lost a home in New Orleans to him. Believe me, when I took out this mortgage, I investigated and made sure Cannan Broussard wasn't involved. I checked all the way from the bottom to the top. There are other things I've being checking, Jake, and I know more than you think I know. I know you're not telling it all. What's your plan? They're my family, man, and I won't allow you to hurt them."

"I want them for my family," Jake said, looking at John Tom. When John Tom laughed, so did Jake. "Okay, I want Torrie. But we both know they're a package deal. I'll take her package along with her. I'm not going to try and convince you, but I just found out a few days ago, when my parents came to town, about the insurance company. It wasn't until Torrie and I were at the house talking that I found out my father owns her bank. You can believe me or not, but I don't know all of my father's business transactions. How the hell would I? The only things I had prior knowledge of before talking with my father was that the entire family had their homes insured through C&J Mutual. And no, I never wondered who C&J were. Torrie was insured by Rediflex Mutual, why would I have made the connection?"

"Jake, that's really hard to swallow."

"It may be hard to swallow, but it's true. When Torrie and I returned here, I didn't know."

The two men stared at each other. Jake submitted to the scrutiny of the older man. "I don't doubt what you're saying. I've told a lot of lies, and I can always spot a liar. You might as well know just in case you don't already. There's more than the insurance company and the bank. Trey wasn't just talking in there. There's been talk that your father is involved with Halliburton, that he's offering the people pennies on the dollars for their land so he can sell to Halliburton. Don't tell me you haven't heard rumors of that man?"

Jake stared at John Tom and shook his head, sighing in defeat. "I've heard a couple of rumors."

"Did you ask your old man about them?"

"I haven't had a chance."

"Jake, man, come on."

"Okay, maybe I didn't want to hear his answer. Besides, I was doing so many damn things I had no business doing, trying to help Torrie, that I wasn't in any position to judge my father."

"Torrie doesn't know, does she?"

Jake waited, wondering what was coming before he answered. "Torrie doesn't know," Jake said. "How the hell do you think I could tell her a thing like that? If you want to tell her, go ahead."

"And if I don't, what are you going to do, Jake Broussard?"

"What I said I would do. I'll do the assessments and give a fair estimate to all of them."

"And Torrie, are you going to overprice her home?"

"Torrie's not stupid, she'd know."

"And she'd hate you for it if you did it. But you want to give her every dime she paid for her home, and then some don't you?" John Tom smiled and glanced toward the house. He walked out the gate and stood there looking up and down the block before walking back to where he'd left Jake standing in the yard.

"Jake you're not that difficult to understand," he continued, "I know the old folk's home wasn't worth much, hell they know it too. And as for Kimmie, I'll take care or her. That kind of leaves you with Trey and Torrie. You don't give a damn about Trey, and no matter what you give him, he's going to think it should be more. So that brings us back to the root of your problem—Torrie. If you could have your way, what would you do about her?"

"If I could have my way, we would be married and none of this would matter. But we're not married and our entire relationship hinges on my wanting to protect her, just because I wanted to help her and couldn't figure out how to do it, I might lose her. Again." Jake said. "I can't stand the thought of losing her. I've waited fourteen years to tell Torrie I love her." He heaved and stared at the older man. "I promised her I wouldn't hurt her."

"Then ask your old man to tell you the complete truth and when you know all there is to know tell her the truth. Better she hears it from you than from Trey."

"Damn."

"Trey's really been busting your chops. Why the hell are you trying to help his dumb ass?" John Tom asked, looking back toward the house.

"Torrie." Jake answered.

"Jake, tell me something. Why are you here steadily kissing everybody's ass? You're acting like a punk in front of your woman. I did a hell of a lot more to hurt Kimmie than the shit you pulled on Torrie and Trey, and they forgave me. Man, don't it just gall the hell out of you that you have to work so hard to get the woman you love?"

"The way I hear it," Jake started, "you had to work hard to get Kimmie to give you another chance. The strongest man is made weak at times by his love for his woman."

"If Kimmie was making me jump through all these damn hoops, I'd tell her to forget it. Sure, I did some groveling to get her back, but I knew my limit. What's yours?"

"Kimmie isn't Torrie. You hurt Kimmie when she was old enough to handle it. Torrie wasn't old enough to handle it, man. I was the first and only man she gave her heart to. I was the first and only man who broke it. Don't you think I know Torrie has me jumping through hoops? Do I like it? Hell no. But I love Torrie, and I want to marry her. Does it piss me off that it was you who came after me and not Torrie? You bet." Jake sucked in his breath. "J.T., the family's not holding stuff against me I did when I was sixteen. They're holding my name against me. If I wasn't Jake Broussard—"

"Yeah, but you are."

"You're right, I am and I can't change that."

"I feel you man, and no amount of groveling and apologizing for who you were born to be will change it. Still, you need to find out if your old man is up to more dirty dealing. Torrie loves you, but if she finds you're involved with anything like covering up for your father, stealing the land here, she'll not worry about loving you. If it's true, you'd better find a way to stop your old man ASAP."

Jake eyes widened as he listened to John Tom. A plan started to unfold in Jake's mind of how to fix the problem. A shudder of self-loathing stopped him. Damn it, now he was thinking like his father. He wouldn't give into it.

His voice shook a little as he shoved his hands in his pockets to calm himself. *Damn, stop it,* he scolded himself. "If my father's planning on selling out to Halliburton, I'll do everything in my power to stop him. I have no plans on letting my father take Torrie's property. And I'm not going to lie to her about it. When I know anything for sure, Torrie will be the first person I tell. But I have to find out the truth. It's not that I don't trust what you say, but like you said, they are just rumors."

"Jake, tell me something. Why are you telling all of this to me when you should be talking to the woman you love?"

"Because I don't care about the look in your eyes," Jake said and shrugged his shoulders. "Good night." Jake got into his truck and drove away. It was time he opened his eyes to who his father was. It was time he became a true son of New Orleans. If his father was really doing what people were accusing him of, Jake was determined to stop him, and that would require doing things Torrie wouldn't like.

Backdoor dealing would be the only thing to beat his father. No, Jake wasn't going to ask him. The old man would probably be more than happy to confirm it. Then he'd go out and try his best to take Torrie's property.

Jake was determined to do his damnest not to allow that to happen. And he would do it without his father finding out anything. He would use the things already available and make them work for him as they had for his father and everyone else who had used New Orleans.

Welcome home, Jake thought as he drove home. This was exactly the kind of shit he'd left home to not become involved in.

Chapter Sixteen

Are you tired, baby?" Jake asked in a quiet voice. He had Torrie pressed against the wall of the hotel room with his hand sliding underneath her dress, his fingers moving her panties aside. He stopped abruptly and brought his hand away, smoothing the silk with his fingers. He sighed and pulled Torrie from the wall.

"What's wrong?" Torrie asked.

"I'm not sure."

For a tenth of a second, Jake thought that might be true. But he knew the reason he'd stopped fondling Torrie. He'd been about to make love to her as an act of desperation. He ran his fingers up the side of her body. The passion he felt for her was overwhelming, he didn't need the desperation.

"You asked if I were tired. Maybe it's you who's tired, Jake"

"I am a little, but I can't envision the day when I'll be too tired to make love to you."

"Envision it now. If you're too tired, maybe you can just lie down and let me do all the work."

"What fun would that be?"

"Trust me, Jake, you'll enjoy it."

Jake finally managed a grin, then turned at the knock on the door. "You're always getting saved by someone delivering food," he said, going to the door and taking the tray from the hands of the Room service personnel. He took the tray to the table and walked back placing bills into the waiting palm.

"You really are tired aren't you?" Torrie asked, uncovering the food and walking back to Jake, kissing him lightly on the lips.

"Yeah, we've been working night and day." He sighed. "This wasn't how I fantasized our being in Louisiana together. For the twelve years I thought about it, this was never part of my plans."

Torrie couldn't help smiling at him, his voice was so sad and his eyes held a question. "I thought you told me we would be together, vision or not." She smiled again teasing him, hoping to pull him out of his funk.

Jake blinked a couple of times in confusion before he gave up trying to figure out what Torrie was talking about. "Would you mind giving me a clue?" he asked.

"You, you're looking so gloomy. Like you've lost your best friend." She braced her hands on the hotel table to keep it sturdy then leaned over and kissed Jake again. "You haven't, Jake." She sat back and waited. This time a smile appeared on his lips. They were on the same page.

"You sure about that?" he asked.

"I'm sure about it."

"What about your parents? Their property has been condemned."

"At least they own the land free and clear. And Daddy told me you advised him to hold on to the land at least until May when we see what's going to happen with the levees, whether they're going to be able to rebuild them in time for next year's hurricane season. He said you advised him that if they're not repaired to hold out for the best price and not to sell it back to the bank. I think by then the federal government will step up their game. The entire world is watching."

"Did you have another vision?"

"So many I'm tired of them." She shrugged her shoulders. "New Orleans will not be the only place that will be hit with a natural disaster…" Torrie stopped in mid-sentence. "You keep getting me off track, Jake. I don't want to talk about the coming months. I want to know if my family should be worried about your father. I'm asking you straight out, and I want a straight answer."

Torrie stood and came to stand in front of Jake, swaying slowly back and forth, wondering how she could be asking Jake questions when all she wanted was to make love to him.

"I didn't come back to make my father richer, Torrie, not at anyone's expense. As far as your family goes, from the little progress I've seen, I wouldn't hold out hope that the levees will be rebuilt in time for the hurricane season. And even if they are, maybe they should think of moving somewhere else."

"This is home, Jake."

"I know. I'm not going to move back here and worry every second. I know when we're married, I'm moving you out of the path of danger," he stared defiantly into her eyes, and she stared just as defiantly back at him.

"Jake, that just sounded as though you'd issued an order. You do know you can't just tell me where to go, and have me follow you like a little lap dog. My home is New Orleans."

"I'm aware of that. It's also my home. But I think we'll do better living somewhere else. I don't like the things I've done since I've been back. I'm beginning to feel too much a part of the things that happen here as just routine."

"I don't think it's the fault of the city."

"Maybe not, but it's been accepted so long it feels almost natural. You know, like it's in my blood."

"What are you talking about, Jake?"

"I'm talking about me playing games, giving favors for information. I may not be doing things on the same level as my father, but I see how easy it is to make that downward spiral. Who knows, maybe my father started out doing wrong things for the right reason. I don't know."

"I don't know what you're talking about."

Jake couldn't help but smile at Torrie. "I thought you always knew what I was talking about."

"Not this time."

260

"Forget it, baby. It's not important. Right now I just want to set things in motion for us, for our family."

"Jacob, you'd better not do anything else to complicate our lives. Do you hear me?" When he didn't answer, Torrie took his face between her hands and held it firmly. "I'm not kidding with you, Jake. I'm not going to lose you to this town or this system. I will not lose my friend."

"The rumors are true, Torrie. My father is buying up land and selling it to investors."

"And you plan to stop him?"

"I plan to stop him."

"How, by doing the same things he's doing? By becoming corrupt? Look, I know you're making deals with people all over town. The talk has already started. Stop it! Do you hear me?"

"He's not getting your land."

"Jake, do you think your father not getting my land is as important to me as you losing that part of yourself I fell in love with? Listen to me. This is what I worried about for us, not you loving me, not your father disapproving of us. This, Jake, I worried about your becoming this person who wants to fight fire with fire."

"What am I supposed to do, just roll over and give my wife's land to my father?"

"We're not married yet, Jake."

"Then let's set a date."

"You think that will change things."

"In a way, yes. Right now you're my fiancée, little more than a girlfriend. I still have no rights. I want rights, Torrie. I want you to be my wife. I'm sick of not waking up with you beside me, not making love to you any damn time I please."

"That's not my fault, Jake. You're the one who's always busy. You're the one who just professed to being too tired to make love. I'm sick of us always talking about everything but us. We don't get to spend much time together as it is. Not now, Jake, let's not talk about anything, but us right now."

Torrie tilted her head just a little, then allowed her gaze to linger on Jake. "It seems you have different ideas than I do about a lot of things. Here you are thinking about our waking up together, and you're missing all the good stuff that happens before we go to sleep."

Desire for her shot through him and created a throb in his groin. "Are you making a suggestion?"

"I'm making an offer, tell me what you want." Torrie dipped the tines of her fork into the mashed potatoes and gravy and brought the fork to her mouth, smiling coyly as she licked the tines clean. "Tell me what you're thinking."

"Can't you read my mind?"

"I could, but I'd like to have you tell me."

"You want to know what I'm thinking right now?"

"Yes, tell me what you're thinking right now."

"I want you, Torrie."

"And?"

"I want to rip your clothes off, right now, and make love to you."

"That sounds so boring, Jake. Same-o, same-o." Torrie dipped her fork into the turkey and smacked her lips appreciatively. "This food is good. You're going to have to offer me something that compares. Whatcha got?"

"I want to kiss your chocolate nipples, and I want to nibble your thighs." He reached for her hand. "I want to run my tongue all over your body, licking you slowly until you go crazy with wanting me."

"You're sparking my interest," Torrie whispered tearing her gaze from Jake to look behind her at the bed. "Go on; tell me what else you want."

"I want to make you so wet you come from watching me." Jake scratched the inside of Torrie's palm lightly with his nails knowing what the sensation was doing to her. "Are you wet, Torrie?"

"I'm wet, Jake."

"Then why don't we leave this food here for later and lay on that soft bed?' Jake's gaze softened with desire and he smiled, glancing at the bed. "Don't you want to make love?"

"We haven't finished lunch. You promised me lunch, now you don't want me to eat it."

"I could care less about eating and neither do you. You're teasing me."

"I'm hungry."

"Yeah right."

"I am, Jake. I'm hungry for you," Torrie whispered seductively.

"Stop looking at me like that, Torrie, or I swear…" His breath hitched. "I want you so damn bad," he whispered. He ran a finger down her arm, felt her shiver and smiled. "Doesn't my plan sound much better?"

Torrie could barely breathe. An electric magnet connected her and Jake; heat sizzled and shimmied down her spine. Sitting across the table from him with a bed behind them and them teasing was having a heady effect on her. At this moment Torrie wanted one thing and one thing only—Jake. "I guess you've made me want something more than turkey. Just make sure you deliver everything you've promised," she said low making her voice sexy and husky, making sure Jake knew how much she wanted him. Before she could move, Jake was helping her from the chair.

"Torrie," Jake moaned, laying her on the bed, moving over her to slide his left hand once again under her dress. He was so damn hungry for Torrie, it gnawed at him like a raw ache. "Tell me you love me, baby."

"I love you."

"Now tell me what you want." He ran the pad of his fingers down the side of her cheek, matching the movements of his right hand with those of his left that was between her thighs.

"I want you to do all the things you promised to do to me when you forced me to stopped eating." A grin broke across Torrie's face. "I love you, Jake."

Forever and a Day

Torrie could barely breathe, being with Jake turned her to mush. She dropped her head back, loving the way Jake's mouth immediately pressed against her neck. He kissed every inch, scorching her skin with his tongue. Lucky for Torrie, Jake wasn't a fictional vampire. She'd just presented him with her throat. Torrie trembled with desire, falling even farther back, knowing Jake's arms would be there to catch her. They always were.

As Torrie fell back he positioned himself to have her fall in his arms. Jake positioned Torrie on the bed, not bothering to pull back the covers. He stared down at her. As he stripped, he watched the desire build in her. He grinned at the hungry look in her eyes that followed his pants, then his briefs as they landed on a chair. Torrie loved looking at him naked. Jake grinned even wider. He loved looking at her in her birthday suit, but he also liked unwrapping the package.

He grinned as he took in the dress Torrie wore just for him, knowing how he liked looking at her shapely legs. When they moved to New York he doubted if she would wear skirts in November. He watched Torrie in fascination as she used one hand to pull the covers down. When she tweaked a finger toward him to come, he was almost panting.

Torrie smiled, her eyelids heavy and hooded with lust. She wondered if she would ever tire of looking at Jake's beautiful sculpted body. She grinned; she didn't think so. As Jake's hand slid under her dress, Torrie moved her legs apart. She wore dresses strictly for Jake. Her normal attire was pants, but pants wouldn't make her have the feeling she was having right now. She loved the feel of Jake's hand sliding under her dress, touching her flesh, peeling the nylons from her legs. She trembled against his hand as need coursed through her. Torrie moaned as Jake slid a finger into her wetness, and then another.

"Jake," she whispered breathless, as the nylons came from her legs. She could feel Jake using his foot to push them away and didn't care that he'd more than likely caused a dozen runs. Maybe she'd just start wearing ripped nylons for him. It would be a lot cheaper. This time Torrie could feel the smile on her face as her body shuddered in ecstasy.

"What are you grinning at?"

"I was just thinking of the money you cost me in stockings."

"I'll buy you more."

"No…yes…you will." Torrie gave in. Why not, he was the one ruining them. She looked into his eyes. "Jake, didn't you say something about my chocolate nipples?" She used her tongue to tease the corner of his mouth.

"I did say something about that, didn't I?" A hard shudder shook Jake's body. Jake's eyes closed as his mouth filled with Torrie's nipple. He caressed the other breast, glad of having her beautiful brown body to make love to.

"Jake," Torrie purred, "I love the feel of your fingers inside me and your mouth…my breast…the feeling is soooo good. But, Jake, my other breast is beginning to feel neglected."

He smiled at Torrie reversing what he was doing. He turned the attention of his mouth and tongue to her right breast caressing the left with his hand. He was, pulling gently on her nipple, biting her lightly. He felt Torrie's hand moving downwards and groaned as her fingers circled his flesh. His penis jerking wildly in her hand, wanting to enter her, but he had so much more loving of her body to do. Besides, her caress felt almost as good as being inside her body. She ran her finger across the tip, and Jake trembled.

Damn, he thought, he shook away the need for release. It was too damn quick. "Torrie, take it down a notch."

"No," she said and slid her finger once again over his tip, making the need rise. He grunted and fell on her body, kissing her harder, tasting every inch of her skin, filling his nostrils with her scent. He worked his tongue down her body. He stopped at her belly and used his tongue to dip into the indention, feeling the reaction against his fingers. As the wetness pooled out onto his fingers, he smiled as she rubbed him again, running her fingers up and down him, playing him for all she was worth.

They'd developed their own game of trying to figure out who would last longer. So far it seemed they both would give at the same time. He could smell Torrie's scent rising to meet him as his head dipped farther and farther south. He felt the shivers chasing each other as he replaced his finger with his tongue and tasted her.

Her fingers twisted in his hair, holding him tighter. He knew what this was doing to her same as she knew what she was doing to him. With her other hand, she cupped him, squeezing gently, and then going up and down the length of him.

"Lord, have mercy," he said. *Damn, Torrie*, he thought as he lifted up and gave Torrie the condom. Since their first time she always wanted to put it on him. This time he was so damn hot he almost couldn't wait. She wasn't playing fair. She was doing more caressing than she was trying to put the condom on. Jake took over sliding it over his swollen flesh in order to enter her. He sank deep into her warmth, almost losing it, glad, as always, that Torrie had saved herself for him. Her legs tightened around his waist, and he thrust into her, looking deep into her eyes. Jake loved looking at her when he came. His orgasm was much more powerful. "I love you, baby."

Torrie's body shuddered and she opened her eyes and blinked. "I love you, too," Torrie answered, barely able to breathe, but knowing she would always tell Jake she loved him, even with her last breath. The feel of Jake filling her body with his hardness made Torrie know there was definitely a connection between them. They were meant for each other. No way Torrie would ever feel like this with another man. She didn't even want to think she could. She'd tasted Jake, and he'd tasted her. She didn't want to be that intimate with another soul. Jake was home for her. She'd been right; she had been born to love him. Her eyes stayed on his face as he thrust deeper and deeper, harder and faster. She could feel the scream welling up, the need overriding everything but the fulfillment of them. Her body arched and the screams came out.

"Jake," Torrie screamed while Jake's heat intensified like an electrical storm moving through her, taking her out of her body and out of her mind. She clung to Jake, breathless with longing.

Her body tensed around Jake's hardness, quivering at the guttural sounds that came from his throat. Only then did his eyes close. His body tensed, and he threw his head back roaring, grunting, groaning. He spilled into her and she clung on for the ride, enjoying it with him, tears spilling at the wonder of it all. She laughed as they came down. And Jake wiped away the moisture on her cheek with a finger that smelled of her.

"Will I always cry when we make love?" she asked, smiling at him.

"As long as they're tears of joy, baby, I don't give a damn." He kissed her hard. "This was just a snack, Torrie. I hate making love to you and getting up and leaving as though we were nothing to each other. The hell with both our families, let's just stay here and make love all night long."

Torrie ran her fingers down the side of Jake's body, touching the heaviness of him that was not inside her. She could feel him harden up again. "Maybe just once more," she answered, and began caressing his testicles, feeling the jerk of his flesh inside her spring back into full attention.

"How about New Year's Eve, Jake?"

"New Year's Eve?"

"Yeah, at the stroke of midnight we get married. What do you say?"

"New year, new beginning, you as my wife. I like it," Jake answered, his voice hoarse with lust. Then the talking ceased and he begin pumping into Torrie. They had a date set. Torrie's features changed. She had a dewy angelic look and he knew the reason. They were sliding toward heaven, the second release quickly coming. She'd done this to him. He was made to love her. He belonged to her, and she belonged to him.

Jake kissed the hollow of her neck. "I love you, baby," he grunted as he thrust toward completion.

Chapter Seventeen

Jake pulled up in front of John Tom's house and walked Torrie up the walkway. They both looked up as the door opened. Trey came out on the porch and stood looking down at them. "Hello, Jake," he said, "Merry Christmas."

Torrie glanced at Jake, and then Trey as a tingle ran from the top of her head down her spine. Jake was holding her close, squeezing her hand tightly, he looked at her, then back up at Trey. "Merry Christmas, Trey," Jake answered. Torrie waited for the shoe to drop.

"So, Jake. I guess it didn't matter much which way you did it. But I was wondering if the fact that your father is buying land left and right is something else you can explain? Of course saying he's buying it when he's only paying about twenty percent of what it's worth is a stretch. Does that sound familiar to you, Jake? The newspaper article said that you're also buying up the land. There are also innuendoes that you're over appraising some of the homes. Would those homes belong to your family Jake?"

Trey turned his attention to Torrie. "You wouldn't listen to me, would you? I've always told you I knew the real Jake Broussard. You only know the part you want to see." He put his hand in his pocket. "Of course I don't expect you to believe my word. I'm only your blood. Here, Torrie, here's the proof."

Torrie didn't move. She glanced at the paper in Trey's hand and raised her gaze to Jake's eyes. "Thanks, Trey; I don't have any need to see your proof."

"Don't be stupid."

"Stay out of my damn business," Torrie screamed. "I didn't ask you to go and investigate Jake. I didn't ask for your proof. You had no cause to investigate Jake anyway. He gave you a lot more than you deserved, so go in the house, Trey."

Instead of Trey going back in, Torrie and Jake watched as one by one Torrie's family came to stand on the porch glaring at Jake. Kimmie was holding a copy of the article. "It was in the paper, Jake." Kimmie hissed and then turned toward Torrie. "If you marry him I'm not coming, you'll marry him alone."

"If that's the way you want it, then that's the way it will be. Jake has done nothing to any of you."

"Are you not listening to us, Torrie? The rumors are true. Cannan Broussard is buying up all the land around here that he can."

"I know," Torrie answered.

"You knew this? Why didn't you tell us?'

"What could you have done about it except try to find some reason to blame Jake?"

"Are you saying you knew about this and you told Jake not to tell?" Kimmie asked in disbelief.

"Yes, and the way you're acting, I'm glad I didn't tell you." She glared at each of them before her eyes fell on John Tom. He was the only one not glaring at Jake. There was pity in his eyes. Torrie blinked, somehow John Tom had already known. It didn't matter.

"You would do this to your family, baby?" Torrie's mother asked with dismay in her voice.

"Mama, I didn't do anything. Jake turned in your claims. He even told Daddy not to sell the land."

Jake stared for a moment at Torrie. "We need to talk," he said softly.

"Jake?" Torrie whispered.

"Baby, we need to talk."

"I said Jake hasn't done anything wrong," Torrie repeated, glaring at her family before turning to look at Jake.

Jake was watching Torrie closely. Tears filled her eyes and her disappointment in him struck him, burning him to the core of his being. This was worst than the look she'd given him when he broke her heart at sixteen. She was trembling in anger, that much he knew, but still she'd backed him up. He should have known this was going to blow up in his face. She took in a deep breath and moved closer to him. He was aware that she was presenting a united front to her family.

"Would you all go in and give us some privacy?" she asked. "You've all had your say: you're not coming to the wedding, you hate Jake, and you think I'm crazy. I think I've covered it all." She waited until they closed the door looking at them.

"Torrie, it's not as bad as it seems. Not what I did anyway. I told you the rumors were true. I found out they were, so I started buying the land to keep it out of my father's hands. I didn't cheat anyone, Torrie. I paid a fair price. I only did it to keep my father from getting the land and selling it to an outside investor. I turned in the appraisal on your family's property. I gave them a lot more than they had coming. It wasn't illegal. I just gave a high appraisal. Hell, it's my money."

"What about all the other people C&J Mutual have insured, Jake?"

"I don't have their claims. I had yours and your family."

"You shouldn't have done this."

"I told you I was going to find a way to fight my father. You knew that."

She walked back toward his truck. "I asked you not to make our lives more complicated. I didn't want you throwing money at my family. If they didn't deserve the money, you shouldn't have given it to them. I told you we didn't want charity, not even from you. Damn, Jake, I could have taken this. I could have. Now everyone is still going to try to make something different out of this. You just couldn't listen could you? It's not your job to take care of my family. It's mine. I want to take care of them. Don't you understand? That's my job, not yours. You said you were going to stop trying to run my life, stop treating me like a child and stop trying to protect me. I've done a damn good job of protecting myself. All you had to do was tell me you were buying up land to keep it out of your father's hands. You could have told me you had over appraised my family's property. Why didn't you trust me?"

"Torrie, baby, I didn't know how to tell you this part. I didn't want you to think I'd become my father."

"You've been so damn busy trying to protect me, Jake. That was my main worry, and you knew it. You're too busy wanting to help me that I think you have the loving me part confused. Is that the reason you gave my parents, Trey, and Kimmie more than they should have received? I want you to fix this, Jake, redo what you've done. I'm not playing. You meet me tomorrow with the appraisal on my property, and all I want to hear from your mouth is how you plan on fixing this mess you've made. I told you not to do this. If my parents aren't due this money, then you're not going to give it to them."

"Torrie, baby," Jake said reaching for her as she backed away. "Torrie please...please...don't look at me like that."

"Don't you dare touch me right now. I'm so damn angry with you I could slap you silly. Go home, Jacob Broussard, and when I see you tomorrow, you tell me how you're going to undo this."

Why the hell couldn't he have just told Torrie that there'd been no other way to fight his father except to fight dirty right with him. That was the only way to stop Cannan Broussard. It was the only language he truly understood. Hell he'd alluded to it but they'd ended the conversation and they'd made love instead. The memory of the newspaper in Kimmie's hand came to Jake's mind. Only one man could have approved that information to get into print, and that one man was trying as hard as possible to ruin Jake's life.

The drive from Harahan wasn't enough to clear his head or quiet the hurt. He wanted to blame it all on his father, but knew the majority of the blame rested solely on his shoulders. He'd had a choice in everything. He could have turned the job over to someone else when he knew he had to assess Torrie's property and that of her family. He could have confirmed the rumors of his father amassing land to sell off at a profit. And he could have just told Torrie he'd become a New Orleans son to save her property, but he hadn't wanted to tell her the lengths he'd gone to accomplish that goal. Undo what he'd done. How the hell was he going to do that? He'd sent the appraisals in already.

Her voice still sang across his nerve endings. It wasn't until this moment that Jake realized what he'd taken from Torrie. Her need to protect her family and take care of them, to provide for them was as strong an instinct for her, as his to protect her. He'd been wrong to treat her like a child trying to take care of her. He'd known that wasn't what she wanted but he'd done it anyway. For the first time he truly understood. "What the hell have I done?" he groaned. "And how the hell will I ever fix this?"

When he opened the door, the fury in his father's face matched the fury in Jake. He was in no mood to be nice, to be the son wanting of his father's approval, wanting to hear his father say again how proud he was of him. Sure, he still wanted those things, but there were other things he wanted more. Not to have hurt Torrie was the most important. Jake didn't have a choice. He had to find a way to fix things.

"Jacob Broussard, for the first time in my life, I'm ashamed of having you for my son and only heir."

"Then I guess we're even, Dad, because for the first time in my life, I'm ashamed of having you for my father."

They stood like twin statues, staring at each other. Jake was trembling with anger, and then the unbelievable happened.

"Jacob, I wasn't trying to hurt you." His father reached out and pulled Jake into his arms, holding tighter as Jake pushed away. "Son, I'm sorry. I just didn't think she was right for you. I've been grooming you to take your rightful place, and this was all a part of it. I didn't plan Hurricane Katrina, Jacob. I didn't blow up the levee, and I didn't know they were going to break. What are you blaming me for?"

Jake swallowed. "The story in the paper, you gave it to them. You could have allowed me to tell Torrie's family. Everything I've done to convince them I've been straight with them has just been shot to hell with that article. Now even the ones who were willing to give me a chance have turned against me."

"I was trying to allow you a chance to handle things, Jacob, and then I got those ridiculous appraisals you gave for that girl's family."

"Torrie, Dad," Jake warned and glared at his father until Cannan shrugged his shoulder.

"Okay, Jacob, Torrie. I asked you to do your job. I even gave you a way out, but you said you could handle it. You and I both know what you did was gave away money they didn't deserve."

"You said the money was mine to do with as I pleased. That it was my company, remember?"

Cannan moved away from his son. He walked to the mantle, took out a cigar from his pocket and lit it with a match from the box. He turned back to Jake. "So was I right, Jacob, is she happy with the appraisals?"

"She was happy."

"Was?"

"Until I told her I'd inflated the appraisals. Now she's not so happy."

"And you."

"And me? And she wants me to fix it. How the hell can I undo what I've done?" He glanced at his father. "Have the checks been cut?"

"They went out yesterday."

"I could replace the money."

"And you think that will fix things. Jacob? Will she be happy you've given her family charity? How will that undo things?"

"I don't know." Jake looked at his father, furring his brow. "I can't believe you'd really try to practically steal people's land to sell to developers."

"I'm not stealing a damn thing. I'm paying for everything I'm getting. I'm not forcing anyone to sell."

"No, but you sure as hell aren't giving them much of a choice. Hell, Dad, you own the damn insurance company a lot of them use and you own the damn bank. Now you're buying the land. It would be different if you wanted to keep the land, but you're not. You're selling it to outsiders. That's really a sore spot with everyone. Everybody's angry and ready to run you out of town."

"So what? Let them sue me if they want. I'm not putting a gun to anyone's head."

"I don't give a damn. You're wrong!"

"What about you, Jacob? You cut quite a few corners and paid more than a few people off to find out what I was doing. I know you paid off Torrie's mortgage on her home and on her business. I know you've gone behind my back and bought up land. Do you think I give a damn? There's more land to buy than hers."

"You've got more than enough money! Why are you doing this?"

"No one can ever have enough money. Besides, Jacob, this is all about business. It's time you learned. If you're going to make a go of it in the business world, then you'd better learn that lesson. And for the record, I don't believe you've never cut a deal to get a contract. You may have signed the legal papers, but every really great deal has a little corruption, someone getting paid off the top. And everyone knows that's how it done, one hand…"

"I don't work like that."

"That's a lie, Jacob. You do, you just don't want to acknowledge it. Look at everything you've done since you came home. You're my son, and you're finally beginning to behave like it. Hell, Jacob, it's made me even prouder of you."

"The things I've done since I've been home were not to make you proud of me. I hated doing it, and Torrie hates it. She likes things done the right way, not the handshake and side deals. So don't be proud of me for that."

"Jacob, I'm not going to tell you I went about this the right way. But I'm a businessman. I'm not the heartless bastard this city thinks I am. But I do have to present that persona or I would find myself in messes like you've made for yourself. There are things in my life I would never trade, Jacob. You and your mother are what I live and work for so ruthlessly, and when I fight tooth and nail to leave you an empire, it's because I have a dream for you. I want you to be able to do and have any damn thing you please."

"I want Torrie, Dad. The rest doesn't matter. "

Cannan puffed on his cigar for a few more moments. "That girl has you whipped. She always has. I never knew a five-year-old boy could be whipped, but you were, Jacob. I didn't like it then, and I don't like it now. I don't want you wanting her. Her family hates you, Jacob. You could have any woman in the world. You don't have to settle for a little girl you rescued like a stray kitten."

His father sounded as bad as Torrie. "What makes you think I rescued Torrie? You've got it wrong, and so does she. She rescued me when she was a four-year-old beauty. Her eyes looked into mine, and she rescued me from never knowing what real love was like. She rescued me from searching aimlessly for that one special person, my soul mate. Torrie is and always was that for me. No, Dad, you have it wrong. Maybe I've done the wrong things trying to prove myself worthy of her love, but I do love her. I may not deserve her, but I want her, and you're doing everything in your power to ruin that. If you can't accept Torrie—"

"That's a lovely speech, but don't you dare issue me any ultimatums, boy."

"Your father is right, Jake." Dee Broussard walked in the room and stood in front of her son. "Don't issue him ultimatums. You weren't raised like that, not to disrespect your father." She continued.

"Mom, do you know what he's done?"

"I know."

Jake stared at his mother in disbelief. He could believe these things of his father, but not his mother. He moved his gaze from her face, looking over her head to the mantle that held the matches for his father's mostly unlit cigars. They had so much he thought, wincing in acknowledgement as his eyes fell upon piece after piece of expensive furniture.

"Torrie's going to be my wife. She's my main concern."

"That's as it should be," his mother answered.

"Then why?"

"Because you were about to walk out of our lives, and I'm not going to allow that. It's my job to issue ultimatums to your father, not yours."

Jake watched his mother as she walked to his father and took the cigar from his hand, giving him a disgusted look.

"Unless you're prepared to lose your entire family tonight, Cannan Broussard, you will start behaving like you've got some sense. I've ignored the things you've done through the years because none of them meant we'd lose our son. You make things right with Jake. And then I want you to make them right with Torrie and her family."

In his thirty years, Jake had never seen his father cower before any man, but the four foot ten inch woman was making the great Cannan Broussard back down. He and his father both watched as his mother snuffed out the cigar, glaring once more at her husband before returning to the kitchen.

"I'll talk to Torrie," Cannan said quietly.

In disbelief, Jake studied his father's face for his angle and found none. "And you have the nerve to call me whipped?" Jake laughed, amused at the look on his father's face. "What's that about?" Jake jerked his thumb toward the direction his mother had gone.

"Your mother's my Achilles heel." Cannan sighed. "And I guess Torrie's yours, Jacob. I truly thought you'd be better off without her."

"You're wrong."

Cannan shrugged his shoulder. "Only time will tell, but I meant what I said. I'll talk to Torrie."

"You talk to Mom, Dad. I'll take care of Torrie. Just tell me why you put that in the paper without telling me."

Forever and a Day

"Torrie's cousin Trey came here to the house before the story appeared in the paper. He had information he'd researched and found. That's why I put it in the paper, Jacob. That man wanted to hurt you. He hates you. He thought he had something on you, so I wanted to show him he didn't. Besides, it was my plan to announce, not his. So I put it in the paper. What I'm doing is legal, Jacob, and in a way I'm just trying to protect you the same as you're trying to protect Torrie from me. Hell, having it in the paper for all to see should have taken some of the sting out of it."

For some crazy reason, Jake could actually imagine his father thinking what he was doing would somehow protect him. It may not have been right, but who the hell was Jake to talk? Everyone did things to protect those they loved, even Jake. "Dad, I don't think that worked. The results were a hell of a lot worse than a sting." What was done was done, and Jake had only himself to blame. "Torrie demanded I undo the things I've done." Jake shook his head and blew out a breath of resignation.

"You know this doesn't change anything, Jacob. I still don't think she's right for you."

"I know what you think, but you know your feelings on the matter don't change how things are. I'm in love with Torrie, and I'm going to marry her. " Jake paused and looked at his father. "I've always loved you, and I've always been proud of you until the things you did to hurt Torrie, those I'm not proud of."

He pulled in a breath. "But as much as I love you, I love Torrie more. I won't allow you to hurt her feelings or her pride. It doesn't matter what you or Torrie think of my protecting her. I'm her friend, and I'm going to be her husband. I will always protect her. But I'm going to have to learn to back off some. She's pissed right now, but in the end we will be together. She loves me." Jake started up the stairs.

Chapter Eighteen

Y ou have got to be kidding."

"Do I look like I'm kidding?" Jake stared at Torrie. "That's the estimate I'm turning in."

"For my house and my business? Why the hell don't you just stick a gun in my face if you want to steal my property for your father?"

Damn that hurt. But it also angered Jake. He was doing what he could to undo the situation, now Torrie was accusing him of doing something she knew he was incapable of doing.

"Do you really think that's what I'm trying to do?"

"Do I think it? I don't have to think, Jacob. It's here on this damn appraisal. You've given me what, ten percent of the value? You're crazy."

"No, you're crazy."

Torrie threw the papers across the desk at Jake. "You're right. I am crazy to have even thought you wouldn't be like your father. You taught me that lesson when I was sixteen, only I was too stupid to get it, too blinded by love for you. Well I'm not blind anymore, Jacob Broussard. God, Jake, I thought you were different. First you overvalue my family's property, and then you undervalue mine. I'm sure you have a good reason for this too, like always, but I've told you not to manipulate me and try to fix things. I don't know what the heck you've done with my money. But whatever you did you didn't have the right to do."

Jake was now as angry as Torrie, if not more so. He took two long strides and stood in front of her. "Are you saying this is about money? That if I had given you charity, you would have taken it?" he growled.

"Charity? I've never asked you for charity, Jacob Broussard." Tears spilled down her cheeks. "But I didn't want you to steal from me either."

"Stop calling me Jacob. What the hell do you want me to do, Torrie?"

"Try standing up to your father. Stop being so damn worried about what he thinks of you."

"You think that's what this is about?"

"Yes. You're too old to be seeking parental approval, Jake. I know your father got you the job at the insurance company. I know he secured your loans for your business. You didn't do any of it on your own."

"He didn't do anymore than your father would have if he had the money. Good or bad, right or wrong, he's my father."

"But he's not mine, Jake. And I don't want him as a part of my family. Tell him he's won. He doesn't want me in his family, and I don't want him in mine. You're right about families being a package deal."

"He's my father, Torrie. He was just trying to help me." Jake reached for her and shook her as she attempted to move away from him. "You're being unreasonable."

Torrie pulled the ring from her finger and snatched Jake's hand, putting the ring into the center of his palm. "I don't want the package."

Torrie was determined not to cry, at least not until she was alone. She had never hurt this badly: not in her dreams, not when her visions had come true, not when she'd first seen her destroyed home. Now it was as though her soul had been wrenched apart from her body. If she could curl into a ball and die, she would at that moment. She could feel Jake's glaring after her. If he dared to come near her, she would pick up a brick and bash him over the head.

How dare she accuse him of trying to steal from her to give to his father? If she didn't know him any better than that, then maybe they didn't belong together. Soul mate or not he'd lived without her for twelve years; if he had to he would live the rest of his life without her. Pain filled him and a burning claimed him. Jake's chest hurt from the lie. He didn't want to live without Torrie, but he was so damn angry with her. She didn't even wait to see if he'd done the right thing, if he'd fixed it, she had no idea.

Maybe if she'd given him half a chance, he would have told her. Jake shoved the ring into his pocket, and then he knocked over everything that wasn't nailed down in the office he was using. To hell with it. He would still undo all that he'd done. If Torrie didn't know in her heart he loved her...*if you lie to a woman, even a lie detector test won't help*. Out of the blue his father's words came to him.

Determination fueled Jake's steps. He was getting tired of everyone second-guessing him. He was still determined to do exactly what he'd said he was going to do. He was going to undo the wrongs he'd done, and his next step was with Trey.

Jake waited in the teacher's lounge of St Mary's school for Trey. He wasn't inclined to shout in a school. He wasn't inclined to fight with Trey, but this was the first mistake he'd made in his relationship with Torrie. This was what he would have to undo.

"What the hell do you want, Broussard? They told me it was important."

"It is." Jake moved away from the desk where he was perched. "I need to talk to you."

"What do you want, for me to talk to Torrie? Get real. Do you think I'd lie to save your ass? Torrie finally knows the truth, Jake, she's done with you."

Jake swallowed. Today wasn't exactly about Torrie, but it was about righting a wrong."What I did to you was wrong, Trey," he said softly, waiting as Trey's hand slid from the door.

"What the hell are you talking about now, Broussard?"

"We were friends. I was wrong. I was a disloyal friend to you. I'm sorry. I shouldn't have taken that job from you. I knew it then, and I know it now." Jake blinked at the glare that was on Trey's face. "I'm sorry for calling you out of your name, for saying you were too black to get the job. I'm sorry I used my skin color to take something you wanted and you should have had. We were both qualified for the job, you maybe a little more. I knew I would get the job, and I didn't even stop to consider your feelings. I wanted to make money to buy a gift for Torrie, a gift I never even gave her."

"Why the hell are you telling me this shit now?"

"Because the first time I tried, you decked me. I wanted to try again. I'm not asking you to forget what I did, Trey, and I'm not asking for your forgiveness. I'm just trying to undo what I've done."

"You can't undo what you've done anymore than you can undo how you hurt my cousin. She's not going to marry you, Jake. If you think coming here to me after fourteen years is going to change things, think again. Torrie sees you for what you are, the son of Cannan Broussard, light, bright, and almost white, wanting the girl who can't pass a paper bag test. She doesn't want you, Jake. None of us are ever going to let you get close enough to Torrie to hurt her again."

He'd known it wouldn't be easy; just something he had to do, something he should have done fourteen years ago. Jake watched

Trey for a few seconds. "I didn't come here because of Torrie, Trey. I came because of us. I didn't have illusions of us being friends again. Too much has happened between us. As hard as you might find this to believe, Trey, I'm doing this strictly for myself. I want to feel better. I was wrong in what I did to you, period. I'm apologizing, you don't have to accept it, and I don't expect you to, but I've done it." Jake stood for a moment his gaze fixed on Trey, and then he turned and walked away.

"I don't accept it, Broussard," Trey shouted after him. "I'll never accept it and as for this little stunt, I won't even tell Torrie you came, so you're not going to get points from it."

"I don't want you to tell Torrie. I didn't do this because of her. I did it because it's the right thing to do. I want this kept between us." Jake continued walking, ignoring as best he could the words Trey was shouting. He'd done what he came to do. He walked into the parking lot, got in his SUV and drove away.

New Year came and went. Jake didn't call Torrie, and she didn't call him. Instead, Jake did what he'd come to New Orleans to do. He worked day and night, clearing debris. January came and went and still he'd not spoken to Torrie. She'd come out a couple a times and looked at her house with different people, but always walked away when she saw him. Through it all, Jake worked until the aching hunger in him became too much to bear. He hurt just as much as Torrie but he wasn't going to keep running after her. Just like he didn't expect forgiveness from Trey, he wasn't working his behind off now for Torrie's forgiveness or her approval. He was helping to clean up New Orleans because it was the right thing to do.

Forever and a Day

Despite his working night and day, there wasn't nearly the improvement Jake had wanted to see, and it was time he returned to New York. He'd thought about just leaving and not even telling Torrie he was going. But the knowledge of what they'd meant to each other kept him from it. He was determined not to chase her, but he wasn't leaving Louisiana without her at least knowing the truth. Jake knocked on the door and waited, he wasn't leaving without seeing Torrie.

"What the hell do you want, Jake? I told you not to hurt my sister, and you did it anyway."

He ignored the look of fury on Kimmie's face. "I need to talk to Torrie. Would you please tell her I'm here?"

"She doesn't want to see you."

"How do you know? You haven't told her I'm here."

Torrie's mother came out the door. "Jake, I told you if you hurt my baby you wouldn't have to worry about what her daddy would do to you. I'm giving you fair warning, Jake Broussard, get off the porch or I will go and get my husband's gun, and I will put a bullet in the center of your head. I'm a very good shot, Jake."

"I need to talk to, Torrie."

"Torrie doesn't need to talk to you, go away."

"Mama, go get the gun." Kimmie glared at Jake, her hands on her hips and a no-nonsense look on her face.

Jake refused to blink or look away. Even if they got the gun, he wasn't moving from the spot until he'd undone what he'd done.

Jake watched as Torrie's mother went back in the house, no doubt to get the gun she'd threatened to use. But before she'd had a chance to return, her husband was there and he had his shotgun in his hand. This was crazy. Jake couldn't believe this. Yes, he knew the man had pulled the shotgun on many people. Yes, he knew more than half of New Orleans's residents carried guns, but did he know someone would stand there holding a gun on him ordering him to leave? Hell no. Still, Jake refused to be dissuaded. "I need to talk to Torrie. If Torrie tells me to leave, I'll go."

"We're not getting Torrie," Kimmie answered.

Footsteps made them all look toward the door, but it was John Tom who came out. He took a look at Jake, then at Torrie's family and the shotgun. "Don't you think you should leave, Jake?" he asked.

"Not until I talk to Torrie." Jake answered.

"She's through with you. She said it. Torrie told us not to get her if you ever came by."

"Would you just tell her I'm here to do what she asked me to do? Just tell her I came to undo what I did."

John Tom sighed and looked at Jake.

"Please," Jake pleaded, knowing the only person he stood a chance with was John Tom.

"No," Kimmie shouted, putting her hand on John Tom's arm to stop him. "You help Jake, and it's over."

"You're threatening me, Kimmie?"

"I'm telling you like it is."

"You can't live your sister's life for her. Hell, you can't even live yours." John Tom looked toward the old man. "If you want to shoot Jake, go ahead. If you think that will make Torrie stop loving him, you're a fool. This is between Jake and Torrie. Kimmie, if you're fool enough to throw away a second chance at happiness after everything that's happened, after all we've been through, then hell, maybe I was wrong about us." He turned on his heels, slamming the door behind him

"She's not going with you, Jake," Kimmie declared loudly. "You can't undo what you've done. You hurt her. How the hell are you going to undo that? You lied to her and you cheated her. Tell me how you're going to fix it. She doesn't want anything to do with you, Jake."

This time two pairs of distinct footsteps sounded and again they all turned toward the sound.

Torrie looked at Jake, then at her father holding a shotgun and at her mother with a gun in her hand, both were aimed at Jake. She thanked God Trey wasn't there, or Jake would have been dead.

"Are all of you crazy?" she asked.

"You said you didn't want to see him," Kimmie replied angrily with her hands on her hips.

"But I didn't tell any of you to kill Jake. God, I don't want him dead. Put those guns away before someone calls the cops. Jake, why did you come here? Daddy's not kidding, you know. I've been having a hell of a time keeping him from coming after you, and now you come here. Jake, you're crazy."

Jake stared at Torrie. The weight of loneliness he carried without her in his life felt as if it were crushing the air from his body. He wanted badly to reach for her, to hold her, one touch, one caress. He pulled in a breath and let it out sharply, ordering his body to not make any sudden moves. He licked his lips. God she was beautiful, but her mother was right, the glow was gone from her eyes replaced by sadness and pain. His entire concentration was on Torrie as she stared at him.

"Put the guns downs," she said, walking down the stairs toward him. She stood for a moment looking into his eyes then she turned positioning her body in front of his. "Go in the house and put the guns away." She ordered in a firm voice that surprised Jake and surprised him even more when they all obeyed.

Maybe the glow was gone, but Torrie was trying to protect him. That meant the love she had for him was still there. Jake waited until her family returned to the house, then he turned Torrie to face him.

"I found a way to undo what I've done."

"How?"

"You asked me to undo it and I have. Give me a chance to prove it. Will you let me prove it to you? I'm not asking you to take me back, Torrie. I'm asking that you allow me to prove something to you, then when I return to New York, at least you will know the truth."

"How are you going to prove it?"

"Are you willing to come with me?"

"What's the use? Will it make a difference in the things that have happened?"

"Maybe, maybe not, will you come with me?" he asked, allowing hope to seep into his voice, making sure not to touch her. She was so fragile, she would break if he did. Besides Jake could see the barrel of the shotgun sticking out the open window.

Torrie looked back toward the window as though she'd read his thoughts. "Go get in the truck, Jake."

He glanced at her, and then at the window, shaking his head at the absurdity of the situation. He walked around to the driver's side, climbed in and opened the passenger door for Torrie. She stood for a moment looking at him, and his heart lurched. She didn't want to come. "Please, Torrie, if nothing more than to close the chapter on us." She tilted her head and squinted at him as though he were an insect that she was inspecting.

"This will close the chapter. And then I don't want to see you again, agreed?"

"Get in," Jake answered not agreeing to anything.

"A polygraph?" Torrie read the sign on the door in disbelief. She looked at Jake, staring at him in astonishment. "I didn't ask you to do this."

"No, but the accusing look in your eyes did. And the fact you're not wearing your engagement ring is reason enough. I never would have believed I would have to do this. All of these years I've always thought we had this connection between us. We've both talked about it. But it seems lately our connection isn't working. Like I said, I want you to know the truth. You're not going to spend the next fourteen years thinking I said or did something I didn't. I'm not kissing your behind, Torrie. I'm clearing my damn name."

"Then you'll clear it with the two of us, Jake. You're being so dense. This was never about me not trusting you. This was about your being so damn overprotective of me you're making it hard for me to trust your decisions. You were treating me like a child, not like the woman you wanted to be your wife. I'm not going in there, so you've wasted your money." Torrie turned around and walked out the door and back to the SUV. For several minutes, they remained like that until Torrie glared at Jake, annoyed that he was sitting there in stony silence.

Jake's gaze was locked on hers. She could see the hope in his golden gaze, and she saw the love. A flicker passed before his eyes shuttered. He'd always worn his heart on his sleeve. He missed her. That much she already knew. She wanted him to stop looking at her that way. She needed to hold out, not allow him back into her life, but the way he was gazing at her was making it awfully hard.

"What did you expect to accomplish with this?" Torrie pointed back toward the office building they'd exited.

"To undo what I've done."

"Stop, it," Torrie snapped as she moved across the seat toward him and put her nose to Jake. "Stop this right now. What is this supposed to be that you're doing? Is this what you meant by undoing?"

"No, Torrie, this is not what I meant by undoing."

Torrie shook her head, she couldn't believe Jake. What was taking a lie detector test supposed to prove? "You don't get it do you? I can tell the way you're looking at me. You don't understand why you can't take care of me even when I tell you not to." She sighed, thinking, *'what was the use.'* "I'm tired of this."

"I love you, Torrie. You know in your heart that I'm telling you the truth. You know I love you," he said. "You know I haven't done any of the things I've done to hurt you. I've never wanted anything but to protect you."

"And therein lies our problem. You can't keep protecting me."

"Torrie, why don't you try being honest with me? You're afraid of something, and I'm not sure what it is, but I don't think you've really been honest with me. I think you're holding it against me that I'm rich. That's something that I was born into. But every single time I've tried to help you financially, you've bitten my head off. "

"Because I haven't asked you for money."

"Why do you think you'd have to? I have money. You have needs. What's wrong with my helping you?"

"I don't want you ever thinking I wanted you for your money."

"I never have and you know that. There must be more."

"That's enough of a reason."

"Are you afraid, Torrie?"

"I'm not afraid, just not interested any longer."

"Have you stopped loving me, Torrie?"

"You didn't need a machine for that one, Jake. No, I haven't stopped loving you, but that doesn't change things."

"You're willing to throw away our future?"

"I also told you I never saw a future for us. Do you mind taking me home now?"

They drove back to John Tom's in silence. When Jake stopped, Torrie got out of the truck. "I'm not running after you again, Torrie. This is it, the last time. This is goodbye."

"Goodbye, Jake," Torrie said and walked up the stairs and into the house without a backwards glance.

Jake sat in his SUV and stared at the house. He was aware of the things he'd done wrong, he'd readily admitted to them. But how the hell did Torrie think he could stand by and watch her hurting and not do something to stop it if it were in his power. He'd seen the way she'd behaved when he'd said she was uncomfortable with his having money. That was one problem Jake couldn't solve for Torrie. He had money. That was a fact.

Forever and a Day

At least he could return to New York knowing he'd done his best to make things right with Torrie. He'd known the polygraph idea was a long shot. Even if she'd agreed to it, he couldn't predict or control the outcome. Besides, he'd known her changing her mind was damn near impossible, and he'd convinced himself that it wasn't the reason he'd gone to such lengths. He'd wanted to believe he was only doing it because of the off-hand remark made by his father about women needing lie detector tests to prove a man's innocence. He'd wanted to believe he hadn't done it, hoping Torrie would change her mind about the two of them. She was so damn stubborn that couldn't have possibly been what he'd wanted. Now as he sat looking at the house Jake knew—he'd had hope.

He'd done his best to show Torrie he loved her and still that was not enough. He thought over the last fourteen years of his life. Torrie had never been far from his thoughts. He wondered if after loving Torrie completely, if he could ever forget her. He didn't believe he could. But he was returning to New York in a couple more weeks, and this time he would not be coming back for Torrie.

For two weeks Torrie walked around in a daze. She had no heart and no soul. Jake Broussard had cut them both out and tossed them away. Her body burned with the ache of the remembered pain. Getting over Jake this time would be much harder. This time Torrie would not write him letters, never mailing them, or saving them in a metal box. This time she would forget him.

With each day that passed, Torrie grew numb. She didn't believe she would ever feel again. She was growing tired of hearing her family tell her to snap out of it, to forget Jake, as if she could. Maybe if they would stop downing him and forcing her to defend him, she could forget quicker. Since they wouldn't stop talking about Jake, she stopped listening to anything her family had to say.

Finally, Torrie breathed a sigh of relief, glad she would once again be living on her own. She'd been told she was finally getting a FEMA trailer. The catch, she had to have somewhere to put it. Her parents were also getting a trailer. John Tom, the saint that Torrie was rapidly thinking he was, told them they could put the trailers on his land. Trey found a small two-room efficiency apartment over in Tremae. It took him a little longer to get to school, but at least they were all moving on with their lives.

If Torrie could convince herself not to dream about Jake, not to have her body ache from not having him buried inside her, not to look into his golden brown eyes and know that he loved her, if she could stop dreaming of those things she would be fine.

"Hello my name's Jake. You don't have to be afraid. I'll protect you."

Those were the words she heard in her brain each night she fell asleep. She thought of the twelve long years without Jake, and the tears flowed. Part of her was to blame, she knew that now. Yes, she'd always loved knowing she had Jake's protection, but more than that, she knew she wanted his love.

Torrie looked up. The house was oddly silent. Her mother was watching her and her father was watching her mother. John Tom and Kimmie had gone out somewhere. Her mother's scrutiny was unnerving. "What, Mom?" Torrie finally asked when she could take the inquisitive looks no longer. Her mother glanced at her father then stood up and came over to her.

"Baby, we need to talk," she said, heading for Torrie's bedroom.

"What's wrong?" Torrie asked when the door was closed.

"You're not happy. Jake's leaving and your heart is broken."

"Why do you care, Mommie? You all hate Jake."

"But you don't baby. You love him."

"Mommie—"

"Don't Mommie me, baby. I've been watching you moping around here, and it's breaking my heart to see you like this. I want you happy."

"I want to be happy."

"You can't, baby, or you'd try harder. There's been something eating at you and Jake for a long time, tearing away at your relationship."

"I know his father—"

"It's not Cannan Broussard, Torrie, it's you."

"Me, how?"

"Baby, I wanted you to come to this conclusion on your own. You've been trying for so many years to be good enough for Jake." She put her hand up to stop Torrie's protest. "Yes, you have baby, and that's okay. It's never a bad thing to try and better yourself. But you've got to know you were always good enough for Jake. You were born good enough for Jake. Jake may be rich but that doesn't make him any better than you are."

"I never thought that."

"Yes you did, baby."

"But Jake—"

"Jake nothing. Jake has never thought you weren't worthy of his love. If anything, he's always thought he wasn't worthy of yours. Jake is rich, Torrie. He's always going to be rich. He doesn't hold your not being rich against you. Why are you holding his money against him?"

"His father doesn't want me with Jake."

"But Jake does, baby. He loves you."

"But you and Daddy don't want me with Jake."

"But you want to be with him, and it's your life. You've just got to let go of your pride and admit the truth to yourself. You love that boy. You just can't stand the fact he has money. If this thing with the hurricane hadn't happened and Jake wanted you, you would have gone to him wouldn't you?"

Torrie tried to avoid her mother's gaze.

"Torrie, don't lie to me."

Torrie shook her head.

"Why would it have been okay then and not now?"

Tears filled Torrie's eyes and her throat closed with wanting to shed them. Her mother opened her arms and she rushed into them crying all the tears she hadn't yet shed.

"No, baby, you can't just cry. You've got to say the words. What would have made it different?"

"I had money, Mama. I had a home. I had a business. I wanted Jake to be proud of me, to see all the things I'd done. I didn't want him to feel sorry for me, to have to take care of me."

"Let it go, baby. That's not how Jake feels about things, and never was. Jake wasn't ashamed of you. It was you being ashamed of you. Don't blame Jake for that. He has money, big deal. He wants to spend it on you. He loves you. Don't hold his money against him baby. Don't miss out on your happiness because of your foolish pride. You've got to know you're worth it. You deserve to be happy."

"What about everything that happened?" Torrie pulled at the blue fringes of the bedspread while kicking her foot dangling over the side of the bed in a gentle back and forth motion. She rubbed her hand down the side of her mother's arm before bringing her gaze back up to meet her mother's.

"You're the one who's in love with him. Do you think Jake's to blame for all of that trouble or do you think he was trying to help you?"

"He wasn't to blame, but he was throwing money at me. He was acting like his father."

"Maybe it was the only thing he knew to do." Her mother pulled the fringes of the spread from between Torrie's fingers. "Stop pulling at that spread before you ruin it. Besides, why take your frustrations out on it? It's Jake you should be talking to."

"I can't believe you're talking like this. How about Daddy?"

Her mother smiled and gave a quick look in the direction of the closed door. "If your daddy asks me what we talked about, I haven't decided yet if I'm going to tell him the truth."

Torrie laughed. "Mommy, you'd lie?"

"If I have to." She hugged Torrie to her. "I can't stand seeing you like this. I'm just saying don't let it be because of us that you're staying away from Jake. I've got your father and Kimmie has John Tom. You're beautiful and you're smart, and if you don't want Jake I'm sure you'll find another man. I just don't want you saying we were the cause of your unhappiness. It's your life, baby, whether we want you to be part of the Broussards or not. It's still your life and only you can make that decision."

For several minutes Torrie's mother rocked her back and forth, and then she kissed her forehead and smoothed back her hair, then walked out of the room, leaving Torrie to return to unraveling the blue fringes.

Torrie ached with wanting and missing Jake. She wanted his arms around her. She wanted to marry Jake and have his babies. She just wanted to be with him. As the desire claimed her, Torrie crushed the soft feathered pillow to her face and screamed into it. She wasn't going to Jake. She wasn't going to go running to him, begging him not to hurt her again. She cried until her throat was aching and raw as the rest of her body. Then she climbed out of the bed and got dressed.

Jake lay awake in the king size bed, wishing his parents had not gone back to Texas, while still wishing they had not come back to New Orleans. But they had and he had been glad to see them. A lot had happened in the weeks they'd been there. He'd finally heard the words he'd waited to hear his entire life. Jake couldn't deny that he'd been pleased. Still, that joy was tamped down by the knowledge that the rest of his life would be as lonely as the past twelve years had been.

Jake could feel the agony of his loss overwhelming him. He had a sudden urge to bawl like a baby, but he wouldn't. If Torrie didn't want him, to hell with her, he wasn't going to cry over her.

The tears ran down his cheeks, and he wiped them away angrily. This was crazy, he wished to hell he could sleep. Facing a shotgun party again was damn insane. He wasn't going. Let her come to him if she wanted him. Again he thought, *to hell with her*. He wiped the tears as angrily as he had wiped at their predecessors, and then he got out of the bed cursing and got dressed.

Halfway down his drive, Jake stopped his truck and got out of it. He stood there, watching the car moving slowly toward him. The tears he'd tried to stop before now ran freely down his face. He opened his arms and ran toward Torrie, crushing her in his arms. "You came," he breathed into her ear. "You came to me, baby."

"Yes, I came. I couldn't stay away," Torrie held him close. "Where were you going?" she asked.

"To face your daddy's shotgun again. Why did you come, baby?"

"Why do you think, Jake? I love you. I'm not going to go another twelve years without you in my life." She looked up at him grinning, "and I wasn't about to let you face Daddy's shotgun again." She laughed. "Kiss me, Jake."

Before the words were out, Jake had swung her up into his arms and was almost running with her back into the house. She loved him regardless of everything that had happened. They would work through it. Torrie didn't want to think of another twelve seconds without Jake, let alone another twelve years. She wanted him in her life, good or bad, right or wrong she was in love with Jake. He owned her heart and soul, without him her world was less bright.

In less time than she thought possible, they were in Jake's king size bed, holding each other as though they were afraid to move. They fell asleep after hours of talking, after the healing had begun. He was her future because she wanted him to be. She didn't care if she never had a vision of the two of them together; she would still remain with Jake.

When morning came, they made love...touching, caressing, kissing and taking it slow. They made love over and over until finally they were filled. Jake looked down at her and asked, "Are we doing it?"

"Yes," Torrie answered moving from the bed with Jake to take a shower together, with him.

"Yes," she said every time he looked at her. "Yes," she answered again when he replaced the ring on her finger. "Yes," she said when they went into Father Mike's study and asked the priest to marry them then and there.

When they said their "I do's," Torrie blinked on seeing the five-year-old Jake standing before her. She blinked again and saw him as he was, then she saw him standing beside her with three babies between them. She saw their smiles. "Oh my, God," she moaned. "Jake, I just saw us together. It must have always been there. I guess I had to truly let go of the hurts and open my heart to in order to see the vision. I'm so sorry I allowed your money to come between us. That was all my own doing. I won't worry about how much money you have anymore. I love you."

Jake hugged her to him. "It's our money, and I love you, too, baby. From now on no more Jake the bulldozer. I'll ask before I start fixing things. And I was wrong to just take over your life. You're right. I was treating you like a child. I'm sorry."

Jake grinned at Torrie as he pressed her against the door of his SUV. "I suppose with all the things I've done I'm no longer your hero. It may be a cliché, but it's true, baby, your hero turned out to have feet of clay."

"You're human, Jake, and you'll always be my hero, flawed, but oh so fierce and so very heroic. A flawed husband for a flawed wife. You were right; we were born to save each other from self-destruction."

As man and wife, Torrie and Jake walked back up the driveway of John Tom's house to tell her family the news. They walked in ignoring the startled looks. "We're married," Torrie announced without fanfare. John Tom smiled at her, then came over to Jake and shook his hand. Torrie shrugged her shoulders when no one else said anything and turned to walk from the room.

"Torrie, wait a minute."

"No, Trey, Jake's my husband. I'm not listening to you say anything against him anymore."

"I wasn't going to," Trey spoke quietly, looking at Jake. He swallowed. "You should know this because I don't think Jake plans on telling you, and since you're married, I don't think you need anymore secrets or lies between you, Torrie. You told Jake to undo what he'd done, and he did. He divided what your home should have been worth with the three of us. He gave a low appraisal on your home, I'm guessing, so that you would be the one helping us and not him."

"It wasn't charity he gave, and he didn't give your land to his father," John Tom said. "I checked. Jake paid the entire balance on your land. He paid every dime for it. Your business and your home, may be condemned Torrie, but you own the land. Cannan Broussard doesn't own them."

"I guess I was wrong," Trey said.

"You found a way to have me help my family," Torrie whispered softly, her gaze fastened on Jake. "You could have told me that."

"But I used money that should have been yours to do it."

"And you gave it back when you paid off my mortgages. Thank you, Jake."

"No complaining about me throwing money at your problems?"

"Not anymore. I'm going to just repeat what I should have been saying to you all along. Thank you. This entire thing has been harder than it had to be, more convoluted than a badly written novel." She shook her head slowly, finally understanding Jake's need to help her and her resistance against it.

"Torrie, you're so damn stubborn, I didn't know what I could or couldn't tell you. Telling you I love you was hard enough for you to believe." He took her hand rubbing his thumb over the back of hand as he lead her from the house and back to his SUV. "I love you, baby. I'll love you for forever and a day."

"I love you, too," Torrie said softly, thanking God that she hadn't blown it.

"Stop looking at me like that," Jake cautioned as he started up the truck, "or you're going to make me crash."

"I can't stop looking at you, Jake. Now that I know we're going to be okay."

"Your vision?"

"Your love." she answered. She rubbed her thumb across her ring and smiled. "And the vision. Like Father Mike said, 'in the midst of it all we made it through.'"

Jake glanced in the rearview mirror, then stopped and glanced at Torrie. The black Lincoln pulled up to the house and parked behind Jake's SUV. Almost at the same instant the door to the house opened and Torrie's parents stepped out on the porch.

Ernestine Thibodeaux walked down the stairs of the porch. "Come on," she urged her husband. "We're doing this."

"What the…?" Jake glanced at Torrie. They both stared at their respective parents and got out of the vehicle to see what was going on. Jake hadn't known his parents were coming back, let alone coming to Harahan to John Tom's.

Both mothers turned in their directions.

Ernestine Thibodeaux held her hand out to Jake's mother. "Like it or not, we're family now," she said.

Dee Broussard put her hand out and clasped Ernestine's hand within her own. She looked toward Jake. "So you two got married?"

"Yes," Jake answered.

"Congratulations," she said to Jake and smiled. "Torrie, welcome to the family."

She had to be living in a dream, never in her wildest imagination had she imagined this happening. Torrie held tightly to Jake's hand as they both looked toward their fathers. The men didn't shake hands, didn't speak or even glance at each other but they did nod. Torrie threw her arms around Jake. "It's a start, baby," she whispered. "We've been through a lot, and we're all still standing." She grinned. "Right now, Jacob Broussard, I'm seeing forever and a day."

Note from the Author

Michael Brown resigned from FEMA months before, but in February 2006 he went before Congress, and he had gotten angry. It was also reported that the White House had known before Katrina that the real possibility existed of the levees being breeched.

Different news shows kept the plight of the survivors in the public eye, alerting America to the fact that many thousands of people were still homeless in Louisiana, Mississippi, and Alabama and that thousands upon thousands of FEMA trailers sat empty and unused. Hopefully, by the time you read this story that will have changed. Hopefully, every Katrina survivor will have a home that they no longer have to leave after a few months.

Good stories also came out of the midst of the tragedies. It was reported that over thirty thousand viewers donated money to *The Oprah Winfrey Show*, which Ms. Winfrey had given ten million dollars of her own funds. In Houston Texas, some of the Katrina survivors have begun anew with homes built by Habit for Humanity along with the generous contributions of Ms. Winfrey, her viewers, and Target stores.

I hope you enjoyed the fictionalized account of Torrie and Jake Broussard. As such, I took literary license in the telling of this story. This is not meant to be an entirely factual story, and in that I changed some of the events to heighten the tension.

In one of the greatest natural disasters in terms of the toll on the lives of an entire American city, I want to leave you with this thought: Hurricane Katrina was not a respecter of persons, regardless of skin color or economic resources. It happened because of the right weather conditions that enabled a storm of that magnitude to grow and turn into a devastating hurricane. A city built five feet below sea level and in a crescent-shaped bowl didn't stand a chance once the protecting levees broke. I want people to also be mindful of the Americans in Mississippi and Alabama whose lives are still on hold along with the citizens of Louisiana.

Regardless of what will, I'm sure, be debated concerning what the Federal Government should or should not have done, the American people pooled together and helped out in this crisis. As far as the American people were concerned, the racial, social and economic lines were blurred if not totally erased and people of all nationalities, creed, and religions came together to show that we are all together on this planet called Earth.

About the Author

Award-winning author, **Dyanne Davis** lives in a Chicago suburb with her husband Bill and their son Bill Jr. She retired from nursing several years ago to pursue her lifelong dream of becoming a published author. She was able to accomplish this with her husband's blessing and financial support.

Her first novel, *The Color of Trouble*, was released July of 2003. The novel was received with high praise and several awards. Dyanne won an Emma for favorite New Author of the year and was presented with the award in NYC in April of 2004.

Her second novel, *The Wedding Gown* was released in February 2004 and has also received much praise. The book was chosen by Blackexpressions, a subsidiary of Doubleday Book club as a monthly club pick. The book was an Emma finalist in March 2005 for Steamiest Romance and for Book of the year. *The Wedding Gown* was also a finalist for Affaire de Coeur Reader's poll.

Misty Blue is a sequel to *The Wedding Gown* and hit the bookstores May of 2006. The book received a four star review from *Romantic Times Magazine*. *Forever and a Day* is Dyanne's first book for Parker Publishing.

When not writing you can find Dyanne with a book in her hands, her greatest passion next to spending time with her husband Bill and son Bill Jr. Whenever possible Dyanne loves getting together with friends and family.

A member of Romance Writers of America, a professional organization with over ten thousand members and chapters worldwide. Dyanne now serves as chapter president for Windy City, a local chapter of Romance Writers of America.

Dyanne loves to hear feedback from her readers. You can reach Dyanne at her website. www.dyannedavis.com.She also has an online blog where readers can post questions and photos at http://dyannedavis.blogspot.com.

She also has an online book club with almost two dozen of your favorite African American authors. You're welcome to join. Romancing The Book. http://bookmarked.target.com/bookclub.

Parker Publishing, LLC

Celebrating Black
Love Life Literature

Mail or fax orders to:

12523 Limonite Avenue
Suite #440-245
Mira Loma, CA 91752
(866) 205-7902
(951) 685-8036 fax

or order from our Web site:

www.parker-publishing.com
orders@parker-publishing.com

Ship to:
Name: _____

Address: _____

_____

_____

City: _____

State: _____ Zip: _____

Phone: _____

Qty	Title	Price	Total

Shipping and handling is $3.50, Priority Mail shipping is $6.00 | Add S&H
FREE standard shipping for orders over $30

Alaska, Hawaii, and international orders – call for rates | CA residents add 7.75% sales tax

See Website for special discounts and promotions | Total

Payment methods: We accept Visa, MasterCard, Discovery, or money orders. NO PERSONAL CHECKS.

Payment Method: (circle one):   VISA   MC   DISC   Money Order

Name on Card: _____

Card Number: _____ Exp Date: _____

Billing Address: _____

_____

City: _____

State: _____ Zip: _____